PLEASANTVILLE STORIES

PLEASANTVILLE STORIES

SEX, DANCING, AND SHOOTING U.S. NAVY JETS

(Growing Up in South Jersey in the 1960s)

DAVID W. BETTERTON

PROGRESSIVE COMMUNICATIONS

This is a work of fiction based on real events that took place in the author's life.
Out of courtesy and concern for privacy, some names have been changed.

Book design by Eichner | Fukui Design

Published by:

 Progressive Communications

Photograph credits appear on page 269.

Inquiries may be addressed to:
Progressive Communications
2768 Cedar Avenue
Long Beach, CA 90806
progressivecommunications627@gmail.com
dwblit.com

ISBN 979-8-218-37612-3 (paperback)

First printing.

Printed in the United States of America.

CONTENTS

ACKNOWLEDGMENTS ix

CONTENT WARNING xi

1 THE OLD MAN 1

2 COLORS 13

3 LIARS 17

4 THE PIT 29

5 BEEPER LINE 31

6 EASTER SUNDAY 55

7 FRIDAY NIGHT 57

8 SNOTNOSE SNIPERS 81

9 FISTICUFFS 85

10 WHAT IS EASTER? 95

11 THE PERFECT CRIME 99

12 PULLING A TRAIN — 129

13 I REMEMBER — 143

14 THE HURT — 145

15 TITS — 151

16 RACCOON — 169

17 THE BEST SHE COULD — 171

18 CALL MOTHER — 179

19 OLD LOVES — 181

20 VISAGE — 193

21 MYRTLE HOUSE — 195

ACKNOWLEDGMENTS

This collection evolved from a goodly number of stop-and-start efforts over several years. But I do not believe it would have ever come to fruition had I not learned to type. For that, I'd like to thank my old NJ Navy buddy Bobby Dunkirk, for teaching me how to type and for helping me to get out of the boiler room. That little skill alone improved the quality of my working life and gave a nice boost to my income-earning ability and creative expression. A big *mil gracias* to my wife Christine R. Ladewig for reading my stuff, even though she found some of it too painful. I am most grateful for having stumbled upon the California Writers Club, Long Beach, where I learned some craft tools that upped my game to produce a more professional creative product, and where I met Allene Symons, who has been an invaluable ally and whose opinions and suggestions helped to move *Pleasantville Stories* forward to publication. While we fought like cats and dogs, I owe a debt a gratitude to my first-ever editor, Barbara Ardinger. It is a better collection because it ran through her eyes. By now you have noticed that this book looks great! That is all because of Mauna and Lee, the talented inventive minds behind Eichner|Fukui Design. They really make me look good, don't they? A large *thank you* to my "favorite cousin," Russell Borden, whose unexpected financial bequeathal was used to produce this collection. And, lastly, I'd like to thank Pleasantville. I left you, but you never left me.

(Racial slurs, foul language, sexual abuse, and violence)

Whenever I tell people that I am from Pleasantville, New Jersey, they generally tilt their head, squint their eyes, and look off into space, as though they are trying to recall a long-forgotten memory. Then they usually go right to the movie, which is not about my Pleasantville. There was nothing idyllic about my Pleasantville. My growing up in Pleasantville was not pleasant. Don't get me wrong, I had a lot of fun. But that fun came with a price. In many ways, I am still paying. But it's my home. Where I am from. My identity. And the following stories and poems will give you some insight into what it was like growing up in P'ville, as the locals call it. But be forewarned:

If a few racial slurs and foul language will upset you, you might want to take a pass. I can, however, assure you that any derogatory terms are used for expository reasons only and cursing is used for authenticity. That's how we talked. And bigotry? That's how we thought. While there is some graphic violence and sexual abuse, it is not gratuitous. It is my story.

Another thing people do when they find that I'm from Jersey is they immediately conjure up some New Yorky non-rhotic word they carry with them to show that people from New Jersey talk funny. Well, I will have to disabuse you of that stereotype. I'm from South Jersey, and we don't talk like that. New Jersey is only 166 miles long and sixty-five miles at its widest, but travel a mere forty miles north and we'd make fun of how people talked. They called pizza *tomato pie,* for Pete's sake. They called subs *hoagies!* When Mom would get us ready for a trip up to Philly, a whole sixty miles, she'd pack enough food to travel across the country. We were going to the big city. Pleasantville was small-town USA.

In P'ville, it was hard to know someone who didn't know someone you knew. Many years have passed and a goodly number of the people in my stories are pushing up daisies, but some lucky ones are still with us. And because of that, I have changed many names out of respect and to protect the innocent, as well as the guilty. While everything I relate is true, please realize that each story is a fictionalized version of real events. I didn't take notes, and my memory has never been very good. But you can trust that the dialogue I've created is pretty darn close to what was said, in the tone it would have been said.

Pleasantville Stories is my story. At least a slice of it. My hope, dear reader, is that you will take this trip with me with an open mind. Let's visit the crucible from which I was forged. Hopefully you will laugh, perhaps cry, and learn that, for me, growing up in Pleasantville in the 1960s wasn't all black and white, like in the movie.

David W. Betterton
Long Beach, CA

PLEASANTVILLE STORIES

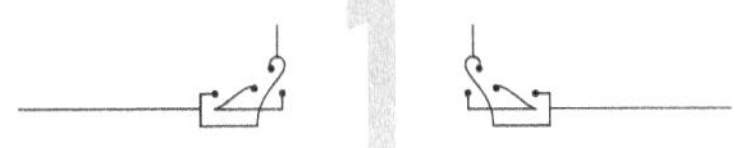

THE OLD MAN

To the best of my recollection, it was a bright, clean, crystal clear, briskly autumn day in what I found out later to be the largest city in Atlantic County: Pleasantville. Ye Olde Pleasantville of New Jersey. Things were a lot different back in 1956. Perhaps there was once a day when things were pleasant enough to warrant such an appellation, but by the time I had reached my then eight years of age, all the pleasantries apparently took to wing. And things only got worse. No matter. On this particular day, in this particular small South Jersey town, everything was all right. Like any other day, it was a good day to hooky school.

Mom had enough troubles of her own. And I was just one of her long-term life complications. The nearest of my half-brother and two half-sisters was eight years older than I. By the time this fortuitous day rolled around, my sisters were off and married and my brother was in the Navy. In essence, I was an only child. The way I see it, something must have happened to me while I was still inside my mother because I was pissed off from the moment I came kicking and screaming into this world.

As a result of my resistance to any and all authority, Mom's life was constantly on edge. On edge because she never knew what was coming, although she always knew *something* was coming. On edge because the "authorities" had threatened to take me away from her because I was a constant disciplinary problem in school. (From day one, I hated school. Somehow I figured out how to play the game and I began playing hooky in kindergarten. While begging not to be thrown into the brier patch, I frequently got kicked out of school.) On edge not only because she worked every day in a sweltering china factory, low pay and drudgery sapping the life out of her, but, also, because she frequently came home to find it smoky from the fires I played with on a regular basis. I was a firebug. On edge because I would steal things; because I would lie; because I was in a constant state of flux, snapping into temper tantrums at the drop of a hat (I would march through the house punching the plaster walls or the refrigerator door until the pain turned numb and blood dripped from my knuckles); and, she was mostly on edge because, combined with all of my other F-student-antisocial anomalies, I had a fetish for knives—I stole money from Mom's purse and kiped coins from her piggy bank to buy them. I stole them from other kids. I lifted knives whenever and wherever I could. I somehow came up with what seemed like millions of them. And Mom found each and every one. When she would ask me where I got the knife in question, I always answered something to the effect of, "Duh . . . , I found it in the street." Or, "I found it on the sidewalk." Or, "I found it in the schoolyard." Or, "I found it by the tracks." Or, "I never saw that knife. Swear t'God." Blah blah blah . . . Or I'd proffer some other equally absurd and unbelievably stupid cock-and-bull story with the best poker face I could muster.

Poor Mom. She must have spent many a night wondering if I were going to kill her in her sleep. I would perfect my knife-throwing skills by tossing them at doors, at the floor, at the baseboard, and at the furniture. Don't ask me why, I just did. There were nicks all over the place. Yep, I had the ol' gal on edge, all right. For all she knew, on the edge of a knife. Oh well, I guess it's true that we reap what we sow and all the rest is a gift. We frequently don't like the gifts we are given, though. She could have aborted me, but she didn't. So I was, I suppose, her special little gift from God—a wrathful god. At least I wasn't boring.

I don't know how it all got started. At this point, after so many years of reflection and analysis, I suppose I'll never know. All I can remember is having these frequent surges of deep throbbing gurgitations of crimson. I would at once become enveloped with mercurial throes of just hating everybody and everything and not knowing what to do with myself. I trusted no one. I loved no one. I hated myself. Although I didn't have the concept of *future* in my experiential vocabulary, I was very aware that mine was to be a bleak one. And my mother's response to all of this was to utter and utter and utter her sweet refrains: "You're never gonna be happy. You're never gonna be satisfied. God help the woman that ends up with you. I don't know what's wrong with you." Well, neither did I. But on this particular syzygial day it really didn't matter. Everything was A-OK. The stars, the moons, and planets, were aligned to a T.

Quite apparently, I had created another ruse to stay home from my personal dungeon, Decatur Avenue Elementary School, as I was home alone, once again, while Mom was slaving away next to the firing kilns at Lenox China, way out in the sticks of Pomona. Anyway, I was at home doing who-knows-what. I don't remember the television being on, which in itself would be unusual, so I surely must have been working out the details of some harebrained scheme or dwelling upon my juvenile agonies whilst in the kitchen, one of my favorite haunts—I ate a lot. I was a plumpster. Or, as kids in school called me, a butterball. (I used to eat everything all at once, saving only the meanest amount for me mammy. I couldn't help it. She tried to hide things from me to make them last, especially cookies and candies, but I would always sniff them out and devour them.) Or, I might have been daydreaming about building a log cabin— a place to escape to and get away from it all, like Davy Crockett and Dan'l Boone. Regardless, whatever it was I was up to on this particular magical day, it was interrupted by the gentlest rapping at the door.

I knew my raps. It wasn't old Dogface Doberman, the truant officer. Nor was it Alice, the neighbor girl from across the street, a few years older than I, who, when she wasn't inciting her boyfriends into having knife fights over her, used to beat my ass on a regular basis. No, it wasn't a knock I recognized. There was something mysterious about that knock; something unique that heightened my interest. Oddly, it did not scare me. So, as I had done myriad times before, I stealthed over to peek around the newel post to see who in the heck was down there.

From my coverture, I could see, through the door's nine small panes, a man looking directly at me as though he could see through the wood behind which I was hiding. Hmm ... He was smiling and waving, saying in a sort of muffled but cheerful tone, "Hello, there. Howdy-do?" I remember feeling suddenly naked, busted, caught-with-my-pants-down-really-stupid. What to do next? He just stood there smiling with the full-glass aluminum storm/screen door resting on his back, squeaking with his every movement of anticipation. *Who is he? What does he want?* He just kept standing there staring up at me with a knowing gaze. He knew I was there, of that I was sure. He tapped lightly once again. Then, on impulse, I stood up to reveal myself, standing at the top of the stairs, akimbo, like Mr. Plumber. It was as though we were pinning one another in a real-life Wild West stare down. With a big friendly smile and an unusually lengthy hand, he beckoned me. I recall that those next few seconds or minutes—however long it took for me to get downstairs—passed in a strange kind of slow-motion. The closer I got to him, the farther I ventured away from my reality—whatever that was. My youthful interiority was directing me. Something was going on. I went to the door.

In a twinkling, I assessed his persona to be that of a hobo. Sans a bindle on a stick slung over his shoulder, he was a living Dorothea Lange tableau—a time-scarred man in timeworn attire. He sported a smartly snapped wide brim grayish slouch hat with a thin black ribbon, a dark brown three-button herringbone tweedy blazer with elbow pads, a light blue denim shirt, and dungarees with very large cuffs. They must have been seven or eight inches high. A thick plain brown leather belt with a brass horseshoe buckle cinched his thin girth to hold them up. And, finally, big old scuffed up brown brogues were his transportation. Somehow, I had gotten the image of the peripatetic tramp mixed up with Pleasantville's one and only bum, J. John the Junkman. Word was that J. John once was a brilliant physician who flipped out after his brother died at his hands on an operating table. Now a ragpicker. Truth? Fiction? Whatever, he was one weird dude around P'ville. The man standing outside was a hobo, but I opened the door without hesitation and greeted him, "Hello, whatcha want?"

There, standing before me, erect, defying gravity, with rounded shoulders that looked as though they had carried all the burdens of the world up to that very moment, was a man—a real man. I had never known one before, being raised by a single mom. All the men I had ever had contact with were marginal at best or paid me no attention at worst. Not a role model in sight. But, intuitively, I knew this man standing before me was a true man. Looking like an errant messenger, the tall lanky gentleman had a long angular swarthy-complexioned visage crosshatched with deep fissures of lost hopes and determination, a desert arroyo that hadn't seen water in a long time, a schnoz big enough to qualify as a ski slope, and ears that could catch fly balls in left and right fields simultaneously. He reached up with his enormous elongated rugged hand to remove his soiled but dignified hat. He smiled, exposing his big white healthy mouthful of teeth. And then, with more courtesy and humility than I had ever experienced, before or since, he addressed me with sincerity and respect: "Good day, young sir. I have a great and overwhelming need for a small bit of sustenance. For the slightest modicum I would be most grateful and promise to pass your kindness on to nurture the universe itself." I hadn't a clue what he had just said, so my only reply was my usual, "Huh?" Smiling even wider, he gave a slight bow, smoothly swinging his felt hat up to his chest with panache, as though it were a plumed helmet, and said more plainly, "Food, man. I'm hungry. Can you spare a little to eat?" I didn't know who Don Quixote was but there he was standing before me.

For what must have been at least half a minute, but seemed more like an hour, I just stared at his giant hands. They were the hands of an inordinately strong man; hands that had known a life of hard labor and fighting for basic survival. They were not the hands of a criminal. They were immense. I couldn't take my eyes off of them. His fingers were incredibly long. I knew that they were special hands; that they were meant for something else in life like playing a piano or a violin or performing surgery—something besides the callused itinerant odd job life they'd been relegated to. Then, he burst my bubble. "Kind sir, is there something the matter? Are you OK?" When my eyes finally alighted on his face I said, "Oh, uh . . . , y-y-yeah. Sure. Come in, mister. Yeah."

It had been planted in my head to never trust strangers: especially men, especially strange older single men, because they would *do* things to young children. *Things* so bad that they went unmentioned. Of course I had no idea what those things were, but I guessed they had something to do with sex and stuff. In spite of the thorough brainwashing I had received regarding strange men, I instinctively knew that none of it applied in this particular situation. So, with alacrity, I led him upstairs.

Today, 40 E. Verona Avenue, which is where this all took place, is just an empty lot. All that remains is a big old oak tree I used to love to climb. Once, though, there stood a grand Italianate-ish mansion on that parcel. But by the time this particularly fine day arrived, it had long since been converted into the American Legion Hall. Behind that former mansion was the former chauffeur's quarters—a two-story red brick dwelling with a loggia on two sides, surrounded by aged dogwood, cedar, and holly trees. Downstairs, a two-car garage. Upstairs, our teeny-weeny home sweet home. The upstairs portion was actually what would qualify these days as a very small bachelor: one room no more than 20′ × 20′, if that, with a microscopic closet, a kitchenette, and a molecule of a bathroom with a pint-sized bathtub. The main room was subdivided into our living room (where my mother slept her years away on a fold-out bed) and my little makeshift bedroom, which was actually an area about 6′ × 10′ partitioned off with ¼″ plywood. All around the top of the partition was a foot of open air, so there never was any real privacy.

In the living room—Mom's bedroom—there was a beautiful unusable red brick fireplace. Unusable because a kerosene heater sat in front of it. Its mantle was populated with novelties galore. In this small living room/bedroom were: a super comfortable olive green Castro Convertible couch that was so dense and sturdy it required two mighty brutes to move it, a semi-matching upholstered arm chair, a massive mahogany black-and-white console television with rabbit ears, a painted black coffee table with golden pothos trailing from the back of a ceramic ebony panther, a walnut freestanding display shelf dedicated to more novelties, two two-tiered Queen Anne round dumbwaiters with doilies for the more prominent knickknacks, and a pink-and-white floral patterned teal upholstered wing chair that cozied up to a walnut telephone table, upon which sat a big fat black rotary phone. Everything sat upon a navy gray salt and pepper carpet. Oh! I almost forgot Mom's hanging wall mirror with its painted scene of a palm tree and two pink flamingos—a singular adornment. As you can imagine, home was ultra-cramped, requiring lots of dusting and furniture polishing. It was like living on a small boat. The interior walls of this erstwhile motor house took on the sloping bevel of its mansard pantile roof and were painted bright peach. The kitchen walls were a pastel yellow and the bathroom shocking scarlet. Upon entering our humble abode, one tramped up a long brilliant lime green stairwell. All the painting was cut out perfectly around high gloss pure white woodwork. The flat part of the ceiling was only seven feet high. Nice bright light entered through four curtained sash windows. One had the claustrophobic sense of being entombed in a truncated pyramid. That's where Mom and I lived. But Mom had a way with things; ergo, the place was brightly decorated, neurotically spotless, and every inch utilized to the max. It was a small place by any standards. But when the old man—who I now believe must have been all of forty years of age—planted his feet (more like two wingtip tugboats) in the living room, I think the place shrunk by two.

Reaching the top of the stairs, he stopped and looked about in a very gentle and deliberate manner. With genuine marvel, he commented on and paid compliment to my mother's collection of descending-in-size ceramic black panthers, the flamingo mirror, and the overall quantity and tidiness of all the knickknacks there were in our itsy-bitsy house. I noticed how neat he kept his slicked back shock of graying brown hair, and that although his clothes had that lived-in-slept-in-not-cleaned-for-a-while sheen, he was tidy—had a dapper style about him. I also observed that his face was a kind face. His eyes were soft and tender. Humbly caressing his hat, he went from item to item, a ballerino elephant dancing in a crystal shop, offering commentary on Mom's prized possessions as though each one a madeleine frothing up fresh memories of bygone days. I knew that those things he was saying, his oohing and aahing, would have made my mother feel real good. If he ever intended to commit any of the heinous things I had been forewarned of, this was his chance. But I knew I could trust him.

After a thorough review of Mom's trove of bric-a-brac, he turned and quietly looked me directly in the eyes. I felt comfortable and uncomfortable at the same time. He looked at me as though he had always known me, as though wherever it was that he was coming from and wherever it was that he was going to, he was, at that moment, right where he was supposed to be—with me. I became self-conscious and looked down at the floor. Speaking in the most loving and instructional voice I've ever heard, he admonished me, "Don't look away, young man. You've done nothing to be ashamed of. You always want to look another man right back true to his eye. That's how you can tell what a man is made of. You can learn all sorts of things from the eyes of a person. Be proud of yourself. If anybody does the looking down, lad, let it be the other person, be they man or woman. Stand your ground. Do you understand what I am talking about, son?" I lied and said yes. No man had ever called me son before. A tingle of pleasure shot through me, a strange and wonderful feeling I did not understand. A feeling that would haunt me for the rest of my life. Never did he, not even once, bend down to talk to me or alter the quality of his voice, the way other adults did when they talked to me. Then, cracking a big smile, he rubbed his belly, "Hmmm . . . , *¿Qué comeremos?* What's for lunch?"

I led him into our peewee kitchen, which had a gray-and-white marbled Formica top table with four teal vinyl chairs, an icebox, a small gas stove, a dinky sink, and a white Maytag round tub wringer washer. I told him to have a seat and that I would fix him something. As he was taking off his jacket he asked me if he could use the bathroom to wash up first. Pausing, pondering the question, I offered, "Uh . . . you wunna take a bath?" He looked at me with those soft moon pie eyes, touched the tip of his aquiline nose with his left index finger and nodded, "Why, yes. That would be nice. That would be very nice, indeed."

Whilst he was splashing away, humming, whistling, and singing songs foreign to my ear, I was in the kitchen being my typical eight-year-old domestic self. I grew up pretty much taking care of myself and had spent a tremendous amount of time alone. Fixin' meals was one of my specialties. 'Twasn't uncommon for me to have dinner ready for Mom when she got home from work. I could sling some hash.

When the old man came out fresh shaven, all clean, spiffy, and smiling, his dirty clothes somehow had taken on a cleaner look, as well. It was then that I learned that a smiling face could obscure tattered fabric and blemish. Later in life I would use the smile to cloak broken hearts and fear. As he opened the bathroom door, still humming some old-timey song, he stopped dead in his tracks stunned by the sight of the table I had set for the two of us: steaming bowls of Campbell's tomato soup, tuna fish sandwiches on plain white Bond bread with plenty of chopped onion and lots of Hellmann's mayonnaise, along with Sunshine Saltines for squishing on the soup. To wash it down, the remains of a half-gallon of ShopRite milk and a kettle of simmering water for either Maxwell House instant coffee or Tetley tea. He went for the tea as did I.

Recovering from his amazement, he leaned over the table eyeballing everything while taking deep whiffs of the soup, which I had cooked with diced onion, a tad of evaporated milk, lots of pepper, and had garnished with a goodly sprinkling of Kraft parmesan cheese. Chafing his hands eagerly, licking his chops, he looked at me with a look that levitated me fifteen feet off the ground. He said, grinning the most giant grin I have ever seen, "You did this all by *yourself*?" "Yep," I said with a grin matching his. "My, my, my, my . . . , I have never had such an epicurean feast before mine eyes in all of my long life. All my long life. And I, most assuredly, have never had anyone do such a nice thing for me. Such a nice thing. Such kindness. I am truly blessed to meet you. Why, I don't even know your name, sire." I told him my name. He told me his, though, I cannot for the life of me remember what it was. What's important is that he made me feel for the first time in my life that I was good; that I was important; that I was capable; that I was a real little man. Spreading his arms as though he were about to take flight, he let out an excited bellow: "I am able to wait no longer to partake of this gustatory delight my olfactories bid me to relish immediately. May I sit, kind sir?" I had no idea what he said, but it made me chuckle.

We sat and ate and talked away the afternoon. I do not recall one specific thing that we talked about. All I know is that it was spontaneous and real and honest—I felt good!—and that was not something I was accustomed to. I don't know if it was because of how he was treating me or because I was feeling the elation people of charity experience when helping others, but whatever it was, it fused us in a bond of space and time and heart that has stayed with me these seventy-plus years. All I remember is that we talked and laughed and ate. We ate and talked and laughed. Slowly. Deliberately. Wherever it was that our conversation wandered, I know that he talked to me man-to-man. He was instructing me, giving me direction. That old man was planting in my bean the seeds of honesty, forthrightness, and self-confidence. I can see his dark leathery face beaming with delight as he slurped his soup, reveling in his meal, asking for seconds. I'm sure he asked me about my life and that he told me about the places he had been and where he was planning to go. I was sharp to the moment that the time I was spending with him was special and not to be repeated—ever. He was the dad I never had; perhaps I was to him the son he never had. Whate'er 'twas goin' on, carpe diem was in order. When we were finished, he offered to help me clean up the mess. I washed and he dried. Then it was time for him to go.

He put on his jacket and grabbed his hat, "Well, friend, it's time for this fiddle-footed bo to be moseying on." Looking at me with a masculine affection I've never experienced since, he extended his hand. As we shook, I felt the controlled raw strength I knew he possessed. Once again he looked me in the eyes and said, "You always want to give a firm handshake, *Don David*. But you don't want to make it unpleasant for the other fella. You can tell a lot about a person from his handshake—not everything, but it's a good start. Personally, I never trust anyone who will not look me in the eyes or who has a flaccid handshake. You, squire, valiant doer of good, now that's a real hardy handshake."

His departure was unlike his arrival. Not like a stranger. More like an old friend who popped in for an impromptu visit. A true fellow traveler. Both of us knowing that it was no big thing and that we would be seeing each other real soon. Still shaking my hand, "Well, kind sir, it has been, indeed, a pure pleasure to make your acquaintance, and I feel truly fortunate to have been the recipient of your gracious hospitality. (There is quite a dearth of largess these days, you know.) Oh, and your expertise in the culinary arts is among the finest, perhaps *the* finest, I have ever had the serendipity to come across in all of my journeys thus far. Ha! And I was told that *xenia* had reached its demise at Troy. Flapdoodle! Baloney! Humbug! Why, I have it standing before mine eyes. I've been misinformed, I tell you. Bamboozled! . . . Rest assured, good lad, that I am well cognizant that I will never be able to repay the 'milk of human kindness' you have extended to me here today. But do know, my lord, that I shall pass your benevolence on to some other necessitous soul when the opportunity presents itself. But for now, my host, off I go. Off I go to stem the universe for a few simoleons and my next prandial pleasure." After his extended good-bye speech, of which I understood practically nothing, all I could think of to say was, "Thanks. See you later."

He donned his hat, pulled it snug, tipping its rim to say good-bye, then turned and walked down the stairs. I watched him walk down and out into the world, a world I now know condemned and ridiculed him for being the hobo that he was. Oh, if that world only knew the love that old man had aroused in this little eight-year-old. He shut the door softly and the storm door creaked itself to a final slam. Later, when Mom came home from work I told her about the old man and she liked to have a conniption fit. Of course she repeated all that stuff about strangers and old men and things and whatnot.

As I ruminate our fateful convivial encounter that long-ago day, I wonder what that old man would think of me now with the life I have lived and all of the mistakes I have made, all of my false starts, all of my incomplete passes, all of my dashed dreams. I wonder what he would think to know that he is the closest thing to a father I have ever known. I wonder if he were to come to my door today, right now, would I invite him in and share as I did then? Oh, how cruel a home truth it is that this life doth throttle the trust and love born of callow youth.

COLORS

Do you remember
The first time
You became
Aware
Of
Genital pleasure?
I do.
I had, of course
Done the usual
You-show-me
I'll-show-you
Routine
But real pleasure . . .?

I was a pup of eight or nine
And learning

How
To shimmy up a flagpole
When it hit me
Damn! *Ooo-oui!*

The flagpole
Was out in front
Of the American Legion
Post 81
On the Black Horse Pike
40 E. Verona Avenue,
Behind which
My mother and I lived
For years now
A flattened unused piece of property

The pole was very accessible
So I began to practice
With discipline
I shimmied every day
Sometimes two or three or four
Or five times a day . . .

I really got quite good at it
Like a Cirque du Soleil acrobat
Aloft

Suspended mid-pole
Looking down at a massive WWII silver torpedo
An advertisement for the Post

Passing cars would beep-beep
In recognition
Of my feat
And I

Legs wrapped around that pole
With all my little strength
Right hand clutching that pole
Left hand waving
Like a seasoned
Politician
My peoples! My peoples . . . !
Smiling
With pure delight
Preorgasmically sentient
Training my little body
My little mind
My little genitals
Right there in front of
God and all the passersby
Of Pleasantville
There was no telling where
This talent would go

Now I know why guys
Like to go to those
Nudie bars
Where exploited women dance
With poles
Brings back fond memories . . .

3

LIARS

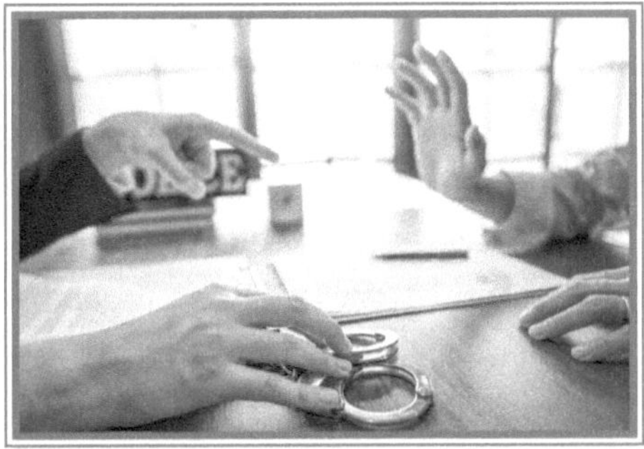

t had to have been a Friday night, because all the conditions were right. My mom was out, so I had the house to myself; Joey DiGiacinto's mom and dad were slurping down the green crème de menthe and listening to Nat King Cole; and, Paul Williams—no, not that Paul Williams—came into Pleasantville from his haunts out around Port Republic way. Paul was Joey's cousin and whenever Paul was around, trouble lurked nearby. He was one crazy fucker.

We were all around fourteen or fifteen and as far as style goes, Joey and I had it. Now, mind you, Joey's folks had money so he always had well-tailored everything and his clothes were always starched and pressed at the cleaners. My mom was poor, but I was keeping up by washing and ironing my own clothes and using spray starch. Back then, our dress would've been categorized as conservative: cuffed, perfectly-creased pants, black nylon socks (sometimes with garters)—Joey liked brown cap toe oxfords, and I was a full brogue cordovan wing tip guy. Whenever we were going out to a dance or a party, we'd wear white or powder blue dress shirts with semi-spread collars, topping everything off with navy blue or burgundy cardigans, which more often than not were folded and slung over our left arm to affect the best sprezzatura we could muster. Princeton haircuts, parted on the left side, were what we were sporting at the time. A constant battle for Joey because his Italian gene kept curling his hair to the point where it looked more like a jet-black sea of turbulence than the pseudopreppy image we were endeavoring to project, no matter how much Brylcreem he lathered on. Thusly configurated would we have been attired this particular hot and humid South Jersey evening, the events of which I am about to relate.

But Paul . . . , style he did not have. To say that he had abominable taste is to put it mildly. Sometimes it appeared that he went out of his way to be goofy. He was a ballsy bumptious bumpkin—a hybridization of a juvenile Ron Howard, a thirtyish Tim Robbins, and Todd on *Breaking Bad*. Innocent, right? Hardly. He really looked and sounded innocent. He was quirky. Out in his species' habitat—the boondocks (i.e., Jersey Devil territory)—a consciousness of things like contemporary clothes and music didn't count for much. I mean he didn't know any of the songs and he dressed like a farm worker and he talked like a square. But the boy sure liked to drink. And when he drank, shit hit the fan. It wasn't a question of *if* there would be trouble; there *would* be. At the very least, he'd come up with outrageous drunken scenarios—of space aliens and vampires and werewolves and you name it—that he'd expect you to believe. One crazy kid, but he was never boring.

So we three set out, one fine Friday night in the summer of 1963, in search of a party Paul had heard about. Very few kids had cars in those days, so walking and hitchhiking was how you got around if you wanted to get around. As Paul assured us that we only needed to walk about a mile or so up Main Street to the edge of Northfield, off a-hoofing we went—three fools into the darkling night.

As I was in possession of a cache of recently heisted booze—a secret I kept from everyone I knew because I knew the dopes I knew would blow my cover—I set us up with some Seagram's VO and warm beer chasers (my secret hiding place not being refrigerated) to get us lubricated, just in case there was nothing to drink at the party—if we even found it. So, happily half-looped, off we wobbled through backyards and side streets, wending our way to where only the gods know. This was a Paul excursion. He said he knew where the party was. The problem was, he couldn't remember. So, like the lamebrains we were, we kept roaming around unfamiliar neighborhoods in the dark of night, searching for the holy party. With the little booze he had in him, Paul became possessed, rabid, and noisy:

"I think it's up here!" Not there. "I think it's over there!" Not there. "I'm sure it's up this street! Yes, up this street!" Nope "OK. OK. I remember now: it's this way. Come on. I've got it this time. Come on." Wrong.

Joey and I exchanged glances and gestures expressing our mutual distrust in Paul's delusionary efforts. All the walking was becoming laborious. It's hard to be cool when you are pooped and looped. Besides, I didn't like wearing my heels down. Joey started complaining. I snapped:

"Paul, you are so fucked up! So fucked up, man. We shouldn't've ever listened to your ass. There ain't no fucking party and you know it—"

"No! No, man . . . There is. I'm telling you. It's around here somewhere. This kid told me about it. A big party. Big party. Lots of booze. And girls!"

Joey chimed in with, "You're full o' shit. Always. full o' shit, Pauly."

"No, man. You gotta trust me. I'm not lyin'. Honest . . ."

Joey started spluttering, "Bullshi'!-bullshi'!-bullshi'! . . ."

It's a wonder no one called the cops on us for just being stupid.

"All right," Paul conceded, "let's get to the next place and if it's not there we'll split. OK? One more try."

"We're gettin' farther and farther away, man. This walkin' shit's gettin' old. You and Joey can keep lookin'. I'm gonna split."

"Ahhh, mannn, one more try. C'mon, mannn . . ."

Well, he was right. There was a party and it was a doozy. We didn't know whose house it was and we didn't know anyone there. Lots of booze, of which we partook. Lots of girls, of which we did not partake. And far too many guys getting shitfaced. But there we were at a party. Paul was feeling pretty good about himself.

Like I said, Paul was, well, uncool. His non-style stood out like a sore thumb. That wasn't bad enough. The clincher was that he had no social filters, so he said whatever was on his drunken or sober mind to whomever. Now, usually I was the guy other guys wanted to pick a fight with. It was a height thing. I was 6′2″ and the little guys, well, you know how that goes.

But this night Paul was getting all the attention. Some kid posed a challenge and Paul duly gave him some lip and *KAblooey!* we had us a tussle. It didn't last long, though. Paul got smacked around and it was quickly broken up. So we relocated ourselves to a safer proximity whereupon Paul effervesced with I-was-about-to-do-this-to-hims and I-was-about-to-do-that-to-hims. Then, of a sudden, he was all jacked up, shadowboxing, beer bottle in hand, prating and prancing around, showing us what his next move would've been, ". . . if only those guys hadn't've broken up the fight—" when, he fell. Bottle shattering to smithereens.

It was dark where he landed and I and Joey and whatever other kids were around exploded laughing. But, somehow, I knew to jump in there telling moaning and groaning Paul not to move, trying to make sure he didn't cut himself. But once he was righted, I could see gushing blood. There was a gash just below his elbow on the inner side of his right arm. Everybody at once started jabbering that we had to call for help, to get him to a doctor, take him to the hospital, but Paul insisted that we should do no such thing, assuring us that he would be just fine. Like some kind of hero, he took off his shirt and wrapped his skinny white arm. Even in the bad light I could see that his T-shirt was dingy—an indication that they didn't use bleach at his house. Posthaste, we three agreed that we should get the hell out of there.

While walking up Dolphin Avenue approaching Shore Road, making Paul hold his right arm up so he didn't bleed to death, I convinced him that we should all go to my place to administer some first aid before he headed on home. We were just passing what we called the crazy house when I lit upon the idea that if we were to be asked by anyone what had happened that we should blame it on a gang of black kids. That was as far as we got with the story.

"C'mon, man, let's hurry. I can't keep holding my fucking arm up . . ."

As expected, and seriously hoped for, Mom wasn't home yet, so we were in the clear. Paul was showing definite signs of weakness and whining like a baby. We needed to act fast. But what to do? Joey was atwitter in the calmest of times, but once we were confined within my tiny home, he became a useless twirling whirling dervish. Where the presence of mind came from, I don't know, but it came and I went into solutions mode:

"OK, Paul! In t'da bathroom."

"Bathroom? I don't have to go t'd' bathroom, mannn. What's wrong with you? I think I'm dying, man. I think I'm dying . . ."

"We gotta get'im to a hospital . . . ," Joey, like the schizo he could be at times, started repeating over and over, pacing aimlessly uttering, "Ooo! Ooo! Ooo!" between his get-him-to-the-hospitals.

"Cut it out, Joey! I'm trying to think, goddamnit! Stop being a jerk-off."

"Who made you the boss? Who made you the boss, huh?"

"Shut up! Shut up! Shut up! Joey. You're not helping. Paul! Into the bathroom, now! Come on!"

Joey was freaking out and Paul, well, he did look like he was dying. But he was drunk and I was, too. It was hard to discern what the reality really was. But I had had a goodly number of injuries growing up and Mom always knew what to do. With that experience under my belt, I knew I could manage this little life-threatening affair. I would simply emulate Mom. No problem.

Now, being that Mom and I lived above the garage of an old chauffeur's quarters, and being that it was lodging for a bachelor hired man, things were tight and sparse. So, our humble bathroom was no more than 5′×7′ with a tiny claw-foot tub, a small sink, and a commode. I herded Paul in there and sat him on the toilet seat. As I was unraveling his makeshift shirt-bandage, he began bemoaning his lacerated arm:

"Oh! Shit! Man! . . . I'm gonna fuckin' die. I fucked up! Oh, I fucked up. I fucked up, man . . ."

"No, you're not. Calm down, now, Paul. Help me out, here. Look at me. Look me in the eyes. Look at me!" He did look at me and he didn't look good.

"Ooo! Ooo! We got t'call the police," Joey blurted. "The hospital. A doctor. He needs a doctor! If he dies—oh, shit! Ooo! Ooo! If he dies, we'll be charged with manslaughter. Manslaughter! I ain't goin'ta jail, man. I ain't goin'ta jail . . ." And in this manner did Joey continue incessantly blathering on all the while in the background, unable to contain his growing case of the whim-whams.

Like some pitiful animal in the throes of death, Paul lets out a whimpering caterwaul, "Nooo! Nooo poliiice . . ."

"He's not going to *fucking* die, Joey. I can fix this. Cut it out, will *ya!*"

When Joey wasn't scuttling around the kitchen like a lunatic, he was hovering over my shoulder, making it difficult to inspect Paul's inadvertent self-inflicted damage. His *Car 54, Where Are You?* Gunther Toody *ooo*-ing thing was driving me nuts. He would get so close I could feel his foul breath on my neck. He was useless. Just in the way. A nervous wreck. I thought about killing him. But I had a life to save. So that was out of the question. His fidgeting was contagious. *Focus!* I had to focus.

Tuning Joey out, I assessed the situation. Paul *was* beginning to fade. Slouching against the tank, he cradled his broken wing while mumbling incoherencies. He was of a deathly hue. His head was tilted back, as were his eyes. All I could see were zombie white orbs. But Paul was prone to drama and I was wondering how much of it was put-on. He had a history of feigning. But, in that bantam bathroom, that my mother had artistically painted scarlet red, he was looking pretty pale. Too pale. Finally, he uttered something I could understand, "Whaaadaya gonna dooo? . . ." His slur was clearly worsening.

Joey burst out, "Ohhh, mannn! Shit man! Shit! I'm callin' the cops. Ooo! Ooo! . . ."

Paul snapped to life, articulating, "No! No cops, Joey! I'll kick your ass . . ."

I was right. Part of it was theatrical. But there was no getting around it, the kid was hurt. "I have the perfect thing, see. My mom's used it on me a million times. First, I have to clean that wound. Sit up."

I had already gotten one of our clean rags we used to clean the house and sopped it with hot tap water. (Yes, we washed our rags. Mom was a clean*nik*.) But every time I only slightly touched him he'd flinch, yell, pull away, whimpering all the while. I went to the medicine cabinet and took out a small white milk glass jar and opened it. Showing Paul its pitch black viscous content, I said, "Look, Paul. I need to put a coat of this on your wound. This stuff works miracles. My mother uses it for everything."

"What is it?"

"Black salve, ma'mans. It'll fix ya right up. This shit is like magic!" (Turns out this black salve Mom used to cure pretty much everything was an old snake oil escharotic concoction. Under the wrong circumstances, it could do more harm than good. I don't, however, remember her ever applying it to an open wound, so I was being less than honest with Paul.)

Gazing down at his injury, coddling his wounded wing as though it were a scared puppy, Paul says in a forced stage whisper, "But it hurts when you touch—"

"I know. I know, man . . . Hmmm . . ." A long pause ensues. Pure quiet. A hissing white noise swells. No motion whatsoever taking place. We three were petrified. I could feel Joey's vision penetrating my shoulder blades. Then I could feel and hear his breathing. My eyes were locked on Paul's physiognomy. It was talking to me. His eyes widened in response to my unusual glances and head tilts. Then—"I know what to do. I got it."

"Wha-wha-what?"

"I'm gonna have t' knock ya out."

"What?"

Joey started chiming in, "Oh, shit! Oh, shit! Ooo! Ooo! . . . Now you're gonna knock'im out?"

"Joey! *Shut* up, will ya . . ."

"Knock me out? OK. Wudda'ya want me t'do?"

"OK. Sit up straight and put your chin out. Close your eyes." And he did.

I pulled back my right and bam! Landed one right square on his left chin. But he just shivered, screamed, and recovered, "Goddamn! Goddamn, man!"

"OK, I know what to do. I'll get it this time. Sit up."

"I don't know about this, man . . ."

Joey's behind me, "Ooo . . . this is nuts, man. You are insane. This is crazy, David . . ."

"No-no-no-no, it's OK. I know what I did wrong." So Paul sits forward, hugs his arm, pokes his head forward, closes his eyes, and tenses up. "Relax, Paul. You need to relax. That's why it didn't work. You're all tensed up." He relaxed and bam! I laid another solid blow to his willing chin. But this time he stood up and got in my face.

"I'm gonna fuckin' kill you! I'm gonna fuckin' kill you! That's it! No fuckin' more! . . . That shithurtsman! . . . You dohn know wuda fuck ya doin'. . ."

Joey began laughing hysterically, *ooo*-ing and pacing around the kitchen, "This is insane, man! Totally fucking insane! Nex'y'gonna wunna *ampu*tate! . . ."

"Hmmm . . . , I don't know why it isn't working. But we *do* need to get the salve on you."

"Just put it on, man. Just put it **on** me. I'll deal with the pain. No more knocking me the fuck out, though . . ."

So I got myself organized and sat on the rim of the tub to ply my craft with Joey hovering in the doorway kvetching and rambling on. Paul held out his arm exposing a wound about two inches long that looked about as wide. Raw meat. Pressuring the back of his wrist to an old towel on my thigh I cleaned the area, rinsing the blood rag with hot running water from the bathtub, bloody water swirling down the drain was reminiscent of *Psycho*, only in living color. After applying Mercurochrome, I slathered on a coat of black salve. Writhing, grinding teeth, growling, and grimacing with pain, Paul managed to keep his arm perfectly still for me. Mom kept our medicine cabinet well supplied, so we had everything we needed. I bandaged him up with plenty of gauze and adhesive tape and gave him a couple of aspirins and told him to call me in the morning, in which he saw no humor. That was that and off they went.

I went to bed. Out like a light.

Floating somewhere amidst slumber, drunken stupor, and hypnopompic hallucinations, I was becoming aware of thumping. No, it was a booming noise. Boom! Boom! Boom! Each *boom!* a little louder, a little clearer. Then it became: Ratatat! Ratatat! Ratatat! . . . Then I put two and two together—someone was knocking at the door. I got up.

In my briefs and T-shirt, I eased over to take a look down the stairs. Peeking around the newel post, I couldn't see anything. Then a flood of light blinded me.

"David Betterton. Officer Daniels, Pleasantville Police. Please open the door."

Shit! The police. What the fuck! . . .

I put on some pants and went down.

"Sorry to bother you. Are you David Betterton?"

"Yes."

"Mr. Betterton, are your parents here?"

"No. No, my my mom'll be home in a while."

"Well, we need you to come down to the station to make a statement about the incident tonight involving Paul Williams. It won't take long. We'll have you back home in no time."

"Ah, OK. Gimme a minute." *Shit! Fuck! Damn!*

When we arrived at the police station, I think it was about 1 a.m., Paul and Joey were sitting on a bench looking scared as shit. The officer marched me directly into a room, so we didn't even get to say a word. He told me to have a seat and that he'd be back shortly. There I sat, freaking out but trying not to show it. When he returned he had a partner. They were nice, but I knew they were playing me. I was just a dumb kid. That's what they wanted. That's what I gave. They both sat down. The new cop, Cop Number Two, started the questioning, ready to write everything down:

"Dave, tonight you were out with Paul Williams and Joseph DiGiacinto. Is that right?"

"Yes."

"Mr. Williams was the victim of a savage assault. Did you witness it?"

"Yes."

"Can you tell us what happened?"

"Umm . . . We were, ahh, walking home—"

Cop Number One asks, "What street were you on?

"Dolphin. By the crazy house."

Cop Two: "What time was it?"

"I guess it was about, oh, I, I don't know. Ten . . . ten thirty?"

Cop One: "Where were you coming from?"

"A party."

Cop Two: "Where was the party?"

"I don't know. Some kid's house. We just went with Paul. Paul knew."

Cop Two: "Were you drinking?"

"No."

Cop One: "OK. What happened?"

"We were just walking by the crazy house when these black kids came up and started messing with us."

Cop Two: "Were you on the sidewalk or in the street?"

"On the sidewalk. Yeah—No! No. In the street. We were walking down the middle of the street."

Cop One: "How many were there?"

"I don't know. Five? Six? It seemed like a lot. Seven?"

Cop Two: "What did they look like? Can you describe them?"

"Oh. They were black. It was dark."

Cop One: "Were they tall? Short? Fat? Dark skin? Light skin? Light clothes? Dark clothes? You must've noticed something."

"Well, there was one who was tall. As tall as me. He was pretty light. One was kinda heavy and dark. But it was dark. I was scared."

Cop One: "What about the others?"

"Two of them seemed little. Maybe eleven or twelve. A couple of them seemed like fourteen or fifteen. But the big one and tall light-skinned kids I think were more like sixteen or seventeen."

Cop One: "Good. That's a lot of detail for not being able to see."

"I'm just guessing . . ."

Cop Two: "OK, so what happened?"

"I don't know. They just walked up and—"

Cop Two: "What did they say?"

"I don't know. It was, like, 'What chu *doin'* here? You in the *wrong* place' or something like that."

Cop Two: "Who said that?"

"The tall light one."

Cop One: "Then what happened?"

"Paul started arguing with him. Telling him to leave us alone and stuff."

Cop Two: "Then what happened?"

"I don't know. The kid pushed Paul and a fight started. The kid pulled out a knife and started swinging it around. The other kids were all yelling and jumping around. It was hard to tell what was going on."

Cop One: "What were they yelling?"

"I don't know. Stuff like: 'Get'im!' 'Kick'is ass!' 'White motherfuckers!' and stuff like that."

Cop Two: "What were you and Mr. DiGiacinto doing?"

"Just watching."

Both cops paused and gave each other a telling glance.

What the hell does that mean? Oh, shit . . .

Cop Two: "Then what happened?"

"Ahh-umm . . . I don't know. Um, the kid-a was-a swishing the knife around and—"

Cop One: "What kind of knife was it? Switchblade? Hunting knife?"

"I-I-I don't know. It was shiny. Silver, I think. It was hard to see . . ."

Another pregnant pause. They glimpsed at one another. Their gimlet eyes alighted upon me dripping with suspicion. The penetration was sharp. They were boring holes all over my story, I was sure. Cop Number Two started tapping out an aggressive paradiddle on the tabletop with his right index and middle fingers. *Oh shit! Uh-oh . . . Damn! What the fuck! . . .* All six of our eyes were unshakably locked. I concentrated on looking innocent, allowing myself to blink a time or two to look natural. But I did not swallow. *Don't swallow!* From one to the other, I looked with inquiry, wrinkling my forehead, squinting, lifting my shoulders, slightly tilting my head, gesticulating curiously with my face. Years of watching *Perry Mason* was paying off—I hoped. Suddenly, the finger drumming stopped with a loud pop. He jotted something down. Again, they looked at each other. This all took a thousand years or one minute.

Cop Two: "Then what happened, David?"

"Uh-uhm, all of a sudden Paul started yelling, 'You cut me! You cut me! I'm bleeding! I'm bleeding!' and the black kid just froze. He just stood there staring. Then he, then he, he-he closed up his knife and then and then he turned and took off. They, they all just took off running."

Cop One: "Then what happened?"

"We walked back to my house and I fixed'im up."

Cop Two: "OK, that pretty much does it. Anything else you want to say about it?"

"No, sir."

Cop Two: "Oh, one more question: why didn't you call the police?"

"Oh-ah-oh-ah-ummm—"

Cop One: "We know you all were drinking. If we *catch* you . . . we **will** arrest you. Understand?"

"Ah, yes, sir."

Cop Two: "Thank you for your cooperation. Wait here and we'll be back to finalize everything."

"Yes, sir."

So there I was. Sitting alone. In a dismal room. Where I had just fabricated the night's happenings to two Pleasantville police officers. Blaming Paul's idiocy on some black kids that didn't exist. What kind of crime might that be? What kind of trouble was I about to get in? The waiting was taking a long . . . long . . . long time. I could hear muffled conversations. Doors opening and closing. Occasional bursts of laughter. The tapping of a typewriter. Phones ringing. I wasn't sure, but I thought I heard a boy crying. Paul? Joey?

After about fifteen or twenty minutes, Cop Number One comes in carrying a file folder. He just stands there, silent, staring at me. *Don't react. Be innocent. Don't swallow. Don't react.* Then:

"OK, David. We got everything we need. All three of your stories match. We'll scour that area. See if we can make that kid pay for what he did. Let's go. I'll take you home."

On our way, he gives me a lecture about being safe and keeping out of black neighborhoods and watching myself with the booze. The radio squawked incomprehensible monotony. The ride is surreal. I can't believe I just hoodwinked the cops and am getting away with it. He drops me off. We say our goodbyes. Mom's not home yet—thank God! I go to bed. (She never finds out until forty or so years later when I reveal some of my shenanigans.)

The next day, I go over to Joey's and he commences to tell me all about how when Paul got home he caved in to his Nazi mother, who basically tortured him into divulging the night's events and participants. And she called the police. Why the fool had to tell her he was with Joey and me, I don't know. All I know is that the cops got each one of us in separate rooms and grilled us for what happened and we all told the same damned story. Sure, we'd all agreed to blame it on blacks, but the alibi died aborning. When Joey and Paul and I later compared notes, we were amazed to find that we had all unwittingly participated in telling a perfect lie.

4

THE PIT

What can I say about that pit
Big old hole in the woods
With lots of water in it
Sleepy kelly green
Sargasso jewel to behold
Never have I seen a more beautiful hole
Borrowed to build the roads
Cape May to New York
Door to door
Hidden off of Coolidge Avenue
From public sight
Quarry forlorn
Cardiff kids' delight

Redolent stagnation I occasionally do smell
When lazy old LA River ceases to swell

Its flocks alighting for a reposeful spell
Ding! Ding! Goes memory's bell
Ding! Ding! Goes memory's bell

A sweet algal whiff stirs the old tickler:
Rafts of purloined four-by-fours
Or anything thicker
Pirate galleons afar from shore
Privateersmen ploughing
With no sails, no oars
Just cool summer dives and
Pit monster kelpies galore
Run for your lives, men!
Swim for your lives!

What small boy pleasures ye olde Cardiff pit
Held in store
Motley crews of temerarious urchins
Heading for the safety of shore
Alack! 7-10 traffic dashes my thoughts
Poof!
Kids can't play like that—
        Anymore
Kids *can't* play like that—
        Anymore . . .

5

BEEPER LINE

Long before email or Facebook or Vine or Textfree or Spillit or Tumblr or Keek or MySpace or Twitter or the myriad social media coming into existence as I write these words—which means those just mentioned will be passé by the time I finish writing this confabulated piece of faction; long before all the contemporary instant impersonal nonhuman technological human interactions devoid of grammar, orthography, tenderness, inhibition, courtesy, awareness, manners, and humanity—long long ago, way back yonder in the 1960s was the beeper line. Some kid somewhere, somehow would get hold of a number and before you knew it, all the kids had it. It went viral. A beeper line would last for a while until Ma Bell would find out about it and shut it down. Then it would start all over again with a new secret number. I never spent much time on the beeper line because it seemed more trouble than it was worth. I did, however, spend enough time on it to sufficiently suffer an experience that has seethed in my soul all these many many years. A real chink in my character.

To join a beeper line conversation, you would dial a number that would ring you through to an alternate universe of eternal busyness. Today busy signals are pretty much continuous bizz!-bizz!-bizz!-bizz!, if you can even get one. An annoying voicemailish digital person usually answers, asking us to make a million frustrated decisions. But if we do get a busy signal, we tend to think that something is wrong. Anyway, when I was a kid there was a crackling static hissing pause between each bizz (bizz! … bizz! … bizz! … bizz! …). It was during the pauses where all the action would take place. You had just enough time to spit out one, two, maybe three fast words at max. It would go something like this:

Ring … ring … ring …

Bizz! "Hello." Bizz! "Anybody." Bizz! "There?" Bizz!

"Yes." Bizz! "Who's this?" Bizz! … And it was off to the races.

Unlike the lightning speed social media of today, the beeper line required a willingness to slow down and listen carefully. Patience was key. From those interstitial snippets of conversation one had to decipher if one was cute or ugly, young or old, smart or stupid, black or white, or whatever. And to raise the bar just a little, you had to do this while others were having crosstalk conversations as well. It could get pretty insane. You had to really be focused and lonely enough to put up with the stupid technology. The ultimate goal was to get a girl's phone number. That was the big deal.

Like I said, I didn't spend much time on it. I only tried it a few times. It could get nerve-racking. But I had the number one prerequisite (i.e., I was a lonely goof). And, being thirteen with pretty much nothing to do, I had plenty of time on my hands (i.e., patience). So, this one summer day in 1962, I called and found that I was the only person on the line:

Ring … ring … ring … bizz! … bizz! … bizz! "Hello." Bizz! "Anybody there?" Bizz! "Hello anybody—" Bizz! …

This went on for quite a while. I just sat there in our living room slumped on the couch with this big clunky phone to my ear, staring goggle-eyed through my tortoiseshell-rimmed glasses into nothingness. Bizz! … bizz! … bizz! … Every now and then, I'd throw out a "Hello," and continue staring. (The pinch of loneliness is an odd symptom of life. It is through suffering that we acknowledge life; that we *become—*

completely aware that we are completely alive. Happiness makes us forget. Thoughtlessly, we spend endless hours with people and things and preoccupations we abhor, attempting to anesthetize ourselves: seeking happiness, forgetting, avoiding the sting of life we each must endure—waiting out the busy signals.)

Then, the impossible happened. I was awakened, jarred from my stupor. An intervallic angel appeared. The lovely voice of a lovely girl. Hallelujah! Pay dirt! Manna!

"Hello."

"Hello."

"Who's this?"

"Who's this?"

"David."

"Hi, David."

"What's your name?"

"Marsha . . ."

It turned out that she was a freshman at Pleasantville High. As usual, I lied about my status. Things were going good. We had the beeper line to ourselves. A rare opportunity. And after slogging our way through the swampy bogs of teenage conversation interruptus, I asked the big question: "What's your phone number?" But she was shrewd and asked for mine instead. True to her word, she called me back a few minutes later and we ended up talking for perhaps two hours, maybe three. It being the middle of the day with no parents around, we had free rein. I heard other voices in the background and occasionally she would have quick asides with what she told me were her siblings. There was a lot of giggling and I knew that they were teasing her about talking with a boy. It felt good. The hole in my soul didn't feel so empty. I was talking with a girl who wanted to talk with me. She seemed real nice. She seemed smart and was talking to me like I was somebody worth talking to. I was in uncharted territory. Then, unexpectedly, she ratcheted things up a notch and suggested that we meet in person—vis-à-vis, *cara a cara, faccia a faccia,* in real life! What to do? When? Where? How? Decisions . . .

Batting around ideas, it turned out that she would be hanging out at Bargaintown the next day. How about there? Bargaintown would be a perfect venue. It was a date. So after all that time on the phone, my mind started working on what to do now that we were actually going to meet. Bargaintown was a good place to do it, I figured. A safe place. And I didn't need any money. I loved Bargaintown. One of my all-time favorite places to go swimming. Ahhh . . . , the possibilities. Lying on a beach towel with a girl of my own, making out and listening to a transistor radio. A scene I had seen so many times in the movies and in real life and in my youthful morphing alleged mind. I ached for it.

Bargaintown is a beautiful little cedar lake about five miles from where I lived in Pleasantville. I could ride a bike, thumb a ride, or walk there. It was easy to get to. I had been trucking over there in the summertime ever since I was a little kid. All these years later, whenever I make a nice hot cup of Lipton tea, I see the cool tannic waters of Bargaintown. Sometimes, the mere sight of a gutter puddle can instantly transport me back there if it's the right tawny hue. One of my favorite things to do when I was a kid was to swim up to the Central Avenue wooden dam, rest my arms up on its stringy algae-covered edge, and enjoy the pressure of the cedar water rushing around me. As I watched the sweet fluid of life cascading down into a yellowish roaring soup, I would become mesmerized for God knows how long. All alone, I'd just stay there staring and thinking and listening to the calming turbulence of the churning water. The gleeful yells and laughter of happy kids at the beach barely filtering through. I was there. But I wasn't there. Eyes fixed on teeming harried bubbles drifting away and popping, until the roiling water once again became a smooth lazy flow. Little did I know the provenance of those bubbles or their destination.

Long before the European Encounter, long before Bargaintown was *Bargaintown,* it was a sleepy cedar swamp whose waters oozed into a creek that flowed placidly four miles southward through the marshes before yawning to deposit its rich sedimental nutrients into the estuary of what the Europeans would one day call the Great Egg Harbor Bay. The terra firma around the swamp was a summering place for the indigenal Lenni-Lenape, which means the grandfathers or true original people of the Algonquin-speaking peoples. They would pick berries, collect birds' eggs, hunt, fish, harvest clams and mussels and oysters, and just hang out.

What the Europeans named Nova Caesarea that became West and East Jersey and then New Jersey, the Lenni-Lenape simply called *scheyechbi* (long land water). In the springtime, after planting pumpkin, squash, beans, tobacco, and corn at their inland villages, they headed for the "Jersey Shore"—the original shoobies—where the matriarchal Lenni-Lenape would sojourn the summer growing season enjoying what they simply called *zeewanhacky* (the place of sea fans or shells), or "the shore."

While I knew not to swim in certain areas because of snags, I had no idea that below the surface lay the slash of a primeval cedar forest with stumps five feet in diameter and that the extant woods all about was probably third-growth; that to my left as I rested upon the dam had once stood a thriving grist mill, to my right a sawmill; that the original Central Avenue and its dam were the fruits of slave labor—and some of those slaves very likely Lenni-Lenape; that those bubbles I couldn't take my eyes off of were drifting down Patcong Creek that until the nineteenth century had supported three shipyards that built sloops and schooners that sailed the world; that stylish Victorian era women had ice-skated on the frozen lake wearing full-length coats and wide-brimmed elaborately plumed hats (a fashion that had devastated Florida's bird population). Nor did I have an inkling that gangs of men once sawed blocks of ice from the lake to be stored in sawdust for summer's use. No one at Bargaintown knew any of this stuff. We lived there! Who knows anything about where you live? We were all just out there splashing around and having fun. It was a great place to go spend time with your friends, if you had any. And with your girl, if you had one. I, for the first time in my life, was about to try the latter on for size. But there was a hitch—a flaw with my beach date with Marsha. One chink. A little catch. A major drawback. One insurmountable problem: I was flabby and terribly ashamed of my body. Oh, well . . .

The next day I got ready. I took a bath. Brushed my teeth. Combed my hair a million times (to make sure my Princeton part was just right). Splashed on some Aqua Velva. Put on my favorite frayed faded Levi cutoffs, my well-worn gray sweatshirt with sleeves cut off to mid-upper arm that I wore inside out (my best beatnik/beach bum/Maynard G. Krebs look), and off I went. And, as the Beach Boys' pseudosurfer thing was *in*—

no shoes. I was a modern day firewalker. It was a personal badge of honor to endure stones, hot sidewalks, and to be able to walk for miles barefooted. The heat and humidity were oppressive. I walked and thumbed down Shore Road, but ended up walking most of the way because I only got a couple of short rides. But it gave me time to think.

Marsha had no idea what I looked like or what I would be wearing. But I knew that she'd be wearing a navy blue Annette Funicello two-piece swimsuit, be lying on a pink beach towel, and that she was 5'6" with auburn hair that would be tied back in a ponytail. On the phone, she was witty, intelligent, and articulate. She sounded delicious. I couldn't believe my good fortune. As I walked toward that which I feared the most, high anxiety and anticipation put a lilting lift in my step. A rooster on the march. A little extra pop to the step and swing to the arm. I was a little cockier than usual. It was almost as if my calloused feet were not even touching the ground. To be on the safe side, I decided to hedge my bets and take a circuitous route: Shore Road to Mill Road and hook a right. An oblique left onto Cedar Bridge to Zion. Left on Bargaintown, then left on Central. That meant more time walking on Linwood's sidewalkless country streets of jagged stones and parching asphalt, but it allowed me to approach the beach from the front so I could get a good look at everyone. While I was giddy with prospect, I was equally apprehensive. I had ample reason to be skittish about meeting a girl.

All of my experiences with girls had been rife with mystery, violence, deception, and, ultimately, humiliation. Sure, I had made out with girls at parties, but that's because they were as drunk as I was, or more so. Then we would disappear into the night and never see one another again. And I had danced with some pretty nice girls at dances. But I didn't *go out* with girls. I had no car. I had no money. While I was overwhelmed with wanting to be with them and touch them all over, I had no idea what to actually do with them.

When I was about nine or ten, this girl out in Cardiff named Naomi made me a deal I couldn't resist: she offered to show me her *thing*. So off to the bushes we went. To this day, I clearly see a little dark hairy circular patch about the size of a silver dollar located right where her bellybutton would've been. Hmm . . . , and that's where I start from. Right out of the gate, geography all screwed up. Then, one night, Alice Nasser (who lived across the street from me, who used to beat me up on a fairly regular basis because she was not only pretty but tough as nails, who a few years later would get much older boys to fistfight over her and go out on a date with the winner—who always had a hot car) called me and uncharacteristically invited me to come over and play with her and her friend. Mr. and Mrs. Nasser were not at home.

Her friend was from cosmopolitan Atlantic City. As we sat around shooting the breeze, it became clear that the girl was a couple years older and more experienced than Alice and that Alice looked up to her. She must have been all of twelve or thirteen herself. Then, out of nowhere, she lit up like Times Square: "Hey! Let's play a game. I know this really cool game. It's called lights out." We each took turns at the light switch and the object was to come up with the funniest craziest nuttiest face or physical contortion possible. When it was Alice's turn to man the switch, it went like this: Light off/on, girl with finger in her nose. Light off/on, girl twisted like Egyptian dancer. Light off/on, girl with foot in mouth. Light off/on, girl bent over, butt facing me, skirt up, panties pulled down. POW! It was a setup. Alice left the light on and just stood there smiling, waiting to see what I would do. I did not know what to do. The girl was looking at me through her legs with an upside-down goofy smile. A massive pregnant pause. Then I broke the silence with, "I didn't know that girls had two asses." Their sudden burst of laughter was deskinning, as they rolled on the floor choking with laughter. These are just a couple of the jillion sexual indignities I had experienced that were on my mind as I approached Bargaintown. Whether it was a hormonal cockroach instinct or inherent impavidity, I don't know. But I kept putting one foot in front of the other. I was determined.

I walked toward the beach on the lakeside of the street and made it clear to anyone looking that I was not interested in who was on the beach. I would occasionally look at the folks in the water, but I was just some kid walking down the road. My plan was to walk past the beach as though my destination were well beyond, that I was a completely uninterested party. Nearing my target, I casually craned my head slightly off to the right while seriously and strenuously levogyrating my eyes to scope out the beachgoers. Near the water's edge, I feigned a stubbed toe and bent to attend to my uninjured foot while upgazing inconspicuously. I thought I had espied her earlier. She was sitting alone on a pink beach towel. Two-piece blue bathing suit. I wasn't sure what auburn hair looked like, but it was dark and tied back in a short ponytail. No one else on the beach fit that description and she looked like she was looking for someone. It had to be her. But she was an amalgamation of Shultzy on *Love That Bob*, Zelda on *The Many Loves of Dobie Gillis*, and Miss Jane Hathaway on *The Beverly Hillbillies*. Not even close to the beauty I had been ideating as I walked along rehearsing what I would and would not say. I was disappointed. I stood up and continued walking, watching her in my peripheral vision. At one point, as I was loping past the beach, I felt her piercing gaze rest upon my left shoulder with hopeful prospect. Instinctively, I quickened my step and looked off in the opposite direction until the heat of her laser-like stare waned to an infelicitous chill.

Bargaintowners parked their cars on the weeds and dirt behind the small gravelly swimming area. When I was a safe distance beyond and sure that she was not suspicious, I ducked behind a maroon '51 Mercury Deluxe and gathered myself. *My God. What do I do now? I can't say hi. I don't want to . . .* And so went my thinking for what seemed like forever, as the heat radiated from the Merc's solid steel body. When I finally got it up to take a peek through the car's rear window, she wasn't there. I freaked. Did she see me? Was she going to suddenly walk up to me and say, "Hi, are you David?" I crouched and scanned the area looking for her approach. But she had only walked down to the water and was walking back to her lone pink towel. She had told me that she would be with her siblings, but she was alone. All alone and looking around like a nervous sparrow. I could feel *her* disappointment. It was 1:45 p.m. Like a jellyfish, I slithered away.

August in New Jersey is insufferable. The little chauffeur's quarters my mom and I lived in was a miniature kiln for cooking people. Not even a fan. Just stifling heat and sweat. With still a couple of hours before Mom got home from work, I made myself a giant bowl of cereal with two heaping teaspoonfuls of sugar, and put on one of Mom's movie theme albums. I just sat there dumbstruck listening to "Never on Sunday" and

"A Summer Place," not knowing what to do. Eating. I felt like a creep. I knew I was a creep. Who was I to look down on anyone?

A mosquito spray truck came by and the sweet DDT drifted through the screened windows, reminding me of when I was a kid and liked to run out and follow behind that pea soup of delicious toxicity. *Hypocrisy* was not in my vocabulary at the time, but it was certainly in my feelings; it was in my bones. I didn't do what I said I was going to do. I let Marsha down. I stood her up. I often got beat up because I wouldn't back down from bullies. I stood up to them. I got my ass royally kicked out of principle. But I slank away from facing Marsha like a piece of sopping dripping milquetoast. My mother was right: I was "*never* going to be happy." I was "*never* going to be satisfied." No girl was *ever* going to love me. I stuffed myself with raisin bran, slurped down the warmish Sealtest milk from the bowl, and cried.

I was washing my dishes at about quarter to five when the phone rang. I knew it was Marsha. I let it ring and ring and ring and ring. Then I picked it up and acted out of breath as though I had just run in:

"Hello! . . ."

"What happened, David? Why weren't you there?"

"Oh, Marsha, hi. I'm sorry. I'm really sorry. Listen, my mom is just about to come in. I can't talk now. Can I call you tomorrow?"

"You won't call. You're just a jerk. I waited all afternoon."

"No. I will—I *will* call. I promise. I'm sorry. I promise. What's your phone number? I just can't talk right now, Marsha. I'll call you and explain tomorrow. What time should I call you?"

To this day, I cannot remember what lies I told her the next day, but whatever it was worked. I covered my cowardly tracks. It turned out that she only lived a few blocks away from me on Reading Avenue off Franklin. Did I want to come over?

Her house was one of those plain rundown skinny two-story places that reeked of poverty. It sat at the terminus of Reading Avenue where it tottered on the brink of the salt marshes of Absecon Bay. It stood out. It was hillbilly. It hadn't been painted in so long that its clapboard exterior was mostly weathered naked wood. A yard of dirt and dead weeds with a couple of old bikes, a tire, and miscellaneous stuff strewed about.

As I paused to take in this sight for sore eyes, I could hear wild nonsensical yelling within—siblings antagonizing one another.

Giving it a second thought, I scanned the neighborhood. Not a soul to be seen on this little finger of a street. I was a stranger going into what was clearly the neighborhood's one and only strange house. White trash. I stepped up onto a creaky porch and knocked on a scuffed paint-peeling door that had a kooky hillbilly faded flower curtain in its window that rattled with each rap. The yelling stopped. The curtain flew open and a goofy looking boy peered out, smiled, and yelled with a lisp, "Mar*tha*, your boyf'end i*th* here! Your boyf'end i*th heeere!*" Droplets of spittle from his enthusiastic announcement succumbed to the force of gravity. He dropped the curtain and ran away laughing, "Ha-ha-ha-ha-ha! . . ."

What was I getting into? What was I going to do? What was I going to say? A moment later, the door swung open and there stood Zelda-Shultzy-Miss Jane in all her smiling glory. At the far end of the sparsely furnished bare-walled living room stood her brother and sister all giggly and goofy.

"Hi, David."

"Hi, Marsha."

"Come in. Come in . . ."

There was nothing comfortable about their home. Purely functional. Shelter at the minimum. An old scraped-up dining room table with rickety chairs and no tablecloth. No coffee table. A giant wooden box television set. Everything was dusty. A couple of mismatched upholstered chairs and a couch in tatters with fruit patterned dishtowels as arm covers. A ratty old carpet in need of vacuuming. Tattered peeling wallpaper. An unshaded two-light ceiling fixture with one bare bulb. It was going on noon and the heat was already concentrating a fetid miasma of stale urine and burnt toast. I was poor. I knew poor. But this was something else. I wanted to turn and run away.

After the giggling part was over, they were very nice to me. Marsha introduced us, saying that her brother Georgie was sixteen and that her sister Sally was just a kid of twelve. Age seemed to be very important. Then she fixed me a delicious ham and Velveeta sandwich on white bread with Hellmann's mayonnaise and a glass of ice-cold milk. I ate alone, as they said they had just finished eating French toast. From the looks of the pile of dirty dishes in the sink and the messy kitchen, I had every reason to believe them. So that was the burnt cap gun smell. I sat at that dining room table like a king on display. Marsha tried to carry on a civil conversation, but sporadic barrages of questions and comments from the other two, who stood behind her observing me like a newly discovered species, continually interrupted her. It was clear that Georgie had something special going on and was afflicted by mongolism, as Down's syndrome was called at the time. All things considered, I was with some nice kids having a nice time.

We talked about Chubby Checker and the Beach Boys and Jan and Dean and music in general. The dances of the day. Favorite places to swim. Television shows. School and other kids. They were still kids doing kids' things. I was hanging out with older kids doing older kids' things. They didn't drink and had never been to any of the dances I went to and were completely oblivious to dances in Atlantic City, West Atlantic City, Absecon, Somers Point, and Ocean City. Their style was no style. Like their home, what they wore was function over form. To them, I was a world traveler, a sophisticate. We did not travel in the same circles. But I was an outsider by nature, anyway. I barely made it under the social wire. I knew what it was like to be an unaccepted oddball goof. And I knew that these kids wouldn't last one minute at a dance before the other kids would humiliate them or beat them up or both. But we laughed and had a good time and talked a blue streak. All the while, I was preoccupied by the subtext of an awareness I would come to know for the remainder of my life: that I didn't fit in—anywhere. After that initial visit, we saw each other sub rosa. Mostly I would go over to her house where we'd hang out.

When we were alone, we made out. She was incredibly passionate and in control. While I was completely ignorant of the female anatomy (as well as my own), she knew what to do and how to protect herself. I followed my instincts and pretended to be savvy. I kept trying to get to her and she kept not letting me. What I would have done when I got *there*, no one will ever know.

After seeing her several times, I decided to take a risk and invited her over to my house. This one day (the one and only time she was ever in my home), our making out reached new heights. It was glorious. She had magical powers. Played me like a sweet violin. Touched me as I had never been touched. Aroused blissful frissons and made me feel things I had never felt. Told me that I was delicious. And after a few hours of that, she went home, leaving me exhausted, drained, and bewildered. I languished in my little makeshift bedroom, ethereal with an unrecognized pleasure that slowly and inexplicably segued into all-embracing ungodly pain. My testicles ached as though they had been punched and kicked—a feeling I knew well from ending up on the losing end of too many fights. When a bit later I told her about this on the phone, she casually informed me that I was merely suffering from a common affliction called "blue balls" and that I would recover from it shortly. Not to worry. That it was due to me wanting to have sex with her so much that my body couldn't stand it. How did she know this stuff!

One of the things we liked to do was to take walks around her neighborhood holding hands. For fear of being seen, I was always keen to stay off the main drag. But one day, when we were walking down a desolate side street off Delilah Road over by the Pleasantville Apartments, I spotted someone walking in our direction on the same side of the street. It was an odd sight. You never saw anyone walking around there. But no problem. I didn't know anyone in them thar parts. As the figure got closer and closer and closer, though, it started to look familiar and by the time I realized who it was, it was too late to duck out of sight, but I cast loose Marsha's hand. Shit! It was Jake Carnet. What the hell was he doing there?

At the time, I was hanging around with these older kids, the Delacroix brothers, and Jake Carnet was their friend. He was popular, handsome, always had beautiful girlfriends, and he knew me. The jig was up:

"David! David Betterton! What are you doing over here? Who's your friend?"

Humiliation sucked my tongue and my eyeballs down to my feet, where I began stepping all over them like an antsy horse. Everything became a blur.

"Hi, Jake. Oh, we're just ah out walking. This is ah . . . this is, um—"

Reaching out with an air of confidence, Marsha shook his hand and filled in the blank that my failed mind had left, "Hi, I'm Marsha. Marsha Wingate."

Jake stood there grinning and engaging us both in long-forgotten polite conversation, during which all I could think about was that he was going to tell Draco and Timmy. Ooh my God. When I made quick guilty eye contact with Marsha, I could see behind the stretched skin of her forced smile that she was internally bleeding with hurt, aware of my embarrassment at being seen with her. Her eyes were glassy and lost. The shell of my character lay bare. A telling moment. We walked back to her place in excruciating silence, aware of a repulsion that would not let us touch—had we wanted to. I was a creep and knew it. She was humiliated. I was ashamed—ashamed of her and ashamed of me. I am convinced that shame is the most repugnant, most undesirable, most pitiful, most god-awful torturous of emotions.

As we neared her house, she took off running, blurting out, "Go away! I never want to see you again!" slamming the door behind her. I heard the windowpane rattle, her bursting into tears, and the crude loud excited yelling of her brother and sister. I simply walked on home. Word spread like wildfire to the Delacroix.

Having kept my shameful romance a secret for most of the summer, I now had the Delacroix prodding me—mostly Draco. Timmy was interested, but Draco became obsessed: "David. You little devil, you. You've been fucking an ugly chick and not telling us? Not sharing? Carnet says she's really ugly—*ooje* ugly . . . ," the slime of juvenile malevolence spewing from his evil smile. Thus began his incessant campaign of pressing me for information about Marsha.

My first recollection of Draco Delacroix is from when I was around nine or ten or so. I was late for school one day, as I frequently was, and rushing to face my regular dose of self-imposed degradation. I hated school and showing up late made me hate it even more. I went to Decatur Avenue public school, which was just a block away from St. Peter's Catholic School. There was a real class thing going on and those Catholic kids always looked down on us public school kids. To top it off, they were known to be tough—girls and boys. Anyway, the street was deserted and I was just passing St. Peter's on the opposite side of the street when this kid jumps up out of a basement stairwell and runs at me like greased lighting. My mind was on other things when all of a sudden, there he was in my face. Shoulders hunched. Fists clenched. Ready to fight. Wearing the Catholic uniform: white long-sleeved shirt, dark blue necktie, matching blue pants, and down-at-the-heels scuffed up black shoes.

"You think you're pretty tough. Don't you. You walk like you want to do something. You wanna do something? You act like you're pretty smart."

"What? . . ."

"You think you can take me? You think you can take me?"

"What? . . ."

"Go ahead, I'll give you the first three hits. Hit me as hard as you want. OK? As hard as you want. OK? Go ahead. Go ahead."

"What? . . ."

Pretty much, the entire incident is a disjointed bundle of painfully blurry recollective synapses. Nothing he said made sense. I was terrified. His red face was about to explode. His frothing mouth bore a Humphrey Bogart tusky grin. I didn't know him. Never saw him before. But I had heard about him: the Catholic troll who jumped unsuspecting public school boys. I thought he was a myth. But there he was in my face. The bogeyman, live. Of course, I chickened out and backed down. After all, he wasn't trying to take anything from me. Nothing to defend. He just wanted to fight. There was no way I was going to fight with this madman. And that was my introduction to Draco Delacroix. Of course, I didn't know his name at the time.

I grew up without a dad and I never really knew my mom with a man. After my brother and two sisters took off to build their own lives, it was just Mom and me, so in essence I was an only child. Then my brother introduced Mom to his tree surgeon boss and they started going out together. After a while, it was time for me to meet his family—his *family* of eleven kids that was living in an apartment above Jack's Army Navy on Main Street. It meant nothing to me that this man's name was Art Delacroix, but, *man*, I want to tell you that when I eventually found myself in the company of his tribe of aboriginal Irish ragamuffins and realized that I was in the same room with the bully of St. Pete's, I was just a little bit more than scared. This was a couple of years after Draco had terrorized me. And while I had morphed from being short and chubby with my two front teeth missing to being a tall flaccid snaggletooth kid, Draco had retained the same stocky high forehead square Irish boxer face—think Bob Hope, Jimmy Cagney—and unmistakable ready-to-fight-anyone-anywhere stance. To this day, I am not sure if I ever revealed to him that I was one of his public school victims. And I am pretty sure that he didn't recognize me as one of his many conquests.

Before I met the Delacroix brothers, I was a true loner. I would pretty much go it alone for just about everything. Occasionally, though, I would hang out with this kid or that kid, always someone even more unpopular and with lower self-esteem than I had. I really had no friends. But once I got with the Delacroix brothers, we became a minor version of the Three Musketeers. They took me in. I was the kid. At the time of the Marsha incident, Timmy was nineteen (he had quit school; had a job washing dishes at the Home Plate; was the one who always had money and a car—the responsible one), Draco was seventeen (going to Holy Spirit High), and I was fourteen (just going into the seventh grade because I got left back in the second and fourth grades—a little humiliation I kept secret as much as possible). But I was tall and could pass for much older. And if it was known that I was with "The Delacroix," generally speaking, that is, the other guys wouldn't mess with me. This was in no small way due to the fact that Draco was a real-life badass. He was not hot air, faux bravado, no action. No, sirree! He was the real deal. Even the baddest of the badasses stayed clear of him. I once saw him get into it with our local Pleasantville King Thug, one Nelson Truax, at a periodic impromptu football game in Northfield and it came out to a draw. So for a few years, we were thick as thieves and I followed their lead. And because of that, I got to go places and do things that would have normally been out of my reach, which included becoming a regular in Lonnie's Den, a "dance club" in Atlantic City that had a special *in* on Ed Hurst's television show, *Summertime on the Pier*, an *American Bandstand* type show.

One hot summer day on the Steel Pier, this giant 6′5″ white red-headed football player type jock with a flattop deliberately smashed into me—I'm sure thinking that as the taller of us three I was the baddest—and challenged me to do something about it. We had some words and I backed down. He would have ripped me to pieces. But Draco slyly slipped between the two of us, leaned up into his face and said, in his evilish daring way, eyes glaring, crazy smile, "Maybe he doesn't wanna fight you, but how'bout *me*? How'bout *me*, buddy? Huh? You wanna fight *me*? You wanna fight *meee*?"

The guy's mean visage melted into fear and confusion. An unexpected turn of events. A little guy was challenging him. So right there, with people walking all about us, Draco took him down and made him beg for forgiveness, making fun of his bigness and telling him that he shouldn't go around messing with people. Another time, Draco and I were just coming out of a candy store up on New Road around Wesley or Adams Avenue with ice cream cones, when this big black joker strolled up and planted himself in front of us:

"Gi'me a'lick'a'dat ice creen cone." He was a massive kid.

Draco took a step toward the kid. There was only about ten inches between the two of them and Draco was as calm as calm could be. Wide-eyed, fearless, staring into the feeble brain behind his aggressor's eyes, Draco took a long casual lick, gave a nonchalant smile, and said, "What did you say?"

"I *says*, *gibs*'me som'a'dat mutha'fuckin' ice creen cone! Chump!" giving Draco his best mean look.

Draco took a couple more slow licks around the base of the cone to catch the drips and said, "OK," and shoved the cone in his face, forcing the kid off balance to stumble backward. Flailing his arms wildly to keep from falling, simultaneously trying to wipe the butter pecan from his face, he made a ridiculous slushy mess. Whiteface poorly executed. He was furious. A terrifying situation from which most would flee. But not Draco. He just stood there peacefully with his gritty toothy smile poised to tussle, edging toward the guy:

"There. *That's* what you wanted. *Right?* You wanted some of **my** eyes-creen cone. Now you *gots* it. Whatchu gonna do about it, big fella? You punk! Come on, big man. I'm just a little guy here. Come on. Come on! . . ."

The kid was stunned stupid. He continued frenziedly wiping cone fragments and sticky melting cream to the ground with both hands, trying to maintain whatever dignity he had left in him, while mumbling, "Hey, maaan, I w's jus'sayin' . . ." He, of course, backed down.

Draco was the real psycho deal. You didn't fuck with Draco. But I digress.

Anyway, after finding out about Marsha, Draco was incessant—beseeching, bugging, and just plain badgering me about her. It went on for days. I thought he would eventually give up, but he kept pushing every embarrassment button of mine he could uncover until—and don't ask me what I was thinking, for clearly I was not—until I caved in. I spilled the beans. I told half-truths and lies to bolster up my non-reputation. I made every effort to make myself out to be a philanderer, an exploiter just out to "get me some"; to show that I was smarter and slicker than he and Timmy thought I was; that I always had something cooking on the side; that I had a brain and was using it. With other kids, such bragging was usually sufficient. Just talk—end of story. But not with Draco Delacroix. He actually wanted me to show him where she lived; he wanted to see just how ooje ugly she really was.

We cruised up Franklin Avenue in Timmy's pristine four-door powder blue '55 Ford with the windows open. It was a typical Jersey sweltry day of hellish humidity. Sitting in the back—Draco always got to ride shotgun—I shivered in my dripping stench of humiliation. Why was I letting them in on my secret? Why did I have to run into Carnet that day? Why was I taking them to Marsha's house? Why did I have to be such a loser? What would come of it all?

"Get ready to turn right on Reading. It's at the end on the left."

As we came to an obvious stop in front of her house, Timmy offered his only comment during the entire episode: "Jeez, Dave. It is *really* rundown."

Draco wasn't satisfied having to look across out Timmy's window and hurried him up to turn around so that the house would be on his side of the car. I was just hoping and praying we would get out of this crappy little cul-de-sac without being seen. But it was too late. As Timmy was maneuvering, I looked out the back window and saw the front door curtain fly back. Then the door opened. Out stepped Marsha. *Shit!* Draco was ecstatic. It was what he had come for. Timmy wanted to get out of there and immediately offered, "Let's get out of here," and started to gun it.

But Draco was always in control, "No! No! Stop! Stop! I just wanna see. Come on. Stop. Please stop. Come on, Timmy. I just wanna see . . ."

By this time, she was out on the porch with her sister, her brother, and another girl I didn't know standing behind her. Marsha had her head cocked and was crinkling her brow with curiosity—a scene right out of *The Grapes of Wrath*, a superb Dorothea Lang composition. There they were, dowdy and barefooted. Her brother, for some reason, had his pants rolled up midshin. He looked goofier than usual. Her sister looked like she knew something was up. They all looked apprehensive. Marsha stood there in her new Buster Brown hairdo wearing a plain loose-fitting sack-like dress, eyes flitting from me to Draco to the car and off into the open air, as if help might be coming.

"Hello . . . David?"

"Hi, Marsha." The humidity was crushing me. I was in the middle of my worst nightmare. How could I wake up and have everything be all right? I couldn't.

She stepped off the porch and came toward the car, but stayed on her dirt yard. The others followed but stayed just behind. "Hi? What are you doing? Are these your friends?"

"Oh. Um . . . We was just, ah, going to Atlantic Cit—"

"Hi, Marsha. We were actually just coming by to see you," Draco, leaning out of the window, chin resting on his arm, slimily said.

Timmy knew things didn't bode well, "Come on, Draco, let's just get out of here."

"*Noooo . . . Holdona* minute! I wanna to talk with *Marrrshaaa* for a minute . . ."

She knew me well enough to know that I was into something way over my head. An effluvium of evil was present that could not be ignored.

An abrupt crepitation (a swarm of bees? a distant arcing power line?) filled my ears. The pungent ozonic scent of bumper cars wafted up my nostrils. Lightning was about to strike. This thing would have to play itself out. I jumped in: "Cut it out, Draco. I'm sorry, Marsha, we have to get going. Come on, Timmy, let's go."

As he stepped on the gas, Draco swung around and placed his left hand flat on Timmy's chest. Pursing his lips, he uttered a quick gravelly sinister whisper, drawing out each word—paralingual cues that there would be consequences to pay: "No! No! It's OK. Stop! I just want to talk to Marsha."

Timmy stopped and threw it into reverse with, "OK, but five minutes. I'm leaving in five minutes, Draco."

"OK. OK. Five minutes . . ."

As we rolled to a stop in front of her house, Marsha walked a bit closer but staying her distance.

All I knew to say was, "I'm sorry, Marsha. We shouldn't have stopped . . ."

"Why did you come here? What do you want?"

Draping himself farther out the window, Draco was looking her up and down and drawling—rather, slurring, "Sooo . . . , Marrr*shaaa* . . . , you like to go out with boys?"

"What do you mean, do *I* like to go out with boys? What did you tell them, David?"

In the boxing ring, when you are on the losing end of a three-minute round, it is easy to convince yourself that the referee and timekeeper are conspiring against you; that you have been in there at least an hour or more; that the beating will never end; that you are in the midst of the worst thing that could ever happen to you in your life; that your opponent wants to kill you. Everything becomes a crystal clear blur; nothing makes sense. But there is no doubt that you are in the wrong place at the wrong time.

Thus did I find myself when Draco and Marsha became engaged in their verbal sparring. I was blank with embarrassment. All the girl ever did was be nice to me, and here she was about to be verbally assaulted. And for what? Because we were kids? Because Draco had a mean streak in him? Because she was a girl? Because we were boys? Because she was not pretty? . . .

All I remember today about that eternal three-minute round of aspersions, insults, and sexual crudities is that it was of no lexical value to me whatsoever. I had regressed to some primordial reptilian state where I merely collected sense data to put meaning into my now purely sensate world. Much like an insect or animal in the wild feels the vibrations and radiation of our human evil intent, I sat in the back steeping in the malignancy of the moment. Then I was startled back to the present as the car lurched forward.

Draco swung around and commanded Timmy to stop. Again, he leaned out the window to beckon Marsha even closer with a big drooling Cheshire cat smile and wild eyes, "OK, Marsha. We have to go. But com'ere. I wanna to tell ya somethin' personal. Com'ere . . ."

Her little clan of family and friend just stood there in tableau. Quirky mannequins. Dumbfounded. Defenseless young children witnessing horrid reality. Three mouths agape. Knowing nothing good was going to come of this.

"What? What do you want to tell me?" taking a baby step forward.

"Com'ere, I don't want these guys to hear. You'll want to know this, I promise. Then we'll go. Com'ere . . ."

Of a sudden Marsha's brother spoke up in his thick-tongued Down syndromic kind of falteringly delayed voice of caution and intelligent compassion, "Mar*tha!* C'm'*on!* Le*th* go in*th*ide. Tho*th* bo*yth* ar' mean! . . ."

She turned and gave him a prolonged stare, then turned back to scan me, and then Draco. She ducked to get a look at Timmy whose deadpan gaze was straight ahead. "What do you want to tell me?" edging yet closer.

Leaning even farther out the window almost to his waist, Draco was sporting a big friendly incongruous smile, "*Come here* and I'll whisper it in your ear. No one will hear. It's just something that I heard. Com'ere. Com'*eeeeeere* . . . ," as he waved her toward him and cupped his hands around his mouth to receive her ear.

In a word, Timmy and I were powerless. Draco's gravity was too great. He always won out. He was the indisputable alpha male. We were stuck in a slow thick orbit, like a couple of dimwitted subatomic particles waiting for the inevitable collision. Except for at the very beginning, Timmy and I never looked at one another during the course of this whole pile of mischief. We couldn't. We were both struggling to deal with our pusillanimous selves. He was the beta, and I, of course, the omega. It was our destiny to see how this would unfold according to the Law of Draco.

Georgie started yelling cautionary advice once more at his sister. His animal instincts knew better than to proceed. She turned in his direction for a moment, but summarily ignored him. A motherless lambkin seeking comfort from a wolf, Marsha haltingly shuffled closer to Draco. Stepping onto the blistering macadam, she started hotfooting it like a flamingo about to take flight, performing some sort of mystical suicidal Zulu wedding dance. Draco unctuously assuring her that everything was going to be all right. To come closer. The air had become a thick, dark, stifling syrup—a mephitic asphyxiating cloud of adolescent evildoing. It seemed as though I had stopped breathing. Sweat was streaming down my face; the weight of my goofy tortoiseshells was hurting my nose; my bleeding madras shirt a sop; I felt as though I had peed myself. I was in the middle of some perverse rutting ritual where human sacrifice was impending.

Draco eased her over with his typical display of greasy psychopathic trust and confidence. A wide smile on his face, "Com'*eeere* . . . I'm not gonna bite'ya." Marsha inched closer and paused. Then she took a good long hard curious look at me. Through me. Direct eye contact. And I knew that she was seeing the shame and cowardice I was then knowing. Draco was slowly reeling her in. While words were making no sense to me, while time had turned inside out and upside down, I was very much aware that harm was being done. And I was the cause of it. She turned again and looked back at her silent, motionless clan. Then she stepped up to Draco and offered her left ear to his waiting cupped hands.

While I am sure that we all knew that Draco was up to no good, none of us could have anticipated what he had in mind. He started whispering into Marsha's ear innocently enough, but, all of a sudden, like a bolt out of the blue, he grabbed her in a sort of bear hug growling like a hungry lion or an angry dragon, pulling her toward the car. Marsha struggled to break loose, but Draco's tremendously strong hands held her upper arms so they were perfectly vis-à-vis with an inch to spare. It's amazing how anything so slow can happen so quickly or how something so fast can happen ever so slowly. It couldn't have taken more than a second or two, but I scanned the scene and saw Timmy's wide-eyed look of *What the hell's he doing?* Her sister, brother, and friend all cocking their heads asking the same thing of themselves. Marsha was stricken with horror and Draco's face was red and about to burst from the pent-up anger he always had in tow. And then, like a pissed off camel, he hawked up everything he had from deep down in the bowels of his evil soul to produce a humungous quantity of loogie directly into Marsha's face. Timmy hit the gas and Draco shoved Marsha away like she was some disgusting piece of garbage.

"Damn, Draco! Why'd you have to go and do that for!" Timmy yelled as we sped off.

To this day, I have no idea what Draco's response was to Timmy's question. Perhaps there was none. I was pretty much numb to the whole experience, anyway. As we drove away, I turned and took my last look ever at Marsha. Her kith and kin were animated and moving about like frenzied bees in helpless disbelief. Marsha just stood there stock-still in the middle of the street, her plain straight unstylish brownish cottony dress drooping. Arms down at her side fanning outward. Palms forward. Fingers splayed, asking a stigmatic question. Even at that distance, I could see the humiliation, the hurt, and the tears flowing down her face commingling with the spit. She was in shock. So was I.

Draco and Timmy were saying all kinds of stuff up front, but I have no idea what they were saying. I was too busy trying to hold back my tears by controlling my breath and staring at the flicker of passing clapboards as we drove down Main Street. I was feeling worthless; that I was a bad person; that I should have protected her. I was shamefully aware of how scared I was of Draco. Speechless, stewing in uncourageous puddles of puberty, I did the only thing I knew to do in those days of my callow youth—I chewed the daylights out of my fingernails and cuticles until my fingers bled and hurt real bad.

As my senses were shutting down in self-defense, I felt something large trying to gnaw its way out through my chest. My vision became a translucent one-dimensional plane of scarlet (one of God's favorite colors). The voices up front decayed into barely audible mumbles obscured by the purling of a remote fanciful stream swirling in my thoughts. As we passed Woodland Avenue Elementary School and Uncle Milty's

Bicycle Shop, a chimerical sweet savor of cedar entered the car, jolting my olfactories. Somewhere, way way off in the distance, in the unsure future of adulthood, in between the whir of tires and the Doppler shift of passing structures, as clear as a whistle, I heard a busy signal: Bizz! . . . bizz! . . . bizz! . . . bizz! "Hello." Bizz! "Anybody there?" Bizz! . . . bizz! "Hello." Bizzzzzzzz . . .

6

EASTER SUNDAY

My mother made me go to church
Until I was twelve
Then she told me I didn't have to go anymore
Just wanted me to know there was a god
I remember the fragrance of lilies
The pure white steepled clapboard First Presbyterian Church
Now a plumbing supply business!
Hot as hell and stuffed with people looking for salvation
Whatever that was
Us men in suits and ties
Women with hats and little thingies of net over their eyes
The preacher man talked and talked
About all the usual crap I didn't understand
Afterwards I would catch a bus or hitchhike
Over to Atlantic City with a dollar or two in my pocket
Probably less

All dressed up
To walk up and down on the boardwalk
Past, through, and around the happy pretty girls
Past the happy families
Past the groups of kids having fun
Back and forth for I don't know how long
Hoping not to be seen by anyone who would recognize me
Alone, isolated, confused, wondering what it was all about
Walking like I had somewhere to go
I was pretty good at that; still am
How old was I?—I don't remember
Just a kid
How many times did I do that?—I don't remember
Once was too many
Then I would catch a bus or hitchhike back to Pleasantville
Get off at West Jersey and Main and walk home
To an empty house
Where I'd stuff myself
With yellow marshmallow chickens and jellybeans
And wonder what the fuck all the excitement was about
On Easter Sunday

7

FRIDAY NIGHT

t was just like any other Friday night in Pleasantville, New Jersey—nothing to do but get drunk. My mother had just started seeing this guy, and that turned out to be good for me and my loser friends. That's because drinking quarts of beer and pints of wine out in the bitter cold South Jersey night, down some alley off Main Street or behind a neighbor's home, was grueling business. Something to be avoided at all costs. However, this particular Friday night, she would be out romancing it up and I would be able to effectuate my proprietary foolproof method for acquiring the requisite booze. As I was thirteen (and a half, that is), I needed a foolproof method. But back in the '60s, public awareness of the evils of alcohol was at an all-time moronic low—again, good for me.

There were two main liquor stores in town: Bill Martin's Liquor and Hy-Grade Wines and Liquors. I had lived on top of Mi Lady Dress Shop, which was next door to Martin's (the first and only drive-through liquor store in P'ville—perhaps in the world), until I was about eight years old. Everyone there knew me, my mom, and where we lived. That was a problem. So, Hy-Grade was the mark. I had perfected my scheme down to the minutest detail. And while my lifelong efforts have left me with the scarred recognition of my status as a film and stage director manqué, hindsight brings into sharp focus the fact that I had the knack circulating in my blood since early childhood. I was always quick to orchestrate scenarios, manipulate others, and lie with a smile on my face and a twinkle in my eye.

Perhaps it all started in grade school at Decatur Avenue with my walk-on as a slave in a kindergarten version of *The King and I* (my bow was fantastic!); or it could have been doing the old soft-shoe on stage at Pleasantville Junior High to the tune of "By the Light of the Silvery Moon" when I was a chubby missing-my-two-front-teeth meritless Cub Scout (front-back-shuffle-hop-skip, front-back-shuffle-hop-skip, shuffle-hop-skip, shuffle-hop-skip, one-two, one-two . . .); or, maybe it was that time when I beat Doug Hamm out at an audition for the high school choir—from which I was immediately dismissed due to poor academic performance. Who knows? But I got the bug somehow, and I was pretty good. I could elevate a child's world of pretend from mere hoecake to crème brûlée. Years later, I would endeavor to parlay my self-perceived talent into a profitable career, only to find out how little talent I really had. My own personal un-Manifest Destiny.

But on this fall night in Pleasantville, I had talent and lots of it. And I put it to good use securing all the alcohol I could afford. For it appears that at such a tender age, I was already unwittingly on a path that would lead me to my present destination, that that evening was unalterably foreordained and that I was going to need all the drink I could get to survive the darkness that was about to unfold before me. What an instructive night it would be: a night when a fella would learn just how right and wrong he was about so many things. A night when a young boy would learn exactly what character is and isn't. A night when the impossible would become the possible. A night when Gene Pitney's "Town Without Pity" would really mean something.

On this November night in 1961, I was with three kids I had recently met at a dance at the firehouse up in Absecon. Firehouses were known back then for their dances. There was one in West Atlantic City and one in Somers Point. Kids from all over would go to them and the hormonal electricity would snap, fly, and spark. To this day, some of the sexiest hottest wildest intimacies I've ever experienced were on a dance floor with some girl I didn't know doing the slow grind to "Maybe" by the Chantels or "Could This Be Magic" by the Dubs or "There's No Other (Like My Baby)" by the Crystals, which, by the way, was the first hit for Philles Records, which launched Phil Spector on a career trajectory that led him to the insanity he finally achieved. Anyway, these guys from Absecon never knew it but that night we met I left the dance alone so drunk that when I went out into the woods behind the station to take a pee, I tumbled down a cliffy scarp and landed face foremost in the freezing water's edge of a gravel pit. I could have drowned, but only peed on myself and got all scratched up. Besmirched, in tatters, and soggy, I shivered and slunk four miles home, hoping none of the other kids would see me.

Warming up for our night, I was admiring myself in our wall-mounted pink flamingo mirror, dancing to "Blue Moon" by the Marcels, a Lucky Strike sandwiched between my lips, smoke drifting up under my caramel tortoiseshell rimmed glasses into my watering eyes, when I heard rapping at the door. Actually, I was studying—studying my moves: rhythmically stepping left to right and back again; swirling my forearms in front of me as though I were a human skein winder; every four beats throwing my hands down to my side with loud fillips while thrusting the relevant foot forward; extending my left hand up to an imaginary moon; gesturing that I was all alone in this world by sweeping my crossed hands away from my bosom downward to reveal the emptiness all about me; using musical sign language to indicate that I was suffering by allowing my right hand to tenderly float away from my temple down to meet my left hand where they sadly caressed my heart of despair; hugging airy emptiness to pantomime that I was a man without a love of his own—all performed with suave reserve and style, as I envisioned myself backed up by four clean-shaven male performers (three black, one white). All of us, fine sartorial specimens in gunmetal gray three-piece Italian suits with cuffed pants, powder blue shirts with silver diamond studded cufflinks, matching tie clasps for our five-inch double Windsored muted pink and gray striped ties, with pastel pink three-point pocket squares.

On our feet: black Florsheim cap toe Oxfords, pastel pink nylon socks. On our heads: perfect hair, well pomaded and Brylcreemed. A synchronized team of sophistication and precision.

Although I didn't have a clue what a choreographer was at the time, I was a pretty good dancer and fancied myself a career creating slick dance moves and teaching them to groups (when I got older, of course) because I was always watching their moves and thinking, *I could do better.* Me? A goofy thirteen-year-old white boy with the physical configuration of Baby Huey, who was short and fat and missing my two front teeth until I was twelve, who suddenly and unexpectedly shot up and morphed into a short-fat-tall-skinny-snaggletooth-pimple-faced kid practically over-night, and whose style was pretty much limited to what Mom could afford to buy on time from George, the traveling salesman from Lieberman's Department Store. But I loved music and I loved to dance.

This ne'er-do-well friend of mine, one Joey DiGiacinto, turned me on to a new radio show out of Camden on WCAM 1310 AM. The DJ was this wild guy named Jerry Blavat. I have no idea how Joey found out about him and I have no idea how we even picked up his show. Reception wasn't good or reliable. You had to hunt and play with the dial, and when you did find it, you had to listen through the static. But it was magic static. I re-member hunkering down under the covers at my sister Kitty's house with the radio playing real low and dreaming that I was at a dance with a girl in my arms slow dancing or that I was out there strutting my cool stuff with a beauty following my lead. Blavat opened his show with some really jamming sax tune backing his screeching cry: "Yaou*oooo!* It's the big boss with the hot sauce, the geat*or* with the heat*or*, the yon teenage leader! . . . ," and on and on he would go. He played stuff that no one else would play and would talk throughout his entire set addressing "foxes" (girls) and "coyotes" (boys) and "macking" (making out) and "rhythm talkers" (liars). Between songs, he would rap about the trials and tribulations of teenage-hood, offering advice about broken hearts, growing up, and respecting your fox—making everything relevant to the lyrics of the songs he would segue to and from, composing stories that kids could understand. Thank you, Joey DiGiacinto.

Music was a mixed bag at the time—country, blues, jazz, rock and roll, night club stuff, big band, Cuban mambo, movie themes, gimmicky novelty tunes—you name it, radio was all over the place. On the Top 40 stations, all you heard were Annette Funicello and Ricky Nelson and Patsy Cline and Bobby Darin and Connie Francis and Frankie Avalon and Teresa Brewer and Ferrante and Teicher and, of course, Elvis Presley. Our Podunk WOND in Pleasantville played one entire day of nothing but Brenda Lee's "I'm Sorry."

I went for the stuff that had soul, though. Stuff I could move to. Stuff that toyed with my emotions. Stuff that tapped into how lonely and confused I was—like: The Elegants, "Little Star"; The Drifters, "There Goes My Baby"; The Fiestas, "So Fine"; The Miracles, "Shop Around"; The Marvelettes, "Please Mr. Postman"; Maurice Williams and the Zodiacs, "Stay"; Little Caesar and the Romans, "Those Oldies but Goodies"; The Shirelles, "Mama Said"; Little Anthony and the Imperials, "Tears on My Pillow"; The Diamonds, "The Stroll"; The Fleetwoods, "Come Softly to Me"; The Del-Vikings, "Come Go with Me"; Dion and the Belmonts, "A Teenager in Love"; The Penguins, "Earth Angel"; The Flamingos, "I Only Have Eyes for You"; Rosie and the Originals, "Angel Baby"; The Flares, "Foot Stomping"; The Crests, "Sixteen Candles"; The Skyliners, "Since I Don't Have You"; The Emotions, "I Ran to You"; The Ikettes, "I'm Blue (The Gong Gong Song)"; The Teddy Bears, "To Know Him Is to Love Him"; James Brown and The Famous Flames, "Bewildered"; The Monotones, "The Book of Love"; The Capris, "There's a Moon Out Tonight"; and on and on and on . . . That's the kind of stuff that was whirling around in my head that Friday night.

Nineteen sixty-one was a common year—nothing profound in my view. I had no idea that we had broken off relations with Cuba and that the Bay of Pigs incident had any meaning whatsoever. Not a clue that the Freedom Riders had been doing their thing or that racism was roiling and boiling and that Southern crackers were planting strange fruit. I think I knew that Neil Armstrong flew the X-15 and that it went very fast, and that Alan Shepard was the first American in space. But that Eisenhower warned us about the "military-industrial complex"? That Judy Garland made her comeback (I never knew she left)? That the Six Flags monstrosity came into being, or that Stalin got kicked out of his tomb? I had not an iota of awareness of any of this stuff. That the Berlin Wall went up?—*nada*. Kennedy made it a goal to put a man on the moon?—*nada*. The Peace Corps came into existence?—*nada*. Barbie got a boyfriend?—*nada*. That we had two thousand "military advisers" in Viet Nam and were preparing to slaughter millions of people in Southeast Asia who posed no threat to us?—*nada*. That Dag Hammarskjöld would die and then win the Nobel Peace Prize?—*nada*. Or that one of the most heinous mental retards of our times, Ann Coulter, would be born?—*nada*. I knew nothing of nothing about nothing. I was uninformed about pretty much just about everything a human could be uninformed about. Hell, I was a kid. And my mom was lucky to get me to go to school, much less learn anything.

I turned down the volume on our portable stereophonic hi-fi two-toned beige and cream leatherette-covered record player and went down to let the Absecon kids in. I say *Absecon kids* because kids were defined by where they were from. If you were from Port Republic, you were a hillbilly, a piney. Tough as shit, but a hillbilly, nevertheless, and possibly related to the Jersey Devil. From Atlantic City, or AC? Tough and streetwise. Philly? Definitely tough, hip, sharp dresser—possibly a gangster. Northfield or Linwood? Probably rich and neutral. It didn't matter where you were from—if you were Italian, you were a wop. A Jew? A kike. Latino? A spic. African-American or any shade less than lily white? A nigger. Of course, it was all based on a well-cultivated ignorance that went with the times.

There was nothing pleasant about Pleasantville. It was its own brand. If you were from P'ville, you could be anything. Everyone knew Pleasantville. It was the nexus, the hub, the crossroads—the place you had to pass through on your way to and from Atlantic City, five miles due west across the salt marshes. (It is little known that in 1866 the great American inventor and co-father of the modern submarine, Simon Lake, was born in Pleasantville.) It was a real town, whereas the other places around there were just places to live, communities, suburbs. It had a real Main Street. It had a five-and-dime; Acme and Food Fair supermarkets; Sander's hardware; Jack's Auto Supply; Mike's Sugar Bowl ice cream parlor; Jack's Army/Navy and the Hub men's clothing stores; Mi Lady, the Flamingo, and the Style Center ladies' dress shops; a men's hat shop; appliance repair shops; Pop Dewy's popcorn stand; Stecher's and Lee's jewelry stores; Marco's and McCann's stores for children; beauty parlors and a couple barber shops; the Mainland Sun Ray, and Old Man Megan's drugstores; a couple cleaners; Nick Fazio's shoes; a Sears gift shop; Bolf's and LaRosa's vegetables and Mazzeo's and Melrose's meat markets; Western Union; the electric and gas companies; a bowling alley; the Rialto movie house; the Home Plate restaurant and the "Greasy Spoon" railroad car diner; and, a bunch of bars and those pesky liquor stores. Anything and everything you would need—all within walking distance. Plus, a new bus station was being built. On Friday nights, everyone walked up and down Main Street helloing one another and stimulating the economy. Most important of all, there were places for kids to hang out: the monolithic gray granite First National Bank to lean up against to smoke and be seen, Frankie and Johnny's Sub Shop, Pine's and Dot's soda fountain/hamburger joints, and Pasquinj's Pizzeria—best pizza in the world!—which was directly underneath the apartment at 111 South Main Street, where I was born in the wee hours of a sticky June night in 1948.

When the Three Stooges came upstairs, I turned up the music a little and watched their respective reactions. We didn't know one another well at all, the dance where we met being our only common point of interest. It was our first get-together, so things were a bit awkward. I was internally atwitter, awaiting the inevitable question kids always had when first coming into our home: "You live *here*?" And it did come. They all lived in houses with bedrooms and had brothers and sisters and mothers and fathers. Here, it was just me and Mom. I was the youngest of four siblings. A late comer. An eight-year difference, so the others were off and married. Mom didn't have good luck with men, so she was on her own and slaving away at Lenox China for around $1.15 an hour to make ends meet. And to make those ends meet, we lived in the previously mentioned former chauffeur's quarters behind what was once a turn-of-the-century-mansion-turned-American Legion. It was tiny. Very tiny. There was no privacy. But it was clean and as homey as could be. While I felt the sting of stigma, I never apologized or made excuses. I focused on the fact that it used to be a chauffeur's quarters and that somehow stopped further inquiry. The bottom line was that we were at home alone, which brought us to the reason for our getting together in the first place—booze.

These jokers were so un-cool that they thought I was cool. They didn't know that I was still in the seventh grade because I got left back in second and fourth grades. They didn't know that I didn't have girlfriends. They didn't know that I got my ass kicked on a fairly regular basis because (A) I wasn't tough and (B) I didn't know enough to keep my mouth shut. They didn't know that I was significantly unpopular. And they didn't know what they wanted to drink.

As I shot up to 6'2" overnight when I was twelve, I was taken to be older than I was. I belied my callow youth by emulating older kids and affecting the jive lingo and gestures of the black kids I went to school with and who messed with me to no end. Sort of like the psychological sympathy one reads about that a kidnap victim develops for the kidnapper. It was a survival strategy: walk fast, don't slow down, give the impression that I'll kick your ass if you mess with me.

The only problem with that scenario was that little guys always sought out tall guys to fight with. As I almost always lost, humiliation was a constant factor. Me? I just wanted to spar verbally. But they always wanted to duke it out. Nevertheless, I was an excellent jive talker and walker who could tittup swagger with the best of them—a gentle double bounce and push-off on the ball of the right foot, a smooth outthrow of the left leg, a utilitarian dance with the arms swinging pendulously to and fro as the shoulders thrust and rotate like a proud barnyard rooster. I am confident that some black kids emulated me. So, that Friday night, there we were—four thirteen-, fourteen-, and fifteen-year-olds sitting around making like we were all sophisticated, talking about what we liked to drink.

"Schlitz is good. I like Schlitz."

"Pabst is better—"

"No way! Schaefer is light and has a much better taste."

"Well, I like Schlitz, but I also like Rolling Rock and Ballantine. Ballantine is good and it doesn't give you a hangover . . ."

Then I chimed in, "Iron City is three quarts for a buck."

As none of us had but a couple of dollars, economics dictated our taste for the evening. The question arose, "So, how are we going to get the beer?" I laid out my plan and called Hy-Grade. I placed an order for three quarts of Iron City, a quart of Schlitz, a six-pack of Ballantine, and a six-pack of Rolling Rock. We got ready.

Our tiny little place was laid out in such a way that our itsy-bitsy bathroom was directly over the stairwell that led down to our one and only entrance. Directly next to the bathtub was this crazy little double-hung window. A very cute window. Just a window. As though you could look out into a beautiful garden. But all you could see from there was the rear side of a plywood transom my brother had built, from which hung a tropical floral-fruit patterned barkcloth portiere that separated our cozy home from the freezing stairway. These details and the fifteen steps down to the door were all logistically important to the successful execution of Operation Alcohol. I gave the Absecon kids their directions. We rehearsed. Then we just waited.

When the storm door finally creaked open and the anticipated heavy knocks thrust us into the reality of our criminal intentions, we all jumped up and stared at one another like chickens about to be slaughtered and knowing it. *Showtime!* The kids all went into the bathroom and turned the bath water on. I grabbed the cash and plodded down the steps with my leaden feet, readying my performance.

"Good evening. Delivery forrrrr—" squinting at his order slip, "for George Berr-Berten. $5.82." He was a white man, probably no more than thirty or so. But at the time, sixteen and seventeen was old to me, so anything beyond that was ancient history. Unfathomable.

"That's my dad. It's poker night," as I reached out with confidence to transfer the cardboard box of booty into my loving arms, which he willingly gave up.

"Really? Poker. It is a peculiar mix, this order. Is Mr. B-B-Burrten here?"

"Yeah, but he's in the bathtub right now. He gave this to me for you. It's seven bucks. He said to keep the change." The running water and periodic splashing were producing the desired effect. The delivery guy looked up the stairs, as he accepted the cash.

"In the bath, eh . . ."

"Yep . . ." He was questioning me. My confidence was beginning to weaken. Could he see it in my eyes? Could he hear it in the crackle of my voice? Did he notice my giant enormous loud swallow? Could he see the nerves twitching in my cheeks? Was the jig up?

"Well, kid, I been here before. I thinks a couple times. I'm sure everything's OK. You tell your dad that I said thanks. And you—you be careful. Just be careful. Don't get yourself into any trouble, kid."

"No, sir."

And with that he turned and walked away, allowing the pneumatic door to close, hissing and bouncing. Just as the door was about to shut, he turned and yelled back:

"Hey, kid!"

I pushed the door open with my shoulder, box in hand, "Yes, sir?"

"Tell your dad good luck with the cards tonight, OK."

"I sure will."

As he was walking away I yelled back at him: "Sir!"

"Yes?"

"What's your name?"

"Henry. I'm Henry."

"Thanks, Henry. I'm David . . ."

Ever since that night, I've been asking service people their names. Easiest and surest way to make them feel good. Show that you care about them. Show that you respect them. They become your ally and you get great service.

As you can imagine, I and the Absecon kids were in seventh heaven. They couldn't believe that the plan had worked. It was just one of several clever scams I would successfully pull off in my young life. And on that Friday night, with those kids, I was cool. Hip. Happening. Bad. Slick. With it. Sophisticated. In between peeing and throwing up, we smoked cigarettes, did the Bristol Stomp, Ponied like a bunch of dopes to "Quarter to Three," and did the Slop to The Mar-Keys' "Last Night."

We yarned drunken teenage boy stories about how many times we had had sex. Stitch for stitch, every last word a lie. As I was a pristine virgin, my prepared pat response was that I had only had sex once, and that it occurred on a beach with a girl I had met at a dance in AC and that I got sand on my dick and it hurt and felt good at the same time. I had to say something. You *had* to say something. And as my story was anticlimactic compared to the others, it drew no further scrutiny. A few fun-poker jabs at me, and then they were off bragging about themselves. I wasn't interested in one-upping them. I just wanted to get off the hook. Then it was time for them to go. If they didn't catch the last bus back up to the hinterlands of Absecon, they had a long walk ahead of them.

Drunk or not, I made us all clean up my house. Otherwise, Mom would exact a heavy toll. The bus station was no more than a quarter of a mile away. We there staggered through the dirt no man's land behind my house between Lennox Avenue and Green Street, traversed the split rail fence and cut through the yard between the *Pleasantville Press* and the venetian blind company, dumped ourselves out onto West Jersey Avenue, and headed up to the bus stop. It being Friday night, there was a bunch of kids hanging out when we got up there. Mostly older kids.

The actual official real bus station, an expansive dingy extremely high ceilinged sparse barren shabby dungeon of a place, shared a party wall with Frankie and Johnny's Sub Shop, two places where kids hung out. Both were closed. The bus for Absecon stopped on the opposite side of the street by the railroad tracks, where a new bus station was being built. We stood there in front of all the construction stuff shivering and trying to look cool and talking and smoking and waiting for the bus. There was a bunch of girls on the other side of the street and for no good reason this one girl came over and said something to one of the Absecon kids. I don't recall exactly what she said, but it amounted to calling him a dork or a doofus or a hick—all of which he was, but, nevertheless, he was with me. So, I chimed in:

"Get the fuck out of here, you skank!"

"You can't talk to me like that. My boyfriend will kick your ass. Kick your ass!" And off she went.

I had no idea who she was. But we all laughed uncomfortably, knowing that trouble might be brewing. She disappeared around the corner, heading toward Pasquini's Pizzeria.

A few minutes later, one Timmy O'Brien came strutting up wearing his meanest demeanor and started badgering the Absecon kids, "Which one of you assholes called my girlfriend a slut!"

Now, I have to pause and give you some backstory because Timmy and I had a history. He was a bully. Not a big guy. Just a bully. Would mess with kids to no end, me included. Several years prior, he was menacing me one wintery day and I lost it. Just couldn't take any more. I must have been nine or ten. Out of the blue, I just started flailing and screaming. A response he hadn't planned on. I was a flagellating amoeba gone mad. So, as bullies are wont to do, he ran for it. But I was crazed and followed hot on his heels. He had just enough time to open the door to his house and get inside when I was on the porch, squishing my demented face up against a windowpane, watching him squirm inside, fear dripping from his eyes. It was a lovely sight. A *lovely* sight. It was a bitter cold day with fresh snow on the ground. A beautiful array of icicles draped over the eaves of his home. I reached up and broke one off and stood there waving it at him, yelling, "Come out here! I'll kill you! Come out here, you fucking bastard! I want you to stop fucking with me! Come out here! I'll kill you! I'll stick this in your fucking throat! . . ." Thereafter, we had what you might call a cordial relationship. The bottom line was he no longer messed with me.

Timmy had arbitrarily picked out one of the Absecon kids to be the guilty party and started zeroing in on him. Pushing him and egging him on. We were all so drunk and the Absecon kids were not expecting to be messed with. I took everything in for a couple minutes and then chimed in: "Eh. Timmy. Leave'im alone. He didn't do anything. I'm the one you want. But I didn't call her a slut. Just called'er a skank."

As all of this was going down, some other kids started to congregate on the opposite side of the street. A cluster of girls gawked, his girl one of them. He let loose his obsession with the other kid and directed his attention at me. And though I was insensible with alcohol, pretty much seeing double everything, I noted in his gaze serious apprehension and recollection. I was sure he didn't want to tangle with me. His right cheek twitched under his eye a few times. I took it for fear. But from across the street his gal yelled: "That's the jerk-off, Timmy! He said it . . ."

The pressure was on.

Around the corner at Pasquini's was the older gang of kids—the eighteen-, nineteen-, in-their-twentysome-year-olds. A tough lot. In general, they didn't even acknowledge us younger kids. It was as though we were invisible. That's how it is; we notice our peer group. Babies spy other babies. Four- and five-year-olds pick out other four- and five-year-olds. And the eyes of twelve- and thirteen-year-olds automatically fall upon others in their age group. It doesn't matter what group you're in, you are disdainful of the youngers and in awe of the elite olders. In P'ville, the older kids usually hung out at Pine's just down the street, but it was late and Pasquini's stayed open sometimes until after midnight. On the weekends, it was a beehive of hormonal alcohol laden teenage frenzy. Business was good. Anyway, the de facto leader of the "older" pack was one Nelson Truax. He was, as everyone was, white.

The blacks had their section of town. I never knew exactly where that was, but I did have an innate sense of where not to go. I knew that when I walked up Washington Avenue on my way to Cardiff, I didn't dare turn right and stray up Doughty Road because I was sure to get my ass kicked. It could have been a myth. Nevertheless, I stayed clear. And Latinos? There was no such thing as Latinos back then, nor blacks nor African-Americans—"niggers" and "spics" is what they were—we were victims of regional willing ignorance. To my knowledge, there was only one Latino in P'ville. A Cuban dude. It was like he was this space alien who went back to his ship every night. I had no idea where our resident Latino lived. He was an incarnation of Ritchie Valens. He wore pegged pants and *guayaberas*, and rode a cool English Racer to and from his job at Mainland Drugs, where he wore a very authoritative white smock. All I ever really knew about that guy was that he was neat to a pin, kind and professional to customers, and competent. But such qualities wouldn't get you far in the narrows of South Jersey.

Back to Nelson:

He was a stereotypical small-town thug. In Pleasantville and environs, he was the ruling cock of the walk. My sister, who was ten years my senior, said that there were always groups of toughs hanging out on Main Street when she was a kid back in the '50s. It was just an ongoing rotating crop of juvenile delinquents. Anyway, everything about Nelson reeked of *I'm-in-charge-and-I'll-kick-your-ass-and-I've-been-in-jail-and-I-don't-care-so-don't-fuck-with-me*. Compared to his cronies, he was a short one. He strolled down Main Street with a carriage of arrogance, dare, and challenge, coiffed with this too-cool outrageous slightly top-heavy pompadour that made him look like James Dean on steroids—top-heavy because his head was too large for his dwarfish trunk. I don't believe I ever saw him alone. He was always with at least one or two of his boys. The Pleasantville Gang. He wore black slim fit almost pegged dress slacks that were hiked up to the middle of his belly, à la mode, that were cinched tightly with a silver buckled black belt so that his black nylon socked ankles were amply exposed to show off his two-inch cleated Italian black Oxford Cuban heels that were popular in Pleasantville way before the Beatles came on the scene. Always a perfectly ironed long-sleeved light blue or white starched dress shirt, cuffs double-rolled to mid-forearm. A burgundy or navy blue wool cardigan sweater nicely folded and conspicuously draped over the left arm, held stylishly and delicately chest height, as though it were a tallit or a nation's sacred banner. Right hand at the ready in pant pocket with thumb exposed, hiking the pant leg yet a bit higher. But on this winter's Friday night, he wore a black Italian-cut leather jacket. His boys emulated his style the best they could, but no one came close to his evil proto-Fonzarelli cool.

Who all was hanging out at Pasquini's with him that night, I don't know. They were an elite older group and I was way out on the fringe—young and uncool. But his regular thug partners, the usual suspects, were there. Two in particular, for sure: one Eddie, who was himself somewhat cool and of normal stature. Alone he stood out, but in Nelson's company he faded into the background. And the other, well, I can't remember what his name was, so I'll just call him Bluko (because it fits)—a big ass stocky football player giant type who was blustery and always poking for a fight.

A redheaded bull with a flat top. Loud. He would stand on the corner in front of the First National Bank at Main and Washington and do his best to pick fights with guys walking or driving by and yell crudities at girls. Try as he did, the styles of the day never draped well on him. He affected the requisite styles like all the other guys, but the end result approximated the dressing up of a fireplug. Out of the whole crew, these two guys, Bluko and Eddie, were inseparable. And then there were the girls. I never knew who they were or where they came from, but there was always a bevy of foxy girls hanging around the Truax gang.

Timmy O'Brien knew that he had crossed a personal Rubicon. There was no way of backing out. I could see the fear in his eyes. He did not want to get into it with me. But the girls were practically singing "My Boyfriend's Back"—yelling at him to do something. I was feeling cocky and confident and took a couple steps toward him:

"Hey, Timmy," looking him dead in the eye, trying not to sway to and fro, "nobody did anything. She just came up here and started messing with these guys. I never even seen her befo—" BAM! Before I could get *before* out of my lips, he planted his fist smack in the middle of my face. He sucker punched me! Gone were my glasses. It was perfect. A glorious pain shot up my nose into my brain. My hearing became heightened. I could hear the high-pitched chitter-chatter urging him to take me out. Underneath and behind that was the slow-motion droning wow of kids exclaiming wonder at Timmy's coup. Phosphenes ignited, burst, and danced. My internal universe illumed—an unplanned-for wild New Year's Eve in my head. Warm luminescence enveloped me. Life had suddenly changed for the worse. BAM! He connected again. I staggered back with my hands out in front of me to stem his attack. BAM! BAM! But I didn't go down.

As my brain gathered itself, Timmy came into hypersharp focus. Lights were bright; colors were saturated. The vulture girls squirming off to my right and the Absecon kids standing motionless to my left were out of focus as though I were seeing life through a Vaselined wide-angle lens. Smelling blood, other kids began circling. Now, in the middle of East West Jersey Avenue, instinctively stepping toward Timmy on the offensive, I could see the bus approaching off in the distance. Perhaps its arrival would interrupt and bring to an end the terrible situation in which I found myself. Timmy was hopping and jumping and shuffling like any other black kid in Pleasantville, except he was white. We all knew the routine. When black kids fought, they did it with style, athleticism, and showmanship. The cheering girls were feeding Timmy. Boys were expressing astonishment at the lashing I was taking. The eyes of the world were on me.

Beckoning me with a gravelly timbre of victory, he yelled, "Comeonmotherfucker! Punk! Come on! Co*m'ahnnnn!* . . . Whud'ya gonna do! . . ."

Warm blood gushing from my nose stained my hands and dripped onto my hooded three-quarter length olive green wool coat. My tan desert boots were splattered. So much for style. Foggy brained as I was, I put on my best Cassius Clay and mumbled, "O'Brien, I'm going to fuck you up. I'm going to kick your fucking ass. You fucking jerk-off, you! . . ."

And there we were, dancing around like two black birds bobbing and weaving a jabbing and missing. And then—BAM! He connected. And again! And again! And again! Until I went down.

I wasn't sure what was going on. Everything seemed to come to a complete peaceful and dark stop. I couldn't hear anything, but through my squinting eyes I could see the bus pulling up. Then, Timmy was standing over me with a piece of asphalt about 18″ in diameter that must have weighed five or six or seven pounds. He lifted it up over his head and thrust it full force down onto my face. My attempt to deflect it failed. It connected. BAM! As I lay in the street, struggling to get up, I saw the Absecon kids gawking at me as they got on the bus (I never saw them again, ever.); I saw the bus driver, cigarette hanging out of his mouth, completely unaware that a fight was going on as he drove off. Then, Timmy began kicking me. I was trying to double up into a fetal position, but I couldn't. Thump! In the head. Thump! In the side. Thump! In the legs. I knew he was inflicting pain, but I couldn't feel it. I had become a human wet noodle. When I looked up, there he was again launching his chunk of asphalt. He had been waiting for me to look in his direction. I thought, *He's trying to kill me.* BAM! And again. Three direct hits in the face.

Then he walked away. All the other kids left, too. To this day, I have no idea how long I lay there in the middle of the street or how I eventually got myself over by the construction site, where I stood and swayed in a bloody daze trying to put some sense into what had just happened. I was alone. All I could think of was that those bastard Absecon kids had abandoned me; that I had been humiliated; that that punk Timmy O'Brien had caught me drunk and off guard; and, that I would show him he couldn't fuck with Betterton. So, off I staggered toward Pasquini's, where I believed he would be hanging out with the older crowd. I had to navigate mostly by memory because my vision had been reduced to seeing through a turgid slit on my right eye.

As I limped past Baker's Five & Dime, approaching the crowd hanging out in front of Pasquini's, a dark formless hulk of a figure appeared before me and began pushing me and yelling foul degrading aspersions. Visually and auditorially, I had been reduced to a near-insect. I couldn't see, and sound had become a mere persistent dull hum. I was coursing my way based on vibrations and heat. Coming from behind my evil ghost attacker, I could make out the purring murmurs of a frenzied pod of juvenile sharks shouting everything from "Leave him alone, he's had enough!" to "Get'im! Fuck'im up!" I have never been able to prove it and no one has ever fessed up, but I always believed my assailant, the formless hulk, was Bluko.

I slurred something lame like, "I don't have anything to do with you. I'm after O'Brien," and the hulk said something like, "You pussy motherfucker. You gotta get past me first if you want Timmy. You chump motherfucker—"

And then it started all over again. BAM! His giant fist smack in the middle of my face. Every time he smashed me with his enormous fists, he connected square in the middle of my face. He hit me and he hit me and he hit me. I was a human punching bag. I was being hurt bad, real bad, and knew it. But I could not feel his blows—each one a light puffy breeze. After each impact, I heard a dull noise that sounded like a door being slammed at the far end of a large empty metal warehouse. I had slipped into some involuntary psychological immunoreactive state of numbness. I was supercognizant that I was being pulverized and disgraced in front of everyone. I was the town freak. That, I could feel. But giving up was not an option. I staggered and stumbled to remain upright, feebly holding my hands up as though I were going to hit someone. Blind-man's bluff. I no longer attempted to block punches. I just absorbed them. From some mysterious insane place deep down inside of my thirteen-and-a-half-year-old soul, I was still able to muster up a futile cockiness that fueled my incessant mumbling and slobbering, "Fuck you asshole. I'll kick your ass, too. You jerk-off motherfucker . . ." Each word and thought interrupted and punctuated by a Gatling gun of haymakers—Thwack! Thump! Phipt! Thud! Splitch! I thought, *He's trying to kill me.* How long the beating went on, I have no idea. But Nelson and his minions got quite a show—a communal stoning.

Directly across from Pasquini's was the entrance to Green Street, a tiny lane that led off to where I lived. If you stood at Green Street look-ing back toward the pizzeria, you would see a little grocery store to its left and to the store's left a narrow alleyway. When consciousness started to fade in, I was in that alley and this guy named Walter had his hand on my chest, holding me up against the wall. He was telling some other kids to get out of there and to leave us alone. I immediately switched on auto-matic and started trying to walk away, mumbling that I was going to kick Timmy O'Brien's ass. Walter threw me back up against the wall, pinning my shoulders so I couldn't move. I never knew much about Walter. All I knew was that he was a cool good-looking older (eighteen? nineteen?) guy who seemed to have a long-term stable relationship with a beautiful gal; that he had class and wore a really nice double-breasted three-quarter length black wool Italian style overcoat; that he was one of the good guys; that he was independent (i.e., he did not run with the Truax morons); that none of the Truax boys messed with him; and, that Truax himself paid Walter a certain obvious deference. That's all I knew.

"Look, kid. It's over. You're beat. It's done. You're fucked up, man. You can't do anything. You little jerk-off. You're really fucked up, kid . . ."

Spent as I was, I attempted to wriggle my way back out onto Main Street, muttering, "I'm gonna get Timmy. That little—"

Again, Walter slammed me against the wall like a wet towel. I wasn't going anywhere. Granules from the Insulbrick siding trickled down the back of my shirt. Through wheezing gurgles of blood and sputum, the aroma of pizza enveloped my brain. I was safe.

"Boy! If you don't stay here and calm down, I'm gonna kick your ass and—"

When just then, the shrill gut-wrenching wailing screams of a woman silenced everyone. In seconds, a little woman, a Warner Brothers Tasmanian devilized bantam rooster of a woman—my mother!—came whirling though the crowd of kids, pushing and pulling and yanking them out of the way, yelling, "That's my son! That's my son! Get out of the way! That's my son! Oh, my God! Oh, my God! . . ."

I am confident that each and every nocturnal creature foraging dinner for miles around, the whole of Atlantic County, paused to note the never-before-heard guttural yowling that pierced the night and wondered what it could be. All I could think about was, *Oh no, double humiliation. Oh, no . . .* Not really able to move my lips, speaking from somewhere in the back of my throat, lamely, I asked, "*Ohhh . . . Ma . . . wh-wha-wha-du'ya doin' here, Mom?*" Nevertheless, on this Friday night, Mom was a welcome dea ex machina. Coming home in a taxi that slowed down to see what was going on, she had espied my spindle-shanked lanky thirteen-year-old-6′2″-self towering above everyone in the alley.

After some mumbled discussion with Walter, she paraded me through the drooling pack of kids. "Get back! Get out of the way! Move! Get! Get outta the way, you kids! Why didn't somebody help him?. . ." Holding my arm, she escorted my wobbly ass up Green Street in silence, stifling the lecture I knew she wanted to give me. At home, she washed my face, put iodine on my wounds, and assured me that I was going to be all right. I slept well that Friday night.

When I started to ooze back to life next morning, Mom was already out in our tiny kitchen fussing around, trying to be quiet. With an uncanny intuitiveness, like a crow that knows you are watching it, she sensed that I was awake, "Good morning, Son. The water's on. Tea will be ready in a couple of minutes." Tetley's tea with two spoonfuls of sugar and Borden's evaporated milk was exactly what I needed. Physically, well, I felt like I had a hangover. Otherwise, nothing unusual. It was just another Saturday morning.

When I stepped before our flamingoed mirror, I mentally jumped back with a convulsive twitch. The raw meatball face I saw on top of my powder-blue-and-white checkered pajamas was not mine! My heart stopped. I did not breathe. I stood there motionless, listening to the clatter of Mom putzing around in the kitchen. Everything I had ever known was suddenly unknown. Up was down. Out was in. Nothing made sense. A grotesque creature was staring back at me. Its pate, a mangy matted mess. If it had ears, they were hidden somewhere behind the bloated flesh. A timid, squinty-eyed monster. Its pork chop nose, recessed within puffy distended cheeks, was almost impossible to discern. It was not quite a physiognomy, rather, a scraped and lacerated and bruised tumescence of mutilated flesh with daubs of mercurochrome here and there. When I lifted my hand to my face, the creature pantomimed me with exact precision. When I whispered, "Oh, my God!" its sausagelike mouth attempted to lip-sync my words. I could barely detect movement where a mouth should be. I tried again, "Oh, my God . . . ," when I realized *I was* that meatball faced creature. As I stood there amazed that there was not one recognizable feature, not a single clue, not the slightest hint that I was me, Mom hollered out, "Oh, stop looking in the mirror. Come on. Tea's ready. You're gonna make it. I made some oatmeal."

At Somers Point Hospital, I was to experience yet another humiliation. This beautiful girl who was a candy striper and the girlfriend of this guy who always had beautiful girlfriends recognized my name. When we arrived, the staff was aghast. I was sort of an ugly Jack, of Jack in the Box West Coast fast food fame. I looked bad. Bad bad. But I was up and chipper, as though nothing had happened. I was still trapped in some sort of time warp continuum where up was down and in was out. I was as helpless as a newborn. It was probably the only time in my life when I did exactly what my mom told me to do—mostly, that is. Several compassionate nurses and technicians tended to me, checking this and that. The doctor did his prodding and probing and X-raying and testing and then left Mom and me sitting alone in a sterile little windowless light guacamole colored room that smelled of hospital chemicals. We sat in silence waiting for the verdict. Mom was making her trademark chucking sounds, where she would create a vacuum between the roof of her mouth and her tongue that resulted in a birdlike chirp or a horselike clop when she'd pull her tongue away: "T'k-d'unk-t'k-d'unk-t'k-d'unk . . ." It meant she was thinking. It meant she was worrying. It meant this was serious business. I now know that at $1.15 an hour, it also meant that I was putting a dent in her extremely tight budget with hospital costs, glasses, taxi fares, and other yet-to-be-known expenses.

When the doctor returned, he casually leaned up against a table holding a file folder to his chest and just stood there gazing at me without saying a word. I, sitting on the examination gurney. Mom, cradling her pocketbook on a chair in the corner. He scrutinized me, cocking his head this way and that while humming and uh-huhing pensively, as though he were a sculptor trying to decide where to start chipping away next. Then he shook his head and cleared his throat:

"Mrs. Betterton," he said, while staring at me with wild wide-eyed disbelief, "I have been a physician for twenty-five years. I have seen a lot of things in my time. Terrible things. It's amazing what the human body can endure. But I have never seen anyone beat—physically beaten as bad as your son has been beaten. It is a miracle that he was not killed last night. But what is even more miraculous is that there is nothing wrong with David. He has no broken bones. No fractures. No concussion. No eye damage. No ear damage. Just an abnormally distended face, some mean-looking contusions, and some pretty ugly lesions." Still unable to take his eyes off of me, he explained, "Young man, I have no explanation for it. It makes no sense to me or my colleagues. But you're going to be just fine. The only explanation we can come up with is that you were so drunk that you were in some advanced state of relaxation where your body went on automatic and absorbed and compensated for the impacts and pounding. Don't drink! Don't get into any more fights! Be sure to get plenty of rest. You can go home now."

Next stop—the Pleasantville police station. Definitely not my idea. But, like I said, I was doing what Mom told me. I was minimally cooperative and as vague as can be: "A kid—don't know his name; just some kid—beat me up, and, another bigger kid—don't know who he was because I couldn't see him—finished me off . . ." The cop kept taking notes and Mom kept using adult rationale on me, explaining that the kids' parents would be liable and that they had to take responsibility for their behavior and that it was wrong to do what they had done to me, that it was a crime. I told them it was actually my own fault. That I had insulted the first kid's girlfriend. That had I just taken my beating and gone home, things wouldn't have gotten so out of control. That I was bullheaded and just kept going back for revenge and getting my butt kicked. All the cops had to come in and comment on how bad I looked. I was a walking talking freak show.

I played dumb. They gave up. We went home. I recovered. Timmy and I kept out of each other's way. Whenever I passed by Bluko, I would surreptitiously look for a glint of recognition in his eyes, an admission of guilt. But he never even acknowledged me. In fact, not one of that gang ever gave a hint that they even recognized me. It was as if it had never happened.

When I got out of the Navy in '69, it was hippie time. I like to say that quitting high school and getting out of Dodge was the best mistake I ever made. I shiver at the thought of who I might have become had I stayed in Pleasantville. Brrrrrrrrrr . . . But getting out was exactly what I needed. While I did not see in-country combat—thank the gods! O! thank the gods!—I was a medevac for a year on the good ship USS *Valley Forge* (LPH-8), "The Happy Valley," carrying litters loaded with body parts, mutilated, comatose, moaning, screaming, insane young men, plus an unremitting excretion of cadavers. Huey and Chinook helicopters became giant parturient insects desperately depositing their foul eggs on the flight deck in their futile attempts to save a dying species. It was in the Navy that I witnessed just how stupid wealthy, educated, powerful men—professional bullies—can be when making decisions affecting our tax dollars, our planet, and our lives.

The good news is, though, that while I ran through a bunch of come-and-go friends during my three years, eight months, five days, and fourteen hours of "defending" our country from those dirty commies, I ended up hanging out with a couple of good guys who actually had morals and ethics and who introduced me to concepts such as peace and love and brotherhood. Pretty much every night, sailors and marines would congregate to get high on all sorts of drugs and discuss music, war, and what we all were going to do when we got out. So, as you might expect, when I returned to Pleasantville, I was a very different David.

Over the course of my first year back, I, and a girl I had met in California, ended up renting an apartment in downtown Pleasantville, where we lived and loved and partied, biding our time trying to figure out what to do next. Then, one day, and don't ask me how, I found myself in the company of Timmy O'Brien. A chance reencounter. It's all rather vague. But I distinctly recall that I felt not one iota of animosity or resentment or ill feeling toward him. None whatsoever. We met, we talked, and the next thing I knew we were sitting in my apartment at the kitchen table rolling and smoking joints and laughing, *The White Album* drifting in from the living room. That Friday night never came up in our conversation. He was a nice guy, and our thinking was parallel. That was the last time I ever saw him. I didn't quite know what to make of my feelings, but I did know that things were right. I was on a path I wanted to be on, going in a direction I wanted to go in.

Our apartment was on the corner of Washington Avenue and Main Street above Megan's Pharmacy, right across from the First National Bank. That's where all the kids traditionally hung out waiting for Godot. Most everyone had moved on, and hardly anyone ever hung out there anymore. Bluko and Eddie, though, usually drunk as skunks, would still make regular pilgrimages. But while I was away, old Bluko had been in a car accident and was tooling around in a wheelchair with old Eddie as his chauffeur. It was a ridiculously pitiful sight. Absolute buffoons. From his wheelchair, Bluko would try to start fights, yelling at kids across the street or who were driving by, "Come'eeer! You punk! You pussy! I'll kick your fucking ass! You chump! You jerk-off! Come back here! Come back here! Who you lookin' at!" Well, whether that joker is alive or dead today, I don't know. But as sure as I send him loving-kindness, I'm sure that it was he who was the dark formless hulk who pulverized me that Friday night. The bastard.

8

SNOTNOSE SNIPERS

We lay on our backs
In the flight path
Dirt and twigs and leaves in our hair
On our foreheads
And the backs of our hands
Sweaty grime-ball smudges
Above us—blue
Just blue
Hot blue
Sunny blue
The earth radiating a steamy, thick heat
Piney pungent verdancy enveloping us
New Jersey being cooked

By the beating summer sun
A cosmic stew
Of wildness
And little boys:
Snotnose snipers

The air is still
Silence . . .
Except for the buzz of insects
The distant clink of dishes
And a bobwhite
"phwoot-phwoot-phwoot-phhweet!"
"phwoot-phwoot-phwoot-phhweet!"
Trying to notify the authorities
We talked in hushed tones
As though anyone could hear us
Or even cared.
We lay on our backs
Concealed
In Cardiff
In Birdland
In copsewood
Third or fourth year growth, at least
Acres,
For years awaiting development
Two boys,
Awaiting the next takeoff
From the Navy Station

We lay on our backs
And then, it came . . .
Roaring over the last stand
Of pines and scrub oaks
"The woods"
Into the open

Kronos in flight
Thundering, rumbling, growling
A massive contraption
Of steel and stuff
That ain't supposed to fly

Taking aim
With his .22 single-shot rifle,
Albie
Tracked that jet
And then—
Pop! Reload. My turn. Pop!
Reload. His turn. Pop! Reload.
My turn. Pop!
And I wondered: *What if it falls?*
Right here? Right now? On us?
Then, it was off to pick some blueberries

Filling quart milk bottles
Eating as many as possible
In the process
Taking our booty to Albie's mom,
Mrs. Hopcroft,
Who—in her house clothes she wore
All day, every day
Because she never left the house—accepted
The bottles of berries with a smile
From bunches of kids
Us little Jersey hicks
Saying sweetly, "OK, come back in a few hours
When the pies will be ready."

Then Albie and I stood in his front yard
Leaning against his tract home
And peppered the new houses that hadn't been sold

With that .22
Ha! My cousin Buddy bought one we shot up
Real good

And then, we did who knows what
Until it was time
To bite into
The warm, sweet, delicious
Fresh out of the oven blueberry pie.
Fond memories of Robin Road
Back when gravel pits were to swim in
When little kids could walk miles and miles
All alone
And it was OK
To shoot military planes with a .22 . . .

9

FISTICUFFS

My one and only year of high school was, hmmm . . . , let me see—excruciating? That certainly wasn't a word in my uberlimited vocabulary at the time. Getting left back in the second and fourth grades didn't help. I was a snaggletoothed, 6'4" lousy basketball player (not to mention all other sports, as well), a dope with girls, an F-student, and the lousiest fighter perhaps in all of human history. I was, however, a damned good dancer. But that, too, got me into fights. A lot of my thinking time was spent on thinking about how I just couldn't seem to win—anything. So, dear reader, I am confident that you can already imagine that my one and only freshman year at Pleasantville High was no picnic. Man, just the normal stuff itself was too much for me to handle. Add on to that a thick layer of goofy hoodlum bullies, and, well, it was just downright foul.

Bullies. What are they good for? Absolutely nothing! It seemed to me that when some adolescent god or goddess made heaven and earth and hell as some class project that he, she, or it, plucked two of the biggest little shitheads s/he could find from the nether regions and assigned them to me. My own personal bullies: Steaphan and Oakleigh. They were never far away, kindergarten through high school. Steaphan was actually the smarter of the two, but I always felt he felt he had to put on a show because of peer pressure. In our age/class group, especially among the black kids, Oakleigh was the boss. He had that glazed look we see all too often on the faces of our contemporary lost child gangbangers who kill people just because of a perceived insult. One time, oh, I suppose it was about the sixth grade, when our forgettable teacher asked us all to tell what it was we thought we wanted to be when we grew up, Oakleigh said that he wanted to be a "hood an'nah rogue." At least he had a dream—I can't for the life of me recall what I said. Don't get me wrong, it wasn't just these two dunderheads who used to torment me. No, sirree! There was a nimiety of bullies. Erumpent spores of them bursting from the woodwork. My being white and tall was their incentive. Having a reputation for being easy to beat up was an added added-feature. These jokers never messed with tough kids. Nevertheless, fight I did.

I lost about 99.999 percent of all my fights. Oh, there was an occasional win, and I am guilty of picking on a few other kids I knew were weaker than I, but I fought. I got my ass kicked, but I never gave up money or cigarettes or whatever stupid stuff kids might want to plunder. I had the dubious distinction of making whoever wanted to fight with me (my neighbor Alice used to kick my butt) to have to work for his or her ill-gotten victory. I never ran away from a one-on-one fight, but I would back down and walk away from abusive treatment rather than getting my clothes all messed up, which at times was more important than my face or my pride.

Yes, bullies, or as I thought of them in South Jersey parlance, jerk-offs, were in abundant supply. At this point in my career, my home range was wherever a dance might be found: Atlantic City, West Atlantic City, Ventnor, Northfield, Somers Point, Ocean City, or Absecon. That was pretty much it. But it didn't matter where I was or when I went there; I had to be on guard unceasingly. I was a bully magnet. My only safe haven was within the confines of the tiny chauffeur's quarters I shared with Mom, whose subsistence wages as a china inspector at Lenox China just got us by with no surplus allowing for replacement of clothes screwed up by fighting. I don't know how kids make it today with all the gangs and gun violence. It was tough enough when a gang was just a few kids who beat you up, derided you the best their vocabulary would permit, eventually to walk away laughing and feeling mighty fine about the human misery they'd inflicted. Such perpetual maltreatment gave me fantasies of growing up and moving to Philadelphia and becoming a hitman so no one would fuck with me. *And* I would be a sharp dresser for sure. Oh, how distress makes the mind go to strange places . . .

Like I said, Steaphan and Oakleigh weren't the only ones. There was nothing truly special about those two blockheads. It was mere coincidence that we all happened to be following the same dismal trajectory through the Pleasantville elementary, junior high, and high school prison system, for *prison system* is what it felt like to me most of the time. I hated it. Anyway, unless they got left back and I didn't know about it, they were picking on an older kid because technically I was two years behind them. Nevertheless, when we got to high school, their two slim minds were quick to point out to other older black kids that I was an easy mark. So, suddenly, I had a bevy of new black faces in my face challenging me to daily deadly duels and ass whoopin's. Constantly, I was constantly trying to avoid these thugs-in-the-making or trying to find a way to accept the humiliation they meted out at every opportunity—just wanting to make it through the day and get home unscathed. And they didn't talk. They yelled: "You better get on outta here, you chump!" "You string bean motherfucker!" "You four-eyed motherfucker!" "You goofy fuck!". . . , in the halls in front of everybody. Day in and day out. It was tiring. And after a couple of months, I started noticing something a bit peculiar. I couldn't quite make sense of it, but off in the distance one Larry Thomas would be watching—just watching.

Larry Thomas was a star. I didn't follow his career, didn't even know him; but I knew he was one of those varsity quality athletes. The kind that gets: "Hooray! for Thomas / Someone in the crowd yell hooray! for Thomas / One two three four / He's the guy we're rootin' for / Hooray! for Thomas / He's a great guy!" sung to him during assembly. I knew that all the dopes who used to fuck with me kowtowed to him. Nobody gave him shit. He was respected and feared. He was handsome. Girls loved him. He was a sharp dresser. Always pressed pants, starched shirts, clean white undershirts (most kids' were varying shades of dun), always well shined shoes. A conservative dresser. He reeked of strength, but I never saw him fuck with anybody or be mean to anyone. I just started noticing him in the background eyeballing me when the other kids were fooling with me. As I said, he never messed with anyone—until . . .

One day after the lunch bell a group of black kids including Steaphan and Oakleigh began twitting me in the hallway, dredging up whatever vituperations they were capable of, egging me on with high hopes of provoking me into doing something stupid. Humiliation was their sport. All I can remember is that I was focused on the impending danger, trying to figure out my next move, self-conscious that kids galore were watching what was pretty much becoming a daily ritual. Kids love to see other kids suffer. I squeezed the few books I cradled at my right side. It was as though I were looking through a lens Vaselined for a glamor close-up— my peripheral vision a smeared blur. To top it off, my auditory system was breaking down: flaming arrows of insult piercing me frontally while a pack of bloodthirsty hyenas around and behind me were lobbing, "Hit'im!" "Fuck'im up!" "You gonna take that shit!" "What a chump!" "Chump he chump. He ain't nobody." "Hit'at muthafukka!" . . . and on and on. A well-rehearsed routine. It all began to blend together into an evil cacophony of nothingnesss. Fight-or-flight hormones were cascading through my vascular system. Everything was turning red. Things weren't boding well for me. *Think! Think! Think!* Any second now I'd be in pitched battle. So there I was, tunnel-visioned with hell enough to go around when a semi-tractor trailer smashed into me—no! it must have been a locomotive: ka-boom! A collective gasp issued from the mob as everyone took a cautionary step back.

Whatever just happened to me was big and powerful and strong, thrusting me several feet laterally. I nearly lost my balance. When I shook off the impact and gathered myself to the tune of the rabble's delight, what I thought couldn't get any worse just got worse. Surely I must have been goggled-eyed frozen with fearful disbelief, for looming over me was the menacing visage of Larry Thomas—dressed neat as a pin, wearing a very cool navy blue cardigan sweater over his perfectly pressed starched white shirt, meticulously creased cuffed gray wool pants, all bottomed-off with spotlessly polished brown Florsheim cap-toe oxfords—his face in my face. Our eyes were locked upon one another. I felt the fire of his breath. His eyes began searching my face. Oddly, what I noticed was that he was calmly holding a stack of textbooks in his left hand. He knew I wasn't going to do anything. Giving me his meanest vein-bursting look (think Richard Pryor in the YouTube SNL job interview with Chevy Chase), he growled, "What are you going to do about it!" and poked his finger into my chest. It felt like a railroad spike. Oh shits! and damns! and uh-ohs . . . began frothing from the chomping muzzles of the blood sport fans. Snaps! cracks! and popples! Mental chihuahuas nipping at my Achilles' heel. It was deafening. I said nothing.

Larry Thomas came even closer, looking me dead in the eyes with wild abnormally wide orbs that were scanning me, as though looking for something, as though I had a spot on my face that kept moving. Then he bumped me with his shoulder again, like someone bumping you by accident in the hallway, but with such force that it threw me back. He was a powerful kid. It hurt. The crowed oohed and aahed and cast various aspersions. Larry Thomas snapped around and told everyone, "Shut up! Keep your mouths shut or I'll jump on you!" Silence ruled thereafter.

"Betterton, I want to know what you're going to do about it."

I was impressed that he knew my name.

"Look, I don't know why you guys are always messing with me," my nerves beginning to twitch with fear, "I haven't done nothin' to nobody."

"Don't tell *me* to look!" he lashed out, poking me again with his steel finger, making me flinch, then tilting his torso backward like a huge angry question mark, "Son, what are you going to do about it?" He was very articulate—his idiolect not matching the dialect of black Pleasantville.

"I just want to go eat lunch and—" and then he pushed me back toward the stairs.

"What are you going to do? *Betterton!*" And he pushed me again.

"Just leave me alone—" And he pushed me like a shopping cart. I tried to walk away but he grabbed me. "No!" Pushing me even harder, hulking over me, "What are you going to do about it, damn it!"

I turned on my heels, went to the nearby stairs, and threw my books down. I had had it. He had pushed me to my limit. I flipped. When I turned around, there Larry Thomas was, breathing in my face. The throng of wanton delinquents were backing him up, bearing torches and twirling hangman's nooses.

Thrusting my fists straight up in the air, I growled, "Fuck you! Fuck all of you! Come on! . . ." The world was blood red. I was ready for another beating. Ready to be beat to death. I was fed up with this shit. "Come on, motherfucker! . . ." The oohs and aahs and shits and damns ratcheted up.

Larry Thomas spun around snapping at the swarm again, "Shut up!" Then, very calmly, he turned to address me. "OK, Better-*TON* . . . me and you. But not here—up in the third floor bathroom." Throwing me for another loop, he suddenly took an unanticipated step aside and around behind me. "Here, get your books," as he gathered them up and handed them to me, "and let's go."

I wasn't quite sure what to make of it all, so I clenched my books. Heading upstairs, we turned to see a contingent of black kids and a contingent of white kids following us. Larry Thomas mumbled to me, "When I'm done, you tell those white boys to stay down." He stopped and turned around. "Hey! Hey! Hey! Nobody, nobody follow us. If I find anybody following us I'll *beat* you. I *will* beat you. You got that. *Stay* down here. This is between me and Betterton. Y'all keep out of it unless you want an ass kickin'."

Steaphan and Oakleigh, et al., shucked and shuffled, but backed off.

Prompting me with a stern look, Larry Thomas rolled his eyes at the white kids while jerking his head and pointing with his nose in their direction. It was sign language. No words necessary. I understood perfectly. I told the white kids somewhat the same thing, except I didn't say I'd beat anybody.

And off to the third floor we went.

I knew I was in trouble. Larry Thomas had an aura of strength. He was way out of my league, if such a league existed. He was an adult. A man. But what the fuck, I was committed. I would just have to see how it all played out. After all, I'd been beat up many times before. We walked in silence. My thoughts, as usual, went to my clothes: *Shit! I just got these pants. Damn. I'm wearing one of my favorite shirts. Remember. Remember! Take off glasses. Take glasses off.*

Larry Thomas pushed the bathroom door open and very politely held it open for me. He went over and set his books on a sink, making sure it was dry first. I followed suit. He took off his cardigan, smartly folded it, carefully placed it atop his books, then rolled up his sleeves and spun to face me:

"Looky here, Better-*TON*, we're gonna fight, but no hitting in the face. You got that? Chest and body punches only. No tearing clothes. You fuck up my shirt, and I *will* kill you. You understand?"

I stood there, not really believing what was going on. I had been in lots of fights, but things were not going according to what I had expected. It was all very civil and non-threatening. He was actually quite nice. I guess I was looking like a deer transfixed on oncoming headlights because he leaned toward me, snapping, "Betterton! Hey! Son! Do you understand?"

"Uh . . . yeah. Uh . . . uh-huh. Yes. OK. OK . . ."

"Good. Let's go."

He stepped out to the middle of the ring and assumed his fighting stance. He was a southpaw, which really didn't matter to me. Just something I noticed. Most black kids hopped and bopped and skipped and flipped when they were getting ready to fight. Waving their fists and arms every which way was some kind of cultural choreographic meme—a bit of Maori *haka* and peacock mating dance mixed together—dancing to a tune only they could hear. But not Larry Thomas. He stood there, very professional-like, beckoning me:

"Come on, Betterton. Get out here. Get your hands up. Come on, son."

Now, I had taken some boxing lessons when I was about thirteen, which meant I knew that three minutes of getting your ass kicked is a rather long eternity. So I knew a little bit. Up went my hands and in I went, bobbing and weaving and feinting, dancing as though I were Cassius Clay. I threw a few jabs right out of the gate. I faked left. I faked right. Then I let loose a right hook, plastering a solid biff on his left cheek. Bam!

Well, bam! was me. Before I could blink, he thrust a jackhammer punch to my chest, crashing into me like a runaway dump truck loaded with wet beach sand. With me wheezing for dear life, he threw me up against the wall, the institutional fluorescent greenness of the bathroom overwhelming me. As I was sucking in the wind he'd just knocked out of me, he stage whispered a sinister admonishment:

"I told you no hitting in the face. You hit me in the face again and I *will* fuck you up."

Between his aftershave and minty breath, I couldn't help but note that the fella had good hygiene. Standing back, he brushed me off like a valet, then turned and said as he was walking back to the middle of the ring, "Now get out here and fight, son."

This was definitely not how things were supposed to go. Was I actually alive on planet Earth? Had I drunk too much and slipped into some alternate time continuum? Was this really going on? Back in I went. More bobbing and weaving and potshot after potshot from me. Then, like lightning, splap! thwack!—he pasted my chest. Then, thump! whack!— excruciating punches to my left shoulder; then clobbering my right. I was fighting a Brahman bull. This was not a boxing match; it was a bullring, and I was about to be banderillaed to death. I could hardly lift my arms. He kept talking to me throughout the whole thing. One minute, taunting me, using me as a punching bag. The next, coaching me:

"Keep your hands up. Keep your eyes on my eyes. The eyes tell you everything. Hit me. Hit me hard. We're not leaving here until you start laying into me."

He wasn't cutting me any slack, but I started getting pissed and wishing I weren't even there. Fucking fighting. What stupid human behavior. Why do guys always want to fight? So, with whatever mind I had left going blank on me, I charged with unbidden primal rage. We became entwined. Arms flailing. Hugging. Pushing. Pulling. Searching for a grip. I was almost overcome by his sweet cologne. Was it Brut? In the midst of grappling, I got hold of his shirt and started twirling him. His arms flew up as though he were about to take flight:

"The shirt! The *shirt!* You pop a button and I *will* kick your ass."

"Aw, oh yeah. Oh yeah. OK. OK. I-I'm sorry. I'm sorry . . . ," and I let go.

"*Damn* Betterton. You were getting scrappy, son. You *are* lucky you did not tear my shirt. That's enough. We call it quits now. But you got some good ones in. I'm impressed. Nice fisticuffs." Then, nonchalantly, he began dusting himself off, going over to the mirror, checking himself out, patting his Smokey Robinson self back into shape, humming and singing "Mickey's Monkey."

I was still mystified. Stunned. Still not sure what was going on. What just happened? He just stopped. Stopped! And me standing there, agape, with my fists half-ass ready to continue fighting.

Casually sprucing up and washing his hands, he paused, looked at me in the mirror, and said, "Put your hands down, Betterton. We call it quits. Comb your hair. Let's go before we miss lunch."

"Larry, I don't get it. I thought you wanted to kick my ass."

"*No*, Betterton, I do not want to kick your ass. It's been tweaking my undies watching you put up with those chumps fucking with you every day. I want you to stand up for yourself. Be a man."

"Huh? . . ."

"Looky here, son. What happened in here is between me and you. No one gets to know how this turned out, you hear? This is our secret. Anybody asks who won, we tell them that it's between me and you and none of their business. They're going to want to know who beat who. I hear tell you told anyone how it all went down—and you *better not* say you kicked my ass—I will kick *your* ass in front of the entire school, you hear?"

I kind of laughed. Let my guard down. Just stood there watching him primp. This guy was decent. No malice whatsoever. He was actually trying to help me. Nobody ever did that.

"OK. That's boss," I conceded.

"Those guys are idiots, Betterton. You could take 'em. Most of them won't even graduate. Don't let them get to you, son. And don't get any ideas—this doesn't mean we're friends or anything. You're a freshman. OK, son. Let's go to lunch."

I tidied myself up and grabbed my books. We exited the bathroom and walked down the steps side by side in good humor talking about who knows what. When we got to the first floor, there were our antsy-pantsy contingents of white and black kids—restive paparazzi. All the utterances flowing from their collective mouth amounted to one question: who won? Larry Thomas and I were still standing three steps above the lynch mob. I looked at him with all the confidence I could muster and raised my eyebrows; he did pretty much the same.

"That's between me and Larry."

But those sharks weren't satisfied. They spit out inquiry after inquiry as Larry Thomas and I stepped down pushing our way through them. We kept walking as we exited our respective tribes, but Larry Thomas turned and walked backward to hurl a piercing Parthian shot:

"Like the man said, it's between him and me. You want to find out? Try one of us."

On that note he smirked and turned and looked at me. We smiled. He put his hand out. We shook, then we tittuped jively on our separate ways. From that day forward, neither Steaphan nor Oakleigh nor any of those other dopes ever messed with me again.

10

WHAT IS EASTER?

What is Easter?
I'll tell you what Easter is.
It's the most coarsely shredded coconut
Pure white ice-cold coconut
Not quite so sweet as you find today
And not so creamy, either
Chewy slivers
Shredded shreds you have to chew
Really have to chew
Hand rolled into a perfectly formed
Bunny egg
About 6″ long
And about 3 ½″ high and wide

Bluntly tapered at the ends
With a double-triple-quadruple thick covering
Of hand-dipped dark chocolate
Not so sweet as you find today
Topped with cute little flourishes
Green and yellow and pink sugary doodads
Flowers and stuff
To be eaten immediately
Just to get it out of the way
So as not to taint the good stuff
Sitting on a saucer
In the refrigerator
Chilling like fine wine
Knowing its destiny
Waiting patiently
For a serrated knife to saw it
Into 1″ thick slices
Like salmon steaks
Easter egg steaks
Better than any steak
Mmm-mmm-mmm . . .
It is this
Homemade
Handmade
In the little candy store on Washington Avenue
Where the Pleasantville Cleaners
Ended up
It is this annual ritual
That my grandfather
Lornenzo D. Borden
Started
A ritual
I do not believe anyone else even remembers
But a ritual of great significance to me
I could not wait to be alone

No Mom around to govern my eating
So I could begin slice by slice devouring
My ambrosial confection
In solitude
Eyes closed
Sitting
At our blue-gray marbleized
Formica-top kitchen table
Slowing chewing stringy meaty morsels
Blending in the chocolate
Of my grandfather's annual Easter egg
Savoring
Pure ecstasy
Complemented
With sips and gulps of ice-cold Sealtest milk
That is what Easter is
And absolutely nothing else matters . . .

THE PERFECT CRIME

One thing I learned when I was a kid growing up in Pleasantville, NJ, was that if you're going to commit a crime, go solo. Don't trust anybody. Don't even trust trust. When I was five, six, and seven, I used to go visit my cousins, and we'd be playing, doing whatever, and then get busted for doing it—"I didn't do it! David did it! It was his idea . . ." Right. And it was never my idea because I was a follower-alonger. As a neighbor recently told me, "You only need to learn your lesson once." Well, it took me more than once, but I finally got it: make sure your accomplice has more blood on his or her hands than you do. Or, better yet, go it alone. I got involved with so many tomfool capers in my youth it's a wonder I'm not typing this from my cell in a big house somewhere. But I'm not, so it must have all along been the intention of the designer of this lovely universe that I relate the following:

You might say that larceny was in my blood. But it must have come from my father's side because Mom was as honest as the sun shines. Honest to a fault. As I would piecemeal reveal the whole truth and nothing but the truth to her in her latter years, well past any possible statutes of limitations, she would have minor coronaries upon hearing the details of my shenanigans that had been theretofore classified top secret and sequestered deep within the vaults of the National Archives.

I was lying and scheming and pilfering from my earliest memories. I would use a dinner knife to slip coins out of a golden glass piggy bank so I could go buy candy. My mom had this clear plastic replica of a bank building that had hollow columns for stacks of nickels, dimes, quarters, and pennies. I learned how to filch those coins unnoticed. Unnoticed that is, until I got carried away and then there were almost no coins left. Of course, I always denied it and said that I had no idea where the money went. Plus, I would steal money from Mom's purse from time to time.

I had this crazy passion for knives—pearl handled stilettos, switchblades, fancy poniards, hunting knives, penknives of all sorts; if it sliced it was nice—and when I would get busted by Mom with one of my weapons of choice (which scared the bejesus out of her), I would say, "I found it!" I always *found* everything. Whenever Mom would make cookies for Christmas, she'd have to hide them around the house, constantly coming up with innovative hiding places because I would ferret them out and little by little they would disappear. I just couldn't help myself. She would send me to the store for whipped cream and I would eat little squirts of it on the way home and by the time she got it there would be nothing left but hiss and sputter—they didn't safety-seal things then the way they do today—and I'd swear that I hadn't touched it. Once her boyfriend Art sent me to the store to get him a Hires root beer. Because I knew how to sneak the top off and put it back on, I took a few sips, replenishing it with water from a neighbor's garden spigot. After I'd done this a couple of times, it looked like weak tea, so I blamed it on the store. Mom took me to her friend's house down on Main Street one day where I stole some pristine mint condition coins from the seventeenth and eighteenth centuries. I ended up heating the coins to red-hot on our gas stove so they'd look old. Certainly, I ruined them.

One sunny summer's day I was shooting marbles with five or six tiny mibsters in the middle of Wabash Avenue over in Bungalow Park on the north end of Atlantic City (or AC, as the locals call it), where my newly married sister Kitty lived. I spontaneously decided to steal this kid's most unusual multi-colored orb—a swirliness of bright purple with splatters of dark green and yellow with flecks of gold peppered with a constellation of cool air bubbles. Never saw anything like it, so I just put it in my pocket. Anyway, its owner started chasing me in pursuit of his property. When I fell, my seven- or eight-year-old left arm lodged itself in a crack in the blacktop, snapping like a brittle twig. Crack! Pain, sharp and so immediate, rendered the marble kid inconsequential. I let out such a savage wail he froze in his tracks. Slowly standing, cradling my little arm, tears flushing, my shattered ulna and radius trying to escape, articulation where none should be, kids all freaking out backing off, moon-eyed, mouths agape—quite the surreal moment. The bones made a downright freakish protrusion. And, man, did it smart. I went right into survival mode. Lucky for me, my sister's neighbor was one Dr. Lee, a very nice Johnny Mathisish-looking man. I ran a block straight for his front door and kicked it, standing there on his porch crying with my deformed arm. I don't remember all the details but I know that when he opened that door, Dr. Lee was the epitome of compassion and confidence. I knew I was going to be OK. That man took gentle good care of me. And that marble was *mine*.

I snuck into a neighbor's garage one time and stole some tools just because I liked tools. One humid sweltering summer day, during a rare extended visit with my sister Doreen and her new family, who were living in Birdland, a new housing development out on Robin Road in the hinterlands of Cardiff, I tagged along with a knot of little country criminals and swiped tons of tools from a construction site above a nearby gravel pit we used to swim and raft in. We hid those tools in the dog house of our de facto leader, Alberto B. Hopcroft. Alberto had this big old friendly black Labrador retriever named Butch, and Butch's house was inordinately large. It would almost qualify as a tiny house for people. Several kids could get in there with plenty of room to move. Anyway, later on that day I snuck back to ol' Butch's house with evil intentions. In its darkness, with its doggie portiere tightly drawn, using strobing bursts of light from a torch spark lighter, I selected the tools of my fancy and stole them. I hid the whole bunch under my bed at my sister's house. But she found them. "David, where did you get all those tools under the bed?" Duh . . . I always thought it was she who had turned us in to the police, but nigh on three score years later I asked her about it and she assured me that she didn't do it; that a neighbor had told her about the theft, leading her to scour the room. Quite clearly, one of the kids had coughed up my name. Aside from a strong dose of humiliation and a stern talking-to, nothing really happened to us. This was when I was about nine. Today, it would be called a gateway crime.

In Pleasantville, we had three supermarkets: Food Fair, Acme, and Starn's ShopRite. One wintery day, this pathological thief and liar I had been hanging around with and I decided to hit ShopRite. He came by my house, "Hey, Dave, let's go steal something." So we headed on over to Starn's. Per our plan, we went in and went our separate ways. The goal was to lift what we could in a ten- or fifteen-minute turnaround and meet up behind Baker's Five and Dime to inventory our pickings. The scheming of twelve-year-old Jersey wannabe ladrones.

I was inconspicuously meandering up and down the aisles, or so I thought, stashing things inside my coat. Important things. Things like a pair of kitchen mittens, socks I would never wear, a bar of Baker's dark chocolate, a metal flip spatula, a bag of Nestlé's semi-sweet Toll House chocolate chips (I would eat the whole bag), and several other forgettable items. While I was plying my trade, I noticed in my peripheral vision a prying eye poking out from behind the end of the aisle to my left. I was being watched. Time to move on to Plan B. So I started acting like I was looking for something and moved on to another aisle. Lo and behold, the peering eye was there slyly peeking, too. On to another aisle, and the same thing. Time to move on to Plan C. I hied myself across several aisles and down toward the back of the store, dipping into the frozen food department. There I was alone. What to do! I was in a real pinch. Raw instinct kicked in. In nanoseconds, I commenced lifting packages of frozen food and dumping my entire stash in the space it had previously occupied, secreting my ill-gotten gains below fish sticks, chicken pot pies, and Swanson TV dinners. Tidying up, composing myself, I headed for the exit.

As I was walking out the door, suddenly before me appeared Stanley Starn. Stanley knew me and my mother. He abruptly stood directly in front of me, "Hi, David . . . ," and began jokingly poking me in the belly with his right forefinger, making me flinch. He was wearing a big smile and messing with me like we were long-lost friends, jabbing me a little higher and a little lower, bracketing for the goods. I knew darn well what he was doing. "How's your mom? Is she here? . . ." I shirked and winced and acted like what-are-you-crazy-why-are-you-messing-with-me? and told him, no, she wasn't; that I thought she was but that I couldn't find her. And that was that. He backed off and told me to tell her that he'd said hi. I left, shaking my head, feigning puzzlement at his behavior. But the other kid got caught. Phew! I decided then and there—no more high-risk stuff. Not because of moral reasons, mind you, but because I couldn't possibly stand the humiliation of getting caught. Hence, that was my first and last foray into the world of shoplifting. Interestingly, a couple months later Mom told me that she ran into Stanley Starn, who'd made it a point to apologize to her because he had thought I was in there shoplifting, but he was wrong; that he felt bad for thinking that of me. Ha!

The ShopRite incident was as close as I cared to get to getting caught. I quit hanging around dopes that were bound to get me in trouble. If I were ever to do anything criminal again, it would have to be foolproof. So I lay low for quite a good while. I heard all kinds of stories and paid attention to how different kids got busted doing their shifty work. Uh-uh, there would be none of that for me. My life of crime was over. I was going straight. After all, I really was an honest trustworthy kid—kinda . . .

From when I was about eight or so, Mom and I lived in that chauffeur's quarters behind what was then American Legion Post 81. The Legion was a once fantastic Victorian-Italianate*ish* mansion that Robert and Laura Willis had built in 1908. Their heirs had sold it to the Legion in 1946, and from then on, the once-palatial residence became a common rental hall for small-town weddings, graduations, and dances, but mostly a place where old vets hung out nightly getting plastered, especially on Fridays and Saturdays. Winter and summer, clatter and jabber oozed through its back door, interrupted now and then by the clang of empty beer kegs being placed outside for pickup. An occasional drunk would stagger past our door or creep to a place he thought was out of sight to take a pee.

I can trace my first orgasm back to the Legion when I was no more than nine or so. Out in front, there was a real silver-painted World War II torpedo emblazoned with American Legion Post 81. It was cradled on a galvanized pipe frame and I loved climbing all over that underwater missile, riding it like a horse, imagining the damage such a monster could do. There was also a flagpole there. One chilly sunny day, I shimmied up that cold pole and right there in high heaven, on the Black Horse Pike, in front of all the passersby, when I was about twenty-five feet up in the air, is when it happened—Whammo! Kablooey! Pow! There I was, clutching that frigid pole. Not a clue whatsoever what was going on. A nutating nystagmic hunk of frenzied juvenility. An on high spasmodic carnal swallowtail flagging in the breeze. I thereafter spent a goodly number of thoughtful moments aloft on that old pole—a would-be steeplejack, I was—the unsuspecting traffic whizzing by me below. But no matter how much I wished for or tried to replicate that most desirous effect, I was never able to achieve a reprise.

On the side of the Legion was a huge oak tree I used to climb to just think and watch the world or to escape the violent intentions of my sister Doreen Mae, who was somewhat a bully. The Legion's backyard—which was our front yard, through which kegs of beer and large canvas bags of chipped ice and tongued blocks of ice were delivered, through which drunks would pass and pass out, or take a heave, or take a piss—would every spring produce a beautiful bordered bloom of King Alfred daffodils that would delineate the central grassy area where our clotheslines were. (It used to gall me that our across-the-street-neighbor Mrs. Nasser would come uninvited into our yard and pick bouquets whenever she darned well felt like it. She treated us like we were poor. Oh, how my nine- or ten-year-old self would unwittingly wish for Hermes to whisk her off to the underworld with one last golden nosegay. Sadly, she ended up committing suicide.)

The back entrance was through a fortresslike claybank rough stucco Mediterranean*ish* wall about a foot thick, ten feet tall or so. It had a couple of empty niches that once had surely displayed religious or classic statuary. Its two massive faded and paint-flaking white timber carriage gates were side hung on capped stucco pillars, fancily adorned with black wrought iron fleur-de-lis strap hinges, pintles, bolts, and thumb latch. I loved climbing up on that wall. Sometimes just sitting there, feeling on top of the world. Other times, testing my ability to walk its length back and forth over and over without falling. There was a stagnant leaf-filled darkling fishpond loaded with miry scum that was no doubt the source of our summer mosquito population—its foul mushy contents slumbering away beneath an ancient massy holly tree that shaded the deteriorating loggia alongside the chauffeur's quarters—our home. Quite a magnificent place in its day, but to Mom and me it was just Ye Olde American Legion—a once-opulent villa, now with the pointing of its efflorescing Dutch bricks spalling and crumbling, its clapboarding rotting in need of paint and repair. Without constant maintenance, New Jersey's seasonal extremes exact a heavy toll on architecture. Architecture aside, one thing every kid in town knew about the Legion was that there was booze within, and lots of it. Hence, the Legion was periodically burgled.

While burglar alarms had been around since the mid-1800s, they weren't all that prevalent in Pleasantville in the 1960s. And if they were, the Legion didn't have one. A fact I was completely unaware of. But the P'ville cops would, nevertheless, now and then, foil some local yokel trying to plunder the Legion's cache of alcohol. It was more than once that Mom and I were awakened in the wee hours by heavy running feet, yelling, and flashlights slicing the night. The last time I remember, one sticky summer's night, it was our resident town thug, one Nelson Truax. He tried to elude the police by squeezing his pompadoured elfin body in the small filthy space behind a boiler in the Legion's frowzy basement.

Nelson Truax was one cool hombre. Always a girl on his arm and a sharp dresser to boot. Probably not the brightest star in any constellation, because he was in and out of jail all the time, but he was a local P'ville legend and a much feared punk. Guys two and three times his size kowtowed to his wishes. Anyway, that night, somewhere around midnight, peeking through the yellow flower pattern café curtain on our downstairs door, our only door in or out, I watched the PPD drag him from the basement of the Legion, all besmirched and sooty. With all flashlights focused on him, ample giggles of derision coming from the police, I could see him treading defiantly in his Cuban heels, tight tapered pants, pinstripe button-down, and one helluva cool Italian black leather car coat—collar flipped up, all the while donning a cocky smirk that said, I'll-beat-this-in-a-Jersey-minute-and-if-I-catch-you-alone-on-the-street-I'll-kick-your-ass. He looked much like a coal miner coming home from a hard day's work, but there was one thing that stood out: his hair was perfect! The way Nelson Truax would drag a comb over his flawless pompadour, it would not surprise me to find out that Henry Winkler had observed his trademark self-pampering to affect his Fonzie character. It also would not surprise me to find out that at that very moment, just before he knew he was going to be nabbed, Nelson Truax did, in fact, drag a comb across his head. As the officers loaded their catch into a squad car, the night returning to stillness, a thought entered my alleged mind, *These smart guys always do it at night and they always get caught.* Mom yelled down to me from her convertible bed in the living room, "Go back to bed, honey. Just another smartass up to no good. I've got to go to work in the morning. C'mon. I'm glad I don't have to worry 'bout you doing stupid things in the middle of the night."

If I had any intelligence when I was a kid, it was all hidden. Generally speaking, I failed at everything. No good with sports whatsoever. A real oaf without a bone of competitiveness. I pretty much garnered Fs in everything at school—when I was there, that is. I was notorious for hookying and getting kicked out. I hated school. A real goofball with girls, who seemed genetically engineered to reject me preemptively because they could intuit my inner defects. I fell in love with turbaned ring-wormed Barbara Bullock in kindergarten and held on to that crush until around eighth grade when Deloris Leeds came along to supplant her. But that means I was already two years older than the rest of the kids because I got left back in the second and fourth grades. When it came to fighting, I pretty much became a human punching bag for my opponents. I always lost. With few exceptions, I didn't back down. I'd fight, but I fought fair.

Ergo, I lost. I just took it. At around twelve, I went from short and chubby to 6'2"—I was short, fat, tall, and skinny all at once. Until I was twelve, every Christmas I had to listen to "All I Want for Christmas Is My Two Front Teeth," which kinda helped divert attention away from my acne. I was a class clown, but my highbrow humor was wasted on the moron thugs in my classes. They ridiculed me for what *they* didn't understand. Getting left back didn't help any. According to the juvenile and teen standards of any generation of any culture, I was a loser. Always on the outside looking in. Never understanding how things worked. Smart and stupid simultaneously.

Then, somewhere in the penumbral days between twelve and thirteen, my mom started going out with this guy who happened to be the father of a local bully. Now I have to redefine *bully* here. Generally, a bully is someone who picks on the weaker and really isn't all that tough himself when someone calls his bluff. Not so with Draco Delacroix. He would challenge anyone, and the bigger and badder the better. He always won. He seemed to lack a fear gene. The only time I know of him not winning a fight was when it came out to a draw with the aforementioned Nelson Truax, who was known far and wide for his prowess. One day, on my way to school, Draco Delacroix ran up to me and challenged me to a fight. In a rare moment of self-preservation, I sensibly chickened out. So it came as quite a fear-ladened surprise when he suddenly became part of my extended family. But that worked itself out, and I began to hang out with Draco and his older brother Timmy. They were, like, sixteen and nineteen, respectively. I was thirteen. My life changed dramatically. I started seeing things and hearing things and going places and meeting people and doing things I had never imagined. Drinking (actually, drinking more). Picking up girls and making out like wild rutting goats. Dressing cool. Going to dances and parties. Staying out late. Wondering if I would die before I had sex.

Now, don't get me wrong. I didn't suddenly become an overnight success. I just got to see things from the other side for a change. Which actually made me feel all the worse. I still got rejected offhand by girls. I still got the crap beat out of me on a routine basis. While my two-front ivories did grow back, with a couple extra extraneous to boot, I ended up joining the ranks of—"Heavens to Murgatroyd!"—the Snaggletooths of the world, which later in life I found out included Sam Shepard. Not bad company. Being older than the average eighth grader because of getting left back twice wasn't cool, but getting massive cysts on my eyes that my ophthalmologist said I needed to let grow to a goodish size before removing them, engendering the sobriquet Butterball Eyes, really made life hard on one already beaten down. I was a walking, talking juvenile Job.

But through life's meaningless and unfair gantlets I could see—I knew—that there were some things at which I was superior: I was a good dancer and one hell of a liar, cheat, and thief. And while the latter three clearly inclined toward the dark arts, they were, after all, arts. Crafts to be honed, requiring spontaneous creative thinking. Talents to be worked upon in pure solitude as accomplices were a liability—even the most loyal of loyal companions is prone to some sort of weakness, corruption, or conscience. So this Legion booze heist business became a personal challenge. Those other jerk-offs, who were supposed to be the older kids, the "smart ones," always got busted. What were they doing wrong? Hmmm. Incubation had begun . . .

Hanging out with Draco and Timmy led to our becoming members of a dance club called Lonnie's Den over in AC. The Den's eponymous founder had inside connections on a TV dance show on entertainment tycoon George Hamid's Steel Pier—"Showplace of the Nation," or simply, "The Pier," as we called it—and had somehow cornered the market on controlling who got to go up on the feature stage during the live show, a highly coveted and sought-after thirty seconds of fame one might experience on camera. In order to get into The Den, in addition to not being a criminal or thug, you had to be able to dance, and the test was for you to show up and be auditioned at the club's hangout over at Charlie Banana's burger/soda joint on the northeast corner of Atlantic Avenue at Delaware. To the left, as you entered Banana's, at the far end of the booths and counter, up four or five steps, there was a door that led into this room where kids congregated. This was the official Lonnie's Den clubroom (Lonnie and his family lived a couple doors directly behind Banana's on Delaware), a rectangular affair about 15′×40′ or so, with long wooden benches affixed to its lengthy walls. Girls sitting on one side; boys on the other. It had a jukebox at one end that was ten cents a pop or three for a quarter. A couple of guys, who were easy with girls or had themselves a girlfriend, would make it a point to linger in distaff territory, acting all too nonchalant, knowing damned well that they were making the rest of us look like the dopes that we were. Now and then, somebody would drop another dime in the jukebox and it was time to go over and ask a girl to dance. This is where the audition took place. If the group liked the way you danced, you were in like Flynn, thenceforth entitled to buy and wear the club's proprietary Mandarin collared off-white cashmere cardigan sweater with dark brown four-hole wooden buttons and/or a full-zip white cotton jacket with hoodie, both very light weight, bearing the club's three-inch navy blue *LD* logo sewn on the left chest over the heart. Right there in that cubbyhole of a refuge, we'd cut loose to "The Loco-Motion," "Mama Said," "Let Me In (wee-oo)," "Mother-in-Law," "I'm Blue (The Gong-Gong Song)," and whatever else was on that juke that gave our sweet youthful bodies the primordial thrill of rhythm for ten cents or two bits. I guess you might say that it was a rehearsal studio where dance moves were worked out for on-air performances.

The show was Ed Hurst's *Summertime on the Pier*, which was broadcast during the summer from the Marine Ballroom on the Steel Pier. The Pier was this phenomenal structure that jutted some two thousand feet out from the Boardwalk across the sugary sand of Virginia Avenue beach into the briny Atlantic. A fantastic place where, once you gained entrance, you had access to all kinds of shows and movies and griddled pork rolls and cotton candy and candied apples and movie stars and singing stars and big bands and diving horses and a diving bell and fun houses and all sorts of revues. Food and attractions galore. Excessive entertainment for the price of admission—one dollar. You had to buy the food, but the buck included all the entertainment. A body could spend the entire day on The Pier and not be able to take in all its offerings.

Hurst had a storied show biz past up Philadelphia way, but his *Summertime* was a big deal for us locals. It came on Saturday afternoons and kids could become local celebrities of *American Bandstand* caliber. As far as me being a member of Lonnie's Den, yes, I got up on that stage a couple of times, but I was an outsider. A nonentity. One of the uncoolest of the uncool in a cool club of Flossies and Floes, Mattie Mattels and Vick Tartaglios. A fly on the wall, I was. Once, one of the hottest girls used me to get even with her boyfriend. She asked me to go to a movie with her. So off we went. After watching for a short while, she said that she had to go to the bathroom. After a long while, I figured out what was going on. When I got up to leave, there she was, making out with her thitherto estranged beau. Exiting up the aisle, massive Jurassic reptilian dermal plates of shame, humiliation, and flat-out confusion began wagging behind me. They mean-eyed me and snickered. Trying to maintain some sort of dignity, I reached deep down and dredged up something that allowed me to maintain eyes forward and stem my welling tears. I marched out of that the theater, and never told Draco or Timmy a thing about it. I was a cipher extraordinaire. A true nebbish. Which brings me to one Gary Ozer.

I never knew anything by being directly informed. I had to acquire my information by fits and starts, bits and pieces, catch-as-catch-can. That meant usually overhearing conversations. Not exactly eavesdropping; rather, taking advantage of a situation. For instance, I knew that Lonnie had worked out a deal with the cops and the Hurst people to run a straight up club: no hoodlums, no bad behavior, no bringing bad publicity to the show or The Pier. No one told me this, I just picked it up in snippets of info happenstance, putting two and two together. I was an intuiter. I never really understood the relationship between Lonnie and Hurst, but I always suspected Lonnie was being compensated for his efforts. Not that that was a bad thing, just that it seemed more like a business relationship than outright altruism.

I was raised in racist Pleasantville, New Jersey, five miles due west of AC, where it was not uncommon to hear "The only good nigger is a dead nigger" fly out of the mouths of kith and kin. That's just how people talked. No one was ever what they were. You were a spic or a kike or a Nip or a wop or a blah blah blah. So, my outlook on life and other people was pretty screwed up. Hence, I thought Lonnie was a real anomaly. He didn't fit any of the stereotypes my Bigotry 101 catechism had covered. He was this man, I'm guessing, in his early-to-mid-twenties of Polynesian extraction of a somewhat smallish stature. Small but buff. Incredibly buff. During the day, he was a fish lumper at Captain Starn's Restaurant on the inlet, doing humble and labor intensive stinky work. But come night or a Saturday show, Lonnie Kockiana made John Travolta and *Saturday Night Fever* look like mere child's play. Only he did it without the garish pomp. The de facto leader of Lonnie's Den, a group of teenagers, he hovered above us all. To some, he walked on water. We were kids; he was a man. Whenever he showed up at a dance or some other event, he always had an absolutely gorgeous taller woman on his arm, both of them impeccably attired. And when he and his partner would begin dancing, there was no doubt in anyone's mind that the man was an artist. While I didn't know what the hell I was doing at the time, I could tell that he did. A gifted soul. From the latest craze to elaborate ballroom dancing, Lonnie did it all with style and professionalism. The man's life itself was a movie, but to us he was just Lonnie, and his mission was to run a club of clean-cut kids he kept out of trouble by keeping us occupied thinking about all things dancing so we didn't get involved with the "bad kids" and gangs. Like Gary Ozer's Brighton Avenue Gang.

When the bad kids showed up at a dance, it was as clear as the Beatles vs. the Rolling Stones. They shone with a different luster. And when bad boy Gary Ozer made an appearance, when the Orlons were cutting loose with "Let Me In" or "South Street" or whatever, he would sashay across Marine Ballroom as though airborne toward some fine chick, doing his special brand of Watusi, arms outstretched and pumping like he was wearing an invisible fancy Mummer's costume, cakewalk-strutting unlike any of the other kids. He was original. With his tall thin agile rhythmic body adorned with sandy suede desert boots, olive green slacks with cuffs resting stylishly just below the boot collar, the top two buttons undone on his starched white dress shirt to expose his spotless tee allowing his Italian spread collar to fly and flop as he pranced, his careful ensemble topped off with a maverick pompadour that fluttered and flowed so flawlessly that it made Elvis's look like a high and tight. His hair more perfect than a werewolf's at Trader Vic's. Flitting and flinging his grinning aquiline blemish-free baby soft white epicene face that sat precariously atop a wiry lashing chicken neck, one could almost hear the rote of his perpetually cresting wave of hair crashing and splashing to the beat of the music—Gary Ozer was pure cool. A chick magnate. A hoodlum. A someone to stay away from.

I don't believe I ever had two words with Gary Ozer, but I certainly observed him and caught a few of his words here and there. And I certainly knew he was bad news. Whenever he arrived on a scene, there took place simultaneously a parting of the seas and a crashing in of all things drawn into his gravity. While an attractor of impressionable personalities, he too evoked a palpable repulsion—kids (especially kids from The Den) would sidle away from him, casting furtive glances, murmuring in hushed tones. Gary Ozer was a veritable persona non grata—an authentic desperado. And it was my overhearing—eavesdropping, actually—one of his outlaw conversations (he was spewing Macheathian advice to one of his acolytes one day during a commercial break) when I harvested a golden nugget of information that would prove absolutely useless to me. Trying to act like I was paying attention to the kids I was with, combined with the Lombard effect of crowd din, I couldn't make out but every few words or so. Sort of like having a conversation on a cell phone with a bad connection.

Apparently, the kid he was talking to was an aspiring hoodlum, and Gary Ozer was explaining to him the makings of an ideal tool kit for a housebreaker. Through the racket I picked up valuable fragments: Tool kit should be lightweight. Tools should be packed so as not to make noise. Should be able to carry kit on back or over shoulder to work hands-free. Flat-blade and Phillips head screwdrivers. Flashlight with fresh batteries. And absolutely necessary, a crowbar. Something blah-blah about jimmying a door or window. And that's pretty much all I could pick up. But it was enough for me to try to figure out a few things on my own.

So the jokers in P'ville always got busted trying to rip off the American Legion. I can't remember how many times—Mom and I lived behind it from, say, the late-1950s, and I joined the Navy in 1965—but before I left home, perhaps four or six kids got nabbed trying to pull late night booze heists. Each ending in humiliation and probable jail time. But, overall, it just never really meant anything to me. It just was. And it was nothing of interest to me. Or so I thought.

I started drinking at about age twelve. (Actually, I got my first taste of getting high much earlier, around eight or nine, but that's another story involving hallucinations, a dog, and the duping of our family doctor. About twelve is when I started drinking and smoking regularly.) And when you're a kid and your mom drudges away inspecting china for slave wages and just barely making ends meet, well, money is not plentiful. While I wasn't born with a plastic tablespoon in my mouth, we were nevertheless poor. Even though booze was pretty darn cheap then and easy enough to get, I could never really get enough. It's not like I was an alcoholic in-the-making; rather, it seems I was one right out of the gate. Throwing up, passing out, lipping off, screwing up, and getting into fights I couldn't win—all this was so much easier to handle under the influence. Booze was the good stuff. The magic elixir. Teenage wasteland fixer.

Now, I did do odd jobs in the neighborhood from time to time, but, mostly, whatever money I had came from Mom's meager earnings. I really didn't have an allowance per se, but she ponied up a buck or two now and then out of the goodness of her heart (or to get me out of the house so she could have some alone time with her "boyfriend," Art, Draco and Timmy Delacroix's dad). Or I outright stole it from her on the stownlins.

Alcohol had gained such a wide enough currency amongst the kids I was hanging around with that we were constantly aware of just how much currency we did *not* have. Whenever there was an opportunity to buy booze, whether by having it delivered to one of our homes or by having some older guy buy it for us, we were reduced to chipping in a quarter here, fifty cents there, or a buck or two if one was flush with cash. The end result was usually pukes and pitiful. Drunks, after all, have to start somewhere.

One lovely spring day, I was hanging around the house doing my usual nothing, Mom sweat-shopping at Lenox to bring home the bacon, all was quiet on the neighborhood front, when this thought popped into my alleged mind: *I know why those guys always get caught. They always do it at night and are drunk when they do it. What if?—What if I were to do it in broad daylight? Hmmm . . .* So right then and there I devised a plan based upon and inspired by Gary Ozer's B&E tutorial. Why, I had everything in-house to pull off a clean job, and no dopy joker but myself to screw things up. So, first things first—make sure the coast is clear. As I lived there, I could get away with screwing around the Legion where another kid would be suspect.

The first thing I did was just kind of lounge around, unobtrusively checking for watchful eyes. I'd place myself at different locations outside the Legion, listening to make sure no one was inside. I'd lie on the grass and pretend to be napping or just thinking. I'd straddle the torpedo. I'd shimmy up the flagpole a bit. I'd sit on the fancy molded concrete bench under the giant oak tree. I stooged around the backyard, which was Mom's and my front yard, softly walking up and down the concrete walkway on the opposite side of the building—always acting like I was doing something else but listening, tentacles up, searching for inaudible vibrations of human movement or voice or hidden observant eyes. Again, because I lived there, such behavior was not uncommon. I knew no one was there, but for the project I had in mind, extra precautionary measures were called for. My last test was going up to both the front and back doors and knocking. Should anyone answer, I was all ready to ask if Frank was there and then I'd figure out what stupid thing I'd say off the hip, should anyone actually answer. But no one did. The coast was clear. So I stood in the backyard, leaning against a 4″× 4″ clothesline post scoping out the situation, scouring every inch of that dying old mansion. I worked out my entrance and exit, mentally rehearsing my impendent activities.

The arrangement we had with the Legion was that we rented and lived in the chauffeur's quarters above a two-car garage. It was a cruel coincidence that our technical address was 40 E. Verona Avenue (in the rear), while the sliding garage doors of our humble abode actually opened out onto Lennox Avenue, and Mom spent her life toiling away for Lenox China out in Pomona. Anyway, part of the arrangement was that one half of the garage was ours and the other half was rented out to Jenkins Plumbing and Heating. That meant their side was loaded to the gills with all sorts of plumbing and heating-related paraphernalia. As my sinister brain was conjuring criminal intentions, this little garage sharing situation began looming large—a boon for my caper. As the great Willis house had been built just after the turn of the twentieth century—Peter Lunati's rotary lift was yet two decades in the offing—mechanical work on the undercarriage of a car was usually done by either scrunching oneself under the vehicle or driving it up a makeshift ramp or working from the comfort of a grease pit. As chauffeurs at the time were expected to be mechanically capable and were responsible for general motorcar maintenance, it was my good fortune that such a grease pit existed on the Jenkins side of the garage, a subterrane about 6′×4′ and some 5′ deep. It was hatched by four ancient grease-soaked 3″×12″ roughhewn slab planks that had all sorts of plumbing and heating crap stored atop them. To my scheming eyes, that long-forgotten hollow was a perfect accomplice for my mens rea. A pirate's cave awaiting booty.

I gathered up the necessary tools per Gary Ozer's instructions given on that day who knows how long before. It was all so crystal clear, as though he had spoken only moments ago. It seems that from an early age I was eager to be good at something—anything, so long as I was good at it: to be competent, to be capable, to be professional—whatever that meant. As a kid, I took this unusual pride in making sure I made straight handsawn cuts; that whatever I affixed was plumb and level; that I colored within the lines; that I outwitted the other kids. Sports and fisticuffing were out, though, because I was lousy at every sport and was pretty regularly getting my butt kicked. So, I had to seek other endeavors in which to excel. I was a proven F-student and not quite ruthless enough to be a streetwise criminal. I had to find a Middle Way. Lying and deception came naturally and suited me well. But I wasn't a cheat. If I failed, I deserved it. If I succeeded, I deserved it. My merits were my merits, and I had somehow learned to accept them, along with my bounteous demerits, with all their fruitage of emotional pain. As a result, I was neither a braggart nor blatant about anything (except maybe my dancing capabilities). Somehow, I had evolved into a low-key maneuvering-behind-the-scenes operator.

As I was going to jimmy open a back door, making my entrée via the look-out basement, I would only need a screwdriver and crowbar. From my assessment of things, the task would be easy enough. So I grabbed a flathead and a crow and slipped out the storm door. Holding the tools unobtrusively vertical by my side, I sauntered over to the stairwell that descended five or six steps beneath a service entrance that jettied out some 10′ to 12′ over an open area about 10′×10′. A great place to do my stealthy deed. Again, had anyone from the Legion seen me going anywhere or doing anything, it would not have been suspicious. For years I had been playing all over that building's exterior. I knew every nook and cranny. So going down under the steps would not be out of the ordinary. I was *above suspicion*. I laid my tools on a carpet of decaying foliage. I sat on the concrete by the door, listening. Just listening . . .

As I sat there, imagining how I would get that door open, I speculated on what I would find on the other side. What kind of prize awaited me and how much? How would I get whatever I would get out of there? And then—reality. Another reality had to come and enter my picture. One of the many possible realities that were zooming through my addled mind was the specter of someone, anyone, waiting on the other side of that door. My enturbulated conscience exteriorating manifestations of authority figures laying for me. Fear looming large. Could I be wrong? Was someone on the other side just waiting to beat the daylights out of me and throw me in jail and send me into a life of criminal exile? Had someone been peeking through the curtains as I cased the joint and suspected that I was up to no good? I had to admit that it was true—I might be making a mistake. I tried to come up with a good lie for why I was in there, were I to get caught, but my conniving mind wasn't coming up with anything viable. I would just have to wait and see and do some serious thinking on my feet, a feat I was usually fairly good at. I would just have to jump into the deep end and see what would happen. I was making my life into an adventure. Enough time had passed. Had I been there one minute? Five minutes? Ten? Whatever—it was showtime. No more checking or inspecting or waiting or other cautionary measures to be taken. I grabbed the screwdriver and rose to my knees.

According to Gary Ozer, it should be as simple as pie to jimmy a door open. So I started gnawing away at the wood around the doorknob. And I gnawed and I gnawed and I gnawed . . . Nothing. Nothing but metal. It was one of those dang doors you locked and unlocked from the inside. I couldn't gain enough space for my flathead, no less the crow. For all I knew, which clearly wasn't much, the whole door was metal. So I slumped into my pile of chips, a distraught mouse knowing there was cheese to be had but not knowing how to get it. I mixed and mussed chips and leafage and wiped my fingerprints from anything I thought I might have touched. It was time for Plan B. Tools in hand, I casually exited my cubbyhole to reassess the situation.

To add to the ruse of my futzing around, should anyone spot me, I stashed the tools back in the garage and came back out to climb up the sage old dogwood just outside our front-and-only door. I always loved the rough bark of that tree and its little white flowers and the story some forgotten person had told me about how Jesus was crucified on a cross made of dogwood and how God had cursed the tree so it would never again grow large enough to build another cross. I did some of my best thinking up in that tree.

David being up in the dogwood was not unusual, so I acted preoccupied admiring the little white bracts, all the while lifting my eyes panning my surroundings to make sure no one was eyeing me. The coast seemed to be pretty clear. So I thought: *Hmmm . . . that didn't work. What the hell! When Gary Ozer explained to that kid how to jimmy a door, it sounded easy-easy. Whittle away to the latch, work it back, open the door. Easy. But all I got was metal. Oh, well, I did something wrong. There's got to be another way . . .* Surveying the back of the Legion for possible points of entry, I saw a couple of possibilities, but there was no way I was going to climb up to the second floor. What to do? I couldn't *not* do it. I knew I was doing something wrong. If I got caught, I'd be mortified and Mom humiliated, I'd get a police record, and maybe even end up in the "youth reformatory" up in Annandale. *I could quit now and no one would be the wiser, but*—then I noticed one of the look-out basement windows that had been boarded over. *Hmmm . . . never noticed that before. Don't want to break any glass.* So I climbed down to investigate.

I guess I never noticed because I'd never been trying to get into the joint. But it had to have been like that since before we moved there because I would have noticed. I pretty much noticed everything and took a peculiar pride in observation being one of my hidden talents. The old fixed-sash window was just big enough for a good sized adult to crawl through. It had long ago been boarded over with plywood and painted white. Clearly, an attempt to cover a broken window but no attempt at security. Upon closer inspection, it was obvious that the plywood had been simply nailed to the frame and the rusty nails had not been driven home, so I suspected that the original intent was to one day replace the glass. A job unfinished. Regardless, whosever handiwork I was looking at was going to be my ticket in. I assessed the situation, closed the carriage gate so I could work completely unseen, and went back for tools: claw hammer, needle-nose pliers, small flat piece of scrap wood, a rag.

Placing the wood scrap on the plywood near a nail, I began tapping lightly to see what the play might be. One by one, I got the wood and nails to travel in different directions so as to expose just enough nail head to get a good purchase with the needle-nose. Once I had worked a nail out a bit, I used the claw hammer, resting it on the wood scrap to do the rest of the work. Time and weather had worked to my advantage and I was able to work each of the eight nails almost completely out. I wanted to leave them in place because my plan was to replace the wood as though it had never been removed. As it had only been painted with primer, the plywood wasn't all gooped up and sticking to the sash. It came off quite nicely. I lifted it off and set it to one side, leaning up against the building. When I looked inside, the first thing I saw was a brown solid wood five panel door. What I was about to enter was a closet-sized space no more than $6' \times 4'$. It was, oddly, clean as a whistle. Nothing in it. Just a clean little room. Very strange. It was as if someone had cleaned it recently. Furtively looking over my shoulder, I slid in. Dang! The door was locked. Think. *Aha!* . . . No problem. It was an old mortise lock like the one I'd run into on the other door, but this time there was a keyhole on my side, and I just happened to have had a little collection of skeleton keys. So back to the garage I went.

Voilà! It worked. Open sesame. I unlocked that door without a hitch. And using the rag, I opened it to espy a scene as eldritch and dark and scary as any I had ever fancied or seen in a horror film. Stacks and stacks of stuff. Lots of stuff. Old stuff. Cobwebs and dust covered everything. Eerie strands of gossamer dripping from roughhewn floor joists began to flutter from the unexpected draft. The perfect place for Nyby's *The Thing* to be lurking. Tables, chairs, bar stools, in piles under thick decades of dust. Ghostly big things draped with dark, dirty fabric. Directly to my left on a circular banquet table was an old barrel-stave steamer trunk with leather straps. Upon it, a large leather portmanteau, also with straps. Upon it was what I now think might have been an alligator embossed ox leather Gladstone. And, next to that pile of luggage, precariously propped on its end, stood another venerable wayworn leather travel trunk that seemed about to fall off the table. Surely relics of the Willises. These things spoke to me—loud and clear. A natural born snooper, there was nothing I loved more than rummaging through other people's things. I could spend hours picking through abandoned homes, my sister's attic where I found nudie magazines belonging to my brother-in-law, my mom's cedar chest, trash piles, and kitchen middens behind ancient forsaken country homes, or (not proud to admit) the drawers and closets of people's homes my mom would visit. I was a sneak and there, before mine eyes, was my main debility. God, would I have loved knowing what was in all that unremembered trunkage. But I had a job to do and had better get on with it.

It was dark. Did I really want to go in there? I stood there, staring into the gloom to get my bearings. Allowing my eyes to adjust. Thinking: *Do I cross this stygian threshold and step into the dusky abyss of crime? Oh!* A creak on the floor above. *Is someone tiptoeing? Lying in wait for me?* Gazing back at the open window, *I could still call this off.* My eyes adjusted, I stepped into the cellar and marched into the dimness. Slowly, I headed over to the side of the Legion, to where I had been trying to get in at the first door. That's where they loaded stuff in, so I figured there must be steps leading up. It was actually fairly easy to maneuver once my vision had acclimated. But those darn lurid heaps of dusty, cobwebby junk— each a perfect place from behind which a psycho in drag might jump out brandishing a massive sparkling butcher knife and commence to lacerating me into smithereens—were testing my mettle. It was far worse than anything Alfred Hitchcock or Vincent Price could have conjured up. In the span of about one second I had just written, produced, directed, and starred in the most gory horror film ever not seen. But the job! I had a job to do. So I snapped out of it and forged on.

The years of storage of just about everything under the sun had resulted in a maze of paths just wide enough to do my business. Every now and then, I would start to a halt, stock-still, listening for threatening signs of life: *There's that creak again!* In my fearful stillness, I took in short quick silent breaths of the thick air redolent of stale beer, a smell I would come to know all too well in my alcoholic future. When I froze in that frightful murkiness, expecting the worst of the worst, my heart would sink to somewhere down by my thighs and gradually return to its proper residence once the fear subsided. Then I would proceed, slowly, cautiously, making sure to lift each foot straight up and placing it down flat, as I knew the Lenni Lenape did to maximize silence—my one-eighth Blackfoot DNA kicking in. When I finally got to the stairwell, I flatfooted up, knowing that someone might be waiting for me on the other side of that door. I checked behind me to see if I was leaving a dusty trail of footprints and was glad to see that I wasn't. I was impressed with myself for being such a good sneak. I didn't make one squeak on those steps. Using the rag, I gently opened the door that opened into a big bright institutional kitchen. Once again, I had to await ocular adaptation. Everything in there was big: big pots, big pans, big coffee maker, big stove, big sink. *Ah! So this is what my backyard looks like from in here . . .*

I slipped on over to the traffic doors and ever so gently took a peek. There it was, a once elegant display of opulence. Space. Lots of space that in lost times had been occupied by a library and sitting and reading and living and dining rooms. Now, one big hall where banquets, weddings, and dances generated income. One giant tasteless room with big old support columns that surely supplanted the long gone load-bearing walls. Half of it covered with green linoleum that reminded me of the green painted walls in Decatur Avenue Elementary School, which is where I was still stuck in seventh grade. So I knew my institutional shades of green. The other half, or maybe it was a third, was thick old well-worn hardwood. A bunch of round tables were clustered together and chairs were stacked out of the way. At the far end was the mother lode—the bar. It was beautiful. A liquid oasis in the midst of a parched desert.

While I had been in the Legion before, I never paid much attention to the bar. It was just a place where old fellas sat night after night shooting the breeze, drinking away the war, the workday, and their women. Patriotic oblivion. Except for blizzard conditions, the back door was left open, which gave a direct line of sight to the bar. That meant I could hear the unintelligible banter, eruptions of laughter, and occasional yelling. There was a jukebox, a dartboard, shuffleboard, and a pool table, but no television. The Legion was a place where men socialized. A few well-to-do, but most not so. When flowing smoothly, alcohol is a great temporary equalizer of class, race, and religion. A drunk is a drunk. And most of the fellas went to the Legion for the specific purpose of sipping and gulping their nightly dose of Lethe. Not that there were never any women, but it was a man's joint.

The bar must have been twenty-five or thirty feet long. It sat at the far end of the room stretched out between the front and back entrances. A dark elongated stadium affair burnished by years of sorrow and dirty elbows, where a vet could sit across from his pals watching them dissolve into double visions of spittle and incoherence before staggering off to his car or zigzagging home afoot. It was classy. Chicago rail all around with a finely grooved drink rail to match. Its seasoned fine figured bird's-eye-ish surface was studded with clean milk glass ashtrays touting Ballantine Beer. At the end, near the back entrance, its drawbridge door stood open, a welcome sign if I ever saw one. Scattered around it was an army of stately sentinels, double-ringed chrome backless bar stools with thick cushy rouge Naugahyde seats. Seats that in a few hours would be comforting the weary tushies of men who had had a long day at the office, laboring their bodies away, or who just needed to get out of the house—men recovering from WWII and Korea. I had better get busy.

But for the moment, there I was. All alone. Running my hands over the smooth wood, wiping everything I touched with my handy rag—just in case. In bartender character, parading behind the bar on the wood-slatted floor pads, I was cleaning up imaginary messes, pouring air drinks, and taking orders. I sat on a stool, ordered a Tom Collins, and yelled something stupid at the imaginary guy sitting across from me. I burst out laughing at the insanity of what I was doing: acting like a child acting like an adult. But I shuddered thinking about how I would feel or what I would say should someone walk in on me. What lie would I fabricate? Nothing came to mind. Time to get to work. I opened the back door ever so slightly for a peek. I was in luck. With the carriage gate closed

I could do my business without anyone seeing me. I had originally been thinking of making multiple trips out the way I came in. This was a better plan. The concept of a kid in the candy store had been bumped up a few notches. Behind the bar I stood, trying to figure out where to start. Such a cornucopia. I went for volume. Beer. Being pretty big for my age, I was pretty strong for a gangly goof. That meant I could carry two cases of beer at a time. Thus began the transfer of wealth.

In the spirit of efficiency, I set our aluminum storm door's hold-open washer after my first load so I wouldn't have to putz with the door while hauling freebooty in. *What the hell am I doing! Oh, well, I'm into it. Just finish it.* I really can't tell you how many trips I made. It was a lot. A whole bunch. But the time came when I was aware that I was pushing my luck. There were any number of elements that could kick in and bust my caper into a million pieces. The grease pit was stuffed, so I started wrapping things up.

I locked the back door of the Legion and, as I did with everything I thought I might have touched, I used a damp bar rag to wipe fingerprints. I checked for footprints. I tried to make everything like it was. I wanted to be subtle; to leave no trace. The only difference was that almost all the booze was gone now. What a surprise someone was going to get. Except for a couple gallons of wine, some open fifths of whiskey, some strange liqueurs, and sodas, the bar was stripped of anything worth drinking. I didn't mess with anything else. I was focused. Took what I wanted and left everything else undisturbed. I even hung the bar rag back just as I had found it. I went out through the kitchen and back down into the hellish cellar. I found my way back into the little closet and used the skeleton key to lock the door behind me. Exiting the window, I replaced the plywood, making sure the nails were returned to their original holes. Resetting each nail using a reversed tenpenny common to give each a slight countersink, I was sure to dress any freshly exposed metal or wood with dirt and spit, gently massaging the area with my trusty rag, blending away the window's implication as an unwitting accessory before the fact— using skills that would come in handy years in the future when I would be working in film production. Gathering up my tools, I schmazooled up the area around the window to show no signs of disturbance, did a double-idiot check of the areas I had been messing with, checked to make sure the coast was clear, then I opened the carriage gate. Safely in our garage, I put my tools back in place after I cleaned them to make sure there was no telltale paint or wood or rust evidence. Now I was prepared to take stock of my loot.

There it was. A trove of alcohol. A nascent alcoholic's dream come true. I had just accomplished what the badasses of Pleasantville had not been able to accomplish—I had burgled the American Legion and gotten away with a king's ransom quantity of booze in broad daylight! What a sight. I had beer. *Lots* of beer: Schlitz, Schafer, Ballantine, Rolling Rock, Miller High Life, Piels, Budweiser. Ponies, stubbies, long necks. Ambers, greens, clears, of course, all sporting crown caps. All in sturdy cardboard cases with neat little dividers and easy-open split lids. How special it felt slipping my hands into those forbidden perforated handles, feeling the durability of those incredible cases seemingly made to last forever—sleek cartons protected with a waxy laminate finish, each bearing fancy logo artwork. I must have had twelve or fourteen cases of beer. But for this alcoholic-in-the-making that wasn't enough. I had fifths. *Lots* of fifths. Fifths of whiskey, gin, sloe gin, brandy, blackberry brandy, scotch. I didn't know one from another, so I'd just grabbed as many unopened bottles as I could. I don't know, I must have had twenty bottles of the hard stuff. I took a quick inventory and carefully replaced the planks and the Jenkins plumbing/heating crap on top of the grease pit. I checked the garage and my tools to make sure nothing was out of place. Then I went back to the scene of the crime and did another double check. I had screwed up my jimmying of the door, but there was nothing I could do about that. Perhaps it would serve as a distraction. With all my bases covered, the only thing left to do now was to be patient. Do nothing. Wait. And wait I did.

I sat on my haul for a month. The richest kid in the world. Never letting on to anyone that I had anything. I just waited. The crime of the century and not a word. Nothing. Usually, if someone would tell Mom this or that, she'd drop it to me over dinner or tea or ice cream. But *nada*. I sat back, watching Legion life carry on as though nothing had happened. When I felt it was safe, I started to slowly break the stuff out. A little here, a little there. I produced it along with lies about where and how I had come by it. The kids I was hanging around with didn't care a whit where I got it from; they were just glad to be getting bombed. They wondered why the beer was always warm, but I just told them we were going German or that you got drunker that way or something equally stupid. I thus quietly consumed my take in small quantities. Never anything voluminous or splashy to indicate that I was rolling in it. Just enough to get a few kids high.

Up the alley behind my house there was a dirt lot where Bennett Chevrolet stored a bunch of old junkers. When I was a little kid, I loved playing in and on those cars, running in and out and jumping on and off, breaking an occasional window and snooping through seats and glove compartments for treasures. I would spend hours there, alone, fascinated. A vehicular boneyard. A heavenly place. Now such a thing would be considered an attractive nuisance, where children would be found raped and murdered. But that wasn't a problem back then. And now that I was older, that God's acre had become my teenage taproom. We kids would sit in those cars drinking and smoking and doing whatever it was that we did—mostly bragging and talking about girls, drunk as skunks. Afterwards we'd stagger down and get a sub at Frankie and Johnny's or head over to Pasquini's pizzeria or just hang out at the bus station, smoking and generally being stupid. But even in my drunken stupors I always maintained my criminal frame of mind and made sure not to leave any evidence behind. Besides, I didn't want the police to know anyone was drinking in the cars and start watching the place. So once we had all told our respective lies about how much sex we were having; once we had sang all the lyrics to whatever songs were on our polluted minds; once we had dropped every cool name of someone we really didn't know; and once the imbibitional festivities had come to an end, I made sure that we took all our bottles and threw them on the roof of the venetian blind company that was nearby. A good plan well executed.

Then, one day, oh, say, about five months down the road, there came a rat-tat-tat on our storm door in the middle of the day when I was home alone. Having cut school and expecting it to be old Bulldog the truant officer, I tiptoed over to take a peek down the stairs. It was Frank LaRosa, a stellar Legion officer and our de facto landlord. There he stood, as always, in his trademark white shirt, dark suit, and tie, puffing away on his habitual big fat cigar. I thought about it. *What on earth does he want?* Then he leaned on with a few more forceful raps and yelled up, "David! I know you're home. It's Frank LaRosa. Come on down, I want to talk to you."

For you to understand what I was about to face, Frank requires a bit of description. To say that he was an imposing figure is to put it mildly. He was one big mother. I was 6′2″ and looked up to him. Or at least that's the way it felt. And he was big. Not fat, but big. And loud. Loud talk. Loud laugh. Wherever he was, everyone knew Frank was there. He had this big egg-shaped face sporting a Don Fanucci chevron stash, a majorly receding hairline, and long sideburns, all sitting upon his big egg-shaped body. I couldn't quite tell if his smile's provenance was felicity or evil. But there was a special something behind those beady eyes of his that told me he was capable of having a good laugh while breaking my bones with a baseball bat. Frank was always sartorially suited up for business, constantly chomping and puffing and fingering his big fat smelly cigar. My knowledge of Frank only scratches the surface, but he had his fingers in antiques, meat, insurance, and God knows what else. In Pleasantville, he was *somebody*. Around town he was known as The Godfather or Uncle Frank. He was the putative self-elected Mayor of Pleasantville. While he could have been at our door for myriad reasons, my nimble defensive brain snapped to putting two and two together: Frank was married to Jane; Jane and Frank lived just up the alley from us on Green Street; Jane worked at the venetian blind factory on West Jersey Avenue; it was on top of that building we disposed of our empty booze bottles. *Uh-oh. Get ready . . .* So I stepped out into the open and went down. As I opened the door, a chill wafted in:

"Hi, Frank. Whatcha need?"

"Cuttin' school again, huh, David? I don't care. I've got something else on my mind."

It was a casual situation with Frank standing outside, me propping the storm door open while standing inside, several inches above ground so that I was more or less superior, height-wise. He was an old friend of my mom's, and it was probably because of that friendship that we were living in the chauffeur's quarters, so I knew he knew stuff about me. But what and how much, I did not know. The cigar stench reeked, but I stood there respectfully, posing in my most innocent countenance.

"Somebody broke into the Legion a while back and I was wondering if you knew anything about it."

"No, I don't. When'd that happen, Frank?"

"Yeah . . . ," taking a big drag and blowing it up in the air, his eyes never leaving mine; his lecherous stare giving me the creeps, ". . . it was a few months back. Whoever did it took quite a bit of booze. You don't know anything about it?"

"Why would I know anything, Frank? Why you asking me?"

Suddenly he was squinting. His perpetual smile vanished. He was looking for reaction. *Don't blush. Don't swallow. Wrinkle forehead. Don't smile. Look him directly in the eyes. Be curious. Be neutral . . .* The pause was long, the silence deafening.

"You think I did it?"

"Well, David, when they went up to repair the roof of the venetian blind factory over here the other day, they found a whole lot of whiskey and beer bottles. Just seems funny the brands and pony bottles are exactly what was stolen from the Legion. Just thought you might know something about it, that's all. Do you know anything?"

"Nope. Sure don't. This is the first time I heard anything about it."

He stood there vacillating. Scrutinizing. Trying to read my reaction or lack thereof. Twirling his cigar. Twitching his lips. Petting his moustache. Then his Snidely smile returned:

"*Okaaaay* . . . , David. You're a good kid. Jus' thought I'd ask seeins how it's so close and everything. If ya heard anything 'round town. It's a darn mystery, it is. The coppers couldn't figure out how whoever got in got in. The only thing we do know is that they got in; and then they got out with a lot of inventory. But we'll get'em. One day. Whoever did it, one of them will eventually slip up. And then we'll pinch'em."

"Yeah, I hope so, Frank. Seems all the crooks in town want to rob the Legion."

"Yeah . . . OK, David," he said with a mouthful of cigar, as he started to turn away, looking at me askance with an untrusting Snidely stare, "I'll let you get back to hooking school. Sorry to bother you," and off he went. Phew!

I went upstairs and began thinking about fingerprints. But that was the first and last time the topic ever came up. And Mom never mentioned it, so I knew that Frank hadn't told her. And so as not to draw suspicion to myself, I kept on throwing our bottles up on that roof.

I did so many crazy things when I was a kid and lied so much that I carried an invisible suitcase stuffed with secrets for years and years and years. Every now and then, well after any possible statute of limitations, I'd tell Mom about some of the misdeeds and shenanigans I'd been involved with or knew about—just to blow her mind. I think I let, oh, about forty years go by before I shared this little jewel with her. And, as always, her response was disbelief and her usual verbal note: "I don't know why you did that crazy stuff? I didn't raise you that way. I'm glad I didn't know about it . . ."

Mom's been gone for a number of years now. And she was right—she didn't raise me that way. But I was an alcoholic in the making. Who can account for anything in this crazy world? So much is the draw of the cards. Had I been caught for some of the stuff I got away with I'd have a juvie record and my life would be quite different today. But I skated by. As I sit here typing out these words, I've accumulated goodly number of years of sobriety, one day at a time, and I'm doing OK. As I listen to the purling fountain and enjoy the birds enjoying our beautiful Long Beach backyard, my heart has forgotten everything I've just written and swells with sadness for all the kids who have gotten caught up in similar stupidity only to end up dead or in prison and having their lives ruined. OK, I'm sorry for all those kids. But now back to me:

Man, it feels good. It feels *real* good. Ain't nothin' finer than to sit back and let the ol' mind play out a montage of events leading up to this very moment. A sequence of events that is true and honest and real. A good healthy dose of self-gratification comes from knowing that, yes, indeed, I have, in fact, pulled off the perfect crime.

12

PULLING A TRAIN

One thing about life is that it does not come with any instruction manuals. Oh, sure, there's a plethora of self-help books, but we usually get around to them too late, after the damage has been done. And, of course, there's therapy, but by the time we get there, we're already half banged out of our minds. So, it turns out, it's an inside job. On-the-job training. Do what you can. Hold your nose and jump in. Hope for the best. And here I am, six-plus decades later—still learning. It never ends. When it came to sex, I truly assembled the product without reading the instructions.

My goofy upbringing left me perforated with holes and gaps and lacunae galore, not to mention misinformation, misunderstandings, and traumas. All foisted upon me by my peers, older kids, and goofier adults. Stuff enough to fashion a sociopath. But in my case, I was bequeathed enough noodle to grow up, at worst, to be a teary-eyed sad sack at times, and, at other times, to be a mature, well-rounded, sensitive, caring survivor. An intermittent good lover, at best. The journey has been depressing, suicidal, and rife with anxiety, but never boring. The women I have wooed and woven into my life have pretty much all raised a brow of curiosity trying to figure me out, as I never did, still don't, and never will fit the mold that "guys" are supposed to fit into. Growing up—if I ever really did—with my eccentric mom and no male role model to emulate, for good or bad, I have had to fashion me out of all the crap that bombarded me day after day, year after year. And while there was a protracted dark spell in my life where I felt cheated and damaged, I no longer do. Not so much, anyway. Seems that later in life, I find myself meeting more and more men who are recovering from their fathers. And when I see what they are going through and hear what they have to say, I breathe a sigh of relief. I'm thankful that I never had a father.

And so here I am, glad to be the culmination of the accumulations of experiences I have endured all these years. But there are a couple of things that have lingered far too long in the back of my mind, under my skin, inside my bones. Things I have not been able to shake loose of. Things for which there is no rhyme or reason. Things I have wanted to understand. Things that have caused me a great deal of distress over the run of my life, that have shaped my outlook and behavior in the sweet and sour realm of intimate relations.

I suppose that my experiences with sex growing up were not all that different from any other kid on the planet—you show me yours, I'll show you mine. My bringing this up, dear appreciated reader, has probably evoked images and recollections that you have not stirred or entertained in quite a long while.

But there were two singular incidents that befell me in early teenagehood that so indelibly emblazoned themselves on my psyche that they are here and now, vivid and redolent of freshly plucked daisies. Bright and smellful as freshly picked daisies? Of course, that's easy for me to say, now, after years of unrelenting emotional anguish, substantial therapy, screwed up relationships, attempted suicides, and every possible painful behavioral post-traumatic bizarre permutation I could conjure up with the assistance of drugs and alcohol. For a period, things didn't look too good. But what's in a look?

Whenever I'm engaging with children, I am keenly aware of how I look and act. Not only are rightfully cautious parents perpetually on the lookout for perverts, but kids are instinctively looking outward for affirmation and acceptance. I am mindful of the former, but deeply concerned with the latter. When I pull up to a stoplight, oftentimes I look over and there is a deadpan child staring at me as though I am just another bug crawling on the ground. This has happened so many times that I have a well-rehearsed response at the ready. I squeeze out a big happy smile and wave. It's my responsibility as an adult. And it takes on even more significance when the kid is black or Latino or some other non-white variety. I feel—no, I believe—no, I feel and believe—that that one moment, that microsecond brief exchange, could very well form that child's lifelong outlook on men, white people, adults, and humanity in general. When I am involved with kids in a social setting where talking is involved, I am cautious with my words, the tone of my voice, and my gestures. I make it a point to treat them as intelligent, capable, worthy beings. And, playing down the pretty and cute stuff, I pay particular attention to telling little girls that they are intelligent, smart, quick, and capable. Why all this? Again, because I believe a nanosecond can shape one's future. It matters.

Our lives are the accumulation of all our experiences hitherto. True. Fair enough. But is it right to blame one's outlook on a single experience? A spoonful of blue will noticeably tint a gallon of white. Hence, one little act can shade the hue of one's life forever, and a series of similar experiences can either significantly embellish or uglify a person. Two such visits to the underbelly of humanity, which I shall relate here, were enough for me.

When you are in the midst of something, it is often not possible to realize that you are in fact in the midst of it. You have to act. You have to get through it. You have to survive. It is only through hindsight, perhaps many many years later, that you realize that you really were just one of a crazy cast of characters in a phantasmagorical film-in-the-making. That you weren't really a fool, but just acting the part of a fool on the stage of life with a bunch of other budding actor-fools who didn't know their lines or parts any better than you did. That you just happened to end up in the wrong place at the wrong time. Like the realtor says, "Location, location, location." And what's in a location?

Birch Grove got its name from ten-year-old Claire Kreutz, who won a name-the-park contest in the 1951. When I was a kid, I just knew it as a keen place to go and play. I used to walk there to play Davy Crockett and Jim Bowie and let the alleged one-eighth Blackfoot in me run wild in the woods. It seems that back in the '50s and '60s, a kid could range for miles alone without getting molested or chopped up—unless, that is, you walked through a bully's neighborhood. And that did happen from time to time. Ass kickings for no good reason have been an occupational hazard for me ever since—well, ever since I was a kid. Adolescent psychos were abundant when I was young. I guess they're the ones who grew up to be all the adult psycho bullies I now try to avoid on the freeway to and from work every day. Anyways, Birch Grove was a great place. Woods. Lots of woods. An arboreal cornucopia of birch, pine, larch, maple, oak, dogwood, blueberry, laurel apple crab, hemlock, hickory, and on and on and on. A massive maze of trails and mini-lakes galore. Ducks and geese and swans all over the place. There was a picnic area with a set of swings and a sliding board and a little funky zoo, too, but I always headed off to be alone on the trail. I would stealth through the woods and imagine that I was spiritually in tune with and communicating with the flora and fauna—birds and deer and bear and muskrat and beaver and hawks and a whole lot of critters I never, ever saw, except in a book or on television. I would hide motionless for hours, resting on a bed of duff, completely unnoticed by passersby—I was a mountain man/woodsman/Blackfoot-for-a-day. Kid's stuff. It was a simple no-frills wonderful place to play and learn.

From a bird's-eye view, Birch Grove looks like a Titan gardener had made a couple of random swipes this way and that with a massive cultivator, its tines leaving twenty or thirty massive cat scratches scoring Mother Earth. The resulting elongated furrows were destined to become recreational ponds. Some of the trout-stocked pits are thirty feet deep and range from one-quarter to five acres in surface area. The actual provenance of the park dates back to the mid-1800s, when the area became an Earth-marring hubbub of industrial activity. It seems that a crustal uplift that caused the Atlantic Ocean to recede, combined with ancient alluvial deposits from the Miocene Epoch, had blessed this erstwhile Elysian Fields with a rich deposit of glauconite, a clay well suited for manufacturing the eighty thousand Jersey Red Colonial bricks per day that were in demand during Atlantic City's construction heyday. In order to get at the clay, teams of men manually scooped away the topsoil. The long rows of unwanted earth they pitched off to the side became separators that defined a Nazcan-like archipelago of ponds that formed after the brick business went belly-up. Abandoned, Mother Nature began reclaiming what mankind had defiled. As a diversity of flora took root and critters and people took to traversing the overburden, a system of wooded trails emerged. It was on one of these idyllic causeways, on a somewhat brisk Sunday in 1961, that I found myself, at the ripe age of thirteen, an unwitting supernumerary in a Federico Fellini film. There I was. On set. Without a script. Without a director.

It just so happened that on that day I was with the Delacroix brothers, Draco and Timmy, with whom I had been hanging out during that particular facet of my nascent malleable life. They were sixteen and eighteen, respectively, so I was the kid. With us was Draco's friend, one Tommy Barnet. I didn't like Tommy Barnet. And Tommy Barnet certainly didn't like me. He used to endlessly make fun of me and make me cry. He relished humiliating me. He was downright mean-spirited. Anyway, there we were. I remember it being a sunny day, but chilly enough that we were wearing our winter jackets. We had just come from mass at St. Pete's and were there just to hang around—no drinking or anything. We weren't up to any mischief. Just there to check out Birch Grove and walk the trails. Something to do. No agenda beyond that. So we went a-walking.

The hierarchy would have been Draco, Tommy, Timmy, and me. I was last. Sometimes those guys would switch positions for a while, but wherever we went, I was always last. Anyway, every now and then, as he was wont to do, Tommy Barnet would cast some moronic aspersion back at me that would cause Draco and Timmy to erupt with laughter. Occasionally, Timmy would at least offer up, "Hey, Tommy, you shouldn't pick on David so much." Of course that was useless. I cried when it got real bad, but otherwise grinned and bore it. After all, they were older kids, and I got to go places and do things I wouldn't be able to do on my own. It was the price I had to pay.

So there we were, traipsing along out there in the woods when we encountered another group of four or five boys. It turned out that Tommy Barnet knew one of these kids, a freckle-faced lantern-jawed kid with a Princeton hairdo and that certain affected air of privilege I had come to recognize, mostly, in Catholic school kids. All of us were dressed in the style of what at the time we called *conservative*—attire with Ivy League aspirations. There was the typical greeting among us, and then Tommy walked off for a private chat with his friend while we stood around waiting. Whatever they were talking about was all hush-hush and involved a lot of smiling, hand gesturing, and head shaking in disbelief. Then Tommy Barnet headed back to us smiling from ear to ear, and the other kid and his friends headed on down the trail. After they walked a ways, they turned off and headed directly into the woods. Something was up.

Tommy Barnet pranced back with his best pseudo-collegiate cocky self, "Hey, you guys. You guys . . . Guess what! Gentle*mennnn* . . . , guess what! Oh, and you, too, David."

"What's going on, Tommy?" Timmy shot off.

Tommy Barnet just stood there grinning, nodding his head as though he were listening to music that only he could hear.

"Yeah, Tommy," Draco asked, "what's with the secrecy? Where are those guys going? What are they up to? They got some booze?" He was eager to know. He liked to drink. We all did. Anytime was a good time to drink.

"You're not going to believe this, my fellow countrymen, but this girl is going to pull a train and my friend has invited us along for the ride. You guys want in? . . ."

Before anyone could say *Schopenhauerism*, we were leaving the trail and heading into the woods. Into the woods—where a girl was going to pull a train. Out of the sunlight. In the shade of the canopy, it was a bit chilly. But as we stepped away from the footpath, the air became still and warm and moist and musky. The smell of decaying vegetation—the same smell I'd smelled when I was a kid hiding in my leafy twiggy coat of camouflage, watching passersby, breathing in the sweet process of death and decomposition making way for birth and growth.

At first, we didn't see anyone. Draco and Timmy were whispering their doubts. But Tommy Barnet assured them he was following his friend's directions to the letter and that we just needed to continue following him. Then he hushed us. "Listen!" Behind us, we could hear the high-pitched talking of passing hikers. Before us, we could hear soft deep murmuring. His face lit up with satisfaction as he swung his right arm up in an arch, like a soldier leading us into battle, beckoning us in the direction of the furtive whispers. We followed.

After struggling through a thicket, we stepped out into a spacious glade where several clusters of teenage boys stood about. *Surreal* is inadequate to describe what I saw. We very well could have been walking onto a set of *Happy Days* or *Father Knows Best* or *Leave It to Beaver*. Just a bunch of clean-cut white kids standing around in the woods having a Sunday chat, quietly behaving themselves, while another boy with his pants pulled down to his ankles was busily pumping away on a naked girl lying on what apparently was her own clothing to protect her exposed body from the scratches of the litterfall that provided the cushioning for her makeshift mattress. I had never seen—no, I had never even imagined such a thing.

Still at too great a distance to see things in fine detail, we followed Draco's lead and moved in closer. Interrupting all their heavy breathing, thrusting, growling, and yelping (all the while conscious that they needed to subdue their mating sounds), the girl cried out, "Your buttons! Your buttons are hurting me! . . ." Annoyed and maneuvering so as not to pull out of her, the boy pushed himself up frantically contorting his body to unbutton his double-breasted trench coat. Both moaned in pain while this was happening. Then they laughed as he cast aside the lapel flaps of his coat and dove back in. As he began pumping with a vengeance, she latched onto his epaulets and began flailing her legs while uttering a medley of restrained wild grunting moans. The same sounds my mother made the one and only time I ever heard her having sex. While the lovers were rapt with passion, I noticed that the girl's eyes were casting about taking in the thirty or so eyeballs that were fixed upon her. Perhaps wondering who would be next. I thought for a second that she made eye contact with me, but if she did, it was short-lived. Because as soon as the thought entered my frazzled mind, she shut her eyes and slipped back into whatever world she had conjured up for herself. The kind of world that would allow her to endure such exploitation. I don't believe she could have been more than sixteen or seventeen. Maybe eighteen. Whatever. I wasn't sure what I saw in her eyes, but I knew it wasn't happiness.

To me, the girl was a grown woman. Dark complexioned with short dark hair. I imagined Italian or something as exotic. Not thin. Not fat. Voluptuous, as I expect a young Sofia Loren must have been. Youth had blessed her with soft blemish-free skin. She was stark-naked. Not a stitch. A fillet on the cutting board of life. I became heady with a pervasive guilt, cognizant of being involved with something that was wrong. But like the rest of the boys, my eyes were glued on this pagan rite of passage-cum-human sacrifice that was in progress. The event was so atavistic that we very well could have been passing around a gourd of the victim's blood from which to sip.

After that boy finished writhing in his ecstasy, he got up, unceremoniously pulled up his pants, and buckled his belt while staring down at the girl without speaking a word. Paying him no mind, she grabbed something that looked like an article of clothing to wipe herself. Then she pulled her coat around her body for warmth and lay stone still with closed eyes awaiting whoever was to be next.

Sporting a shit-eating grin of extreme satisfaction, the boy swaggered over to his friends. In hushed congratulatory tones, he and his friends giggled and said God only knows what. As the young woman lay there, Tommy Barnet's lantern-jawed friend who had invited us went to a cluster of boys and chose the next taker. Clearly, he was the organizer of this celebration of human degradation. There we were. In the woods. There she was. Banging boy after boy.

Standing around in our voyeuristic clutches, I cannot imagine for the life of me what any of us talked about while this was going on. Surely I was in the midst of a scene that has repeated itself innumerable times throughout human history. It was all so casual. To be expected. No big deal. Happens all the time. Then, after a couple of boys more, old Lantern Jaws ambled over to us:

"One of you guys want to go next?"

Automatically, Tommy Barnet and Draco and Timmy huddled up and began conferring in hushed whispers. I stood a bit off on the periphery, a satellite in stationary orbit. All I knew was that I didn't want to do it. I had no idea what to do, anyway. I never had sex. I lied and said I had, but I hadn't. And while I didn't know how I wanted it to happen, I knew that this was not the way. Besides, the overall experience had aroused not one iota of sexual excitement in me. Quite the contrary. Sex was the last thing I wanted anything to do with. Then, everyone turned with a smile looking at me:

"You go next," Draco piped up, pointing at me, as though doing me a favor.

"Yeah, Dave, you go ahead. We've all had sex," some other boy chimed in.

"This is your chance, Davey Wavy," gibed Tommy Barnet. "If you don't go for it now you may never get another chance."

If I could even imagine what was running through my mind as Lantern Jaws was leading me over to the girl, I would gladly reveal it here and now. But I'm drawing a blank. Black. Empty. Red. Nothing. All I know is that some kid was directing me toward the girl and that each step toward her was long and slow and leaden and I had no idea what was going to happen when I got there. I do recall being aware that I was supposed to *perform* while all these guys were watching. Before I knew it, there I was, just a few feet away from her when she opened her eyes and sat up like a monster come to life with her coat still wrapped around her. Her eyes widened with disgust:

"No! Not him! No! Not him! No! I won't do it with him! . . ."

My psychopomp had to console her. No explanation. She just refused me. While screeching, she was moon-eyed and cringing as though she feared for her life, like an abused dog cowers when it sees its beater. But I didn't even know this girl. Ironically, while tremendous humiliation was enveloping me, I was simultaneously experiencing a great sense of inner relief. I was so glad to be off the hook. A consummate politician and diplomatic pimp in the making, Lantern Jaws compassionately eased me away from her:

"Friend. Don't take it personal. Who knows what's going on in her mind? She's all fucked up. I don't know what it is about you, but she just doesn't want to do it with you. Do you know her?"

"No. I never saw her before."

Walking back to my cluster, to my place, to my clan, in some sort of tunnel vision of humiliation, I could feel more than hear the snickers scratching at my back. Piercing eyeballs. But that was OK. I got out of it. I would have to put up with endless teasing from Tommy Barnet, but it was over—or so I thought. Rather than it being a conclusion, it turned out to be the beginning of something that would indelibly impose itself upon the rest of my life.

At dances, there always seemed to be a girl who was the official "slut" of the floor. I mean, she was the one who did the dirtiest of dirty dancing. There was this one girl I had seen at several dances and she was good. I don't know how she did it, but she would somehow arch all the way back on her knees down to floor level with her dancing partner a mere fraction of an inch above her. Both of them horizontal, sexually grinding away to the beat of the music; both technically still doing the Twist. Their feats were truly proto-Cirque du Soleil. And when she got into it, everyone would stop and encircle her and her partner marveling at the spectacle. It was quite a show. To us, it was sex on the dance floor. Of course, there were all sorts of stories floating around about how she *did it* with all sorts of boys.

One hot humid sticky summer's night circa 1963, I was at a dance with the Delacroix and another friend, Jimmy De Clemente. We were over at the Ocean City Convention Hall at Sixth and the boards. We paid our buck admission and spent the night doing the Popeye Waddle, Hully Gully, Mashed Potato, Slide, and whatever else we were doing at the time. I was a pretty good dancer and had a reputation for two very specific things: (1) being the first to get up the nerve to go ask the prettiest girl in sight to dance, and, (2) usually ending up dancing with the shortest girls. This height factor is only significant because at my callow age I was already 6'2". Regardless, I was really only good out of the gate for appearance purposes, as I didn't date girls; didn't have a car; didn't have any money; was only mimicking the other guys; and, had been lying about having had sex. In short, I was clueless as to the ways of girls and 99.9 percent of everything else in life.

Timmy was the only one of us who really had any resources. He worked. He was a dishwasher at the Home Plate in Pleasantville, which was an all-American white-bread restaurant on Main Street with cozy booths and delicious smells. My mother would take me there for special occasions when I was a little boy. How I loved their liver and onions and mashed potatoes and string beans followed by chocolate pudding. Timmy was the one who always had money and the all-important car. If we needed to get somewhere, Timmy got us there. Otherwise, we hitchhiked or took a bus.

After the dance, we took off in his 1956 powder blue Ford. A beautiful machine. Oh, yes, I forgot—with us was that girl I mentioned who was the hottest dirty dancer around. Draco had been dancing with her and ended up schmoozing her into coming out with us for a joyride. So there we were, cruising around Ocean City, talking about who knows what, spewing carbon monoxide, hydrocarbons, and nitrogen oxides into the pristine South Jersey air. She was up front, sandwiched between Timmy and Draco, acting as sophisticated as she could. Me and Jimmy De Clemente in the back seat just enjoying the ride. Jimmy De Clemente was never short on corny jokes. And he didn't even need anyone to laugh at them. He was his own adoring audience. Once he got to his punch line he would burst into laughter and yell something like, "Pow!" or "Wham-Bam!" and then almost choke to death laughing at what he had just said. And if you didn't laugh, he'd put on his best Italian gestures and say, "Awww . . . , com'on. Com'on! Don't tell me you don't think that's funny! It's hilarious! It's hilarious! . . . ," and then he'd laugh some more. He had enough laughter in him for the entire world. Of the four of us, he was the most honest, the most innocent, and the most self-directed. While those guys up front were trying to be cool, making idle chitchat with the gal, De Clemente was being his best uninhibited innocent kooky self, showing us just how uncool we all really were. I was doing my usual being-alone-in-the-crowd thing. Just following along. Keeping to myself. I never knew what to do.

At some point in the evening, we ended up pulling into a parking lot. Just an anonymous parking lot. And orders were given that we were all to get out of the car while Draco made out with the gal in the back seat. It turned out that she was going to pull a train and we all would get a turn. But not Jimmy De Clemente. He didn't want one. Not only did he not want one, but he was vociferous about why he didn't want one: "No way! No! It's a sin. It's a sin. I just went to confession. No way. No way. You boys go ahead. Count me out . . ."

So after Draco had done his thing, it was between me and Timmy. Timmy was going to be courteous and let me go. I remember standing. Frozen. Beside the car. In that sultry night. The four of us. A girl lying on the back seat of the car waiting for another round. My insides had been sucked out. I was empty. Not one molecule of my somatic self was sexual. It didn't matter where I was or what time it was. A cool day in a bucolic glen in Birch Grove or a sweaty night in a nondescript parking lot in Ocean City—the fear and shame and lack of character felt exactly the same.

As though I were a puppet with someone controlling my strings, I trudged the seventy-five thousand miles from where we were all standing to the back door of the car. I stood there looking at the shiny chrome handle, mesmerized by the throbbing reflection of a distant red light. Perhaps a forgotten turn signal. I opened the door and started to crawl in. The girl must have been dozing because I startled her. Her eyes popped wide-open with a terror. And there it was, that same moon-eyed look of fear. Cringing and pulling her clothes up around her, yelling, "No! Not him! Not him! I won't do it with him. Draco, come here. *Draay-cohoo!* . . ." Most of what they talked about was inaudible, but I did hear her say, "He probably jerks off," which I was sure she said loudly enough so that I would hear her disdain. Once again, off the hook and humiliated. It had taken me a couple years to muster up a modicum of confidence after the Birch Grove incident. Now, here I was, back at square one.

Both girls' reactions to me planted a series of questions in my mind that would haunt me for the rest of my life. I wish that I could say that years of therapy and self-examination have diluted, resolved, and eliminated the obvious trauma. *Diluted*, yes. *Resolved* and *eliminated*, certainly not. Is there something wrong with me? Did they see something in me that I didn't see? What's wrong with me? These and a whole slew of other thoughts of self-doubt and -worth are the questions I have pondered entirely too often during my precious life. These questions have made it difficult for me to have long-term intimate loving relationships. Of course, now I know that those young ladies had some serious emotional issues going on. I wonder how they turned out. And I thank them for saving me from the guilt I would have carried these so many years had I participated in their exploitation. A big fat weight off my back. Yet I can't stop wondering, Why didn't they want to be with me?

13

I REMEMBER

I remember your controlled uncontrollable
Laughter
Your extended arms
Outstretched with flailing, twitching fingers
Your smiling face
I remember awakening
Reaching over your warm sleeping body
To touch
Your radiating, ubiquitous flannel robe
I remember how you gave me
Room to move
And never, never cramped
My style,
Or lack thereof
I remember how terrified I was
Standing in that telephone booth

In front of Megan's Drug Store
On Main Street
In Pleasantville
When you said,
"I love you.
I don't want to lose you.
I'm coming to New Jersey to be with you.
I'm leaving tomorrow."
I remember
The fear
No one in that dismal, friendless town
Had ever seen me
With a woman,
A girl,
A female
Oh my God!
I remember it all
And my heart wells, and wells, and wells . . .
You were my first girlfriend
At age twenty-one
How stupid I was
How stupid I still am
But there is no such thing as
"New Love."
Only "Additional Love."
How I appreciate you now
Oh, how I do appreciate . . .

14

THE HURT

Hazel eyes blurring, Itzel speeds through South Jersey piney woods, careening down a tire-worn sugary dirt road, in a race for life, white birches flagging her passage. The summer season has only been over slightly more than a month, but, without the come-and-go traffic of the lake party crowd, Mother Nature has begun her annual reclamation. Weeds in the center of the road are half way up to the windshield of the turquoise '69 VW Bug Itzel struggles to control. Any onlooker might think that by the way she whips the steering wheel and guns the VW toward the picnic area that she has every intention of driving off the bank into Lake Lenape. But she knows this campsite everyone calls "the pit" like the back of her hand. She has made these maneuvers many times in various states of intoxication and knows exactly what she is doing. Traversing a familiar summer haunts, she's on automatic pilot. Downshifting, hitting the brakes, this tearful young woman skids across the soil and duff until, just shy of the picnic table, that Bug comes to a standstill at the edge of the embankment. Another few feet and she'd've been flying through the air on her way to the dock some twenty-five feet below. A gliding Cooper's hawk preparing for its southern migration observes this unusual human activity.

She turns off the ignition, removing the keys out of habit. Dust and litterfall settle. Trembling, gasping for air, she lets out the roaring uninhibited cries of a woman who has just sustained a gruesome trauma of the heart. Woodland creatures and workmen across the lake recognize these sounds of a tortured soul. For a longish while, this otherwise statuesque young lady, now a complete shivering wreck, just sits—sobbing, convulsing, gulping for air, her gold rimmed hippie glasses having slidden to the tip of her nose, lenses fogged and smudgy. Arms limp. Shoulders drooping. Her face a cascade of tears, snot, and spittle. Her beautiful long straight black hair a tousle of wet knots. Nothing about pain is subtle.

Less than two hours before switching off the engine, Itzel had walked across the backyard of the First Presbyterian Church of Pleasantville looking for her husband. He had taken the dogs out for a walk and been gone much longer than usual. She became worried and went looking for him. What she discovered was him spread out on the grass behind the church making out with their upstairs neighbor—a wild, strange woman everyone suspected of being a lesbian who very likely had sex with dogs.

First, shock, then, out of thin air, appeared an evil hand, a chest penetrating invisible hand, a yanking hand. A sensation of vertigo affected her while it yanked! and yanked! and yanked! until it had succeeded in yanking! out her heart—shredded, bloody, broken. Rising vomit singed her throat. There was no doubt in this twenty-year-old's mind that this very moment was the worst disaster of her life. Perfidy, indeed, is the most distasteful of disappointments.

Her paisley blouse and expertly patched faded bell-bottom jeans were sopping from the steady flow of sadness she'd been gushing for the last couple of hours while unconsciously driving aimlessly up one country road and down another until she ended up here—at the lake. A familiar place where she would feel safe to let it all out. She sits. Limp. Her face flushing. Her rheumy eyes of glass stare at nothing. Her body twitches as though sundry nerves have been crushed, pinched, and ripped. Infidelity, that most pestilent of parasites, gnawing her insides. All she can think of is how wrong she had been about David; how she had moved from Los Angeles to be with him; how she actually loved him; how he was the only person she thought she could really ever trust; how she was the outsider with no friends or allies in this little hick town of Pleasantville; how she had been working at a shit job to make ends meet while he screwed off getting stoned and partying during the days; and, how fucked her life was. *Fucking New Jersey!* What was she going to do? She lit a Winston hoping to settle her agitation.

The lake appeared uninhabited and placid. Itzel had the place to herself, so she thought. But its population of small forest creatures instinctively froze in stark silence until this wailing suffering fellow creature could be regarded as nonthreatening. Even then, they kept their happy chatter to a minimum. Taking deep sobbing drags on her cigarette, she wished she had thought to snatch a joint before flying out of the apartment. She also wished that the filter king had more of a calming effect on her than it did. She would just have to ride this one out, that's all there was to it. She had been dealt hard blows before and not shattered, so this too would pass. But she had sustained a real jolt and was in shock. Right now, all she could do was sit there trying to get her scrambled brain to tell her what her next step should be—to show her the best way to handle this juggernaut of reality. Through her eyes, it looked like it was raining on the windshield. All her weeping had soaked her fag, and there was an odd sort of humidity that accompanied each puff. Then it broke. *Damn!* She lit another. The fresh pull was soothing.

Across the way, Itzel could see the workmen in the park. She knew that they could hear her because noise carries on the lake. But nothing mattered. Nothing made sense. She searched the VW, hoping David had left some pot stashed there. No such luck.

She met him several months prior in a semi-hippie commune-type duplex on Myrtle Street in the black section of Long Beach, California, where everyone was stoned as often as possible. There was a lot of traffic at the Myrtle House—guys and gals coming and going—and there was certainly a selection of hip fellas she could have chosen from, but somehow she took a fancy to David. And now, in retrospect, it seems that she had developed some sort of sick attraction for fucked-up guys. Her last live-in boyfriend had been busted for exposing himself to grade school girls as they walked past their apartment on their way to class. And her non-live-in boyfriend, the one after the live-in one, had been murdered in some sort of never-solved alleged drug deal. So with all the young people coming in and out of the Myrtle House in the autumn of 1970, it took Itzel some time to notice David through the bustle of stoned activity. But when she did, she fell directly in love.

When she allowed her eyes to focus on him, her intuition told her that David was not an average boy. A bit odd. Not bad looking. Definitely not like the guys she had been hanging with. She recognized that he was one of the good guys. Honest. Trustworthy. With a style and snaggletooth smile all his own.

From the get-go, their love was rife with ups and downs. A real emotional torrent. So much so that David's fear of intimacy and responsibility had driven him away—back to New Jersey, with the unconscious pretext that he would return for Itzel when he had earned enough money. But she insightfully knew that he'd never return. Not because he intended not to, no, not that. It was simply that David was so inexperienced and didn't know what to do: how to be a man, how to be a lover, how to be an intimate friend. So, he skedaddled. That's all. And Itzel knew it.

Yes, David was definitely good, special, honest, a true one-of-a-kind young man. He was all of these things and more. Perhaps the last trustworthy man on earth, she thought. And so, based on this, she had hightailed it out of the Myrtle House and had flown to New Jersey to be with him. She was a woman in love, and there was no stopping her. She would do whatever was necessary to be with the man she loved.

And now this. What was she going to do?

Half a pack of smokes later and a bit calmer, she slips the long slender key back into the ignition. The Bug purrs to a smooth start. Its toy-like vibrations and shrill revving engine offer succor. She wends her way out of the camping pit back onto the dirt road. As the VW passes him, a nervous little skink skitters out onto the road to watch it disappear. The intruder gone, the faunal symphony resumes. Heading slowly home, Itzel aches with pangs of disenchantment, feeling a tad less innocent, a tad more jaded—it's the sting of knowing that her man isn't so special after all; that he's just like all the rest. Such dashed hopes . . .

As the Bug hums along past pine and oak and long stretches of yellow gravel road shoulder, Itzel realizes that she just went through all this without the comfort of her most loyal and best friend, Phoebe, her dog and the mother of six pups at home. David was out supposedly walking Phoebe. In her rashness, she had neglected to take Phoebe along on her emotional rollercoaster ride. A first. She never did anything without Phoebe, who had been with her long before David entered the picture. A sign of strength? Things just might turn out OK after all.

Driving along Route 40 back to *fucking P'ville*, her tender heartache now forged into simmering anger, she swallows the bitter pill of knowledge that it is only a matter of time; that she will have to go through those stages she's gone through before—and will go through again—so many times in her young life. She knows that the wrath will turn to numbness; that the numbness will inevitably become a low key murderous resentment. And even then she knows, too, that for the next ten years their love will wax and wane and eventually fester into oblivion. But for now, she still loves him. A keen warm breeze wafts across her cheek: *Ahhh . . . finally, something feels good*. She will drive home to see what he has to say for himself. Quite simply, she will be a woman and deal with the hurt.

15

TITS

New Jersey has lots of straight roads. So straight and so flawless that sixty percent of the people killed each year in automobile accidents in NJ choose to do so on those straight roads. Of course, they are probably drunk at the time or stoned or both. Regardless, however alert one might be while driving those unvarying, endless, bumpless asphalt backwoods roads shouldered with white sugary sand, it is easy to slip into a catatonic torpor spellbound by the light flicker that slices through the pole forests of pine and oak and birch that peripherally and perpetually frame one's tunnel vision; that stretch out as far as the seemingly never-ending ever receding horizon—a hypnotic strobe of light and shadow—a draftsman's ideal perspective. During daylight hours, the mesmerizing snare of invariability is bad enough driving those straight roads, but at night? Forget it. It's so easy to forget that you are speeding. An innocent deer leaping onto the road, a drunk running a stop sign while dozing off—one false move, and you're mangled road kill. Even if you aren't stoned, chances are good that the Sirens of Monotony will lure you to an untimely demise if you're not vigilant.

It was this latter state (i.e., flat-out boredom) that Timmy and Draco Delacroix and I were seeking to escape one hellaciously hot August morning back in 1961. The sun was still low and the humidity was high, and we were teenagers with nowhere to go and nothing to do—driving and driving and driving. Burning up gasoline and listening to WMID. Curtis Lee had us doing the Bristol Stomp in our seats to "Pretty Little Angel Eyes."

Who knows what was going on in any of our alleged minds? It was just another summer day, and we were tooling along Moss Mill Road up Egg Harbor way when Timmy let out, "Let's do something! I'm tired of just driving nowhere. This is costing me twenty-six cents a gallon."

His complaint was legitimate. He was eighteen, out of school, and working as a dishwasher at the Home Plate in Pleasantville. He had money—and he took us everywhere in his pristine powder blue 1956 Ford. Draco was sixteen and I was a cherry thirteen.

Neither Draco nor I commented on Timmy's frustration. We just let him drive that straight mesmerizing road in the hot silence under the music, rolling past piney trees and an occasional mailbox that signaled a rustic plain-Jane home set back off the road. After a bit, Timmy was mumbling softly again, "This is stupid, I tell you. Stupid . . . ," then, "Let's do something!" More silence. Then Draco piped up, turning to me—I was always in the back—with his famous impish smile, eyes aglow, talking through his teeth, a galaxy of lights incandescing within his head, "What about Sunshine Park, David? You know how to get in there, don't you? You know that place, don't you? . . ."

Sunshine Park. Hmmm . . . What did I know about Sunshine Park?

When I was just a kid back in the mid-1950s, my sister Kitty married this guy, Merv Wescoat, whose father had a cabin up on the Great Egg Harbor River in Mays Landing. I only got to go there a couple-few-several times, but I remember the pure ecstasy of playing on the dock, my little bare feet sucking and sloshing through the bottoms across slippery blackish clayish mud, futzing around the riparian woodland, cattails, jumping fish, mosquitos, and drunk adults. One time, while the big people were partying, I was fishing off the end of the dock with a bamboo pole that had a length of catgut and a hook attached. A hunk of cheese (or was it hot dog?) was my bait. It was such a phony rig and I felt that I was being humored. Something to keep me busy and out of the way. I didn't expect to catch anything. But then, a tug. Then, a stronger tug. And then, the action really began. I lifted my catch upward and was freaked out by this long slimy slender squirming writhing swinging jerking wriggling desperate snake fighting with all its might for its precious life. Holding it out in front of me, I just stared for a few moments at this amazing force of nature. Instinctively, I knew that I was doing something wrong. But then, reality kicked in and I went running up the dock yelling, "A snake! A snake! I caught a snake! . . ." The adults burst out laughing and my sister jumped away shivering wildly, "Ew! Ew! . . . Get that thing outta here! . . ."

Then Merv's dad said, "Boy, that ain't no snake. It's an eel. Don't'cha know an eel, boy? Hee-hee-hee-hee! . . ." He put his highball down, grabbed the string, and wrestled the slimy beast into his gnarly hands. Remarks and snickers filled my little ears. I felt they were all laughing at me for being stupid, for not knowing what I somehow should have known. He removed the hook from the squirming creature's mouth and held it out, still dancing for its life, in front of me, "This is an eel, boy . . ." I fingered my crooked tortoiseshells higher up on my nose and squinched my eyes for a better look. "They live out there," Merv's dad said, "That's their home." Then, belting out a drunken laugh, he cast the terrified glassy-green teleost back into the water. It slithered on the surface a brief moment before disappearing below the cedar water, happy to be home, I was sure, happy to be alive, and skedaddled right back to the Sargasso Sea. Except for a *National Geographic* special or some other nature show on TV, that was the first and last eel I ever saw.

Another day, Merv—who never paid much attention to me—decided that he was going to show me something. I guess I was about nine or ten. He told me to get into the boat, and off we went, just the two of us, in this splendid custom-made 17′ double cockpit Jersey white cedar and mahogany varnish finish 1950s inboard runabout beauty with brown leather upholstery, a windshield, and all sorts of chrome lights and horns. Its 100-horse power engine would grind it through the water at 36 knots per hour. It sounded like the guttural purr of a monstrous lion. A super-duper ski boat. Loud. Fast. Cool. The wind and the spray and the thrust and the jouncing and the excessive noise were all way too exciting. I was afraid of bouncing out of that boat. We were violently slicing our way, planing along at a good clip, but everything else in the world was moving in quiet slow motion. Merv, wearing faded blue mid-thigh swimming trunks, shirtless, shoeless, was silent, staring straight ahead squinting though his black Wayfarer horn-rims. When it came to anything on the water, Merv was a consummate professional—drunk or sober. A hard working, hard drinking bundle of sinewy muscle, he was a badass honey badger of a man. A real curiosity to me. He had never wanted to do anything with me before. What was up now?

We had been churning upriver for about ten minutes when he suddenly dethrottled. As we chugged slowly along, I became hyperacutely aware of the bubbling fuming water abaft and that I was out there with him all alone—floating on the water. I could not then, nor can I today, put my finger on the beauty of the Great Egg Harbor. Its expansive slow tannic effluence at once evoked terror and bliss within me. While I harbored a deep-seated anxiety of being swept away by it or being consumed by a massive creature from its dark depths, I could imagine nothing finer than to be in or on it. Adding Merv's mystery excursion to all this, my little brain was a turmoil of inexplicable fear and grand elation.

As though he were alone in the boat, Merv never looked at me or gave me a clue as to what was up—but I knew something profound was about to happen. I just couldn't assign shape, form, or significance to it. With the engine purring, Merv started arcing to the starboard. A waft of exhaust enveloped us. It smelled good. I took an extra deep breath. We were put-put-putting toward the shore. Not a word had been spoken since we had left the dock. I was just excited to be in the boat, on the river, with him. As we headed shoreward, I could make out ant-sized people lying on and milling about the beach and kids jumping off a dock. Nothing struck me as unusual. Then Merv throttled up a little and arced upstream a bit toward the port, heading us closer toward the woods upriver from where the people were. I didn't ask him what we were doing or what the plan was because Merv wasn't a talker. He was a doer.

When we'd left the cabin he'd just shouted, "David! Get in the boat!" and off we went. Merv sort of grunted and talked loud and laughed loud and looked at one with either delight or derision, but he didn't really talk—not to me, anyway. The mystery finally peaked when he shut the engine off and we began ever so slowly drifting downstream. The instant the motor was shut off, Merv—agile as a squirrel, lean as a greyhound—leapt over the seat back to the cooler—beer for him; soda for me. Taking the church key that was tied to the cooler with a piece of twine, he punctured a can of Miller High Life, pried the cap off a Pepsi, and flew back up front where he planted his butt on the port gunwale. I was on a cushion in the starboard front passenger seat. Even though he was looking forward, toward the shore, I sensed that he was closely observing me in his peripheral vision; that he was thinking about me; that he was looking for a reaction or some sort of expected behavior. I was supposed to do something. But what? And so there we sat. Saying nothing. Just sipping and drifting. God, was that ice-cold Pepsi delicious. Had I known what *surreal* meant at the time, it would have felt that way. Instead, I just felt like I usually felt about almost all situations—strange and odd. Having grown up without a dad or any other male influence in my life, I didn't know how to act with men. Not that I knew how to act with women, understand, just less so with men. Nevertheless, there we floated. It was all so *out there*. But I thought it was wonderful. As cool as cool could be. Just being in a boat was good enough for me. And the fact that I was out there alone with Merv, well, it meant *something*, even though I didn't have a clue what.

As we started drifting past the beach, the sounds of gamboling and splashing kids and happy laughing adult conversation began to fill the looming shrieking silence between us. Then a question entered my little brain and I got up the courage to ask, "Are we waiting for somebody?" "No!" he shot back, taking a swig of his Miller and laughing like a hyena as though I were an idiot, "Look at the beach, man. Use those four eyes. *Huht!* Look at those tits . . ."

And that was the sum total of what I knew about Sunshine Park. Period. But I had surely at some point in time shot my mouth off to Draco and Timmy, trying to sound like I was more experienced than I was. And there we were, three kids with nothing to do but to look for some sort of mischief to get ourselves into. So, off to Mays Landing we went. Timmy and Draco—all excited at the prospect. I—less than enthusiastic.

Back in 1931, Dutch Reformed Reverend Ilsley "Uncle Danny" Boone purchased a sizable parcel of acreage just south of Mays Landing along the east side of the Great Egg Harbor River. His intention was to establish a spiritual health community, which came to be known as Sunshine Park. Influenced by the European naturalist movement, Uncle Danny shifted the community's focus toward spiritual nudism, and Sunshine Park became the national headquarters for the American Sunbathing Association. An ensuing constitutional battle with the U.S. Postal Service over the distribution of its unerotic airbrushed *Sunshine and Health* nudist magazine resulted in a U.S. Supreme Court decision that paved the way for *Playboy* and the multitude of fleshzines that would follow. But there was nothing lascivious about Uncle Danny's publication—the Sunshine Park crowd was all about a natural regimen of vegetarianism, calisthenics, nudism rain or shine, abstinence from alcohol, and generally being good folk. Nudity was not only health-enhancing, it was also a way of breaking down social distinctions. But we local yokels had no idea that what was going on there was a progressive experiment to create a healthier, more just, spiritually equanimous world. To us, it was just the weird old Sunshine Nudist Colony. An anomaly. A place where freaky people went. A cult. A source of titillation for our benighted collective prurient interests. And who could have ever guessed that in 1963 Diane Arbus would focus her lens on little almost-thirteen-year-old Lorna Anton, who was working at her summer job in Sunshine Park as a waitress? In the photo, Anton wears merely a silver hairband and a very cute starched frilly round-cut white Frenchy demi-apron, its sole pocket containing her order pad. That's it. Nothing else. A pure-hearted river nymph, she was. Prints of *A Young Waitress at a Nudist Camp, N.J., 1963* go for hundreds of thousands of dollars today. It turns out that Sunshine Park was a fount of a whole lot of highfalutin stuff. But to me and Draco and Timmy, it was just something to do on a hot summer day. So what did I know about Sunshine Park? Well, I knew where it was.

We had gone up to Port Republic looking for some kid Draco wanted to hook up with. For whatever reason, we couldn't find him, so Timmy just drove on following his nose down country roads until we found our-selves approaching the Renault Winery. That's when the big decision was made to hit Sunshine Park, to satisfy Timmy's need to "do something." Draco's craftiness had put the spotlight on me. I had to deliver. Except for that one time on the boat with Merv, I had never had anything to do with Sunshine Park. Didn't know anything. All I knew was that it was about a five-minute drive from Merv's dad's cabin. I was in the hot seat. I had plenty of experience with lying and making things up, so I just took it one step at a time. My evil mind had served me well in the past; why wouldn't it this time? But I was a little more than a little scared.

We hooked a left onto Philadelphia and followed Route 50 into Mays Landing to River Road—one of the most gorgeous drives on the planet—then headed over to Summers Point-Mays Landing Road and down to-ward the park. We did a reconnoiter up and down the road past the park's entrance a few times and selected a parking spot, a gravel spit just below Ocean Heights Avenue that had several other commuter workmen's cars parked there. A perfect spot. With other cars there, Timmy's baby blue would blend in just fine. The plan was quite simple: Walk down the road a bit away from the park's entrance. Enter the woods. Double back.

While Timmy's car fit in OK, we certainly didn't. Wearing our all-the-rage madras short-sleeved shirts with the tails hanging out, cotton khaki and black skinny ankle tapper pants a bit short for the express purpose of exposing our white socks and showing off our Cuban heels, coifed with our Princentons—and me, the tallest at 6′2″—we were three sore thumbs walking down a hot lonely stretch of wooded road. No, nothing unusual about that. We knew that we were a little more than conspicuous, and Draco's solution was that when the cars that passed us by were just about to pass us by, he would stick out his thumb to make it look like we were just passing through, like we were lackadaisical hitchhikers. After the sec-ond or third car, Timmy said, "Geez, Draco. What if somebody stops?" At that, Draco stopped thumbing. He just stood there, staring at us, not saying a word. A crazy look we were all too familiar with lit up his face, and we knew that something was up. Pursing his lips, he looked at me; then switched his gaze to Timmy; then toward the forest; then, like a discharged bullet, he shot off running into the woods yelling, "Come on!..." As though he were charging up San Juan Hill or something, he turned looking back at us motioning with his right arm to follow him, "Come on, you guys! Come on!..."

We ran like hell following him to who knows where. Once in the woods and away from the road, we stopped and huffed and puffed and gathered ourselves with a rare excitement. A titillating fear. We knew we were up to no good, but the mission had begun. Draco was utterly enthused, exuberant, exalted, and enthralled with the idea of getting on with the business of eyeballing some naked women. He was a fearless lion. It was as if he had some special gene that prevented him from considering failure or loss in any situation. Timmy seemed equally willing-hearted and expressed a nervous eagerness. But an uneasy shifting of his eyes belied what I gathered to be a chafing apprehension, a realization that he had gotten more than he had bargained for with his wish to "do something." And me? I felt like what an eighteenth-century front-line infantryman must have felt like facing ranks of enemy infantrymen, looking down the barrels of their hostile flintlocks. I was doomed. I was going to get shot. I just didn't know when. But I knew it was coming. So off we went, tiptoeing line abreast back toward the park's entrance. Pausing every now and then. Listening...

Stalking deeper into the woods on our way toward Mecca, we began to hear the muffled sounds of chatter and giggling. Then the thud-thud of volleyball came into earshot, but it was coming from a slightly different direction than we had been heading. We reoriented our course using the sounds as our magnetic north. Our sensory radar snapped into a heightened state. Our instincts cautioned us to tread lightly on the forest duff, to dampen out steps. Soon enough, we could see flecks of fleshy movement in the distance. The mother lode. We were like three springer spaniels with our noses locked onto game birds, taking one delicate single silent step at a time, then freezing—three Giacometti pointing men in the woods. Piecemeal, we advanced.

As we forged ahead, the happy sounds of people having a good time grew louder. The sweet shrills of excited females was too much for us. Through the tapestry of scrub pine, white cedar, maple, blueberry, and underbrush, perforations and slashes of light revealed swatches of hopping bobbing skin tone—a volleyball game was in progress, and it turned out to be all ladies playing. We intuitively broke away from our squad line formation and slipped into our normal hierarchal single file: Draco on point, Timmy following up, and I the sweep. The thought entered my mind, *If we can see them, they can see us*, so I "psst" to Timmy, whispering, "They're gonna see us." He nodded and "psst" to Draco. Suddenly we took on a flying wedge formation. I, behind one tree. Timmy, to my left behind another. Draco, hunching down, steadily moving forward, heedless of the crunching noise he was now making. He stopped and turned toward Timmy who was whisper-screaming and waving his hands, "Hey! Draco! Get back! Get back here. They're gonna see us. You're too close. We're gonna get caught." Draco, contorting his face with furrowed brow, pursed lips, and twitching nose, gave him a disdainful look as he shook his head lipping, "No, they're not. No, they're not," giving us a come-hither wave, mouthing, "Come on, you guys," as he turned his back on us, crouched down and continued his advance—inch by inch, tree by tree, bush by bush, closer and closer . . .

From around the juvenile pine behind which I was hiding, I could peekingly see all I needed to see. It was a real social affair. Very casual. Clusters of naked men and women standing around here and there or sitting on lounge chairs by twos and threes. Beverages in hand, chatting, nodding of heads in agreement, laughing, and cheering the bare-bottomed volleyball players whose bulbously large breasts flopped hither and thither. Everyone had on tennis shoes of some sort or flip-flops, and the men wore these foul-looking jockstraps. For sure, the most unsightly vista I had ever encountered in my hitherto young life. No way was I getting any closer. And Timmy was obviously of the same mind. If I was ever to have an unerotic moment in my life, this was surely going to be it. There I was, in the bush with all this frolicsome gamboling and scampering around, but it was anything but sexy. I don't know what we were expecting to see when we started out, but I am pretty sure none of us had envisioned unshapely naiads, drooping breasts, and goofy guys in jockstraps. Definitely not a scene from *The Immoral Mr. Teas.*

Truth was, I was standing there shaking in my boots. Sweating to high heaven. My madras soaked. And then, in the blink of an eye, I became inexplicably relaxed and slipped into an eerie state of consciousness. A lone bobwhite whistled admonishingly in the offing. A souped-up car beckoned as it raced along the Point road. An uncharacteristic breeze reared up, wafting the canopy, and the nude volleyball crowd became an indecipherable cacophony of muffled mumbling. Except for that solitary quail, not a bird was to be heard, not a chirp or a trill. As I took in all that was going on before my eyes, I sensed that every creature in the forest was watching me; that even the nocturnal critters had roused themselves to secure a ringside seat. The insects seemed to have backed off—not a buzz or a bite. Trying to make sense of it all, I stood there crouched and popeyed, breathing in the pungent steamy hot aroma of vegetal decay and fresh pine. While my mind was inordinately relaxed, my body was inordinately taut. I looked over at Timmy. He looked back and smiled. I looked at Draco, who had by this time assumed a soldier's low crawl and was positioning himself behind a bush. Far too close for my taste. But there we were, *voyeurs extraordinaires.* What a scene. Now what?

The nudists were carrying on ever so nonchalantly. Then I noticed a jock-strapped man walking over to a cluster of men and women, where he stood with his back to us in apparent general conversation. At one point, though, I thought I noticed the men he was talking to sneak a glance in our direction. Then he ambled over to another group of men and women and did the same thing. The men he had previously chatted with left the women behind, and strolled over to a sort of tiki bar on the far side of the volleyball court and just stood there, talking and gesturing. After the traveling man finished talking to the next group, he moved on to another knot of socializers while the men from that last group headed, ever so slowly and casually, over to the tiki bar. This went on until all the men, perhaps twelve or thirteen or so, were all huddling around the tiki bar.

I got Timmy's attention, whispering, "Psst . . . psst . . . Hey! I think they see us—" and then all hell broke loose:

A massive uproar of tribal yelling and screaming erupted from the tiki bar gang and every last one of them came charging in our direction. Clearly, it was every man for himself. As it turned out, Timmy and Draco stayed together and headed laterally toward the road. I, in all my wisdom, fraught with terror, turned and ran in the opposite direction, deeper into the woods. I was on automatic—a runaway slave with bloodthirsty baying hounds on my heels.

Tearing through the woods, I saw a large thicket of brush coming up ahead. I quickly assessed my situation and thought, *They'll be expecting me to keep running; they'd never expect me to stop and be hiding right in their path*, so I looked over my shoulder, and when I didn't see anyone who could see me, I leapt like Superman into the midst of that shrubbery. Safe at last. Somehow, through flight and tumbling, I ended up supine propped up on my elbows. I lay motionless, thoroughly surrounded by dense foliage. A great hiding place. They were out there yelling, "They went that way!" and "One of them went that way!" and so on and so forth. They were beating the bushes and had some sort of drum they were pounding on. They were trying to flush us out. I felt like a fugitive—Noah Cullen set free. They were heading in my direction. But all I had to do was be still.

The elasticity of time started wreaking havoc on me. It seemed like hours had passed. While the yelling voices seemed to be drifting farther and farther away, that damned drum they were beating seemed right on top of me and it was driving me crazy: Boom-boom! Boom-boom! Boom-boom! My God, what savages. *Just stay put. Don't move. They're probably standing right outside of this bush all waiting to pounce on me. They're just trying to scare me with that drum.* Then, as my quivering body began to calm itself, I realized that that was no damned drum. It was my own heart! Boom-boom! Boom-boom! Boom-boom! How could I have ever thought that that was a drum? My God, what an idiot. But I stayed still for the longest time to make doubly sure that no one was out there waiting to bust me. When it felt like my shoulders were about to puncture their way through my flesh, I knew it was time to move. There was one small problem, though—that nice thicket I'd chosen to hide in turned out to be a tremendous brier patch. There was absolutely no movement I could make without scratching the dickens out of myself.

While the pounding of my heart subsided and a certain calmness washed over me, I was sure that those jock-strapper beasts were out there laying for me. But now I wasn't so afraid anymore, and rather than give them the satisfaction of tackling me and roughing me up, I decided to surrender with dignity: "OK. You got me! I'm coming out! . . ." I ooched and ouched my way up and stood there in the middle of my barbed wire prison and took a good look around. I was ready for the consequences. There I stood. Alone. Deadly silence pervaded the forest. The critters were still watching me, I was sure. I was also sure that the jock-strappers were hiding and waiting to jump me. What to do? Whatever my fate was to be, I had to first extricate myself from that damned thornbush. So, as gingerly as possible, I began disentangling myself, expressing pain all the way. You would have thought that under the circumstances I would have been more concerned with the protection of my body, but all I could think about was not tearing my clothes. That was usually the case with me—a little over-the-topishly concerned with materialism for someone who had a whole lot of nothing.

Anyway, once out, I combed my hair, dusted myself off, and surveyed the woods to get my bearings. Still thinking the jock-strappers were hiding close by, I offered my surrender a second time: "OK! You got me! Come on out . . ." Once again, nothing. So, totally disoriented, I took off in what I felt was the direction as far away from the volleyball court as possible, toward the road. Every step loaded with leaden fear. In spite of the melting heat, I was chilled. I was trembling. The flora and fauna were in cahoots with those jock-strappers and all eyes were on me—I just knew it. Mother Nature was snickering at my folly. Suddenly, I could hear those creatures sniggering with wild delight. Unmolested, tiptoeing, I continued until I saw a viable exit. Stepping out from the shelter of the woods, into what easily could have been a sub-Saharan veldt straddling the road, I stood there, exposed, motionless, vulnerable. Had anyone driven by, it would have made a most bizarre scene to behold—a lanky-cum-chubby white kid clad in plaid against a matted forest, looking like a cognizant deer staring down the barrel of a Beanfield Sniper. All I knew was that I was somewhere downstream from where we had entered and somewhere upstream from Merv's dad's place.

There I stood, terrified, pursy, thinking about what the heck I should do. Begin hitchhiking back home or go back and look for Draco and Timmy? Knowing full well that I was walking into a possible prison sentence, I hied myself off toward the car. Heading across the right-of-way for the road with forced confidence, I took a tumble, crash landing across weeds and earth. Some evil-minded highway engineer had placed an unseen swale in my path as retribution for my lewd behavior, I was sure. As my sliding came to a halt, a belting song of laughter, a joyous uproar of pent up schadenfreude, burst forth from the wood beasts that had all along been watching my tomfoolery. I stood up and gave myself a good brushing off. There was no time for dwelling upon the grass stains on my pants or the burns on my elbows, so off I trudged doing my best to wipe off the schmazool that was all over me.

My walk was lonely and fretting. I was doing my best to control the nervous twitch that had taken possession of me. Those unclothed, unattractive, unsavory volley-ballers were lodged in my head like dirty thoughts I couldn't get rid of. The onslaught by those wild buck jock-strappers seemed eons ago, ancient memories. How could the so recent past become so distant so fast? The present was a grueling plodding onward toward a terrifyingly unknown future that might hold jail time or at least a good lashing, should those jock-strapper jokers get hold of me. Clearly, I was traumatized, dazed. It was as if I were in the midst of some discombobulated time travel continuum.

There I was, a fish out of water tittuping up the road with bravado as though suspicion could not possibly fall upon me as having just been running through the briers and bushes where even the rabbits couldn't go. What an image my Baby Hueyesque self jive-strutting up the road must have made, putting on my best soulful carriage; my cleated Cuban heels shattering the peaceful calm, assaulting the lonely road. Walking along wondering what on earth I had gotten myself into, I began to hear the urgent whining strain of an engine and the shifting of gears ahead in the distance. The speck of a car was heading my way. Something about the sounds told me that the driver was in a hurry and looking for something. It could be the jock-strappers.

As the car drew closer, it looked blue and I thought it might be Timmy and Draco. But as it neared, I saw that it was a lighter shade of blue. Suddenly I was musing that Timmy's Ford had more green in it; more of a teal. Even closer, I saw that it was a two-toned powder blue and white '53 Chevy Bel Air. Now practically on top of me, I saw that it had four doors and four guys in it. I plucked myself up. What if they stopped? I didn't have a story. Whatever. I would just do what I did when I was walking to and from school or walking down the street in Pleasantville or Atlantic City—walk like I was going somewhere, be intent, be confident, act like I didn't care, and no one would ever guess that moments ago I had been ensnarled within a thorny bosk quaking in fear of a tribe of nudists. Uh-oh . . . They were slowing down and crossing the lane. Clearly, they were interested in me. Frowning, I acted as insouciant as I could muster, taking exaggerated exception to their behavior by walking a bit more off the road indicating that I was wary of their being on the wrong side of the road. They pulled to a stop just ahead of me. I could see that all four guys were white, fully clothed, fair-haired, and tan—very tan, as though they had all come from the same cookie cutter. The driver leaned out the window, "Hey, buddy. Where you goin'?" I made sure my posture was upright, my step strong, and kept on walking, giving them a look as though they were the odd ones out as I responded, "Jus'sup ahead. Have a nice day." As I passed them, I heard the Chevy go into reverse and it started creeping backward as all four guys started saying things—not quite yelling or shouting: "We know you were snoopin' in the park." "You might as well give up." "We got your friends . . ." *We got your friends* caught my attention. Oh, shoot! But I just kept strutting along.

The Chevy backed up a bit farther so it was a couple-few car lengths ahead of me and stopped. When I got up to it the driver asked:

"Where'd you get all those scratches?"

"Look, I don't know what you guys are talkin' about, jus' leave me alone."

"So whatcha'ya doin' out here if you weren't in the camp? Nobody just takes a walk out here."

By this time, I had stopped and was holding a face to face with the driver who was leaning his chin on his arms resting on the open window. One of the guys in the back seat blurted out, "How come you're all scratched up? How'd your clothes get all nicked up?"

"Look . . . ," a blast of genius struck me, ". . . I'm visiting my brother-in-law's father's cabin up the road and I'm out for a walk. I don't know what you guys are talking about."

The driver asked, "Oh, yeah? And who would that be?"

"Merv Wescoat," I retorted without blinking an eyelash, which caused a bit of a ruckus in the car. Suddenly they were all consulting one another.

Then the driver turned back to me with: "It's true. Wescoat has a cabin up the road. You're right about that. But we know you was in the park sneaky peeking. Look at you, man, you're a mess. All scratched up. Your clothes are all torn up. We got your friends back at the car. You might as well come clean. C'mon. We'll take'ya back to'em. They're waitin' for ya . . ."

I stood there listening to his persuasions, looking at those guys donning my best archaic smile wondering what to do. No one said a word. There was nothing more to say. I was aware of the idling engine and exhaust. The woods seemed to be in a high pitch of felicity. Its denizens roaring with hilarity. The jock-strappers didn't look like bad guys. They didn't do anything mean or threatening. So I wrinkled my face, rolled my eyes, spun my head around, wished I had a Lucky Strike, and walked over and got in the back of the Bel Air. "OK . . . I was there . . ."

On the way back they were all reasonably nice to me, poking fun and having a lot of laughs at my expense. They told me not to feel too bad because they were always busting guys sneaking into the park for a peek. Slowing as we approached the turnoff, we rolled off the pavement onto the crunchy yellow gravel. There was Timmy's baby blue, agape like a submissive dental patient—its hood up and five or six guys standing around intent on whatever was going on under the hood. An incongruous MASH unit—everyone watching the guy leaning over the passenger side fender doing whatever it was he was doing. They all looked up upon hearing us, but immediately turned their attention back to their vehicular patient.

When Timmy and Draco had taken flight from the attacking jock-strappers, their primal instinct was to stick together. After all, they were Irish-Italian-French Catholics from a family of eleven siblings. That's what you do—stick together. And so off they went, running through the jungle. Now, during such an unplanned for life experience as they were then presently involved with, one would never—especially during the heat of things—imagine that one would, could, or should, think, *Hmm . . . it's a small world, isn't it.* But in this particular unlikely situation, it would not have been inappropriate. Not at all.

Because Timmy could run like a wing-footed hungry cheetah, he was bushwhacking a trail with Draco bringing up the rear. As they were cutting, dashing, and zigzagging their way to hoped-for safety, Draco heard what he could never have guessed he would ever have heard in a million years at that moment in time. With his determined athletic Golden Gloves boxer's focus on the task at hand—survival—he bolted and hurdled and dodged through the woods. While showing the soles of his shoes to his pursuers, a soft high-pitched dreamlike cry began to drift over him from behind, a summonsing: "Draco Delacroix! . . . Draco Delacroix! . . . You can't get away! . . . We got you! . . . Draco Delacroix! . . . I know who you are! . . ." Dang! Dang! A knockout punch. How could this be? Accepting that absurdity had trumped reality as he knew it; accepting that he was running away from a bunch of guys in jock-straps in the middle of the woods and that one of them knew him—Draco decided to obey the mysterious ethereal mandate emanating from behind. And so he gave up, an act contrary to his defiant competitive nature. At the same time he put the kibosh on his questionable escape, he yelled ahead for Timmy to do the same. Timmy, trusting his brother's judgment, screeched to a halt. The jig was up.

As I and my entourage of bounty hunters approached the Ford, Draco, Timmy, and I went all gimlet-eyed sharing our collective vulnerability, apprehension, and disbelief. Our presence was hushed, timid even. This thing wasn't over yet. What would become of us? For the moment, we were hostages, prisoners, trespassers, captives, perverts, the accused.

The operation at hand was being performed by some guy replacing the rotor he had pulled so we couldn't drive away.

It was a solemn event. Everyone's attention was on the fumbling fingers of the guy tidying things up and securing the distributor cap. I looked at the other cars parked there and wondered how on earth they'd figured out that that was our car. So I asked the guy next to me, "How'd you guys know this was our car?" Without taking his eyes off the handiwork in progress, he deadpanned, "This is where all the peepers park. We just come here and check for the hottest engine. The other cars show up early in the morning and are all cooled down. Besides, we kinda know the cars that park here every day, anyway." Timmy and Draco and I fired off quick glances of so-much-for-our-perfect-original-clever-plan . . .

Mission accomplished. The hood crashed down. Conversation ensued that verged on admonition. We all stood in a cluster sharing uneasy smiles as we three were told that it wasn't necessary to sneak in. The guy who knew Draco from Holy Spirit High invited us back anytime we wanted; an open invitation was extended. One proviso, though—we would have to experience our visitation in the buff. At that, there was some light tittering, but, from the expressions on the faces of the others, I got the distinct feeling that Draco's new best friend was the only one actually welcoming us back. To the others, we were only the latest in a long line of pains in the butt they had to deal with from time to time. The good news, though, was that we were off the hook. No police. No hard time.

After a round of shaking hands and good-byes, they were in their cars and off into the sunset, plumes of dusty yellow particulates kicking up as the sped away. Phew! That was a close one. Somewhat nonplused, we stood there in peaceful silence watching them drive off. Then, blasting our pregnant pause and bursting our bubble of relief, Timmy, scaring the daylights out of us, exclaimed, "Come on! Let's get the hell out of here before they change their mind! . . ."

We headed toward Somers Point swapping stories of our individual experiences and observations. What I didn't know when the rotor was being replaced was that that was the third rotor!— that that jock-strapper joker had broken two others and that they'd had to make two trips into Mays Landing, where Timmy'd had to shell out two dollars two times to buy two new rotors. How one breaks a rotor is beyond me, but the guy managed to do it. Timmy told of magically becoming Pheidippides flying through the woods. Draco told of his otherworldly shock at hearing his name called out as he was coursing through the bushes. I told about how I thought my own heartbeat was a drum and how I lied when they stopped me on the road. Then Timmy and I both blamed Draco for getting us busted because he kept creeping too close. We ended up at the Dairy Queen on Shore Road, where we continued rehashing our adventures. Out of harm's way, licking our wounds and soft serve, we felt pretty confident and proud of ourselves. A lot of been there, done that.

Repasted, refreshed, and raring to go, we loaded back into the Ford and headed up Northfield way. With the recounting of our respective Sunshine Park adventures pretty much spent, we listened to the radio as we cruised up Shore Road where the well-to-do lived. What did we know about Gothic, Queen Anne, Foursquare, and Colonial Revival architecture or ornate two- and three-story Victorian affairs, remnants of the area's once thriving maritime and farming past? Nothing. With whatever shortcomings and lackings we had to contend with in our respective lives, little did we know just how good we had it then or just how privileged we actually were. Those were our *Happy Days*.

The Mar-Keys' "Last Night" was bringing out the black in us as we jumped and jived and convulsed through Somers Point, Linwood, and Northfield. We were cool. Then Timmy lowered the volume, "God, this is all we ever do! Just drive around. Let's do something! . . ." Draco craned around with his devilish bug-eyed look and we cracked up laughing as Timmy hooked a quick right onto Mill Road for no good reason repeating, "What? What? What's so funny? . . ."

Three teenagers with nowhere to go and nothing to do. As we rolled across the marshes, on the beautiful long straight causeway to Margate, Gary U.S. Bonds's "Quarter to Three" gave us a severe jolt of youthful life. With the cool paludal breeze blowing in the window, I could taste the bay salt depositing on my lips and smell the pungent muddy decay of the marshy islands. Life was good. Then Draco turned down the radio, "OK, maybe I got too close—but did you *see* those tits on that one girl?..."

16

RACCOON

It was a cold freezing New Jersey
Winter night—
No,
It was a hot sultry—
No,
I don't remember
But it was night
I was driving my '50 Chevy
Down a flat, narrow country road
I was loaded
Feeling pretty good
And there it was
BAM!
I hit it
What?
What did I hit?

I stopped
I could see it in my rearview mirror
Movement
I got out
Went back
A raccoon!
Quietly screaming out in pain
Not a whimper
It just stared with those big
Eyes
And without anthropomorphizing
I knew it was begging me
To put it out of its misery
I agreed
I got in my Chevy
I put it in gear
I slowly backed up
Gonna crush the life out of it
Do it a big favor
I aligned my back left tire with the creature
I could see it staring at me
I stopped
I looked at those begging eyes
We stared at one another for a while
Then
I slowly drove away
Like a coward
I left it in the middle of the road
To die
A slow and painful
Death
I left the scene
And chalked it up
To
Nature

17

THE BEST
SHE COULD

Corn and crackers were her favorite. Regular old ShopRite canned corn brought to a bubbling boil, left to simmer with a gob of butter, salt and pepper, and a little evaporated milk—to be consumed with a crunchy topping of Sunshine Saltines. Another time, just for variety, it might be canned peas or canned string beans or frozen Brussels sprouts. Just one thing all doctored up. And, after a hot day's work sitting next to those life-sucking china kilns looking for vision-stealing defects on pieces of ware that sold for more than Elsie earned in two weeks, corn was all she wanted to eat. That's all she had the energy to fix. To eat her corn and go to bed was all she really wanted to do. But she still had David to think about, so she usually made what she thought was a complete meal for his sake, because she wanted to be a responsible mother: fried chicken, Spam (which, for some unknown reason, David grew up calling steak), or pork chops with Campbell's baked beans with a little dark Karo, mashed potatoes, perhaps beets or lima beans, and a salad of iceberg lettuce, onion, and fresh Jersey beefsteak tomatoes. Salad dressing would be Hellmann's mayonnaise hand-whipped with evaporated milk and a little olive oil. Mom would have a hot cup of Tetley tea and David a glass of milk (which, for most of his early life, was actually a glass of water with some evaporated milk and a spoonful of sugar). They would eat and not talk much about anything as Elsie watched with utter astonishment as David shoveled in vast quantities of food.

At thirty-eight, with eight-year-old David, another son, Billy, in the Navy, and two daughters, Elsie and Doreen, off and married, Elsie was feeling like there was no end; that she would never be free to be free; that she'd never be able to start over again—alone. That aspiration had been dashed when, eight years after her last kid, along had come David. While she had a healthy appetite for male companionship, men were anathema to her: drunks, cheats, liars out for their own good, useless, physical abusers. And for damned sure, not providers.

There were almost never leftovers after meals. David made sure of that. Afterwards, the two of them would do the dishes. David usually washing and Mom drying, though sometimes they switched. He liked the texture and foaming of Brillo and S.O.S pads and knowing that he had produced a sparkling clean dish or frying pan. She liked the help.

It was a daily struggle for Elsie. It was a daily struggle for David, too, but she could not understand why. He had food on the table, a roof over his head, clothes, and occasionally some spending money—a quarter or fifty cents or even a dollar—when she could afford it. Life had not been easy for her. Consequently, personhood was no bowl of cherries for David, either. Of that, he was all too aware. So far, for the eight years he had been on this planet, David had not been able to find a single reason to be happy. And since he was a *little* little boy, he had been unconsciously trying to fill his perpetual feelings of emptiness and less-than with food.

Elsie had dropped out of school when she was sixteen because she'd gotten herself knocked up. From then on, she was the black sheep of the large family from which she came. Society today is not kindly toward young girls getting themselves pregnant—in the 1930s, it was ruthless toward them. While the high school sweetheart who popped her did marry her, the illusion of being loved and being married only lasted one week. His true colors came out: he was a drunken craven bully.

Coming home drenched with alcohol and the stink of other women, Bill would rouse Elsie from a deep sleep by choking and punching her while screaming, "You whore! You goddamned fucking whore! You fucking slut! Motherfucker! Bitch! Cheap tramp motherfucker!" His rules were: no makeup, no pretty clothes, no friends in the house when he wasn't there (and few wanted to be there when he was there), no more money than was needed to run the house (which itself was a pipe dream because he frequently drank up his pay as soon as he got it). The physical and emotional abuse went on and on. That's just how it was for her. Elsie was on her own. Her family's motto—and they knew exactly what was going on—was, "You made your bed. Sleep in it." The one time she stooped to ask her mother for a nickel for a loaf of bread, she was turned down. And the few friends she had were broke and struggling themselves. The 1930s was not a good time for many people. Succor was in short supply.

One sultry night in the wee hours of 1947, old Billy boy, a tall, hair-slicked-back-proto-rockabilly-philandering-drunken-handsome-fool-of-a-man, came home in one of his usual rows and began chasing Elsie around the apartment with every intention of beating her senseless. It was routine for her and the little ones to be jolted awake by Bill's blustery blathering drunkenness: slamming doors, cursing, laughing, falling up the steps, spilling and dropping things in the kitchen, hollering, and the foul smell of cigarettes or an occasional cigar, the apartment suddenly reeking to high heaven, "Hey! You! Goddam bitch, you! Where the fuck is my beer? Can't even keep a goddam house right. Stupid fuckin' cunt. Shmshitmothersupsup ansy whatthefuckgoddamshitfuck . . . Oh! There it is. Good thing for you, you—Hey! Get your skinny little ass out here! Goddamnit! I'm hungry . . ."

On any random night, at two or three or four or five o'clock in the morning, the bloodcurdling howls of a real-life fire-breathing Chimera would suddenly and at once inflate the younglings' imaginations with super-heated fear and trauma. The two littlest ones, Billy and Doreen, would hug each other in bed, while the eldest, ten-year-old little Elsie, would do the peeking, keeping them apprised. They had been through it so many times. They knew exactly what they were to do—nothing. Just stay in their room like Mother told them, and everything would be all right.

Thus it seemed that this night would simply be a refrain in the horrid dismal musical of their lives, destined to be repeated in perpetuity. This was their life. This was the way it was. The way it was always to be. But neither Bill nor Elsie nor the kids were aware that there are forces at work in this universe and that things do, at times, have a way of working themselves out.

Elsie had done her share of crying and praying and beseeching the old bearded white guy up in the sky only to receive more punches in the face, bruises all over her body, and the vilest deprecations from Bill. But there is a system of deep orderliness so much more profound than the simple crutching-concept of God. For sure, this reality was not something Bill had ever considered, for he was *King* Bill. So he went about his business as usual, throwing Elsie around like a rag doll and calling her every misogynistic epithet his addled brain could dredge up. He had Elsie up against the refrigerator about to brain her when out of the blue he was halted dead in his tracks:

"Stop it!" screamed little Elsie at the top of her lungs, "You leave Mommy alone!" There she was in her little felt nightgown, leaning forward on the tips of her little toes with her little fists clenched ready for battle. Her brother and sister were crouching down, watching from behind the doorjamb. Releasing years of pent-up rage, her little face flushing with determination—the child Elsie possessed not one ounce of fear. The world as they all had known it was in the midst of a seismic shift. For the moment, little Elsie was in complete control of the situation, "You are the *tramp!* You are the *whore!* You are the *liar!* You are a *lush!* A dirty stinky *lush!* Stinky! And I *hate* you! Everybody *hates* you! You are not a good man! You are a *bad* man! You are *not* a daddy! A daddy would *love* us and take *care* of us! Don't you touch-Mommy-ever-*again!* Not *ever! Never!* Stop! Stop! Stop! Stop! Stop! *Staaahhh'p!*"

And then, a blaring silence. A silence so loud that even the neighbors could hear it. A pinging white noise was hissing in everyone's ears. Bill and Elsie stood motionless, mouths agape, in a golden *tableau vivant*, shocked still by the wrath of a ten-year-old. Giants nonplused.

Bill shook his head. For an instant the alcohol stopped coursing through his noggin, affording him a moment of insane clarity. Then, he chose his reaction, "Why you little sonofabitch, you! . . . ," and off he went after her.

Well, after three kids, one after another, and ten years of Bill using her as a punching bag, Elsie had had enough. Beating her was one thing. She lumped it and rationalized it as punishment due for her sins. But Bill had never gone after the kids before—a fatal mistake. Before her eyes, the blackness of fear began transcending all of her normal instincts. A raging calmness settled upon her. A tinge of scarlet began seeping in, toning up her vision and thought. A heretofore unknown maternal impulse, something primal, was ferrying her across the imperceptible line that separates fear from anger. She would protect her children. She *would* protect her children. No other options; no room for negotiating. Like a thunderbolt of Jove, this diminutive twenty-nine-year-old woman began morphing into a titan. Now, her transformation complete, with every thought and vision in boiling vermilion, off *she* went.

When she finally caught up with Bill in the kids' bedroom, he was kneeling and reaching under a bed, trying to grab his child adversary, who was outmaneuvering his drunken efforts. Then, for the second time in one night, Bill had his tantrum interrupted by an unfamiliar demanding voice. A raspy voice he had never heard before. A hellhound's growl:

"Bill!" screamed his wife, with a guttural stentorian tone of authority. Turning to look up at her with a rictus of annoyed disgust, he scarcely had time to see the circular black bottom of a ten-inch cast-iron frying pan closing in on him. The next thing he saw was stars. And that was that.

When Bill came to, he skulkingly absquatulated posthaste, tail between his legs, slurring parting shots. Elsie and the kids clustered together, all of them standing tall and brave, witnessing his ignominious exit. The king was no longer king. After that night, never did Scaramouch return. Thenceforth, Elsie punished herself for not having resisted the besotted dastard earlier. A decade of beatings, beratings, terror, intimidation, mental and physical isolation, virtual enslavement, rape, endless sleepless nights, and, above all, the traumatization of her kids, was over. And the crying. So much crying. Alone. In secret. So as not to scare the kids any more than they already were. Never again would she trust another man.

Life really didn't get any better for Elsie, but at least she wasn't getting bopped around anymore. To survive, she took on any menial jobs she could get: she cleaned peoples' houses, mostly scrubbing floors. She did maid's work for the motels out on the pike in West Atlantic City (which required walking a few miles to and from work—with the kids), mostly cleaning up drunken messes. She sold apples on street corners and worked in a stocking factory. When there wasn't any work, she stole chickens and firewood to keep her kids fed and warm. As the years went by, she began looking forward to when the kids would be grown and off and on their own. Then—*oh* . . . that blissful *then*—she'd be able to begin life anew. Maybe go back and finish high school. Maybe travel. Maybe not have to work so hard. Maybe not have to worry so much. Just maybe . . .

Her plan was to come up with a plan. And so she worked tirelessly toward that *maybe* day doing unskilled factory labor and odd jobs to make ends meet and to provide for her kids; to be the best mother she knew how. Once the kids were gone, she would tell herself, she'd finally be able to get ahead. She had hope.

But then, seven years after what she thought was her last kid, she went and did it again. Men. Damned men. Needs. Damned needs. When David came along, she had to start all over. The price of weakness. Bad luck with men. Every time she looked at him she saw a reflection of failure and unfulfilled dreams—an emotional glitch the boy could sense, loud and clear.

David knew only a couple of things about *his* drunken jerk of a father: one was that he was not the father of his brother and two sisters. The other was that, except for the actual act of conception, his sire had never been present in his life—not even for one lousy second. About his mother, David knew basically two things, also: one was that she never really wanted him; that he was her biggest mistake; that he was the ruination of a future she was never to know. The other was that all she ever really wanted for dinner was boiled creamed corn with crackers.

Much later in life, David came to learn a third thing about his mother. It came to him slowly in a trickle of intuition. Similar to thinking about the definition of a word over a long period of time when, suddenly, without warning, it all makes perfect sense: you understand. You know the meaning. You've solved the problem. You get it. It took nearly half a century, but David eventually came to know that in spite of whatever he might have thought throughout the years about his mother and her motives, in spite of her nightly exhaustion, in spite of her desire to just eat corn and crackers, in spite of all the rough edges of her life, it finally became clear to him that his mother had fixed a full and complete dinner every night—just for his sake. It really didn't fix or make up for the bashings of his life. But it was, after all, something. Something that, when he thought about it, gave him a sort of peaceful feeling in the cockles of his heart.

Elsie never got to finish high school. She worked her fingers to the bone bringing up her kids, and she never earned more than five dollars an hour. Through all her hardships, she ended up a jolly yeasaying Mrs. Malaprop and a queen of mondegreens, whistling and making up goofy happy lyrics, singing her way through life. Relying on street smarts and innate intelligence, she also possessed a very large sense of humor. She was a good soul. Everybody liked Elsie. She never let her lack of education hold her back. She always found a way to get done what needed to be done, which was—caring for her children.

These were the thoughts swirling around David's mind as he gently patted his mom's forehead and stroked her cheeks, whispering words of comfort to her as she lay on her hospice bed, struggling for one last breath. Elsie died peacefully with David and her two daughters at her side, knowing that she was loved and appreciated for doing the best she could for all of her ninety-two years.

18

CALL MOTHER

Whenever there is
A spare moment in the day
Finishing up a project or
Commuting to or from work
There it is
There she is
An ancient impulse
Inculcated by guilt and
Reluctant affinity:
Call mother!
A clang of a thought
That pops up unexpectedly
Like clockwork
Talk to her about nothing
Get my feelings hurt
Talk more about nothing
Make up stupid stuff that
Will get us laughing uncontrollably

Poke fun at her
While dodging her barbs and threats of
"I'm going to bop you one when I see you!"
Resent her "I love yous"
At the end of each and every call
Stilted obligatory I love yous
That came far too late in my life
I love yous
I never heard
As a child
Get pissed off and swear:
"I will never ever call her again.
I do not love her.
Why do I do this to myself?"
But then I do, again and again and again . . .
And more so lately
Since she's been in a nursing home
Driving down Tilton Road
My two sisters in tow
On our way to meet our brother
At Adams-Perfect
To make arrangements
For mother's funeral
And while driving there
There it is
There's that thought:
Call mother!
Loud and clear
As if she needs to be informed
Of what we are about to do
On her behalf
And the girls agree
That they, too
Suffer the same affliction.
It's hard to break old habits.

OLD LOVES

P'VILLE, NJ (1954)

Oh, how I miss my old loves
Ah . . . , Barbara . . .
That beauty . . .
How my love endured—
      kindergarten through the fifth grade
She never paid me one iota of attention
Was convinced I had cooties
Believed those other kids
How dare her!
And it was she who had a ringworm
      who wore a turban
      the first time I laid my adoring eyes on her
      on the playground
      at Decatur Avenue Elementary

My first true love.
For her,
I would while away busy hours
At Lyons Court
Playing in the little polluted creek
That paralleled West Jersey Avenue
Across from her house
Mesmerized by the pond scum
That slothfully followed the railroad cinders
To the reedy marshes
Of West Atlantic City
Hopeful of a glimpse
That never came
An experience
That put an early end
To whatever stalking inclinations
I might have had
Then, an atomic blast: Deloris
What can I say: fine, fine, fine, fine . . .
Good-bye, Barbara.
Hello, classy Deloris.
And as I recall, she was at least cordial toward me
In fact,
She might have inspired my first lines
Of poetry
For her, I used to bleed devotion, desire, and
   deific line after deific line after deific line . . .
Some of which I discovered when I
Got out of the Navy
Pure schlock
But I could kick myself for not keeping it
Clear through the eighth grade
She filled my hormonal aspirations
Side by side with Jacqueline Lee Bouvier Kennedy.

Then, Nancy
About fourteen
Hot
Petite
Great dancer
Great legs
Teased bouffant beehive hairdo
One night on the front steps
Of her house on Delilah at Main
While my friend made out with—
Was it her older sister?
She blackened my neck with hickeys
And another night she let me "touch" her
On the back seat of a buddy's sky blue
'56 Ford
But she had this Port Republic boyfriend
What we called back then
A farm boy
Who wanted to and could easily
Beat my ass
So she really wasn't available
Nor did she care about me.
Enters Phyllis from Philly
Sublime . . .
An Ocean City shoobie from Philly
Very cool, very conservative, very Catholic
Whom I met at the Saturday
OC Convention Center dances
On the boardwalk
Handsome college jocks with cars and money
Pursued her
And the guys I knew
Wondered
How I landed such a fox

Whose father privately
Informed me
Like a mafia godfather
How he would dismember me
Were I to defile or disappoint
His precious offspring
And that I better not bring her home
Late
Which I did
Traveling by bus
From OC
To AC
To see
The Pink Panther
But at least we danced
And kissed
And talked
About what I haven't a clue
Until fate
Made me late
And terminate . . .

OLONGAPO, PI (1966)

Now, the prostitutes in the Philippines.
They were great loves, too
Who cared if they were screwing
The entire Seventh Fleet
They rubbed my feet
And treated me sweet
It was from them
That I learned
How to be (or not to be)
With a woman.
While my shipmates

Denigrated them
I fell in love
I wrote them
Nice letters
And bought them what I could
I visited their homes
And played with their children
And for that
There were times
When they would pay
Their own way
Out of the bar
Not charging me a cent
For their affections.
Sometimes
They would buy me
A Filipino size medium shirt
Which, of course, wouldn't fit
Or other little gifts
And for that
I have always stoked
A warm spot in my heart
For them
And their collective predicament
They helped me
To become
The
Sexually
Dysfunctional
Man
I
Was
Destined
To become . . .

LONG BEACH, CA > P'VILLE, NJ > ROGUE RIVER/ROSEBURG, OR > SF > LA (1971)

Which brings me to
Elizabeth.
Ah . . . , Liz . . .
What a saint
In reality
My first *real* girlfriend
She loved me
When I was so unable
To love myself
A little chore I am still working on.
We actually got married
Tried to make a go of it
But after eleven years
(Not bad for a first girlfriend.)
Immaturity, false values, drugs, and alcohol
Made short work of us
Things got ugly.
But now
I only remember the good stuff
How hard she worked
How she tried to make a good home
How she made me delicious lunches
To take to the million jobs
I quit or got fired from
How she gave me the only real birthday party
I have ever had
How she coddled me
And rocked me
So many times
As I lay in her arms
Asking me
What she could do to help

As I cried
As I whimpered
Enigmatically
That I
Was
A *bad* person
Writhing in the pain in my brain
In the dark of my heart
Oh, how I so regret
Disappointing her
Not being able
To be
A better man for her
But I was
But a boy . . .

MIAMI (1982)

Polita
Wanted me
And she got me
And it was as intense
As it was brief
For she caught me
In the middle of a suicidal
Alcoholic crossroads
To protect herself
She did what she had to do
She dumped me
From the great heights
To which she took me
Onto the wet
Dense sand
Of Miami Beach
Splat! Ouch!
Man, that hurt . . .

Worse than divorce
Death was the desirable
But I am still here
And it was she who
Against all odds
Helped me
To get sober.
Which means
I hooked-up with Lee
Yum, yum, yum Lee
A sober chick-on-a-stick
A decisive factor in my sobriety
Never once
Did we have
Intercourse
But, man, did we make out
Dry fucking
Like fourteen-year-olds
On the back seat of somebody else's car
Wet and wild and wonderful and exhausting
With her
I forgot about my wounded soul
She got me thinking
Of commitment
Of better things to come
Of strong love, soft love, true love
And then . . .
Abruptly
In the middle of the heat
She announced matter-of-factly:
"I'm sorry. I can't see you anymore.
        My old boyfriend and I will be
        moving in together."
Oooh . . . man, that hurt! . . .
Then, Bonnie bounced into

My life
Like a happy tennis ball
Joyous and full of life
A kindred soul
She made me feel legitimate
Awoke a political awareness in me
Made me feel worthy of love
And I loved her
Hard
But for all our efforts
All our best intentions
It didn't work.
And after we ended
It was a good six years
Of being alone
With only an occasional date
With nut cases
I was finished with love
I would let no one hurt me
Again

ANTIGUA, GUATEMALA (1998)

As a gift to me
From me
For my fiftieth birthday
It was off to Guatemala
To study Spanish
Where I met the love
To end all loves
My raison d'être
Where I stood
In a marketplace
That we had unexpectedly
Stumbled upon
A tapestry of sunny colors

Woven patterns
Mountains of tropical fruits
And vegetables on blankets
A palette of lovely possibilities
And it was right there
In this movie scene
From the greatest love story ever told
In front of God and all of Guatemala
I kissed her
Knowing
That this Québécoise
This Marie in my arms
Was a *divine* birthday gift
And for a blissful year
We talked and visited and planned
Our future
Our love
Our new lives together.
And when we met in Texas
On our way to Perú
I sensed something awry
But she dismissed it
And thirty days later
At the end of our trip
One night after dinner in Cuzco
She informed me matter-of-factly
That she would be
Getting back
With her
Estranged husband
While she sipped coffee and eviscerated
My heart and soul
It was crying time
Again . . .

LONG BEACH, CA (2001)

But the pains
Pushed me
Molded me
Opened me
Tenderized me
Made me ready
For new love
For Christine
For the hard love she gives me
Deeply
In spite of
My scales
My armor
My scars
My defenses
My fears
My numbness
My inadequacies
My rough edges
  And she loves my love
My, my . . .
  Finally,
   I am home.

PLANET EARTH (1948–2024)

Such is love
And the lack thereof
To paraphrase Willie Nelson:
There are no ex-loves
Only additional loves.

20

VISAGE

I shaved my Van Dyke off last night
Diminishing returns for vanity
Or at least that's my excuse
Always starts off low maintenance
Man!
That is not my face
That is not me
That is an old man
      with a square face
These can't be my eyes
      because they do not see
                    me
That is not my mouth
Those are not my cheeks
There is something almost perverse
      about me

So square
So aged
But it *is* me
Not really, me
My mother
Oh, how I see my mother
My brother
Oh, how I see my brother
My oldest friend
Oh, how I see Alberto
I got it! I got it. I got it . . .
New Jersey
It's the Jersey look
Timeworn
Urban country stock.

21

MYRTLE HOUSE

The concept of life is overwhelming. At least it always has been for me. *To be.* What a mind blower. To actually be alive. To be cognizant. To be sentient. To be responsible for one's actions. When one cogitates the immensity of the universe and the odds of ever coming into being at all, from the dutiful bee collecting pollen to me—life is truly a gift. Rare, fleeting, transitory. It is no wonder that no matter where you might travel on this exploited and defiled planet, you will most assuredly encounter peoples who have customs and memes that enshrine a Godhead within their individual and collective being. It might be in the form of a tree or a volcano or water. It might be a Higher Power, Divine Intelligence, Inti, or the Lord Jesus. Me? I call it Magoo.

From my sober coign of vantage forty-some years *post factum*, hindsight is 20/20. When I got out of the Navy in June of 1969, I do not think there was a more confused, unprepared, scared—no, terrified person walking on Mother Earth. I never got along well with my mother, and here I was twenty-one years old, absolutely clueless, and living with her in her tiny apartment in Pleasantville, New Jersey. In July, I sat on my bed consulting an eighth-grade science book I had swiped from Washington Avenue Junior High as the literal man on the moon on TV described its sandy powdery surface that in no way resembled the crusty rocky geography the textbook authoritatively limned. In August, I decided not to go to Woodstock because my gut feeling told me that it would be no big thing. And somewhere in the midst of all that, I met a gal at the Albany-Winchester Avenues bus stop in Atlantic City. When we got to P'ville, we got off at the East West Jersey Avenue bus station and continued to talk while standing in front of Frankie and Johnny's Sub Shop. Somehow, I got her to come back to my mother's place, where we had awkward sex. With her, I experienced my first American non-drunk cunnilingus. Later, she told me on the phone that she never wanted to see me again; that she "knew my type"; that she had "been hurt by my kind before," and that she was "never going to let it happen again." What on earth was she talking about? Was I a psycho and didn't know it, but she did? Things were not looking too good. But now I can see that Magoo was guiding me all the while—gently prodding me with an ice pick in my brain.

Psycho or not, I needed to pay my keep and help Mom. So I got a job. More precisely, I got smacked in the back of the head by one. My loving sister Kitty put in a good word for me with her then-husband Merv to get me on his gang of water workers. His dad owned a marine engineering company in Atlantic City, the A. C. Wescoat Company (the *A* stood for Albert), where Merv had pretty much worked all his life. Merv was a "man's man," a term that has always struck me as a mite homo. Anyway, he was one tough sonofabitch. A pip-squeak of a man who overcompensated for his diminutiveness by handily drinking a case of beer; mentally and physically abusing my sister; winning endless sailboat and water skiing competitions; messing around with other women; taking big tough men down while laughing loudly, making them cry uncle and beg for release from his killer leg-lock; and, humiliating me when I was a little boy for not being able to read the roadside billboards as we drove down the highway.

It would take some twenty years before my sister would dump out on Merv, and I would find out that he was a functional illiterate. In many ways, he was a working man's savant, a genius. He could build a house. A dock. Dredge a waterway. Read blueprints. Build precise, trophy-winning sailboats. Hunt deer, duck, mud hen, and bear. Merv could figure anything out. But he couldn't read. All those Sundays, I remember him sitting at the kitchen table browsing the *Atlantic City Press* with his morning coffee. As a kid, I thought he was reading—but he was just looking at pictures and checking scores. Anyway, he got me on with his crew. Clearly, he got me the job at the behest of my sister because he never once lifted a finger to help or teach or guide me in any direction. Being fresh meat with only my clerical yeomanly skills at hand, I took the job.

Out of the gate, we were off towing a scow from Atlantic City up the Delaware Bay. Captain Sharpy, a tawny plug of a man in the obligatory nautical khakis, sporting a matching salty ball cap cocked to the right, gazed up at my youthful six-foot-fourness, his head tilted in skepticism. With about an inch of Lucky Strike and as much ash hanging out of the left nook of his mouth, he squinted and inquired, "You don't get seasick, d'ya boy?"

"Seasick? I just got out of the Navy."

"Good. Can't use nobody gets seasick."

And off we went.

Another company had rented a scow and was finished with it. They'd left it anchored in the waters off of Atlantic City's then still-somewhat-famous Steel Pier, and had hired A. C. Wescoat to tow it back to its owner. We delicately approached the vessel and Captain Sharpy's crew of three hopped to like a bunch of agile grasshoppers doing this and doing that—everyone knowing what everyone else was knowing. All action. Monosyllables. Hand signals. I stood there, useless. The scow bobbed up. The tug bobbed down. Beautifully coiled hawsers were attached to the scow.

Merv was in his element. With lightning speed, his lithe sinewy frame flitted from chore to chore like a determined butterfly. One day, when I was working with him alone on a barge, a cloudless sunny day, he paused and looked skyward. I looked up, too, wondering what he was looking at. After a bit he grunted, "Huht! Gonna rain. Put the tools away, David." Shortly thereafter, clouds began to scud in and by the time we wrapped things up, it was pouring. Driven by an innate love for the outdoors, Merv was the essence of a real-life shark hunter Quint.

I don't think we had passed Margate yet when I got sick as a dog, which turned out to be great entertainment for the crew who yuk-yukked and te-heed and made stupid jokes. Captain Sharpy told me to go below and sleep it off.

As I lay in my bunk, humiliated, I focused on not throwing up. After a while, I started to feel a little better. I opened my eyes and allowed my gaze to rest on the pure azure I could see though the open door that led out to the main deck aft. Nothing but beautiful sky. That is, until the damned scow bobbed up. Scow up. Tug down. Tug up. Scow down. The nausea intensified. I lost it.

After a good nap, I awoke fresh as a daisy. The bobbing scow had no effect on me now. I felt fine. The storm had passed. I put my best sea legs on and went up to the bridge. Captain Sharpy had probably told the boys to go easy on me because they all hushed and restrained their smiles and snickers as I entered the wheelhouse, chin held high. Captain Sharpy, with a Lucky hanging out of his mouth, squinting through a trail of smoke, gave me a kindly smile, "Feeling better, boy?"

"Yes, sir. I think I'm OK now," as I tamped and opened a pack of Winstons.

"Awww . . . , that's OK, kid. We all get sick at first," one of the crew offered.

"Huht-huht. This ain't no Navy boat," Merv pointed out.

"Yep, this is a little different than being on one of those big Navy barges," Captain Sharpy agreed.

I lit a cigarette and took a deep hit as I scanned the beautiful ocean before us. They were right. The Navy was nothing like this. Except for the low thrumming rumble of the engine, we all stood in pure silence. Then, like a sucker punch, it hit me. Something about the smoke made me sick all over. The vomit shot up. I had to clasp my hand over my mouth to keep from puking. As I ran outside, the roar of uncontrolled laughter followed me to the gunwale, where, heaving my guts out, I could hear:

"Go aft! Go aft!"

"Don't do it on the windward! Go leeward!"

"Huht! You make a mess, you clean it up!"

We came around Cape May that night. Captain Sharpy piloted us into the Delaware, guided by years of experience and a spotlight that swept the dark calm waters before us. I was amazed to see so many trees growing in the bay. I had never seen anything like it. Trees were everywhere. I later learned that the waters were very shallow and that the locals stuck saplings all over the bay to mark their respective oyster beds.

On the way back, I was sitting on the main deck with Merv doing some sort of nautical chore. While we worked, he expounded on his highly scientific reasoning why it was not natural for a man, i.e., hippies, to have long hair. Women were designed to have long hair; men were not. Hence, were I to persist in allowing my locks to grow, I should soon be bald. That voyage with Merv was my own personal heart of darkness. But it wasn't over yet.

A. C. Wescoat got a job building bulkheads for a housing development that was being created out of thin air on the Intracoastal Waterway in Ventnor, just south of the Albany Avenue Bridge. This involved driving pilings behind which bulkheads were built. Once the specified area was enclosed, the bay would be dredged and its toxic sludge deposited behind the bulkheads—and voilà!—real estate where there had been none. Pile driving is hard work. And while my abilities were limited, I was willing to jump in and do my share and more of the work. My first day on the job; I wanted to prove myself. I was on my best behavior. After the chill of the morning wore off, it got hot, so I took off my shirt. Jersey heat is profound. I worked hard. Show me what to do and I'll do it. I hugged pilings and pushed and shoved planks. The sun beat down and creosote from the treated wood lathered my arms, my face, and my chest. I was a water worker.

That day, they hired a guy named Joey DiGiacinto, with whom I used to hang out when we were teenagers. He just walked up to the site and asked about work. I couldn't believe my eyes or ears as I listened to the on-site pre-hire interview. Joey DiGiacinto? A qualified dock builder? He whom I knew as a helpless incompetent and shameless liar when I left off with him back in '65? Who could hardly tie his own shoelaces? Whose most salient talents were building AMT model cars and accurately mimicking the engines of various souped-up cars? About twenty minutes after he started, they canned his ass because he didn't know the first thing about pile driving.

Anyway, a good day's work had been done and it was time to go home. Four of us crammed into a pickup with our lunchboxes. I would be the first dropped off in Pleasantville. The rest would continue on to Absecon. As we drove across the rotten-egg-smelling tidal marshes along the Black Horse Pike, the boys started talking quite cheerfully about what a bad idea it was for me to have taken off my shirt and allowing myself to get covered with creosote; that creosote combined with a good sunburn, well, I was in for an interesting experience.

"What do you mean, an interesting experience?"

"Huht. Hell, David, you never want to take your shirt off when you're working with creosote," Merv sagely informed me.

"Damn, everybody knows that," the driver chimed in.

"But what do you mean, I'll be in for an *interesting* night?"

The other joker chimed in, "When'ya get'cha home what'cha wanna do is get'cha in the hot bathtub, real hot, now, with lotsa Epsom salts. Make it hot. Real hot. Hot as ya c'n take it. Let ya'self soak in that as long as ya c'n take it. That'll take care v'ya. Hee-hee! ... "

As the billboards flashed by, I practiced reading them. The chills started coming on. The crew giggled and te-heed all the way and talked in their special water worker cant: goofy boyish guttural sounds, arcane technical remarks, and poking fun—all followed by riotous gales of laughter. Something primal. Though I was sandwiched inside the cab with them, I felt like I was in the midst of an out-of-body experience. The heat and chills were intensifying. Their voices were a million miles away. I was keenly aware that I was an unwelcome outsider. I could never be one of them. That night, I suffered excruciating pain, just as they'd all known I would the moment they saw me take off my shirt.

Needless to say, I wasn't cut out to be a water worker. One morning, after about three weeks with A. C. Wescoat Company, I was handed my little manila envelope with about $86 cash for the previous week's work and was told that I was no longer needed; that they were "cutting back." Right.

Pie was a Navy buddy. His last name was Pietrias. For the life of me, I can't remember his first name. It really doesn't matter, though, because in the Navy everyone calls you something else. (For a while, I was Billy, but that's another story.) Pie was just a buddy. Not a great buddy. Not a friend. Just a buddy. He freaked out one time during a sparring match on our ship and beat the shit out of me. I still have a crushed right pinkie metacarpal head as a souvenir from blasting his insane glassy-eyed stoic cinder block of a face that day. Violence was not uncommon while cruising the South China Sea. In fact, violence was the very reason we were plying the South China Sea. War, even if you're just floating around safely on a ship, makes people crazy. Anyway, Pie was a just-got-out-of-the-Navy-too-New Jersey-home-boy buddy.

During those first couple of months of post-Navy fear-inducing freedom, I went up to Pie's place in Camden a few times. In his world, I learned about kielbasa. I met his sister, who impressed the hell out of me because she loved to travel alone and make friends when she got to wherever she was going. And I got to take in a couple of concerts at Rutgers. Wired on amphetamines one time, I watched Janis Joplin guzzle half a bottle of Southern Comfort in the wings where she had sought refuge during the instrumental portion of whatever song she was singing. Another time, I almost shook my head off in a frenzy of speed as the Guess Who nearly rocked the small venue off its foundation. Somehow, Pie found an advertisement in the local paper where some guy was looking for someone to help drive his car to LA and share the expenses. We took that as our cue.

I don't remember much about the drive out. But I do know that while Pie and that other guy slept, I got that massive luxurious glacier blue four-door chrome-laden 1960 Chrysler Imperial with its space-age taillight fins and giant donut whitewall tires up to about 120 mph driving across those flat barren states, without them ever knowing the jeopardy they were in. I remember hearing Bobby Dylan's "Lay Lady Lay" for the first time on that trip, with cacti, mesas, and pinnacles slowly passing us by in the distance as I glided us into our respective futures. And I remember the two of those guys freaking out about not wanting to drive through LA during rush hour. Fibber that I was, I lied to them and said that I had driven in LA's crazy traffic many times; that I would be glad to do it for them. Like a pro, blinkered like a dopy horse, I drove through Hollywood and on to Long Beach without them having any idea how scared I was. That was my first time. Thankfully, that little lie has paid me big dividends. For years, I drove sixty miles round trip—Long Beach to Burbank—every day for work. Pure insanity.

I have no idea how it all came about, but Pie and I ended up renting an apartment in Long Beach. It was a nice little clapboard two-bedroom affair above a garage behind a home on Molino, just off of Seventh Street. My first time ever sharing living quarters with anyone besides my mother and the two thousand guys I'd bunked with on the USS *Valley Forge* (LPH-8).

I don't think we had a sheet or pillowcase in that place. What in the hell did we sleep on, bare mattresses? I'm sure we went out and bought some household items, like a trash can and a couple of throw rugs, but our apartment had all the trappings of two guys without a clue. I remember wandering the streets of Long Beach trying to figure out how to get a job. I had no idea how to go about looking for work. I was quite the functional illiterate at the time myself, and I painfully recall sitting in offices at my wits' end, trying to fill out job applications. I always ended up leaving humiliated, especially whenever there was a little math or spelling test. I was also ashamed of my scratchy penmanship.

And Pie was no help. He went his way, and I went mine. I had hippie aspirations and dropped acid, smoked dope, and got speedy. Pie, he drank and got loud. Booze made him squinty-eyed and belligerent. At times, I was scared of him because he would get mean and egg for a fight. It was like he had a need to strike out. Hit something. Anything. I don't think we ever had one serious conversation about anything. Ever. Our connection was tenuous. It wasn't even like we needed or depended upon one another. Sure, we had some good laughs, but we were just two free-floating souls, untethered and far from our mother ships. Essentially, I was alone. Nevertheless, rooming with Pie was instructive.

As my discharge date from the Navy had neared, I feared with looming suspicion that I was ill-prepared for life as a civilian. I had been left back in the second and fourth grades and was about to be left back again, at age seventeen, in my freshman year. Fs and Ds were my favorite grades. A fine motivation to join the Navy. Escape P'ville. The Molino sojourn with Pie left no doubt—I was flat-out helpless. While I had passed my high school GED by one-tenth of one percent of one point in the Navy, I was aware that quitting school in the ninth grade was not exactly helping me out. So, in a fruitless effort to do something about that, I spent a few of my fast dwindling dollars on *High School Subjects Self Taught*. But I never did anything serious with that book. I couldn't—couldn't read, couldn't write, couldn't cipher. But I still have that book, and I recently started reading it in earnest. I think of it as the cup of water that was necessary to prime the pump.

It finally got down to no money. Couldn't pay the rent. Wheaties, mayonnaise, and orange slices made a delicious meal. I don't even remember how we parted ways, but I know that I stuck my thumb out and was back at Mom's house in no time, tail wagging between my legs. But before I left, I told my Navy buddy Brother Larry that I was only going back to NJ for one year to make some money; that I would be back. One step forward; two steps back.

BACK

It wasn't easy on Mom, which means it wasn't easy on me. Our chauffeur's quarters at 40 East Verona Avenue—"in the rear"—was a tiny turn-of-the-century red-brick with dark brown shake shingle siding on its upper story, and a roof of red clay pantiles that matched the once-palazzo-turned-American Legion, behind which we resided from the time I was about eight years old. What the old mansion didn't have that we had was this quaint portico on two sides that was supported by concrete Tuscan columns that sat on an unslushed red brick herringbone walkway. As you approached our front door, a couple of white dogwoods sentineled the left entrance. To the right, a good-sized fishpond was shaded by a large ancient holly tree and an even larger oak. As a kid, I spent a lot of time up in those dogwoods and that old oak figuring out the meaning of life, or at least scheming on how to get out of whatever trouble I had managed to get myself into. The erstwhile chateau's back yard was our front yard.

A substantial Mediterranean-Spanish-Moorish-Italian stucco wall with statuary niches and ponderous gates with oversized hand-wrought hardware had been erected to keep out the commonalty. Seasonally, the perimeter of the yard would explode into a perfect square of blinding lemon yellow daffodils.

But the fishpond was a turbid bog—a stagnant breeding ground for mosquitos, filled with years of decaying holly leaves. There was no statuary. The stucco wall was crumbling. The gates hung warped from years of disuse and gravity. The portico's roof was decaying, its tarry stony surface constantly crashing to pepper the brick herringbone walkway that was missing bricks here, there, and everywhere. Several windows on the Legion had been boarded up. Its paint was peeling and the mortar between its two stories of red brick was succumbing to weather and time. But the world inside our tiny home was immaculate. "Just because you're poor doesn't mean you have to dress like a bum or live in filth," was one of Mom's favorite mantras. The house was Mom's kingdom. She ruled. And I was an unwelcome guest. There were rules. I followed them or I knew where the door was. But I had never followed the rules before—why would I want to start? My return to P'ville in scared retreat from Long Beach was the beginning of a good stretch of frustration for us both. Under the circumstances, we did the best we could. While she drove me to the brink of matricide, we also had lots of laughs. Always lots of laughs.

I must have gotten straightaway into looking for work because somehow I managed to get a job as a carpenter's helper with a small framing crew out of Mays Landing. I remember driving Mom's green 1961 Pontiac Tempest back home from my job interview. South Jersey has lots of long straight narrow country roads, and it's real easy to get caught up in the monotony that, year after year, lulls hundreds of folks to their early demise. At some point as I was driving, a spider dropped down in front of me and I freaked. A blast of bitter cold air filled the car as I swished, flailed, and swatted, trying to wrangle the little guy out the window. When I finally looked up, a brief eon later, I was on the wrong side of the road with a car coming at me. *Where the hell did that come from!* A rather attractive thirty-something white woman was the sole occupant of the oncoming projectile. Her face was bleeding with fear. As we approached our respective moments of death—eyes locked upon one another—I could clearly see, in slow motion, that she was screaming in silence and that her bulging insect eyes were about to pop out and flop down onto her cheeks. Following some primal instinct, I whipped to my left, drove up onto the yellow gravel embankment, came back down behind her, and got back into my lane. No harm done. Off I went. A harbinger of things to come.

My first day on that job introduced me to the concept that anything is possible. When I joined the Navy, I wanted to be an aviation jet mechanic. Why? Not because I knew anything about jets or engines. Nope. I asked for that because my brother had been a jet mechanic. But my eyes were bad and they wouldn't even consider me. Before I got "shit-canned" down to the boiler room, which was akin to doing time on a chain gang, I was a plumber's helper. Eventually, though, with help from my buddy Bobby Dunkirk, who just happened to be from Camden and who saved my rear end on many occasions, I learned to type and got a job as a yeoman in the Engineering Office. A yeoman is really a glorified clerk typist, but it's a position, nevertheless, of certain cachet, limited power, and privilege. So, my skill set upon discharge as regards the handicraft trades was pretty much, well, nothing. When I arrived on site my first day up in Mays Landing, the boss man he says, "David, you see that big stack of lumber over there?" which was about half a block away from the foundation, "Well, they dropped it off in the wrong place. It needs to be over here. Right here. In this spot." So, that's what I did for the first couple of days. I physically carried an entire four-bedroom two-story double garage house from one place to the other. And to this day, I am grateful for that experience because I can pretty much carry anything and move heavy awkward objects without any help.

I knew I was crazy. I knew I had problems. My thinking was twisted. I needed help. So I worked it out with boss man for me to take some time off to get some professional help. I had originally tracked down Dr. Fields, who had been my childhood psychiatrist, and had explained to him that I had lied to him when I was a kid, but that I was ready to work with him now and that I really wanted and needed help. He was very kind, but explained that he was afraid that I wouldn't be able to afford his $125/hr. rate, so he referred me to a county clinic in Atlantic City. (Many years later, I would learn that Dr. Fields had committed suicide in a motel off the White Horse Pike in Absecon, where he had been living alone for several years.)

When I showed up at the clinic, I went into an office with a woman who started asking me questions. I poured out my heart and soul. This time I was going to do it right. I forced myself to talk about sex thoughts and inferiority and confusion and anger and being crazy and being stupid. I cried. I cried a lot. Then, after all of that dumping, she smiled and asked, "Would you like a man or a woman as your therapist?"

I was dumbfounded. "What do you mean? Aren't you my therapist?"

"Oh, no. I'm the secretary. I just do the intake and assign you to a therapist. Would you prefer a man or a woman?"

"You fucking let me sit here and spill my fucking guts out and you don't tell me that you're the fucking secretary! What the fuck's wrong with you! . . ."

Everything was pretty much a fog between her and me sitting in the therapist's office. There were forms to be filled out. Waiting to be done. Clearly, I had ended up at either a mafia therapy clinic or was in the *Twilight Zone*. I remember the therapist being a white scruffy short-bearded man in his mid to late thirties. He sat and listened to me intently. I told him how the secretary had deceived me. I tried my best to muster up the drama of my life's story. He listened more intently. He squinted. He leaned in toward me and skrinkled his brow. He nodded and gave me little grunts of acknowledgment. When I had finished listing my concerns, he paused, leaned back in his chair, and looked up at the ceiling. After a bit, I looked up to see what he was looking at. Then he swooped down and looked me right dead in the eye:

"I know what your problem is, David. It's a common problem. I see it all the time these days. Are you ready? OK. I'm going to tell you. You're lazy. You're lazy. You're lazy and you expect the world to baby you. You think society owes you something. Well, I'll tell you something, mister—nobody owes you shit! You're in here taking up my time and wasting taxpayers' money on your petty little insignificant selfish needs. You should be ashamed of yourself for even coming here and wasting our time. My secretary should have kicked you out. Get out of here and don't come back! Stop taking drugs!" So I left, nonplussed, pissed, demoralized, and all the worse for my effort.

I had gotten to be a pretty good rough carpenter. Built my own toolbox. I could cut a straight line and drive a sixteenpenny common with two smacks. I was liked. I was productive. I was trusted and had received a couple of unsolicited pay raises. But there were some big *buts* to the whole affair. For instance, I would far too frequently smack my left thumb with my 22 ounce framing hammer in the bitter freezing cold winter, and the humid sweltering life-sucking New Jersey summer made death look appealing. Then there was the fact that I wasn't any too sharp in the math department. Thus my career as a budding carpenter didn't last long—setting a precedent for the myriad jobs I would bulldoze through for the rest of my life. So my mom, having a vested interest—namely, paying the rent—in my being employed intervened and got me a job at Lenox China.

Word always was that in the early 1950s Lenox had closed up shop in Trenton in response to labor demands for better pay and better working conditions. Whether there is any truth to this or not, I don't know, but there was ample negative attitude amongst the locals toward the company. Lenox, along with Wheaton Glass, controlled the labor market in South Jersey. If you didn't work for one of them, you knew someone who knew someone who worked for one of them. It was considered a good job to have.

I worked in shipping. As it would turn out, I ended up doing less work and making more money than my mother, and she had been working there about ten years or so. On top of that, my work was easier all around. In a parching environment, she spent all day next to hot kilns performing the mind-deadening repetitive eye-straining task of inspecting china while dancing to the tune of the ever-increasing production line. Inspection was where the buck stopped. For this highly skilled but underappreciated talent that sucked the life out of her each and every day, she was paid $1.75/hr., while I got to screw off for $1.98/hr. Those were the times, and that was Lenox.

I don't think more than a few days had passed when Albie showed up on the job. Hop. Hoppy. AB. Alberto. A. B. Hopcroft. Hustler. Petty ex-con.

Artist. Was I glad to see him! As it would turn out, we secretly became the ruination of the shipping department. We were on somewhat similar paths in life and we had absolutely no respect or appreciation for Lenox China. It was a job, and we needed a job.

The last time I saw Alberto was when we were somewhere in our early teens in the waiting room at Dr. Slotoroff's office in Pleasantville. Dr. George Slotoroff, an old-fashioned family doctor. He had delivered me and practically everyone I have ever known in P'ville and environs. My mom told me that for Dr. Slotoroff to come to our apartment (at 111 South Main Street, on top of Bolf's Meat Market) in the wee hours of June 27, 1948, and bring me into this lovely world, at about 1 a.m., she had paid him $60 cold cash. The Slotoroffs had it covered. For eyes, you went to a Slotoroff. For teeth, you went to a Slotoroff. A Slotoroff was tangentially taking care of my mom right up to the time she died at Meadowview Nursing Home a few years ago. I say *tangentially* because now the kindly family practitioner has gone by the wayside. While care came through a young Slotoroff's office, Mom was most often seen by one of his "associates." It gave her comfort, knowing that a Slotoroff was somewhere in the dimming picture.

Anyway, I had just dropped from Planet Navy back into the doldrums of South Jersey and was in need of the insane creativity Alberto would bring into my life. He had an energy that was robust and the last thing he needed was the amphetamines I was holding at the time.

Alberto was married to Briana. They lived with their baby Derrick in a trailer park out past Cardiff on the Black Horse Pike under the Forest Fire Service fire tower. Briana was intelligent. Tall and blond and beautiful and strong and classy. And I loved her because she treated me with a special tender deference that said she knew that of all the men in her Albie's life, I was, in fact, his friend, and to be trusted. She put up with a lot. Alberto was wild. An untamed pony suffering from emotional damages too numerous to be catalogued, all blent up with extreme intelligence and creativity. Now, mind you, I've never felt very talented myself, but I have never doubted my ability, my special knack, to recognize talent in others. Alberto was a painter and my gut told me that he had the potential to be a great painter.

From the get-go, we started hanging out and getting high. Sometimes I would drive Mom's Tempest, sometimes I would hitchhike out to Alberto and Briana's to hang out. Alberto and I would get wired up, smoke a little dope, and quietly listen to Joe Cocker, *Let it Bleed* and such (keeping it down for the baby), and talk talk talk talk talk about who knows what, and smoke cigarettes. All the while, Briana would be in the bedroom smoking and watching TV or reading. Every now and then, she'd make appearances to get something from the fridge or whatever. It was a bit strange, but it was what it was. They were my friends.

Then came the Walkers—Alberto's cousins: Ronnie and Danny (aka the Moose). They were of the famous Macalister clan that had lived for years out at the end of English Creek Road in McKee City on what used to be Granny and Pop Macalister's pig farm. Always on the scene were Martha (Ronnie and the Moose's mom who knew everything about everybody all the time) and Uncle Chet, who drank hard, spoke in his proprietary idiolect about things like shinnywanators, wore gumboots, and had built swimming pools with a pick and shovel back in the '60s and '70s. Each an interesting character worthy of a story. Ronnie was married to Hera, and they lived with their five kids in a trailer next to Granny and Pop—and they weren't but twenty-three or twenty-four years old at the time. The Moose was living with an unmemorable gal named Mattie with whom he had a child in a trailer park at the end of Washington Avenue, just before the circle. But that was all very fleeting for the Moose. I always thought of him as single and unattached. Anyway, we all ended up hanging out and getting loaded together.

Ronnie was one of those lucky types who seemed to always win, always land on his feet. He was a talented carpenter with a good union job that would allow him to retire at fifty-five with a tidy pension. The Moose seemed to be in and out of work, but mostly out. Ronnie always had wads of money. The Moose usually had only enough to buy too much junk food. And Alberto and I were hovering somewhere in between because we had our excellent low-paying jobs at Lenox. All relationships are hierarchical, like it or not. Pecking order is a reality. Ronnie was a good-looking, smart, amoral Robert Redford-type New Jersey hick to whom women were attracted. He was always screwing someone somewhere—an indulgence that caused his head to be smashed on the concrete stoop outside of John's Bar on the Black Horse Pike one night, by an enraged cuckold. The Moose, well, he had a kid when I first met him, but that was that. Short lived. The child stayed with his ex. His real romance was dope and food. Alberto, he had beautiful Briana and beautiful little Derrick. And then, there was me. I had no female contact whatsoever. Other than my mother, that is, and we pretty much fought all the time. In fact, aside from making out with some girls after dances and at parties in my teens and sexual relations with prostitutes when I was in the Philippines, I had never had a girlfriend. My first sex was with a thirty-five-year-old gentle and caring Filipina prostitute in Manila. I had no idea how to interact with women. All of my notions were the product of listening to other stupid guys and a goofball woman at Dot's soda shop on Main Street in P'ville who showed us boys grotesque photos of men and women afflicted with elephantiasis, which she assured us was the result of masturbation and having sex. Per her, another consequence to sexual *anything*—thoughts, masturbation, intercourse, or whatever—was pimples.

From that post-Navy affectionally arid period of my life, I learned that an utter lack of feminine contact can distort a man's personality so much so as to reverse the natural order of things. It will snatch from him the opportunity to develop into a well-adjusted sexual being by wringing the life out of him, leaving him to suffer quietly in a neurotic state of asexual beinghood rife with confusion, doubt, and self-abasement; to walk around feeling like an anomaly, a defective twisted freak. Mix all that up with pot, acid, barbiturates, hash, lots of beer, blackberry brandy, immaturity, and plain old hillbilly ignorance—man, what an *amour-propre* I had going on for me then. But the times were formative and I was growing in spite of my own worst efforts.

I enrolled in a sketching course at an adult school in Atlantic City. The instructor and her husband would take a trip every year, and after each trip, the husband would do watercolors of what they had seen. Then they would revisit those locations to see how close he had gotten. He did beautiful stuff. Of all the media, though, watercolors and reverse glass painting seem to be the most difficult to me. I've tried them both. I might as well be a three-year-old. As far as the course went, however, I wasn't half-bad.

While I was a hack with no real talent, Alberto was forging ahead in real time. He had met this guy named Milty, who was studying art in AC and who had invited Alberto to work with him sometime. Alberto asked me if I wouldn't mind modeling nude because my lank angular sharp-boned amphetamined body would be a good workout for a charcoal session. I remember having a millisecond's worth of hesitation. Uncharacteristic of me, I immediately put it to rest. Nothing funny was going on. I trusted Alberto implicitly. It was one of the few times in my life that I didn't allow inhibition to cheat me out of experience. This was *art*.

Over in the Inlet at the north end of Atlantic City, Milty and his lady had one of those nice airy bay-windowed clapboard seaside apartments just down the street from Captain Starn's seafood restaurant. The night Alberto and I went over there to Milty's, it was all business. As I held my positions on a sheet on the floor, lit by practical table lamps, I watched and listened intently as they did their thing. Silently, they scratched their pads, smudging and blending their fusain renderings; Milty offering a quiet comment or suggestion now and then. I was a little mouse in the presence of Rembrandt and Van Gogh—a metaphor that history may one day prove to be accurate. While I always had artistic inclinations (writing forlorn love poems to girls who rejected me that I never gave to them), I can pinpoint that night as the exact moment when I realized that art is not just a flaky pastime; that it is something innate, worthy of being cultivated and nurtured.

Alberto pushed himself. He studied art at a community center in Linwood, took courses at Stockton State, and, through a friend, finagled himself into classes at the Art Institute of Philadelphia without being enrolled. Years later, when he skidded to a full dead stop in a puddle of life's exigencies and doubt, I told him on the phone that the one talent I had was the talent to recognize talent in others; that he had talent; that he would be a fool to give up and let his talent go to waste. As I write these words so many years down the pike, while he has not received wild acclaim and riches, Alberto Bishop Hopcroft has indeed developed into a world-class plein-airist.

Me? I somehow stumbled upon a compilation of Kenneth Rexroth poems back then and began writing poetry in earnest. The only problem was that amphetamines had my mind inhibited, diluted, and deluded. I knew enough to use writing as an escape valve for my self-diagnosed insanity, but I obscured my every thought; every word was cloaked for fear of being *found out*. I thought I was clever. But when I shared some of my work with Alberto, being the good and ruthless friend that he was, he loudly lambasted me with, "Dude! A lot of good fucking words scribbled here, but what the *fuck* does it *meeean*? Great exercise, but what good is it if nobody knows what you're talking about? It doesn't mean anything!" Hmmm . . . I'm still working on it.

How I "stumbled upon a compilation of Kenneth Rexroth poems" is an interesting sidebar. You see, Pleasantville was a very segregated town. It has been a lifelong ongoing joke for me to tell people that I am from the South—South Jersey, that is. But Pleasantville was and is more South than many would like to admit. There were some places black people just did not live. East West Jersey Avenue was one of those places. However, a few doors east of the El Lidro bar, I discovered this obscure little bookstore one day. It wasn't exactly a storefront. It was more like a just-off-the-street-in-a-driveway front. If it had a sign at all, it was just some piece of cardboard thrown in the window. I don't even know how I noticed it. I had walked past that way millions of times when I was a kid and it had always been a residential dwelling. It had been converted into a tiny storefront, a little personal cornucopia of literature; a world of ideas and words and concepts. But for whom? It was so out of place in Pleasantville. I only went there a handful of times, but I don't believe I ever saw another customer there. It was as though it had appeared just for me. Something out of *The Twilight Zone*. To top it off, it was owned and operated by a black man who looked just like a therapist I would have many years later in San Francisco. I remember him being helpful, gentle, and very reasonable about his pricing. Somehow, it had filtered down to me that he was a "child molester," but I never gave credence to the accusation, considering, well, considering that he was an intellectual black man living on East West Jersey Avenue in not-so-Pleasantville. The place had a good vibe, and it was in that anachoristic pint-sized nameless bookstore that I chanced upon Kenneth Rexroth. The poetry bar instantly rose from arm's length to the distant gravipause toward which my eyes are still cast.

Lenox was a joke. At least it was for Alberto and me. Al the security guard entertained us with stories about Eddie Rickenbacker, while doing the soft shoe and singing "Loving You Has Made Me Bananas" and "Flat Foot Floogie (with a Floy Floy)." In the warehouse, there was a mountain of baled newspapers that were constantly being shredded for packing orders. When we had down time, us shippin' guys would have to help stack that mountain. One day, I got the bright idea to build a bulwark around the top to make the giant stack of bundles look higher than it was, leaving a recessed area where one could hide out and take a nap. Kind of a fort. Alberto and I kept it a secret from the other guys and would take our turns up there. Sometimes we'd both hide out and hear the foreman walking through the warehouse yelling, "Hopcroft! Betterton! Anyone seen those two?"

Because we were both wired on amphetamines fairly frequently, we talked a blue streak, causing the other workers to think we actually *knew something*. Union negotiations were coming up, and they asked us to represent the Brotherhood of Potters Local 236. Alberto and I had to convince them that we didn't know what we were talking about half the time and that we were no match for the army of corporate lawyers Lenox would use to whittle away our wages and benefits.

One day, Alberto and I contrived a joke whereby I would scrunch down inside a shipping box and he would wheel me over on a hand truck to the smoke/break area where the fellas hung out by the vending machines that dispensed coffee, cocoa, a most delicious toxic chicken soup, and peanut butter crackers—all at twenty cents a pop. When he set the box down, that would be my cue to leap out. As he trundled me across the expansive warehouse floor, I devised and rehearsed my planned *Wizard of Oz* scarecrow routine, chomping at the bit to do my thing. This would be one of our most creative endeavors to date. Then, precipitously, the world stopped. I heard muffled unintelligible conversation. The box slowly arced down to rest on the floor. Showtime! I closed my eyes, went into deep concentration, and mustered all of my energy to explode like a volcano up and out of that box, yelling my best bestial theatrical, *"Surprise!"* Then I stood there with my arms outstretched and flopping for maximum effect. When I opened my eyes, directly in front of me stood our general manager calmly staring at me. Directly behind him were about seven or eight Japanese businessmen, each one moon-eyed and agape. And about fifty feet behind them stood all the guys on break, silently cracking up. With suave reserve, the GM said, "Betterton, I will talk to you about this later." Then, turning to his astonished guests, "Gentlemen, now, if we may continue . . . ," and he led them away touting the Lenox system. He pulled me aside later for the obligatory reprimand that amounted to, "If it wasn't for your mother, I would fire you. Don't ever do anything like that again." And that was the end of it.

Another thing we would have to do, when there were no trucks to be loaded or orders to be lined up on the warehouse floor, was to store the ware on the shelves. It was an incredibly boring job, so we would have to create ways of making it tolerable. One of the ways Alberto and I would do that was to play a game in which we'd toss ware to one another because one of us would be closer to the storage bin. It went something like, oh!-here-comes-a-$70-bowl-oops!-I-missed-it-crash!-smash! . . . oh!-here-comes-a-$120-vase-oops!-I'm-sorry-I-missed-that-too-smash!-to-smithereens! We were horrible. All these other poor schmucks working to make a living, and here we were with no respect for any of it. We knew that Lenox—"China of the US Presidents"—was just a capitalist pig exploiting the vulnerable masses of South Jersey. A couple of years before my mother's death, Lenox would send her a polite letter telling her that they could no longer afford to pay for the healthcare she had worked twenty-five years for. Just like that. Health insurance gone. Once she made a money-saving suggestion that was implemented and has saved Lenox many millions. They gave her a five-dollar gift certificate. The company has been bought and sold, with each transaction surely maximizing profits for the new owners by outsourcing and cutting back on wages and benefits. I just went online to see how Lenox is doing. It's now part of Clarion Capital Partners, LLC, who bought the "bankrupt" Lenox for $100 million. Bastards.

So, there I was . . . stuck in P'ville. Learning what, I did not know. Twenty-one and living at home with my mom. Transitioning from the stupidity of war to being a civilian. Driving around in a black, four-door-half-alive-puttering 1950 Chevy I'd bought for ninety bucks. I was a rat on a treadmill. Going nowhere. Going nowhere, and aware of it.

Then the phone rang. The instantly recognizable voice on the other end said, "H-h-h-hey, Billy . . . , a year's up, man. When you comin' back, brother? . . ." It was my Brother Larry. Gabriel blowing his message: Do something! Do something! Do something! His reference to me as *Billy* was in reference to the sobriquet some Navy boys in R-Division had bestowed upon me because I once smacked a guy in the head with a billy club in a dispute over three dollars. Nothing I'm proud of.

At night, after work, it was always something to figure out what to do. Mom was early to bed and our tiny apartment had to be quiet. Had I not been just an inch this side of being a functional illiterate, I could have read books. But getting loaded was always the goal. Much easier than getting laid. After my tenure as a water worker with Merv and the boys, I hooked-up with old Joey DiGiacinto and his Atlantic City crowd, a merry band of misfits and up-and-coming junkies. Joey was the most unfaithful, traitorous, backstabbing friend I ever had. When I was about thirteen or so, I told him about a job I had gotten on my own over in AC cleaning dirty auto parts. When I showed up on the job the following Monday, there he was, sitting over a tub of kerosene washing generators. When he saw me, he went into his typical Joe E. Ross *Car 54, Where Are You?*, "Oooh! Oooh! Hee-hee-hee! . . . ," snickering with grease all over his hands and arms and face. He stole my job! The guy who hired me shot a cold, "Sorry, kid. I needed someone real early and he showed up first."

"But you told me to be here at eight. It's quarter to."

"That's the way it goes, kid. Check back in a week or two."

Deceit and betrayal were Joey's stock in trade. We used to hang out in our early teens building model cars. Joey could replicate the sound of any engine in existence. He knew a lot about real-life cars—engine sizes, horsepower, blowers, carburation, rpm's, and stuff like that, or so I thought. It was only in retrospect that I realized that while we spent hours and hours customizing AMT plastic hot rods and listening to the Beach Boys and Jan and Dean, that we were really getting high on the glue. Years later in the Navy, I would realize this when Chris Matson and

Dennis Wooten and I got into sniffing naphtha. (You'd have to have a buddy ready to smack the bag out of your hand because you'd keep sniffing for the unreachable naphtha high until you'd kill yourself.) Anyway, Joey and his wife and their twin baby girls had one of those cool Atlantic City sidewalk-level apartments where a mélange of young people on their way down would congregate.

I was there one night when Joey was particularly frenetic. It was just me, him, and his wife. The kids were asleep. While Joey was a pathological liar, he was lousy at facial deception. I knew something was up because he kept trying to hold back this devilish smile I recognized from when we were kids. As we smoked some hash, his smile turned to giggles. Finally, he burst out in a choke of laughter and stomped his feet. Like a whirling dervish and with no explanation whatsoever, he began cleaning and drying an area of their gray-white marbled Formica top dining table. His wife, a pretty woman who had allowed herself to become incredibly obese, roused herself from her smoky stupor and yelled, "Joey, what are you doing?" He turned to us, scrubbing his hands together in front of his face, and smiled, "Ooo! Ooo! Get ready for the most *spectacular* thing ever in your life," and ran off into the bedroom. "He's really stoned," she quipped. When he returned, he meticulously laid out a goodly number of lines of heroin on the table, informing us, "This is some good shit . . ." The sight of all that dope propelled his wife into a fight with gravity as she fought her way off the couch. "Joey! Where the fuck did you get money for that!" As he scampered around to and fro, not able to contain himself, blurting, "Ooo! Ooo! You are going to *love* this! Hee-hee-hee! Man, you have no idea how much you are going to *love* this. Ooo! Ooo! . . ." It was quite an orchestration. He had it all planned. He guided us. First, we snorted the heroin. I had trepidations because of all the drugs I had done; I had studiously stayed away from heroin. I knew that I was susceptible to addiction. But being the good lemming that I was, I took my share. Then we stood in the middle of the room and passed a hash pipe around for a few hits. Then Joey announced, "I have a surprise. Close your eyes. Close your eyes!" and off he shuffled into the bedroom again. "Here I come," he called a minute later. "Don't peek now . . ." We complied and stood there, close-eyed. Waiting. Giggling. Ripped. His wife blurted, "Joey, what the fuck are you up to! He's gone fucking crazy, I tell you . . ." And where'd you get the fucking money!" Then she mumbled to herself, as though she were alone, thinking out loud, "Asshole. We don't even have the rent this month. Jerk-off . . ."

We heard his exit, but we didn't hear him return. "Open your eyes," he whispered. And there before us, he stood with that shit-eating grin of his practically frothing at the mouth, hands behind his back. I could see the long gone veneer of painful scarring acne of his youth. I was so stoned; I just kept quiet and took in the showmanship roll he seemed to be on. He was having such fun. But his wife, she was pushy. "Joey, what's this shit! Stop fucking with us! . . ." He just smiled and calmly said, "Ladies and gentlemen, I present to you . . ." unfurling his arms to reveal a re-cord album in his right hand, ". . . the Beatles' just released today—*Abbey Road*," and he stood there smiling and watching us for our reactions, gently pinching the top left and bottom right corners for optimum view-ing of that famous photo of the Fab Four walking across the street at 3 Abbey Road. He presented the album, still wrapped in cellophane, as though he were a Smithsonian librarian handling a rare delicate one-of-a-kind document that only a few chosen people ever get to see. Then we got even more stoned and had our collective mind blown by the Beatles' last recorded album.

Joey's environment was negative. It had been that way ever since we were kids. His family life was exceptionally dysfunctional. Something was always going wrong. Someone was always getting screwed. Scheming, lying—some form of deception was de rigueur to any transaction with Joey.

I watched the disintegration of two sweet young girls as their souls and bodies dissipated into the vortex of heroin. One time, they came over and coached us all to participate in a deal they were putting down. This girl was going to come over to buy a lid of pot from them. But they didn't have a lid of pot. They only had a couple of joints. The plan was that when she arrived we would all pass around the good joints to get her high. After she was sufficiently loaded, they'd do the transaction. When the young lady finally bought her fat bag of catnip, she turned out to be generous soul and insisted on sharing joint after joint with us. So there we were, all smoking catnip, shooting one another stoned telling looks.

It was a petty and sad moment. It would have been more efficient just to have robbed her. Then there arose outside the open ground-floor windows a cacophonous chorus of caterwauling cats pawing at the screens as they swirled around like catfish in a bucket. That, in itself, was mind blowing. As I knew all along, even from teenhood, I was in the wrong place whenever I was with Joey. There was a constant sleaze and ooze to my every visit. I always left Joey's feeling dirty, guilty, used, wrong, bad, defective. But I kept going back. Loneliness makes for strange bedfellows. I snorted heroin a few times with Joey and his wife and it never did anything for me, so my belt remained tightly cinched. But I knew that if I kept forcing it, I too would succumb to the degradation of dirty needles. Guided by some higher power, I stopped going over there. Not long after, I heard that Joey had died.

As a kid in the Navy, when I began to get into drugs, I was keenly aware that there were the good guys and the not-so-good guys. Good and bad, right and wrong—these had always been clear concepts with me, even in childhood. But the ingesting of drugs was allowing my character-forming mind to burst forth from a lifetime of intellectual fallowness into a field of sprouting and blooming thoughts, rank and verdant—a process, a gift, an opportunity I did not want to waste. On the one hand, drugs opened my mind and made me think. On the other hand, they made my mind malleable and susceptible to the moral and ethical toxins of others. I knew this as I constantly walked a fine line feeling fearful of the dark side. Hannah Arendt observed that, "The sad truth is that most evil is done by people who never make up their minds to be either good or evil." Fortunately for me, I had my good Brothers RB and Larry to get high with in the Navy, and Alberto when I got out. With those guys, I actually participated in stoned conversations about peace and love and art and human advancement and other thought-provoking topics that elevated our minds and our humanity.

Alberto had a family. Ronnie and I weren't close and, besides, he had a family and was always screwing someone in his spare time. That left me and the Moose to entertain one another. When you were in the company of the Moose, you were very aware that you were in the company of a very large chunk of humanness—an older Hoyt Axton on steroids. He hovered at around three hundred pounds. The boy liked to eat. While most humans I knew lost their appetite on amphetamines and stayed up for hours on end, the Moose was able to eat a horse and then go to sleep. Barbiturates kept him up all night wanting to talk, but smoking pot pushed him over to the other side of the humanly impossible. Now, I eat a lot. Always have. But the Moose made me look like I was on a perpetual diet. After smoking some pot, we'd go over to McDonald's in Pleasantville and he'd order two Big Macs, two fries, a vanilla milkshake, along with a regular burger and a cheeseburger, to boot. Then, after scarfing all that down, he'd say, "You know, Dave, I could really go for a Whopper . . ." So, we'd drive the couple hundred feet across the street to Burger King, where he'd get two Whoppers, more fries, and another milkshake. I would watch in utter amazement. And then—nope, it's not over yet—we'd go back to his trailer or to Granny and Pop's, depending on where he was living at the time, and then he'd eat up another storm. An incredible metabolism.

While in many respects the Moose was amoral, he possessed a sensitivity and consciousness for which he received no credit. When we got stoned, we would have these worldly-wise conversations that revealed a level of sophisticated thought that belied his Moose persona. Considering his crazy metabolism and his less-than-desirable personal hygiene—one thing everyone would agree on is that the Moose had stinky, no, foul-smelling, feet. But he was my friend, and because he was my friend, I naturally discussed Brother Larry's calling me back to California. He wanted to go with me. He wanted out. I wasn't sure I wanted to go. But Magoo made the decision for me.

My mother had told me time and time again not to bring drugs into her home. That as long as I was under her roof, she made the rules. Of course, I didn't listen. I was careless, left stuff out in plain sight, and smelled the place up with pot and cigarettes. Then, one day, I came home and there on the kitchen table was a chicken scratch note:

"David,

"I do not live your kind of life and I do not talk your kind of talk. Please be out by tomorrow morning.

"Love,

"Mother"

That night I crashed at Granny and Pop's in McKee City.

Because my '50 Chevy was constantly appearing to be at its choking end, I calculated that it might make it as far as Ohio someplace before it crapped out. Then we would have to hitchhike the rest of the way to Long Beach, California. I think I had about $200 or $300 myself, and the Moose had around $90. That seemed more than sufficient for a cross-country trip. Off into the wild blue yonder we went to discover our futures, our fortunes—our fates. Besides, knowing that the car would eventually conk out and that gas was going for $.26/gallon at the time, we had more money than we needed. I can remember so well that $10 was a lot in 1970. So, there were only a few essentials we needed to get ourselves on the road: toiletries, a change of clothes, and a few emergency items like a knife, flashlight, can opener, matches, roach clip, and pot.

Ed Townser was a guy from Pleasantville who traveled from time to time within our orbit. I knew him from pre-Navy days—I think—but I can't remember where I met him. Anyway, I don't think he ever really liked or respected us. He was something of a snob and always put on an air of superiority, as though he should have or could have been at Harvard, but instead was hanging around with us. It was a dope thing. He came from a self-described "good family," and his dad had high expectations of him. He was bright, drolly dryasdust, and, like Joey, a pathological liar. Before I went into the Navy, he and I snuck into the Absecon Drive-In one night and got busted. Security held us, and when Ed's dad came to pick him up he said that he'd only done it because I had talked him into it. We hooked up again after I got out of the Navy, and one night he showed up all flustered and told all in attendance that he had been robbed at gunpoint. They'd taken everything. He was quite shaken. Later, as we all sat around smoking joints and drinking whatever, we decided to order some pizza. He whipped out his wallet—the very one the robber had taken—and chipped in. When we called him on it, he just lied again. Always that sort of stuff. He had this absolutely beautiful girlfriend who was completely unaware of his bullshit. I still blame him for not returning the formula for LSD I loaned him, which he completely denied ever borrowing from me.

Considering my ineptness, he most assuredly did me one very large favor. At some point, he got hold of some bootleg Beatles albums and was trying to peddle them for $5 a pop. One was *Let It Be*. To this day, I kick myself every now and then for not buying one. He had cried wolf so many times that I just didn't believe that the bootleg was a bootleg. I was worried that the fake wasn't fake. What kind of thinking was that? Anyway, Ed was quite the entrepreneur. He cultivated hundreds of marijuana plants in nursery starter flats and sheltered them in the cockpit of his dad's 30-foot Chris-Craft cabin cruiser that was parked on the sunny side of their house. He convinced his pop that they were tomato plants. He was very professional and cautious about all of his underhanded and illicit endeavors.

Before the Moose and I split for California, Ed recruited me into helping him with the next facet of his pot business. Granny and Pop's property out in McKee City had been a pig farm years prior. Beyond a spit of woods behind their house was a sprinkling of dilapidated chicken shacks, tool sheds, and rusty farm equipment—everything being reclaimed by nature. When you ventured back in them thar parts, you'd encounter the most outrageously giant sturdy massive paleoplant life. The soil was a fine wine getting better with age. Ed had worked out a deal with Granny and Pop to use some of that soil for his "tomato project." That's where I came in. Ed had a cool VW bus, and one day we took it out to the end of English Creek Road and pulled it back into the Jurassic McKee City pig dung forest to collect soil specimens. That amounted to lining the bottom of the entire back of the bus with plastic and putting up a ¾″ wall of plywood about 24″ high that would keep the dirt in but allow the sliding door to close. Then, we shoveled and shoveled and shoveled until that bus was loaded to the max with the sweet moist humus of *sus scrofa domesticus*. And off we went. Slowly. Steadily. Low riding and smoking a joint. Hoping the damned tires didn't blow. Had War's *Low Rider* existed at the time, it would have been apropos of our departure. Instead, we drove away damaging our ears with *Tommy* at peak volume.

As I said, Ed was very calculating, so as part of his well-worked-out strategy, he shared some of his more potent pot with me that day. Why?

So I wouldn't be able to remember where in the hell we were going. I am sure that he drove up and back and back again and around in circles repeatedly just to confuse me. Down those long straight, smooth South Jersey roads through endless woods. Then off-road on what seemed like endless miles of bumpy unpaved white sandy roads through woods and swamps of scrub oak and pitch pine, making lefts and rights and turn-arounds galore. We was done deep in the bowels of New Jersey's famous Pine Barrens. Then we stopped.

As we sat there with the engine off, Ed asked, "What do you see, David?

"Woods, man. Lots of woods."

"What else do you see?

Scouring the vista up and down and every which way, knowing that there was something there to be seen but not seeable, "Nothing, man, just woods. Beautiful woods."

"Exactly. Come with me."

We walked a bit back into the bush, and soon we began to see a small army of strategically placed wooden produce crates. Ed began to expound: "You see, they can't be seen from the road and each will get maximum sunlight. Because they are so well dispersed, they will take on the cover of their neighbor tree and no one will notice any difference in the foliage as they drive by or from the air, even . . ." He explained how this was so far out that no one had any reason to come there and that, for whatever reason, not even piney hunters would pass that way. *How did he know?* One by one, we toted the crates over to the bus, lined them with plastic, poked a few holes in the bottoms, filled them up with rich earth, and lugged them back into position. When we were done, Ed drove a good distance away and then we walked back to dress the area where we had been working. As though a murder had been committed, he scrutinized everything and made sure that all traces of human activity were camouflaged. Using leafy branches, we dusted the sandy road to obliterate our footprints. We mussed up any signs of our travels to the crates. After that, we walked just off the side of the road and got back into the bus, which he then drove backward and forward past his pot farm to make it appear that no vehicle had stopped there. On the way back, he gave me the lowdown on how he was going to tell his father that the tomatoes had gotten some sort of rot and that he'd had to dispose of them, and that within a few days he would transplant them to their new homes, where he would tenderly feed them a diet of Miracle-Gro. And grow they did.

In my world of drugs, Ed was the first to come up with the concept of "one-hit pot." It looked good. It smelled good. It was damned good. And he was always peddling it. Of course, before the Moose and I left for Long Beach, I stocked up on some of Ed's good stuff.

One of the most important things to take care of in preparation for our departure was to figure out how to handle the dope. We decided that we'd use some on the road and stash the bulk of it. We made a solemn oath that we wouldn't touch the stash, no matter what, until we set foot in Long Beach. Thinking like a cop, I pondered my '50 Chevy long and hard and considered every possible place one might look for contraband. *Ah-ha!* I figured it out. By lying on my back on the floor, I could squiggle and force my arm up into a really inconvenient small space between the dashboard and the top of the interior of the glove box. I took a couple of fat lids and squished them down into a really compact log and wrapped it tightly with Reynolds Wrap, tightly wrapped that with Saran Wrap, and tightly rewrapped it again with tinfoil. Then I contorted my body and forced the sacred log up into its little sacred hiding space. On the driver's side, there was a small hole in the floor that I worked a bit more so it could serve as an evidence disposal; then I created another hiding place inside the driver's door to house our trip stash, from which we'd make withdrawals as needed. Just what we'd do with all that dope when the car broke down in Ohio, well, one step at a time. We were ready. This was an era before dope and bomb-sniffing dogs and computerized everything, so our world was a world of wide-open possibilities. It was a time when the bad guys could actually outrun the cops because they had faster cars. But that wouldn't be happening with my Chevy.

GETTING OUT OF DODGE

We hopped on the Black Horse Pike and headed west toward Interstate 80, Eisenhower's modernized replacement of our nation's first great transcontinental auto trail, the Great Lincoln Highway. Our first stop for gas was in a small rolling sleepy town in western Pennsylvania. We were getting ready to make our foray into Ohio, where the Chevy would surely die. It had slowly poked its way that far, grinding up and over inclines that had seriously tested its stamina. As we sat waiting for the attendant to fill'er up, he cleaned our windshield and popped the hood to check the oil and water, as was common in the '70s. I contemplated the red-penciled route I had mapped out for us and predicted that, if we were lucky, we would make it to Toledo before we had to start thumbing it.

The gas guy leaned in my window, "That'll be $2.34 for the gas and your oil and water's OK, buddy. Where you boys headed for?"

As if rehearsed, the Moose and I shot back an alacritous and very stoned "California!" as I threw the map over my shoulder onto the back seat. "Or as far as we can get in this baby," I added.

"Now, that sounds like a real nice trip," the guy said. "Someday I'd like to go out that way. Well, good luck with your trip, boys. Have some fun for me. Oh, by the way, one of your sparkplug wires was loose. I snugged it back on for you, though. It should be OK. Happy trails."

I thanked him and thought nothing of it. But as soon as I started the engine, I could tell that something major had happened. The Chevy was running like brand new. A happy curring kitten. For the rest of the trip, the Chevy Five-O ran like a finely tuned Swiss watch. Smoking a joint, we waved hello and good-bye to Toledo as we skirted just south of her, zooming ever so slowly and confidently onward to California.

The truth is that our road trip was uneventful. Nothing Kerouacian about it. I was Dean Moriarty in slow motion—a tenacious control freak driver who erred on the side of caution. Besides, the Five-O wasn't exactly a hot rod and we were smoking pot, the safest intoxicant on the planet. If everyone smoked pot while they drove, traffic fatalities would seriously plummet, our insurance rates would go down, and we'd use less gasoline. Anyway, the Moose slept and ate and ate and slept, and when he got done with that, he done did some more. While we were dazzled by geography all along the way, what really amazed us was how clean Salt Lake City was. It was spotless. It was like being in a lab or something. And then when we were floating on the surface of the Great Salt Lake, that blew us away. We got loaded and floated and giggled like teenage hyenas.

Driving that Five-O with no radio and no air conditioning down the I-15 on the searing outback through Utah, Nevada, and the Mojave, man, that was like driving ourselves to the center of Hell for the fun of it. Each little salt-eaten rust hole in the floorboards shot a laser stream of hot air at our legs. Opening the windows was like sitting inside a blast furnace. Closing the windows was like cooking ourselves in an oven. Two cognizant Thanksgiving Day turkeys. It all seemed too much for the old Chevy to take. I was worried that we would break down and become a page-three newspaper article: "Hippies Found Dead in Desert in Vintage Jalopy." The heat from the engine was so intense we could have fried eggs on the dashboard. We were out of water. The sun seemed to be focusing all its light on us through a gigantic magnifying glass, trying to make us explode like a kid does to an innocent insect in a jar. Aside from the possibility of death, I was concerned about the heat damaging our pot stash above the glove compartment.

Driving down the Long Beach Expressway—which is what we called it when I was in the Navy back in the '60s, which is really the 710 Freeway—with a cool ocean breeze flooding though our wide-open windows, I stared ahead in deep quiet thought. The Moose lay sleeping on the back seat. My nose enjoyed long slow wafts of the delicious pungent sulfuric tinged sea breeze.

Pollution from the Navy shipyard and oil refineries stung my eyes and stimulated my olfactory sense memory. I was driving into my own personal heart of darkness. I had joined the Navy to get out of Pleasantville, and Long Beach had become my homeport. For approximately three years, eight months, five days, and fourteen hours, my life in the United States Navy was one continuous life-lab experiment. And I was the human rat. Long Beach, my personal Petri dish, was where I experimented with sex; where I experimented with drugs; where I experimented with personal relationships; where I experimented with yoga; where I experimented with vegetarianism; where I entertained thoughts of suicide and murder. I couldn't put my finger on it, but there was something magical about Long Beach, something that would continue to draw me back time and time again over the years. I was attracted to the city and scared of it at the same time. Had Brother Larry not called me, I probably would have stayed in New Jersey and suffered a fate of unfathomable dysfunction. But here I was, driving down Anaheim headed for Stanley Avenue.

"Moose. Wake up. Lay-to, lad. We're here. Shake your shinnywanator. We are in *Longa* Beach . . ."

I have no idea what our plan was. Our plan was to get there. That's about as far as we'd thought it out. My inability to imagine failure was equal only to my inability to imagine success. Neither computed. I had no reference point. I had no idea what my options in life might be. In my unformulated state of being, anything was possible. But what was possible? The only thing I was sure of was that I wasn't sure of anything. I am sure, though, that reaching the ripe mature age of seventy-six was a notion that never crossed my mind. Youth has no time for such considerations.

When we drove to California, it was a time when $10 in my pocket made me feel secure enough to hitchhike across the country; when putting one foot in front of the other was all I needed to get to wherever I needed to go. While I had lived all my life, all those twenty-two years, with a certain sadness of soul, with a heart full of a certain lonely desperation, and certainly without a belief in a god way up high in the sky, I had possessed a certain inexplicable faith that propelled me through time and space and allowed me to take risks and trust that things would turn out OK. Intuitively, I knew that the universe would take care of me. How does one know these things?

Thus, with this childlike faith, no more than a couple hundred bucks between the two of us, a 1950 Chevrolet, a stash of Ed's kick-ass pot, and not much of anything else, did the Moose and I arrive in Long Beach. We found a parking spot waiting for us directly in front of Larry and Sharon's apartment on Stanley.

LONG BEACH

It was good to be with my old friend. While I'd had had other friends in the Navy, Larry was a particularly good one. I'm not going to say he was my best friend because I think the concept of *best friend* is highly overrated. He was a *good friend*. Not complicated. Straightforward. With an intuition unlike any I have ever seen. On a number of occasions we'd been involved in some sort of transaction or another or in the company of someone who would laugh and smile and be friendly, someone who would make certain overtures, and Larry would say, "I don't know. Something's not right. I don't trust him," or her or them. And, later, that person would prove to be a bum, just as he suspected. Larry was gifted with a deep soul of perceptive compassion, and I trusted him implicitly.

There had been a time in the Philippines when my libido became terribly excited but my penis had shrunk to the size of a peanut, making sex absolutely impossible with the lovely prostitutes—a little side effect (I eventually put two and two together) of the bennies I had become accustomed to consuming like Pez candies. I thought I had been "turned into a queer," as was commonly thought possible in those days. The Navy, in fact, showed us poorly produced films in boot camp, warning us that the Communists would do such a thing to us sailors so that they could blackmail us into spying for them. Mix that up with the story I grew up with, that a "good boy" in Pleasantville had been turned into a queer because someone had slipped a pill—a heroin pill!—into his Coke at a pool hall he frequented. As Paul Simon pondered in "Kodachrome," with the goofy crap I was fed growing up, it truly is a wonder that I can think.

Anyway, Larry was the only person I confided in on that topic, and I asked him if he would accompany me to the Subic Bay base shrink. I made an appointment, and he waited outside while I went in for my session. After the office formalities, I was shown into the therapist officer's office, where he sat impatiently behind a messy large desk. He began reading from my file before him:

"Betterton, David W. YN three. Valley Forge. 27 June 1948. Have a seat, Betterton. What can I help you with today, sailor?"

"Well, sir. I have this, ah . . . Well, you see, I'm not . . . um . . . I just—"

"Just what are you here for, Mr. Betterton? What *is* your problem?"

"Well, I can't seem to . . . I have this problem—"

"Betterton, what the fuck are you here to see me about? I have many people to see today and I don't have time to fuck around with you. What can I do for you?"

"You see, sir. I-I-I-I th-th-think I-I-I'm a queer. I think I might be a queer."

"Queer, eh? You think you're a queer. Just what makes you think you're a fucking queer, Betterton?"

"I think I've been turned into one, sir. I was doing OK, but suddenly I just can't get a hard-on with any, ah, of the girls, no, ah, no matter how pretty, ah, or nice they are to me."

His superior face reddened. He gritted his teeth. His mouth stretched, tensed, and twitched. Elongated lengths of thin stringy whatevers rose to the surface of his throat. I thought he was going to explode and yell at me. But in an almost calm gentle whisper he began to console me. "So. You think you're a queer. A faggot. Betterton, I have guys who are ready to blow their fucking brains out. I have young men who have gone insane from this fucking stupid war we're in that need my help. And you're in here because you think you're a fucking queer! Get the fuck out of here. You're wasting my time. Everybody has issues like this. Go back out there and figure it out, sailor. It's called growing up. You are dismissed."

Larry was sitting on the curb with his white sailor's monkey hat tilted profoundly forward just above his eyebrows—the sign of a salt—with his arms resting on his knees:

"Hi, how'd it go?"

"Oh, pretty good. Let's go. Thanks for waiting."

"Sure. No problem."

We walked along quietly for a bit.

"He told me to get the fuck out. Said I was wasting his time; that he had more important psychos to take care of than me."

"Oh."

And that was that. We never discussed that incident again.

As Moose and I sat there in Larry and Sharon's living room on Stanley, passing a Jersey joint, I realized that whatever I might have had in my mind about coming back to Long Beach, some sort of expectation with regard to Larry, to picking up where we'd left off, well, it was going to be nothing of the sort. The Navy was the Navy, and it was over. He was with Sharon now, and they had cute as a bug little baby Heather.

Sharon was a pretty petite pixie with disheveled reddish hair and a sprinkling of translucent Irish freckles that spilled off of her nose and onto her glowing face. Even early in the morning, she wore a perpetual smile that easily broke into jerky happy guffaws—the kind of laughter used to express joy as well as conceal a lack of understanding. The way she coddled and bobbed baby Heather made it clear that the child was loved and well cared for. When we first met that morning, Sharon's hug was rigid and a bit distant as she kept her neck stiff and her head turned slightly away, the way women do, because they do not want to send the wrong message. But as we sat and talked and smoked and sipped coffee, I could tell by her soft gaze that she loved me instantly because I was Larry's friend—the way you love your friend's spouse or lover when you don't even know the first thing about them, just because you know your friend loves them. Later on, there would even be talk of me being Heather's godfather, which never came to fruition. Naturally, I was hurt that I was passed over for someone else and I held a resentment for quite a while. But years later, when I learned what a brat Heather had grown to be—a Trump supporter!—I was absolutely grateful for not having that little honor bestowed upon me.

If you didn't know Larry, you'd think he was a badass biker. He was short and stocky, had a full dark beard with redneck longish hair combed straight back à la Wolfman Jack, with a set of constantly darting information-gathering suspicious beady eyes. When he stood talking with you, he always tilted his entire body to the right and looked askance as though at the ready to envelop any possible opponent in his iron grip bear hug, a technique that would years later come in handy during his career as a psych nurse. But Brother Larry was a gentle biker, and as we sat there and got caught up, he talked of putting his GI benefits to good use, of registering at Long Beach City College to study nursing, of responsibility. The Moose and I were in the presence of a happy family. They lived in a small one-bedroom apartment on the top floor of a really cool 1930s stucco quadruplex, just a short walk from old Joe Jost's tavern. It was a nice neighborhood then in which to build a new life. We could sleep on their floor for a few days, but that was it. We understood.

After a few chatty hours, Larry, the Moose, and I headed over to Wilmington to see Brother RB. That would complete the triumvirate. I had only hooked up with RB and Larry during my last couple of years in the Navy. During that time, I think I fancied us as the mighty Three

Musketeers or the bumbling Three Stooges, depending on the mood. We were three. For whatever reason, of the several "friends" I had while in the service, RB and Larry were the ones who stuck like glue. I always looked up to those guys. They had it together. Me? I was a lost boy. I never fit in anywhere with anyone. A perpetual fifth wheel.

Driving across the Gerald Desmond Bridge to Terminal Island was a visual feast. The sea breeze made for good visibility, but the pollution teared our eyes and the Moose was turned off by the rotten egg smell that made Long Beach smell like home to me. For me, it was akin to the salt marshes of West Atlantic City at low tide. We could see the beauty and industry that made Long Beach *Long Beach*: the U.S. Navy shipyard, the Port of Los Angeles, San Pedro, the rise of Palos Verdes, the sunken flatlands of Wilmington, the herds of pumping oil wells, the futuristic towers and pipes for the refining and storage of petroleum. The Gerald Desmond was built in 1968 to replace the two-lane World War II era pontoon bridge that had caused a traffic bottleneck every morning for us sailors rushing back to our ships.

Aside from the beauty I was drinking in as the Five-O purred along, I nurtured a sadness in my heart for an old Navy buddy, who was smart and funny and kind and dead. One Richard E. Ball. He had always said that the *E* really didn't stand for anything, but that he liked to tell people it stood for Euripides. Ball had the distinct honor of being the first traffic fatality on the Gerald Desmond. He was taking the Pier E exit one morning when his little white convertible '63 Austin-Healey rolled over. He was with a guy named McClatchy, who survived unscathed. Our division, A-Division at the time, got the word that someone needed to go ID the body, but none of the other guys would do it, so I volunteered. As would prove to be the case time after time in my life, I wasn't prepared for the wry humor of reality. I was taken to a cold room where Richard Euripides Ball's naked, unbruised, scratchless, very clean body lay before me on a stainless steel table. Pure white. Lily-white. Alabastrine. Apparently, when his car rolled his head had gotten freakishly squished like a fruit. His cranium was misshapen and his deformed face wore a tender smile. A devilish I-don't-give-a-fuck smile. A damned smile! Sometime later, I played around with a Ouija board and the damned planchette spelled out that McClatchy was responsible. Blew my mind.

Ball had been an Ivy Leaguer-type guy who had a kind heart. He was so smart that not even the top ranking offers made him feel insecure. He knew he was smarter than most of them, and on a dime would challenge anyone anywhere to a few rounds of intellectual sparring. He could have been an officer, but he'd enlisted to get the ordeal over with quicker. He was always nice to me and told me once that he knew that I was smarter than other people gave me credit for and that he loved talking with me because, he said, I had *something* to say. I have no idea what that was. I know now that he was just being kind to me. Perhaps he did see potential. At that time, though, I was just an ignorant, uneducated, New Jersey hick. Nevertheless, his kindness went a long way and I was honored to tell the coroner, "Yes. That is my friend. Richard E. Ball. No doubt about it."

Wilmington has always had a bad reputation. A place you didn't want to go. A badlands. A wasteland. An industrial ghetto. A city that subsided in places below sea level because they didn't know to replace the oil being pumped out with water. An urban barrens. Definitely, a place where you did not want to have car trouble at night. But it was also the home of the first Der Wienerschnitzel, Wilson College (the first coed college west of the Mississippi), and Camp Drum, the only significant U.S. Army outpost in California during the Civil War. And that's where we were headed to hook up with RB.

If you had to track down RB right now, I mean this very moment, literally, find him somewhere on this green globe—dead or alive—one thing I could guarantee you is that you'd find him someplace interesting. Like some sort of alchemist, he always had a knack for turning the mundane into the extraordinary. Nothing he touched, did, or said was pedestrian. It wasn't that the world suddenly changed and became something that it wasn't. No. It was just that he perceived the world in a special way and had the ability to help you see it through his eyes. Of course, this meant that he was also a bullshitter extraordinaire. Especially when he had pharmaceuticals coursing through his brain.

In the shadows of a long gone Model-T factory, under the gaze of the Commodore Schuyler F. Heim vertical-lift and Henry Ford double-leaf trunnion bascule bridges, serenaded by a symphony of moored masts and clinking halyards, guarded by a cavalcade of oil-sucking pumpjacks that stretched off in a great distance, into the cool breeze that wafted across the Cerritos Channel from Terminal Island, we drove. Behind an old funky chain link fence, next to a massive trimaran that looked as though Noah himself were building it, and in an unpainted plywood trailer that he had constructed with his very own nimble fingers—this is where we found RB Porter that fine September day in 1970. Living in such an exotic downright Bohemian place with a woman seemed like a charmed life to me. Like RB had done died and gone to Heaven. It was good to see him. I was touching bases with my recent past and trying to figure out what my future might be. Having picked up and just left Jersey, I was a leaf blowing in the wind. I remember thinking, *How on earth did he get it so together?*

First thing, RB gave us the obligatory fifty-cent tour of his estate: a fenced-in plot that was occupied and surrounded by threadbare worn-at-the-edges people amongst a hodgepodge of industrial-type gear, the trappings of all things nautical. He was renting from an eccentric gent named Marcus, who claimed to be one of the original ten thousand Nazis. Marcus said that after he joined the party, it was all downhill from there for the movement. A split second after RB introduced us, Marcus commenced to tell us about the trimaran he had been building for a couple of years and his plan to sail it around the world with a magnificent crew of beautiful young women—he being the only man. His wife just smiled and took in his bull with a grain of salt. As we stood around laughing and chatting, I noticed that the starboard hull of his distaffian Ark was about two feet longer than the other two hulls. I asked Marcus why that was. With confidence and a sudden emphatic German accent, he assured me, "No. They're all the same. I measured them all exactly. I know this boat inside and out."

Eyeballing it with a squint, I said, "I don't know. Come over here. Look. Isn't this one longer?"

He absolutely freaked. Whether or not he ever got that boat to float, I haven't a clue. But if he did, he did it with one hull too long.

Sitting around RB and Wendy's trailer, we passed a joint and caught up on what all had transpired since we three had mustered out of the Navy. It seemed like years had already passed us by. It seemed as though Larry and RB had been out *living, experiencing,* while I had been stuck back in Jersey pretty much doing nothing. The Moose sat in silence with a stoned smile, taking in the California exotica. He wasn't in McKee City anymore. We were now in the land of the Beach Boys, Jan and Dean, surfers, hippies. The dope we brought with us was potent and had us all nicely loaded. Wendy sat quietly and stared, nodding periodically with smiles of approbation. Still relatively new to California, she, too, had escaped from her own personal McKee City, somewhere back in Minnesota.

After a while, Brother Larry broached the subject, "RB, you know where we can get some *L*?"

RB cocked his head, rolled his shoulders, flicked the ash off the joint, took a deep hit, then passed the joint on to me. After a pregnant pause, he allowed a shit-eating grin to spread across his face as he held his breath and closed his eyes. Then he exhaled, saying, "Suuuure . . . I think so . . . that just might be a possibility. There's this house over in Long Beach . . . Jeff's scored some pretty good dope from this guy over there. I went with him a couple times. We can swing by and see what happens. If the vibe is right, we could be high tonight."

So the four of us jumped in the Five-O and headed back to Long Beach.

We cruised up Anaheim, turned left on Atlantic, crossed PCH, and turned right at 20th. Suddenly, everything went dark. Still stoned and driving with all the slow motion caution that pot elicits, I had a heightened awareness that we were four white boys driving slowly in a black 1950 Chevrolet through a colored neighborhood. Every face was a black face.

RB navigated: "Turn left on Myrtle . . . Keep going . . . Past 21st . . . It should be a couple doors down here on the right. There it is. That's it. Park here. OK, here's the plan, man. I'll go in solo, and you guys wait for me out here. I don't want to freak'im out with a bunch of guys who look like narcs."

I parked directly in front of the house, then we three sat in dead silence and watched RB walk through the chain-link gate that had been left open. With his pelvis thrust forward, he swaggered onward like some lanky sea-legged runway model, pendulous arms swinging back and forth, head cocked to one side. It was a familiar walk. He called it truckin'. Something he had cultivated while floating around the West Pacific. I had a similar walk. Only my strut was imbued with black jive cockiness and had been cultivated to display an attitude of don't-mess-with-me to avoid the ass-kickings that seemed to come my way all too frequently when I was a kid.

All of the homes in the neighborhood had been built right up to the sidewalk. Most had a porch and a tiny front yard. But RB was walking down a long concrete walkway that hugged the far left of an unusually long stretch of treeless, bushless, flowerless, unkempt lawn, toward a 1930s light brown two-story Spanish-style stucco duplex with a stylish run of weatherworn terra cotta coping around its parapet. A shoebox-like structure that sat all the way back at the edge of an alley, leaving a tremendous vacant lot in front. Clearly, the place had seen better days. It stood there, alone, straight, erect—self-conscious of its status as an architectural outsider. A wooden flight of stairs rose up the middle, splitting off in a perfect Y with separate staircases going to each apartment. Each door had a little canopy of terra cotta pantiles. RB trucked on up to the apartment on the right, knocked, and disappeared inside. We waited. And waited . . .

The Moose asked, "Hey, Dave. Can I have a cigarette?"

I gave him a Winston and lit up one for myself. Larry lit a Marlboro. The Five-O soaked up the warm California sun. It was getting to be a hot day. We all must have dozed off because RB scared the crap out of us when he leaned in the window, "Come on in, boys. Come on up. It's cool. Get your money ready."

As we walked through the yard, something about the other apartment kept demanding my attention. Its door was wide-open. It seemed to be a refuge of quiet calm. The sun was beating. So was my heart. When we got to our connection's apartment, RB opened the door and we all filed in after him. Sly and the Family Stone's "Everyday People" softly emanated from a tinny radio. The sparsely furnished apartment's walls were bare; a well-worn earth tone 1950s floral-patterned carpet delineated the social area. On a somewhat tattered overstuffed couch sat a sweetly smiling plain-faced blond beauty uninhibitedly nursing a baby. Rising from a cushy Art Deco club chair (that looked so out of place but at the same time appropriate) was a surfer blond longhair guy sporting a big friendly smile.

RB introduced us to Mick and his wife, Deanna. We all shook hands with Mick and nodded our greetings to Deanna who smiled and greeted us as the child suckled her beautiful breast. I had never seen such a thing and all of my resources went immediately into acting like it wasn't happening before my very eyes. Mick got a couple of spindle-back chairs from the kitchen and we all had a seat. Both of them were dressed rather straight and there was nothing in their environment that said *hippie.* Aside from Mick's long hair, they looked like a couple of good kids from Anywhere, USA. It didn't take but a few milliseconds to realize that Deanna worshiped the ground Mick walked on. I remember my prejudicial thinking kicking in and wondering, *What in the hell is this fine looking gal doing with this guy? What's his secret?* What can I say? I was young and shallow.

We engaged in some general chitchat and talked about our trip out from New Jersey. After a while, RB broached the subject, "So, Mick, these gentlemen who just drove all the way from the East Coast would like to score some lysergic acid diethylamide-25, and I told them that you might be able to help them out?"

"Hee-hee." Mick giggled looking me square in the eyes, "You guys aren't narcs, are you? You're not like trying to bust me, are you?"

He was selling delicious barrels of Orange Sunshine for fifty cents a hit. I got five bucks worth and RB and Larry bought a few hits as well. The Moose would mooch mine. As we were ponying up our dinero, a terrifying knock came at the door. But our fears were quickly allayed when we heard, "Deanna, it's Linda. You guys got a—"

"Come in, Linda. It's open. Come in," Deanna euphoniously answered.

The door opened and in stepped a pale thin barefoot little woman wearing a baggy tee shirt and jeans with rolled up cuffs. There was something very Appalachian about Linda Bevins. Her brown hair was straight and unattended. She had a gentle sweet glow about her that belied a hardscrabble existence. While she projected the image of a tough ass biker mamma, she radiated a mature femininity and tenderness. "Have you by any chance got two eggs I can—Ohhh!" Midsentence, she realized that she was interrupting something. Her delicate lips puckered to form a childlike crooked smile of embarrassment on her petite mouth, "Oh! I'm sorry. I didn't realize—"

"Naw," Mick said, "come on in, man. Have a seat. We're just doing a little business, and I was thinking we might want to smoke a joint. You want to smoke some pot?"

"Sure. But have you got a couple eggs I can borrow? I'll get'em back to you as soon as I get my food stamps this month. Do you mind if I leave the door open a bit so I can hear the kids?"

Deanna told her that would be fine, and Mick introduced her to everyone. And, because I was grateful for the acid and the good company, I suggested that we smoke some pot just in from the Garden State. The idea was an immediate hit, so I went out to the Five-O to get some dope. As I stepped out onto the porch, I paused to take a long look at the long empty yard in front of me, noting several people passing by in different directions. A couple of kids on bicycles. A few people in cars. Several pedestrians. None of them white.

As we passed a couple of joints around, the background music got better and better: Hendrix, Joplin, Traffic, Chicken Shack, Country Joe, and on and on. It sounded too good to be true, so I had to ask, "What are we listening to? They're playing some outrageous tunes."

"Yeah, man . . . that's *underground*, man. KPPC. 106.7. FM, man. Is really cool 'cuz I never have to buy no records, man. They just play everything I want to hear. For free. Hee-hee. We're going to miss it when we move up to Kern County."

That got Larry's attention. "Far out. You're movin' up Kern County, are ya? Good fishing and camping up there . . ."

"Yeah, man, I'm bummed with the city. Man, as soon as I make enough money, we're getting out of here. We're going up north, man."

Linda blew out an uncontrolled, "Phyooo! This marijuana is kickass. Where did you get this?" she asked with her most exaggerated Ohio accent.

I smiled at the compliment. "This friend of ours back in Jersey grew it," I answered with my most exaggerated South Jersey accent. "It was grown in the soil of an old pig farm that Moose here's grandparents used to run."

"Pig farm? . . ." Mick wheezed after taking a hit and passing the joint over to Deanna. Unsuccessfully trying to hold it in, he burst out into a laughing cough, "Ha-cha-ha-cha-ha-cha-cha-cha . . . Man! Pig farm? Ha! Man, that's different. That's really different. We're smoking pig. New Jersey pig . . ." And so the little stash that we'd brought with us—or, rather, I brought with us—which amounted to about two or three lids, came to be known as Jersey Pig. It was definitely pretty good. Little did we know that it would only get better.

As we rambled on, with all of us telling stories and forgetting midstream what the hell we were saying, it came up that the Moose and I needed to find a place to live. Once that little cat was out of the bag, Linda told us that we could stay in her garage. She had a policy of letting anyone who needed a place to stay to stay there, and whoever stayed there would get one meal a day at dinnertime. She didn't charge anything, but whoever stayed there had to help out with household chores and if they got food stamps or earned any money, they needed to chip in for food. There was a toilet and sink down there, but we could use her shower. She also said she had two kids, so no violence or funny stuff; that there was a guy named Danny already staying there; that others might come and go at any time; and that we had to work out any conflict issues peacefully among ourselves—or leave. Those were the rules, and they applied to everyone. The Moose and I looked at one another as though we had died and gone to Heaven and immediately accepted her offer.

"Welcome to Myrtle House, gentlemen. The garage door is always unlocked, so just go in whenever you're ready. Same goes for my door. I never lock it. How about those eggs, Deanna?"

During the first couple months at Myrtle House, a lot happened. Danny was this pint-sized longhair who truly lived on another planet in a parallel universe. He had a gig where this guy who was straight and who didn't do drugs but who sold drugs would give Danny samples of everything he was thinking about investing in so Danny could evaluate the quality of the product. One time it would be reds, another time it would be Dexedrine, another time acid, pot, PCP, hash, and you name it. Danny felt that he had been touched by the finger of God and was constantly doing research, which meant he was always stoned on something. That wasn't so bad, but he had a tendency to come home in the wee hours all cranked up in the mood to listen to music in the dark. In his own way, he tried to be considerate by keeping the volume low. This never bothered the Moose. He could sleep through anything.

But I was an anomaly around there. I was actually picking up low paying odd jobs. So I needed to sleep. Every night it was the Kinks, Three Dog Night, Canned Heat, Guess Who, Sly and the Family Stone. It was "The Ballad of John and Yoko," "Going Up the Country," and "Lola," his favorites, over and over and over, ad infinitum. Not exactly a sound track to sleep by, no matter how low the volume.

On top of that, there were strangers who just popped up out of nowhere and flopped for a period of time. In and out at all hours. They would make a mess, not contribute anything, and then disappear. I was always cleaning the bathroom, buying toilet paper, sweeping, and taking out the trash—the very issues Linda had warned us about. And none of the transients did anything to help Linda with the household chores.

Then—there was the Moose. I knew that he wasn't exactly an energetic fella. But once we got to Long Beach and his meager funds ran out, a whole other Moose came to light. At first, I defended him. But he quickly became an embarrassment, and I was sorry I had brought him along. The accusations were undeniable: he was a lazy bum, a thief, and a liar to boot.

On the most elementary level, he wouldn't help around the house with anything. The only thing you could rely on him for was to be there when it was time to eat. People started suspecting and then they started accusing him of stealing cigarettes. Several said that they had actually pretended to be asleep while he raided their smokes. One guy said that the Moose had snuck up on him while he was sleeping and slowly and gently removed the cigarettes from his shirt pocket—the shirt he was wearing—and did his deed. Then, just as gently and slowly, he put the pack back. And he wouldn't just take a few, either. He would pretty much clean you out, leaving only a couple. Everyone started hiding their smokes. The air became thick and humid with ill feelings.

Then there was the food issue. Not only would he eat more than his fill at dinner and disappear when it came time to clean up, but he also started raiding Linda's refrigerator during off hours. Different folks who came and went reported that food and smokes and dope and whatever would be missing from their backpacks or their little personal areas in the garage. Linda ended up putting a padlock on her refrigerator and began locking her front door. She had a talk with me: the Moose had to go.

Some people are just idiots. It's like they're born with stupid disease. And in the midst of their minefield of ignorance, selfishness, rudeness, and lack of consideration for others, if you look real hard, you are likely to find a tender spot—something about them that almost cancels out the rest of their bad character. And, as I am confident that Hitler, Stalin, and Pol Pot had their tender sides, so too did the Moose have his.

One day, he came back to Myrtle House with a three-legged German shepherd that had been manifestly living a hard life. That dog freaked everyone out. But the Moose and Brick, as he named it, got on like the best of buds and the dog became very protective of the Moose. I believe it would have killed for him on command. However, Brick turned out to be a cool dog, and the fact that it had three legs gave it an advantage when playing with the rest of the pack of dogs that seemed to come and go at Myrtle House. Brick was named *Brick* because he used an eight-inch cinder block as a chewy toy.

A group of us would frequently find ourselves frolicking over at the Seventh Street Park drinking Red Mountain, smoking joints, and listening to someone strum away on their guitar. And the dogs would play like there was no tomorrow. When one got hold of a Frisbee or a rag or a ball or whatever, all the other dogs would chase after it as if they had a definite plan to take the object away from its possessor. Eventually, they would catch up and in a scuffle, one of them would gain control. But when Brick got hold of something, he would run in a straight line and then, like a bolt of lightning, he'd push off with his one front leg in one direction or another and make and immediate ninety-degree turn. The other dogs, caught up in their momentum, would have to make a wide arc, slipping and tumbling, trying to respond to Brick's unbeatable athletic agility.

One day, the Moose called home and got money from his mom to fly back to Jersey. He found someone to take Brick off his hands, and we said our good-byes. He knew that he had been a jerk; that he didn't know how to take care of himself; that he was lazy. He knew he didn't fit in and that he needed to be back in McKee City, where there was plenty to eat, and his mom would take care of him. So we parted on friendly terms without burning our bridges. We were friends. And off he went. Everyone was relieved. But Linda continued to padlock the refrigerator and lock her front door.

Speaking of dogs, there was a gorgeous brindled mixed breed named Phoebe, aka the Wonder Dog, which came into my life in a big way. She was as petite and as feminine a lady dog one could ever hope to meet. If you knew her and took a good look at her, you would see that she was a real beauty. But her unique mix threw most people for a loop, because of her exotic wild look. Not a large dog by any means. She had an elongated coyote-like snout, large sound-collecting ears, long slender legs, a trim hunting body of the sub-Saharan black-backed jackal, and a delicately refined friendly tail of a mutt. She carried herself with poise, was incredibly intelligent, and was the de facto leader of the pack on forays into the neighborhood to raid trashcans. (Depending on the floating population, four or six or eight dogs would drag trash back to the Myrtle House and rip everything to shreds in the front yard. It was Disneyland for dogs. We'd let them go at it for a while and have some fun; then a few of us would clean it up. Not a popular event with the neighbors, for sure.) Phoebe had this extreme catlike super ability to leap up onto a five- or six-foot concrete wall from a standstill. She'd look up, do her calculations, and whammo! There she'd be perched on the damned wall. I remember the day I met her quite well.

I hadn't been at Myrtle House but a couple of days and was sitting on the couch at Linda's when in came about three or four hippie chicks. The room exploded with femininity. The energy was kinetic. It seemed as though the furniture and anything else in the apartment was being bumped and jiggled by their presence. They were incredibly nonchalant and seemed worldlier than any girls I had ever been in the company of. They were on their way somewhere, and Linda was a key contact before their departure.

One of them struck me. She made my chest feel empty, and I suddenly became small and insignificant. Totally incompetent. All I knew was that I wanted to be with her. She was a svelte 5'9" gal with big hazel eyes behind gold wire rim glasses and straight hippie chick hair clear down to her butt. She wore well-worn gray corduroy bell-bottoms, Dr. Scholl's wooden sandals with blue straps, and a variegated paisley patterned airy blouse (under which she was braless) that flared out and hung loosely over her hips. She had this contagious laugh that she hyenaed as she stood with good posture convulsing and extending her arms out in front of her while telling her story, making circular motions and pointing and flicking her fingers as though she were controlling a marionette that only she could see. She was *cool*. She was Elizabeth Anne Barber from Duluth, Minnesota, but everyone called her Lizard, or Liz. It turned out that she lived with Linda and the living room couch was her bedroom whenever the social activities died down.

If we said anything to one another that day, it was merely "Hello" in passing. It turned out that Liz was the mistress of Phoebe. I found that out when later that day she opened the garage door and let Phoebe in and announced to anyone in earshot, "Don't let Phoebe out for about twenty minutes, OK? I'll be back tomorrow. Linda will feed her." She bent down, gave the dog a kiss and a big hug and said, "You be good, OK? I'll be back tomorrow. You be good." Then she shut the door and split. She needed to leave Phoebe at Myrtle House overnight so that she and the girls could make their trip to wherever, unencumbered. So, Phoebe and I made our acquaintance. Not only was she a lovely creature, but, as I immediately recognized and began to scheme, she was also a direct linkage to Liz. My fixation was in motion.

In what amounted to a mere speck of time, a few months at most, I experienced a century's worth of experiences while living at Myrtle House: I saw things there, I heard things there, and I learned things there—most all now forgotten and lodged somewhere deep in the fiber and recesses of my being. One of the most shocking things happened one day in broad daylight. Brother Larry and I were over at Mick and Deanna's, talking away, when a squad car pulled up and double-parked out front. I was sitting on the couch and had a clear view out the open door. I sort of freaked and alerted Mick, who calmly took a look and said, "Wow . . . man . . . don't freak, man. That's one of my customers, man."

So through the gate, up the steps, and into the apartment came this LBPD in full uniform with his car running out in front, with another cop sitting shotgun. We did a round of introductions and while we engaged in some idle chitchat, the cop took one of the hits of acid Mick had produced for him and popped it into his mouth. He told us that his partner thought that he was checking in with one of his snitches and that he didn't have a clue what was going on. He paid Mick and then left to finish his shift.

In order to support his family, Mick dealt drugs and took occasional day labor jobs through the Manpower agency to pick up some legit cash now and then so he could hop on and off of unemployment. One day he got involved with a job where some welding was being done and he tripped out watching the arc without any eye protection. Of course, his terrible state of pain didn't kick in until after he got home. We threw him in the Five-O, and a few of us took him up to County General Hospital in LA. It was a zoo. It was like being at a casting call with would-be extras waiting to audition for Dante's *Divine Comedy*. People with gunshot wounds, knife wounds, broken appendages. Kids screaming and crying. People moaning and writhing in pain. Tough looking characters. Unless you were near death, you just took a number and waited.

That was the last straw for Mick. He and Deanna and their kid split and went up country to Kern County. But in those days you didn't just up and give notice and leave. You turned your place on to someone else. So, as Mick and Deanna moved out, Jeff Ellig and Linda Decker moved in. With them, I had some history.

I had dropped acid for the first time in 1968 with RB, Larry (we were still in the Navy), and Jeff Ellig (who had gotten out six months prior), at an apartment on Orange Avenue in Long Beach that Jeff and RB shared. Not knowing diddly about the process, I, of course, just followed RB and Larry's lead. I knew Jeff through them because they were my friends. Jeff had a sort of snobbish mystical side to him that I didn't quite get. He seemed to be in a perpetual state of aloofness. He was just too cool. Anyway, he had scored the requisite hits of Orange Sunshine that we would all drop on a Saturday morning. In those days, you needed a good eighteen to twenty-one hours if you wanted to trip.

When we got off ship and showed up at the apartment, Jeff went to the refrigerator to get the acid and freaked when he discovered that he had left the hits on a saucer below a package of hamburger that had dripped blood. Everyone was momentarily bummed. A saucer of bloody mushy LSD. What to do? Jeff was quick on his feet and came up with a solution: He poured some orange juice—apropos, now that I think of it—into a large glass and then drained the bloody saucer into the juice, thoroughly swishing that saucer to make sure that every molecule of acid ended up in the juicy electric concoction. He stirred and stirred and stirred and stirred and then he stirred some more to make sure the acid was evenly distributed. Then, as though he were a lab technician building a bomb, he poured precise portions of the bloody brew into four jelly glasses, each bearing colorful Disney characters. That way, we would all be taking the same trip.

Sometime after we dropped, or drank, we must have had some sort of an acidy agreement to take off on our own and then meet back at the apartment later, because I found myself alone, barefooted, walking the streets of Long Beach totally ripped, imbued with peace, love, and brotherhood. A real psychedelic *flâneur*. During my traipsing, I came upon one Linda Decker, with whom I had a nice conversation about what I have no idea. But I was meeting a girl. So, I invited her back to the apartment later.

Cheap Thrills was new to me and I was enamored of one song in particular. The apartment had a full-length mirror and on that fateful day, while the others were still out doing whatever they were doing, I must have watched myself dance "like no one was watching" to "Combination of the Two" thirty-two thousand times. After the boys came back, we watched some TV, and it was then that I became aware of just how much violence there was in kids' programming. Later, Linda Decker showed up at the door. I did the introductions. From the get-go, it was clear that she wasn't interested in me in the least. She had immediate eyes for Jeff, who proceeded to move on her. Once again, I put some time and thought into wondering why it was that I couldn't get a girl interested in me. But it turned out to be some great emotional training for my first time out on L.

Mick and Deanna moved out and Jeff and Linda moved in. Not even a speed bump of an interruption. Things carried on at Myrtle House. Linda Bevins was steady as a rock. People came and went down in the garage. It was common for me to come upon Liz reading what to me were these impossibly big fat books. She went through them like hot cakes. I never saw anyone read so much. Hmmm . . . Books. Another link. I, too, would read something. Perhaps she'd see me and we'd strike up a conversation. I went in search of something to read and purchased a paperback novel titled *Sailor* about a merchant marine who continued to run into women who wanted to have wild sex with him. Exactly something I knew nothing about. I tried to put myself into reading situations where Liz would come upon me, but nothing worked. Nevertheless, I kept pecking away at that book like a patient and determined chicken, waiting for my opportunity. I still am a slow reader, so it was no problem for me to stretch that baby out for months if I had to.

After Jeff and Linda had been there for a while, Linda's mother came out from New Jersey for a visit. She was in her early to mid-thirties, which was old to me at the time. I cannot for the life of me remember her name, but she was simultaneously trying to break away from an unhappy marriage and the clutches of Scientology. Somehow, through no conscious effort on my part, we began hanging around together. Perhaps it was because I had the Five-O. Ha! Anyway, I went to a few Scientology meetings with her up in Hollywood, and then we ended on a mattress on the floor in the garage having blissful sex. One time, when everything was working just perfectly for us—she was astride me as I lay supine, deep up inside her, our hands vised together with interlocking fingers—she looked down directly into my eyes and whispered, "David, right now, I love you more than anybody in the world." Until that moment, aside from my sister, which doesn't count, I had never had anyone say they loved me.

One day, I caught Linda Decker on the steps going up to her apartment and broached the subject of me and her mother messing around. I felt awkward about having sex with *her* mother. Linda just smiled, "Oh, that's no problem, David. It's cool. She can do whatever she wants."

And that was that. It all didn't last too long because she went back to New Jersey to face her demons and, by the way, she never told me that she loved me again.

Jeff got antsy and had a need to go on the road. I'm not sure, but I think Linda was pregnant and it was freaking him out. I ended up being the only one who could and would go with him. Our ultimate destination was Denver, but I can't remember why. Larry loaned me some camping cooking utensils and Liz loaned me her Duluth canoe portage backpack. We loaded up with plenty of rice and water and off we went, hitchhiking north.

We stopped off for a couple days in Berkeley, and when we were downtown, I commented that I had expected riots and whatnot; that it was so calm. No sooner had I opened my mouth about that, though, when several provocateurs started running between the various knots of people standing around, informing us of some misdeeds the police or other government officials were doing or about to do. And there, before my eyes, the makings of a Berkeley riot began. Stuff was thrown into a bonfire, and protesters started chanting and waving signs that said, *Hooray for Our Side!* The police showed up with paddy wagons and stood by calmly in riot gear, letting everyone do their thing. After about twenty minutes or so, they calmly moved in, dispersed the crowd, and put out the fire. Then, without any further fanfare, everyone went home. I have no idea why we were in Berkeley, who we were visiting, or where we stayed. But I saw a Berkeley riot, sort of.

With our business, whatever that was, done in Berkeley, we started hitching onward to Denver. After a few rides, we found ourselves out in the boonies, when we got picked up by a guy and gal who told us they were going all the way to Denver. They were driving a 1960 white Ford Falcon that made clunking sounds and had the baldest tires I have ever seen in my life. There wasn't a tread to be found. And we were heading for snow country, the Rockies. Well, they had a whole lot of really good pot, so we put our lives in their hands. A really nice couple. Good people. The guy did all the driving.

It wasn't long after we started our ascent when we found ourselves in what I believe was an unseasonal blizzard. But our host continued on dauntlessly. As we traversed the Rockies, he related to us his philosophy, his secret, if you will, for driving through the snowy mountains: "Just drive slow . . ." That was it. As we climbed to the higher altitudes, ever so slowly, we passed all sorts of cars that had run off the side of the road and big rigs that had jackknifed. People got frustrated with our slowness and would pass us with belligerent impatience and disgust only to have us pass them later where they had skidded off the road. We kept smoking joints and telling stories and singing songs and poking along. Then, before we knew it, we were descending into weather clear and bright. They dropped us off at our address in Denver and we said our good-byes.

I'm not sure why we were in Denver. I guess because we were on the proverbial road. All I remember is that the weather was nice, I never knew whose place we were at, but there was this big longhaired goateed guitarman there who moaned and groaned that he was a better guitarist than James Taylor and that he could play "Fire and Rain" far superior to Taylor and that Taylor was a phony. I have no idea who that guy was, but he was one darn good picker. That much I could tell. But he had emotional problems. That, too, I could tell. So after a couple of days, we headed back to LA. I think we might have cooked rice once or twice the whole trip, just to say that we ate on the road.

When we got back to Long Beach, I was unpacking at Jeff and Linda's place when in walked Liz. One of the things I had sitting on my pile of stuff was *Sailor*. She picked the book up and asked, "Any good?" As they say in Spanish, *"¡Enganche!"* The hook, the connection, the link had been made. I gave her my take on it and thanked her for loaning me the backpack. Time is relevant, but in our world at the time, our relationship-to-be would be a slow burn.

Of course, I still had my eyes open for love and was plotting my radar. One day, when a bunch of us were hanging out at the Seventh Street Park, I was up in a tree when I met this girl. (We'd climb trees and smoke joints aloft to avoid the narcs that would sneak up on us now and then.) I was stoned, but I realized then and there that I had no idea how to interact with an American non-prostitute woman. It has now been confirmed for me, numerous times, that knowing what the question is, is quite often more valuable than knowing what the answer is. A little something I learned at the Seventh Street Park up in a tree.

Another day at the park, I got so drunk on Red Mountain wine that I had to be driven back to Myrtle House and was left to sleep it off on the back seat of the Five-O. When I finally got up, everyone was ripped on acid, which bummed me out. Then Liz sidled up to me, extending her dainty long forefinger and thumb, pinching something. "Here, I saved this for you. They wanted to do it all, but I saved this for you." One of the guys yelled out, "Yeah! She wouldn't let us do it all. She's looking out for your ass, man. She wouldn't let us do it all." That was the nicest thing a girl had ever done for me.

This little gesture would be just one of many acts of kindness and generosity Liz would extend to me over the next few months, from sewing cool patches on my tattered jeans to sharing cigarettes to feeding me at Taco Bell. Not only was I interacting with an American non-prostitute girl, but she seemed to genuinely care about me. But the road we were embarking on would not be bump-and-pothole-free.

One day, when the Moose was still there, we were sitting in the Five-O in the parking lot of a business across the street from Larry and Sharon's apartment. We had obviously smoked up all of our dope, because all I had was a tiny tightly wrapped clear plastic pouch of seeds in the pocket of my hunter red plaid shirt. The pouch was no larger than a typical jawbreaker. The hopeful beginnings of an heirloom dynasty of Jersey Pig. We had all just dropped acid and were washing it down with a quart of beer, when up pulled the police. They asked us to step out of the car and while one searched us, the other searched the car. My style then was rough-cut work boots, Levi's, plaid work shirts, a brownish herringbone tweed blazer, and gold rim "granny" or "John Lennon" glasses. Pretty much the same way I dress all these fifty-plus years later. But at the time, it screamed hippie and drug head. Aside from the beer, nothing was found in the car and nothing was found on the Moose or Larry. After rifling through all thirteen of my pockets, though, the cops found the little bladder of seeds. And it baffled them. They weren't quite sure what it was or what to do about it, so they stepped a few feet away to discuss it, hush-hush:

"It looks like it."

"I don't know. It doesn't look like it to me."

"It's got to be something."

"What do you think it is?"

"I don't know . . ."

So they busted me for having an open container in the car. They were pretty nice about it, though. They could have impounded the Five-O, but they let the Moose take responsibility for it. Now, this was before patrol cars had the now-ubiquitous screens separating arrestees from the arrestors. They put me in the back seat without cuffs, and off we went to downtown Long Beach. On the way, we had friendly conversations. The acid was coming on nice and strong.

The cop riding shotgun turned around and eyeballed me, "You're high on pot, aren't you?"

"No, sir. I'm not. We don't have any pot. Those seeds are it," and so on and so forth.

When we got to the station, we all walked into this big processing room, where I was asked to empty out my pockets and take off my belt. As the two cops stood by, I took off my boots, smacked the heels on the floor and turned each boot upside down with a big shake to show that I wasn't hiding anything inside. Then I took my socks off and turned them inside out.

One of the cops said, "You've been through this before."

"No, sir. Just figured you'd want to look there, anyway." As I waited for them to do their paperwork, my hearing became hyper-acute and extremely focused. I sat on a wall bench while they did their administrative work at a sort of stand-up desk attached to the wall, just to my left. The room was abustle with the business of "Protecting and Serving." My eyes must have looked like moon pies. I could make out their mutterings:

"Did you get that big knife?" one cop whispered.

"You mean the one he had under his front seat?"

"Hey! I didn't have any knife in my car. That's not right!"

They cracked up laughing. "We know. We know. We just wanted to see if you were paying attention."

So off to jail I went. I don't remember what the holiday was, but I got busted on a weekend that had a holiday tagged onto it, so I was in there for three days. The acid came on nicely, and I was able to appreciate the fact that I was on my way to a nice peak and was handling it just fine. For some reason, speaking of *three*, I got the Three Dog Night song "Out in the Country" stuck in my brain.

I just couldn't stop singing that damned thing. All night long. Not real loud, but not real quiet, either—over and over and over. The really bad part was that I got all the lyrics wrong. A little singing malady I inherited from my mother. It's called the Elsie disease. No matter what the song, she would butcher the lyrics, God bless her soul.

During the wee hours, there was quite a commotion when two cholos were brought in:

"*Ese* . . . You took my M&Ms, man. That's not right. "

"I did not, man. I did not take them."

"Yes, you did. You had to, man."

"I swear, man, I did not take your M&Ms . . ."

They went on for quite a while. They argued and I sang, and before we knew it, it was time to move out into the holding tank where we ate breakfast. It was a good night and the acid was leveling off nicely. I was still humming my song when this guy walked up to me and said, "So you're the asshole that was singing all night." He actually said it in kind of a nice way, but that was all I needed and the song was gone.

The two Mexican guys were still going at it about their M&Ms when one of them reached into his pant pocket and when he pulled his hand out all of these yellow M&M shaped pills bounced onto the floor.

"Hey, *ese*, my M&Ms! My M&Ms!"

"I told you, man. I did not take your M&Ms . . ."

Incredibly, the police had missed them. So, for the next couple of days those two got loaded on barbiturates and kept us all entertained. I received some minor fine and went on my merry way.

While I was ostensibly pursuing hippiedom, I was really a pseudo-hippie. Even to this day, I have never been able to be one hundred percent anything, except, I guess, *me*. Always tiptoeing around things. Trying this on for size, that on for size. Wanting to be liked, respected, and accepted, but not wanting to conform. Don't tell me what to do!

My now-deceased brother-in-law Harry asked me once back in '69, "How come all nonconformists dress alike?" Hmm . . . good question, Harry. Got me thinking. It's as though my genetic makeup is to not ever be a member of any group. Or perhaps it's just because no one ever wanted me on their team when I was a kid. Who knows? But I liked the mind altering chemicals, I liked the music, and I was attracted to the basic tenets of peace, love, and brotherhood. But that was pretty much where things ended for me. Of the mostly guys who came and went at Myrtle House, I was an oddball because I sought to earn an income. I had a goodly number of odd jobs. But the subtext of that, I now see, was that I was earnestly trying to get something going with Liz.

One crazy job I had was working for Purple Heart Veterans. Early each morning, a bunch of derelicts, down-and-outers, drunks, and dopers would show up and pile into a rickety old van that would deposit us one by one in neighborhoods that didn't want us there, to solicit for donations of clothes and furniture and the like. If someone wanted to make a donation, I'd fill out a ticket for them to affix to their contributions and schedule a pickup. At the end of the day, I'd hand in my ticket stubs that numerically matched the contribution pledges. If—and it was a might big *if*—a contribution was actually collected, I would get a walloping twenty-five cents per donation.

This one day, I decided to drop acid for the fun of it first thing in the morning. The route that day was in Laguna Hills in Orange County. I had all kinds of great experiences. A crazy sexy woman showing me her breasts from behind a chained door, hateful dogs and their hateful owners, and this guy, a teenager, who came running up to me, breathless, thinking that I was, well, John Lennon just walking down the street in his neighborhood. It was a good hot day. The most profound encounter, though, was this family that invited me in for some refreshment. Really nice people. Big house. Lots of stuff. But what a story.

When they had moved into that house several years prior, they had stuck to themselves and weren't very outgoing with their neighbors. And shortly after they moved in, they went on vacation. But no one in the neighborhood knew that. So, when a massive moving van pulled up one day and a crew started loading up, no one thought anything of it. When the family returned, they found: no furniture, no carpets, no art on the walls, no refrigerator, no stove, no tools in the garage, no family photos, no files, no important documents, no towels, no clothes—nothing. Everything gone. And they weren't rich and they didn't have any insurance. But as I sat there peaking my brains out, drinking some ice cold lemonade, that happy lovely couple, somewhere in their forties, laughed about the whole thing and told me how their painful losses gave them a whole new valuable perspective on life and how happy they were to have each other. That day I learned that stuff was just stuff. And to let your neighbors know when you go out of town.

Clearly, I wasn't going to get rich doing the Purple Heart Veterans thing, so I somehow found Joe. Old Joe. Or did he find me? Whatever the case, we found each other, Joe and his wife. We'll just call her Mrs. Joe because I can't remember what her name was. Joe. An educated hill-billy. A talented cabinetmaker. A carpenter. A mason. A plumber. A house painter. An ex-con. A well-built big muscular guy with a flat squarish face who wore intellectual dark-rimmed glasses, a Ned Flanders moustache, work khakis with his shirtsleeves rolled up James Dean-like, and who, in his soft-spoken manner, oozed condescension toward all humankind. When he'd been in Folsom for a forgotten felony, he said that Charles Manson was a patsy-pussy boy who got pushed around a lot by the other inmates way before he achieved infamy.

At the end of a hard day's work, Joe and Mrs. Joe loved to sit in their smallish airy 1920s clapboard Long Beach bungalow and drink neat glass after neat glass of Seagram's 7. Joe and Mrs. Joe claimed that they could drink liquor all day and all night and never get drunk. It didn't affect them and only helped him to think clearly. Right. They were something. But I could see that behind Joe's transparently controlled façade of calmness, he was capable of horrible violence. He seemed to be in a constant state of trying to keep his temper under control because he knew that one slip would land him back in the big house. I have no idea how I ended up working for Joe.

On a very petty level, he was always hustling. And I, for a while, was a mere tessera in his endless mosaic of schemes. Working *for him* might not be an accurate way of looking at our relationship, though. Indentured servitude was more like it. Shortly after I began the standard I-work-for-you-you-pay-me-for-the-work-that-I-do relationship, he talked me into renting his garage where I could have privacy and solitude and be ready for work, lickety-split. They would simply deduct my rent from my wages, which I think was around $2.50/hr. Then they threw in breakfast and occasional other meals, which Mrs. Joe kept track of and deducted from my pay as well. Coffee by the cup. Bread by the slice. Sugar, jam, butter—she kept track of every morsel I consumed. I had no idea how detailed she was. But when I started hinting that I hadn't been paid for a while, she got out the ledger that showed I was eating and renting up all of my earnings. I could never catch up. So every now and then old Joe would have a heart-to-heart with Mrs. Joe and throw ten or fifteen bucks my way so I'd have some pin money. They owned me.

Joe called himself a general contractor and got all kinds of jobs. We scraped and painted houses. We repaired caved-in garage walls. We replaced hot water heaters. It seemed like every day was a hot clear day, too. We'd go pick up our lumber and cinder blocks or whatever hardware materials we'd need in Joe's 1958 Oldsmobile Super 88. A golden tank of luxury. When necessary, we'd remove the back seat so we could stuff all kinds of crap in there through the trunk. There was one little hitch, though. Every job, every destination, every move we made had to be well thought out because the Olds had no reverse. Everything had to be forward motion. That really made things interesting. The work at times was hard, the relationship was screwy, but I learned some good tips from Joe. He told me that he owed all of his craftsmanship talents to time well spent behind bars.

While I was living in their garage, I had three profound experiences there. The first had to do with me cutting back on eating to keep my company store account to a minimum. In the garage was this big bag of Spanish onions. I got curious and hungry one night and ate a whole onion. A big juicy red and white onion. Yum . . . Yuck! Don't ever do that! Trust me. Another experience was in many ways more painful.

One night I drove over to RB's wooden castle in Wilmington for an impromptu visit. I had parked and was walking toward the trailer and saw Wendy. When she saw me, she perked up and came running at me with her arms wide open and a glorious smile on her face. OK, so she was glad to see me. But she kept running and then she leapt upon me, wrapped her arms around me, and stuck her tongue in my mouth. Whoa! I slipped into one of those prolonged milliseconds of slow motion of extended time like you see in the movies. *What is going on here? How do I react?* I reached up and grabbed her under her armpits and pushed her back without having returned her kiss.

She looked at me, wounded with disappointment, "What's the matter? Don't you like me?"

"What are you doing? You're with RB."

"That doesn't mean I can't like you, too, does it?"

Without RB there, and a looming uncomfortableness between the two of us, I split. The incident weighed heavily on my noggin and I had to do something about it.

The second profundity took place one night when RB was over at my indentured servant's quarters. It was a small garage and my bed was smack in the middle of all sorts of garage clutter. I was sitting on a chair at the foot of the bed, and RB was standing diagonally across from me at the head.

"RB, there's something I have to tell you."

He just looked at me, real serious-like.

"I've been sitting on it for a while trying to figure out how to do it and I don't know how to do it so I'm just going to do it."

He stood silent, looking at me with big puppy dog eyes. His face got sadder.

"The other night I came by to visit you and, well, Wendy just ran up and kissed me. I didn't hit on her or anything. She just did it. You're my friend. I wouldn't mess around with you like that."

"Thanks for telling me," was all he said.

And we've never mentioned it again.

Finally, the pièce de résistance happened one evening when I gave Liz a ride to visit some of her friends in God-knows-where, Long Beach. I remember feeling out of place and unhip with her friends. Unimportant. A fifth wheel. Not really with her. Afterward, stoned and driving her back to Myrtle House, a certain tension came over me. It was something magnetic. Something electrical. Whatever it was, it allowed my vision to pierce the darkness of the Five-O and see her enshrouded in some sort of luminescent aureole. Being close to her was driving me nuts. More than any time before, I just wanted to touch her. I think we might have kissed before, but that was it. I forced myself to say something corny, like, "I have to tell you something. I really like you." Or something like that. Whatever I said, we ended up in my bed back at the Joes'.

Somehow, I managed to scrounge together enough dough to feel independent, and I approached Linda Bevins about renting the downstairs. More and more people kept coming and going and not helping her out and reciprocating in any way. It all just turned out to be a big hassle for her. People were taking advantage of her generosity, and I sensed that she was burning out. Her big soft heart was becoming leathery and resentful. Things had been getting crazy to the point that that's why I'd left Myrtle House and put myself into debt peonage with the Joes for a couple months. But I had to get out of the grips of the company store. Suddenly, just like that, I had my own pad—sort of.

I got wind that Liz thought John Phillips was a fox and I somehow—that's my life's story: *somehow*—found out that he would be playing solo up in Hollywood at the Troubadour. I had never been to the Troubadour and had only driven through Hollywood a few times. Except for asking the beautiful Ocean City summer shoebe Phyllis Conte from Philadelphia to go with me to see *The Pink Panther* in Atlantic City, via bus, when I was fourteen (she was a couple years older than I), I had never asked a girl out on a real date before. I called up the Troubadour and got all the costing information and mapped out our route. Off to Hollywood we went.

On the bill were John Phillips, Barry McGuire, and Doc Watson, which really didn't mean anything to me at the time. All I cared about was that I was on a date with Liz. The club was set up with a series of long tables perpendicular to the stage so that everyone sat askew to watch the show. I sat on one side of our table and Liz sat across from me. In my small, limited, inexperienced, uninitiated, totally confused way, we were a-stylin'. I was high as a kite. On a date. With Liz. At the Troubadour. Then came intermission. When I did my initial reconnoiter, I found out that there would be a two-drink minimum on top of the admission. No problem. So when the hip-hard-edged waitress came to take our order during the break, I told her no thanks, that we were OK. She explained to me that there was a two-drink minimum:

"Yeah, I know. I bought two when we first got here. One for her and one for me." Why was she messing with me? The place was jumping with activity, suddenly the spotlight was on me, and I was trying to keep Liz from hearing what we were talking about.

"Honey, it's two drinks per person, not two drinks total."

I could feel my face blanch and then explode like a mercury thermometer with embarrassment, realizing that I didn't have any more money.

Catching on, smart girl that she was, she leaned to my ear and whispered, "These are on me, honey. Next time, bring enough money."

Linda Bevins hooked up with this guy named David Stein, whom she allegedly stole from her best friend, who had asked her to look in on him while she was out of town. He worked in the refineries, was levelheaded, and seemed to make a ton of money. But they seemed to be happy, and he treated Linda and her kids well. The atmosphere upstairs started taking on the air of a normal family. Things over at Jeff and Linda's were generally low-key. Never much drama there. But they were getting antsy, so they decided to move on. They moved out and Dawn and Carl moved in. Dawn was Liz's friend whom she met up in San Francisco.

If meteorologically Mick and Diana were a periodic squall and Jeff and Linda an occasional cool summer shower, Dawn and Carl were an intermittent F5 tornado. Those guys could fight. Once they moved in, their apartment took on a new life. A new explosive spark came to Myrtle House. While Mick and Diana and Jeff and Linda were more standoffish and less inviting, Dawn and Carl were spirited, open, generous.

Liz made it a condition early on that when she goes to bed, Phoebe goes to bed with her. Meaning: If I wanted to sleep with her, I had to sleep with Phoebe, who was pleasantly uninhibited about stretching out and claiming her space. And, so, that's the way it was when Liz and I decided that we would live together in Linda's garage.

I went to work immediately to make us a home. Somewhere, I had found some sheets of wood to build a wall to make us a little private bedroom, so the outer area could be our living room social area. The wood was very unusual. Extremely heavy. Odd-sized sheets of solid wood—not plywood—about 5'×9'×3/4". I had slammed a framing hammer in my time, so I knew that I was working with something out of the ordinary. It was as if a giant cheese plane had sliced them from an ancient block of tree cheese of immense diameter. It was a bear to work with.

I studded out the bedroom and had a hard time getting things to fit. (My life's story. I was a *rough* carpenter—not a *finish* man, which really means I wasn't all that good.) Every time I measured and cut, something wouldn't fit because the floor and ceiling were cattywampus. And the massive sheets of cheesewood were about to kill me because I was cutting everything by hand with a dull crosscut saw. But I got it done. We had a double bed on box springs on the floor, wooden boxes as bed tables, and a lamp so Liz could read. A funky old couch and a makeshift coffee table were our living room. The bathroom was as fixed up as it could be. No TV. No radio. No record player. But it was home. I had no idea what I was doing, but I was doing it with Liz.

I was picking up work with the Joes here and there (I still had that tab to pay off), and occasional odd jobs. Liz got a job as a waitress at Woolworth's in Long Beach. Kids as we were, we were making a go at it. Myrtle House was still a party place, but things were getting somewhat stable. Liz and I were doing our thing. Linda and Stein and the kids were quietly doing their thing. And Dawn and Carl (who was working making good money as a stationary engineer or something) were doing their thing, albeit not always quietly. But Myrtle House was destined to have spikes of excitement—with or without any of us. It was alive. We were mere participants in a long parade of visitors it had seduced and hosted over who knows how many years. A *Twilight Zone*. A safe place where young folk could go to process through our individual rites of passage and come out on the other side.

Carl and Dawn qualified as periodic spikes of excitement. They had the most tumultuous fights over the stupidest things. No real physical violence to one another, but they sounded like bloody murder. Things would get broken. Dawn was a taunting egger-on fight starter who always went for Carl's jugular—his masculinity. She was good. Crazy. But good. And Carl, he was a stocky frizzy-curly headed Italian Tasmanian devil who had virtually no control over his temper. One time, several of us were standing out by the front gate listening to the hurricane coming from their apartment. It was a particularly bad fight. We started speculating on what would come of it. I bet that within ten minutes they would kiss and make up. We all just stood there listening: Yell! Scream! Crash! Boom! Epithets! Vulgarity! About ten minutes later, dead silence. Then, the front door slowly opened and they both came out onto the porch, unaware of their audience, where they hugged and kissed. We all clapped and cheered.

At some point, Ed Townser, the potologist responsible for the long gone smoked-up Jersey Pig, contacted me to buy him a kilo of dope. He sent me $100. All I had to do was buy it and get it to him. Hmmm? . . . So I bought a key and tried to make a little profit. The problem was that besides Carl and Stein (Stein didn't really do drugs and Carl had his own sources), no one I knew or came in contact with had any money. Everybody was poor. That meant that every time a group would gather and there was no dope, everyone would wear me down with, "Come on, man. You got it. We know you got it. Don't be so tight." There went my profits and Ed's money.

An old merchant marine buddy of Carl's came to visit one time with a couple of his buddies. I think they were from Cincinnati. Apparently, the economy was pretty bad back there, and they'd come out to LA to look for work. What they got was high. They ended up living down in the garage below Dawn and Carl. They were wild guys. One of Dawn's friends had a little sex thing going on, and she got those three guys downstairs and screwed them and screwed them and screwed them. Her screams of pleasure seemed to have no end. While she was doing one guy, the other two would come upstairs for a breather, a beer, a toke, and then go back down for round two or three. Incredible human endurance and stamina. Behavior way out of my league.

Of the three, one was the calmest and sweetest—when he wasn't loaded, that is. But once substances got into his system, he was absolutely feral. He was also married with a couple of kids. One night, he got so ripped on acid that he became the textbook example of a Navy propaganda film's paranoid drug crazed deranged freak. He started thinking that everyone was a narc out to bust him, and he was planning on killing a number of people. For some reason, at first, I was the one he trusted.

After he came down, though, he told me that he later thought I too was a cop and that he would have to kill me as well. Downright scary.

The good news was that he ran away from Myrtle House. The bad news was that Carl and his buddy found him a few blocks away crying and talking into two pay telephones. On one, he was talking to his wife and telling her that he missed her and the kids and that he was coming home. On the other, he was talking with LBPD and telling them that he had a warrant out for his arrest and that he was doing drugs and to come and get him. While Carl and his buddy were trying to get him off the phone and split, the police arrived. Carl and the other guy ended up snowing the cops into believing that their friend was drunk and missing his family and that because he couldn't find work he thought that if he were arrested they would send him back to his hometown. The guy kept insisting that he had a warrant out (which he did) and that they had to arrest him. The police good-naturedly told him that they would, but for him to go home and sleep it off and call back in the morning. They would be glad to arrest him then, but they were having a busy night and had to get going. Things were different then.

While all that nonsense was going on, I went and hid the remainder of my key in a trash can down the alley because I was sure that joker was going to bring the police to Myrtle House—and not to buy any acid. That, thankfully, never came to pass. Making a killing as a drug dealer never came to pass for me, either. I don't remember what flimsy excuse I gave Ed Townser for the loss of his money, but I believe I justified it as payment for his never having returned the recipe for LSD that I loaned him, which he claimed I never did. I suppose I still owe him the dough. Oh, well . . .

Class was always in session at Myrtle House. The lessons were ongoing. Open enrollment was perpetual and everything was pass/fail. While others were out screwing multiple partners or having gangbangs—doing that hippie love thing—I was trying to suss out how to get it right with just one gal. It was not easy being me.

I had never really been intimate with anyone before. I had encounters. I had what passed for sex, but I had never really been *with* anyone before. Never had a girlfriend. What to do? What to say? What to reveal?

What not to reveal? Boundaries—where were they? What did it mean to love someone? Growing up without a father or a male role model around (a blessing for which I am now thankful)—how to be a man? A series of adolescent neurotic specters had suddenly become reality. I was in a relationship:

"What do you mean, *I get out*? I was here before you. Linda is my friend."

"I'm paying the rent. It's my place. She rented it to me. If you don't like how things are, you can just leave."

"I'm not leaving! You're leaving!"

"Oh, yeah!"

"Yeah! . . ."

And so it all began. Living together. We were on. We were off. Sex was up. Sex was down. One day Linda Bevins said that she wanted to talk with me. She took me out to the center of the front yard where we sat on the patchy lawn of weeds and dirt like two skinny Buddhas. She lit a joint, took a deep hit, and passed it to me. With her lungs full, she held her breath and looked me dead in the eyes and uttered a throaty, "It looks like you and Lizard are getting pretty serious."

"Well . . . , yeah. I guess . . ."

"You like her?"

"*Yeah . . .*"

"She likes you, too. You know, we're friends, so, of course, she tells me how things are going, and she says there's a little problem with sex."

Nonplused, I acknowledged this news with a vague, "Uh-huh." Where the hell was she going with this?

"She said that things were going OK with you two, and then they just stopped. She's thinking maybe you don't like her—"

"No, I like her a lot."

"Do you love her?"

"I think so. I don't know."

"What do you think's going on? Are you afraid of commitment? Did something happen to you to traumatize you when you were young? Have you been raped? Was your mother overbearing? Have you been sexually abused? Are you a homosexual? Are you a sex freak?"

Right there in the front yard, levitating above her lotus gun mount, Linda casually let me have it point-blank in the brain with her spiritual Mark 12 5″/38 caliber cannon. Then she reloaded and did it again and again and again. But we talked on. I felt like she was able to see every thought and inhibition I had tried so carefully to dissemble. She was a good person trying to do good by her friends. She didn't mince words. She had a wealth of experience and knowledge and was putting it all to good use for our benefit. She took on a motherly role. She was Liz's friend and my counselor. The upshot was that I no more knew what was going on back then than I do today, fifty-odd years later, but the chat was fruitful and it helped me to zero in on what my priorities were.

So, like I said, Liz and I were on again, off again. During one of those nebulous off times, I took an interest in a girl named Mercedes. That never went anywhere, but she was nice to me and she was, after all, a female—the most pleasing and terrifying creature on earth. I have no recollection whatsoever how I met her, but I definitely recall that she had a couple of brothers who were involved with some shady dealings. One day, she had me over to their big airy two-story Victorian house in Long Beach. Mercedes told me to have a seat and wait for her while she tooled around to do whatever it was she needed to do before we took off to wherever we were going. So I had a seat. Already underway were some heated negotiations between one of her brothers and a Hells Angel.

Though I was sitting just a few feet across from them, they never batted an eye or acknowledged my presence. They were sitting on sturdy scuffed up wooden kitchen chairs at a funky rundown circular drop-leaf table that was half-mooned up against a large bay window that looked out across rooftops and yards and a bright sunny day. The two passed a joint back and forth without offering me any. The pungency of their dope told me that it was something special. Mercedes's longhaired hippie brother was reserved, calm, businesslike, and adamant about cost. The Hells Angel guy was intense, threatening, and pissed. He slapped the table and made bug-eyed facial gestures and shook his fists. But it was clear that Mercedes's brother was not intimidated in the least. After a while, their business became evident: the Hells Angel was wanting to buy dynamite and Mercedes's brother had it to sell. Word was that her brothers were involved with the "Brotherhood," a sort of hippie LSD mafia at the time. Anyway, before they reached an agreement, Mercedes skipped back in, swiped the joint from her brother, took a hit, gave me a hit, gave the joint back, and then dragged me away to frolic. She was a skipper.

A girl that drifted in and out of Myrtle House had a boyfriend who worked in some clerical capacity for the Seal Beach Police Department. He was a big talker. He would just pop in and out now and then, and we all had our suspicions about him. Consequently, we tended to be pretty close-mouthed around him and let him do the blathering. Most of what he said came off as braggadocio. One thing he had been harping on was this alleged "inside information" he had (*because* he worked for the SBPD) about a secret underground hippie subversive dope-dealing plan to launch a revolution at a concert come Christmas in Laguna Beach. From time to time, he would update us about the latest information SBPD undercover cops had gathered. No one believed him. I certainly didn't. It was to be the event, the time, the place, where life as we knew it in the United States of America would change for the better forever. The good guys would win. The bad guys would lose. War would stop. Peace and Love would prevail. Then, on December 24th, someone showed up at Myrtle House with a flyer announcing a *happening* in Laguna Canyon on Christmas Day. The guy was telling the truth after all.

A couple days later, I was over hanging out at Carl and Dawn's, when someone came by and told us that the concert was still going on. I remember it being an unusually sad Christmastime for me because, for whatever reason, Liz and I were on the outs. That meant I was on my own. Music was playing and we were passing a joint and chatterboxing about the usual nothing, while Carl slept like a baby on a single mattress-cum-couch on the living room floor in the midst of it all. He worked really weird hours and amazed us all by how easily he'd fall asleep anywhere, no matter the noise level. Anyway, he hadn't been sleeping all that long when Dawn, in her manic self-centered wisdom, started shaking him, "Carl, wake up! Wake up, Carl! Wake up … Waaake uhhhp! …"

Gritting his teeth and squinting his eyes, he mumbled, "Dawn . . . I'm going to throw you off the porch. What! I gotta get some sleep."

"That concert in Laguna is still going on, Carl. Let's go. It's still Christmas! Let's go."

"It's still going on? I thought it was only for one day. Laguna, huh?" He was in.

Once those two had sorted out their issues with the minimum of bickering, the troops prepared for a sortie. In order to continue the celebration of the birth of our Lord and get into the right frame of mind for a concert, we all dropped acid. All I can say is that I am sure glad Carl was doing the driving because even if you put a gun to my head today, I couldn't tell you where that concert took place. Up in Laguna Canyon somewhere, I'm told.

We all hopped into Carl's brand-new fire engine red Dodge van that had an American flag painted on top of the engine cover between the passenger's and driver's seats. The ride up there was long and slow. Traffic was poking along and people were still pouring in on foot by the hundreds. I only know this because of some innate animal intuitiveness or divine revelation, because otherwise I was so blitzed that everything was a trail or in some prototypal formation of morphing. I have strained recollections that we were listening to Hoyt Axton, and there was the normal drug induced chatter. Or was that in my head? Nothing meant anything, and every little thing meant everything. I know it was Dawn and Carl and me. I know that Liz wasn't with us (She has since told me that she was. If you can remember the '60s and '70s, you know . . .), but I have no idea how many others there were or who they were. We seemed to be a small platoon. We found a place to park, piled out, and trekked the rest of the way up. We passed some cops, but no big deal. Just lots and lots of heads.

When we finally got up to where the action was, we plopped ourselves down on a little knoll that afforded us a good view of everything. There were thousands and thousands of people. Longhairs everywhere. From our vantage point, looking down to our oblique right, we could clearly see the stage where huge-man-with-huge-fro, one Buddy Miles, was slapping the drums as though he were whipping up some cake batter. Or, could it be, he was playing the guitar?

As per usual, I took off wandering alone when I came upon a regiment of Hessians. Their choppers aligned and clean as a whistle. While I knew the bikers themselves were dirty and unkempt—because they were bikers, right?—they appeared through the eyes of LSD to be clinically clean and made of colorful plasticine. They were cool. Too cool. And they had these too cool-looking women hanging on them as they leaned against their modern day Harley horses. As I stood there gawking, agog, unaware that these same bikers, these Hessians, would one day insinuate themselves into our lives in a way that no one could ever have imagined, I was startled into a momentary sense of reality by a face that leapt suddenly and directly to within an inch of my nose. It was Mercedes! Happy as a lark, Mercedes. Brandishing a Cheshire cat smile. Hippety-hoppety on her toes. Genuinely happy to see me:

"David! David! David! You're here! You're here! You're here! . . ." wrapping her arms around me; squeezing me with a big healthy hug. I'm not sure I said anything, or at least I didn't have a chance to say anything before she grabbed my hand and started skipping away through the mass of humanity with me in tow. There I was, spindle-legged, gangly, right hand stretched out, attempting to skip along with her, as we sang the Beatles' "Two of Us" from *Let It Be*. (Actually, my Elsie disease affliction severely accentuated, I mumbled and slurred mondegreens galore.):

"Two of we doing something

Spending something something

Blah blah blah . . ."

As we gamboled through the clusters of hipsters, she would periodically throw a glance over her shoulder and giggle while keeping the song going. Her hand was warm. A special kind of acid warm. I was in seventh heaven. A girl took me by the hand and took me a-skipping. It was pure happiness. I knew there would be no sex with Mercedes, but that was OK with me because it was really Liz I wanted to be with. Once we wound down, she told me how a plane (helicopter?) had flown over the crowd and dropped all these funky sort of greeting cards with tabs of Orange

Sunshine attached to them and how many people had freaked out and how wonderful everything was going . . .

By the time I got back to Carl and crew, the police were announcing that it was all over and to vacate the premises. We talked it over and we decided to clear out to avoid any real trouble. As we headed back to the van, we walked past formations of what seemed like hundreds of menacing cops in dark uniforms with dark anti-riot vests—all standing side by side in a sort of ready position with batons in gloved hands. Under their hard hats and behind their plastic face protectors, not a smile was to be seen. If I had known who Darth Vader was at the time, I would have felt as though we were walking into the bowels of his nasty little mind. As we were leaving, the bulldozers were busy evicting all would-be revolutionaries.

Any day you can do something and escape the wrath of whatever wrath might inflict itself upon life that day, that is a good day. So we headed back to Myrtle House. On the way, I felt lost. I was lonely. Was Liz playing with me? Did she not care? Was I just one of many? Was I a fool to care? Hell—what did it mean to care? Was I some sort of sexual deviant that this clown of a friend in the Navy used to accuse me of being? Was I emotionally damaged and incapable of even being in a love relationship? I didn't have any money. Work was next to nothing. How could I expect to make a go of a relationship when I was a broke, unemployed, uneducated, and scared witless? Life was an endless concatenation of questions. I had no answers. Man, I was stoned. All I really knew was that I could trust Carl to get me back home safely.

While I was still the sole renter of Linda's downstairs garage-apartment, I was falling behind on my rent, as low as it was. Even with gas at $.34 per gallon, I was having a hard time keeping the Five-O running. I was starting to depend on others for my booze and drugs. Liz was always generous with me. Often she bought me Taco Bell, and she shared her cigarettes and anything else she had with me. When I had the money, I would reciprocate and buy her an RC Cola and a Chunky, two of her favorites. But the Joes were having their own problems and work dried up. The door-to-door solicitation and day labor stuff was not panning out, either. And I had proven beyond a doubt to be a totally incompetent drug dealer. Something had to be done.

I thought long and hard. I stared at Liz when she didn't know I was looking at her. I contemplated her. Her and Phoebe. Me. Me and her. Me and her and Phoebe. I wanted her. I wanted Phoebe. But I was at a complete loss how to keep her, to keep them. I didn't know what to do, but I knew that I had, absolutely had, to do something.

Sitting next to her on our makeshift couch in our makeshift living room, as I stroked Phoebe, I announced my plan. "I have been looking and looking," I began, "and I just can't find work. This is no good. I'm living and mooching off you and Linda and everyone else."

"You'll find work," she said. "I know you will. You just have to keep looking. This is temporary."

"I know. Eventually, something will happen. But I can go back to Jersey and get work and save up and come back for you."

"You're going to leave me!"

"I'm not leaving you. I'm just going to go work for a while and save up some money, and then I'll come back for you and Phoebe and . . ."

Winter was coming on. Once again, Liz loaned me her massive Duluth portage knapsack that was made of heavy-duty olive green canvas, with thick leather shoulder straps, a tumpline, copper riveted flap straps, and roller buckles. A fine piece of craftsmanship; I promised to return it. I parked the Five-O in the alley behind Myrtle House. Liz and I cried while hugging and kissing and saying our good-byes. Then, Carl drove me out to Riverside to give me a jump-start, from where I would continue on Interstate 10, taking the southern route to avoid the harsh northern winter.

"See you in a few months, Betterton."

"Thanks, Carl. Thanks a lot. I appreciate this."

"Ah . . . it's nada. If you hitch back and get about this far, give me a call and I'll come and get you."

So, with my tail between my legs, my spirit broken, totally confused, flat busted, lacking social skills galore, I went back to Pleasantville. Not exactly a pleasant experience. Not exactly what my mom was looking forward to. And, as it turned out, I had no better luck finding work there than I had in Long Beach.

One day, after being back for a couple-few weeks, my mom told me that Liz had called and left a phone number. Not wanting to talk with Mom listening, I walked downtown to use the pay phone in front of old man Megan's drug store. I dialed California. The operator came on and told me how much to insert. The coins dropped and tinged. The phone rang several times. *What will I say? What do I have to say?*

Someone answered, "Yeah, hello."

"Is Liz there? This is David."

"Hold on. Hey! Lizard. It's for you. It's David." Whoever answered slammed the phone down and I heard her utter a pleasant "Oh!" of surprise in the background.

"Hi."

"Hi. How you doing?"

"I'm coming to be with you."

"What?"

"I have my airplane ticket and I will be staying with my sister up in Westfield until we can get our own place. I'll be there in two days."

"But Liz—"

"I don't want to lose you. I love you and I am coming to *be with you.* We'll figure it out as we go . . ."

And thus the die was cast. So this is how it would be. After we finished talking and working out the immediate details, I gently put the phone back on its cradle and stood there at Main and Washington, slightly comatose, and slowly scanned my surroundings: the beautiful Greco-Roman gray granite First National Bank with its sparkling flecks of silica, Dr. Jack Slotoroff's dental office, the Atlantic City Electric Company, Jack's Army-Navy, Mike's Sugar Bowel, Martin's Liquor Store. This was *me.* Where I was from. What I knew. My small world. And a girl was coming from California to *be with me!* No one in that town had ever seen me with a girl before. And as I stood there gazing, sleepy-eyed and scared to death of my future, everything gauzy and out of focus, I realized that I would never have made it back to Long Beach on my own. That had Liz not taken the initiative to do what she was so ballsily doing, I would probably never have seen her or Phoebe again.

Standing there and reflecting on our telephone conversation, looking at Pleasantville through a new set of eyes, I was keenly aware that my life was about to experience a sea change. It was on that crispy clear wintery day, lingering there on Main Street in Pleasantville, New Jersey, shaking in my boots, bursting with elation and anticipation, moments after Liz had told me that she was coming to *be with me*, that my life began.

PHOTO CREDITS

Except for the following photographs on the indicated pages, all other photos were taken by family and friends, when cameras actually had film in them.

David W. Betterton was born, grew up, and escaped from Pleasantville. After having his ass kicked so many times, getting "left back" two times, about to be left back a third time, and failing at everything the public school system threw at him, he quit the ninth grade and joined the U.S. Navy during the Vietnam War. It was in the USN that he learned to type, a skill he holds in high esteem above all others. At the behest of his Navy buddies, Betterton earned his GED, passing it by one-tenth of one percent of a passing point.

After the Navy, Betterton had *myriad* jobs, like framing houses, china factory truck loader, boat building, welding, and too many more to list. Thanks to the Navy, he ended up at San Francisco State University, where he earned a BA in Broadcast Communication Arts. After busting around live theater and film/TV production for eleven years, he worked shooting and editing video for the Los Angeles County Department of Public Health, from which he retired after sixteen years. During his time at LAC-DPH, Betterton earned an MA in Latin American Studies from California State University, Los Angeles.

Betterton lives in Long Beach, California, where he endeavors to write entertaining literature and poetry. This is Betterton's first major publication. He has one short story, "Puppy Love," published in the literary journal *Citadel,* and one poem, "War on Poverty," published *in Dissent: An Anthology to End War and Capitalism.*